Star Trek® Online:
The Needs of the Many

STAR TREK®
ONLINE
THE NEEDS OF THE MANY

MICHAEL A. MARTIN
& JAKE SISKO

Based upon *Star Trek*®
and *Star Trek: The Next Generation*®
created by Gene Roddenberry

Star Trek: Deep Space Nine®
created by Rick Berman & Michael Piller

Star Trek: Voyager®
created by Rick Berman & Michael Piller & Jeri Taylor

Star Trek: Enterprise®
created by Rick Berman & Brannon Braga

and Cryptic Studios' *Star Trek*® *Online*
(The Massively Multiplayer Online Role-Playing Game)

POCKET BOOKS
New York   London   Toronto   Sydney   Hobus Nebula

Pocket Books
A Division of Simon & Schuster, Inc.
1230 Avenue of the Americas
New York, NY 10020

This book is a work of fiction. Names, characters, places, and incidents either are products of the author's imagination or are used fictitiously. Any resemblance to actual events or locales or persons, living or dead, is entirely coincidental.

First Pocket Books paperback edition April 2010

POCKET and colophon are registered trademarks of Simon & Schuster, Inc.

For information about special discounts for bulk purchases, please contact Simon & Schuster Special Sales at 1-866-506-1949 or business@simonandschuster.com.

The Simon & Schuster Speakers Bureau can bring authors to your live event. For more information or to book an event, contact the Simon & Schuster Speakers Bureau at 1-866-248-3049 or visit our website at www.simonspeakers.com.

Designed by Jacquelynne Hudson
Cover art: Melvin Yu, Denis Korkh, Chris Legaspi, and Patrick Moore, courtesy of Cryptic Studios

Manufactured in the United States of America

10 9 8 7 6 5 4 3 2 1

ISBN 978-1-4391-8657-2
ISBN 978-1-4391-8658-9 (ebook)

This chronicle is dedicated to Studs Terkel
(1912–2008), who blazed the trail, and to
Congressman Dennis Kucinich of
Ohio, a man centuries ahead of his time,
for proposing the establishment of a
Department of Peace.

FOREWORD

It's been a number of years since I ceased my labors mining a seemingly infinite vein of personal stories about the Federation's war against the Undine—a truly alien race once known to us only by their Borg designation of Species 8472. The many teraquads of stories I spent more time than I could have imagined gathering ran the gamut from heroism and courage to villainy and cowardice, and made stopovers at just about every point in between. During my travels from Earth and Luna to Tau Ceti and Cestus III, from Cardassia Prime and Qo'noS to Galor IV and Altair VI, from Vulcan and Bolarus to Bajor and Omicron Theta, I preserved reminiscences of the best and worst deeds of which sentient beings are capable. This "Undine War history" project, which I undertook at the behest of the Federation's Department of Peace, was both rewarding and exhausting and could have occupied many lifetimes—and that's without reckoning the time and energy it would have taken me to edit those many gigaquads of interviews and other pertinent historical documents into anything resembling a coherent narrative.[*]

Although it meant disappointing my friends in the DoP, the time finally came when I had to recognize that my ambition had finally exceeded my abilities. After all, I had only one lifetime to devote to writing of any kind, and the task of whittling the copious quantity of raw material I had assembled down to even a dozen fat volumes (one wag at the DoP described this venture as a "massively multimind memoir") seemed all but impossible. And there were aspects of the war—nightmare horrors commingled with the gallant heroism—that I frankly had no desire to experience even vicariously yet again, the protective filter of the editorial process notwithstanding.

Most importantly, my long-neglected fiction projects, having grown cold and lonely, were beckoning, and I wasn't getting any younger.

Then E'Shles, my editor on *Collected Stories*, suggested that my Undine War project might not have to remain forever in limbo. S/he suggested that all that might be needed was to "focus a couple of fresh sets of eyestalks" on the material I had gathered. I agreed, and gave hir access to the entirety of my interview collection. E'Shles then brought aboard another scrivener of note, contemporary histori-

---

[*] At one point my office looked like a cityscape crafted out of stacks of the old-style Cardassian data rods I'd gotten into the habit of using during my DS9 years.

ographer Michael A. Martin, who is probably best known for his popular fictionalized accounts of late-twenty-second/third/fourth-century Starfleet missions (and who lacks eyestalks, by the way).

From the very outset, Michael seemed convinced that this book (and the accompanying derivative holoprograms) would indeed see the light of day, once he'd spent a few weeks putting his shoulder to the wheel. His enthusiasm was contagious, so when he began contacting me with historical questions (probably as part of E'Shles's fiendish scheme to lure me back to the project, if only temporarily), I was delighted to help—so much so that I even acceded to Michael's request that I put my name on the book alongside his own.[*]

So now you know how this book came to exist, as well as why: because somebody insisted. In fact, this volume came into being for the very same reason *any* of my works of fiction ever saw completion. Because someone—be it myself, an editor (as in this case), or an irresistible muse—insisted upon it. But this book is no more a work of fiction than it is a mere blow-by-

---

[*] This occurred only after much arm twisting on Michael's part and my receipt of his solemn pledge that my name would appear *after* the ampersand rather than before it. I insisted on this because so much of the literary heavy lifting—the daunting task of imposing some degree of narrative order upon the chaos of my raw record of the war—had fallen across Michael's sturdy back, sparing me the vast majority of the truly hard trench work. Michael will probably try to inflate my contribution to the final version of this work at his own expense, but the reader must bear in mind that he's a filthy liar.

blow recounting of Undine War events with which virtually every contemporary Federation citizen is already more than familiar. It is, rather, a slice-of-life remembrance of the conflict, a decades-spanning chronicle of how profoundly the Undine War affected us all, even when most of us had no earthly idea of what we were really up against.

But before you forge ahead, let's have a word about history.

We're all familiar with the kind of history that gets entombed in textbooks. It is the edited monologue of victors, milled and processed to make the raw stuff of past events digestible for succeeding generations, reducing the warp and weft of human toil and triumph and folly to dry box scores of bloodless dates and places, key battles fought, venerated documents signed. Such "histories" are usually filled with more convenient errors, omissions, and contradictions than even professional historians probably realize. Of course, it could hardly be otherwise. History is all too often an exercise in mythopoeia, the vast, sub rosa, and not-always-conscious self-justification in which every civilization indulges once time's passage has allowed worlds-shaking events to drift to a comfortably safe, numb-nerved temporal distance. Interred deep in the archives of the Federation News Service, the Proxima News Service, the Tellar News Service, or the Ferengi Commercial News, its factual truths lie out of sight, and therefore out of mind.

And then there's the *other* variety of history. The kind that's been branded forever into the living memories of those on whom fate has chosen to bestow history as firsthand experience. It's the kind of history that's the stuff of holonews headlines, and which very often comprises the proverbial "interesting times" that the ancient Chinese regarded as a curse. This variety of history keeps and preserves the journalist's craft—what *Washington Post* owner and publisher Philip L. Graham called "the first rough draft of history that will never really be completed about a world we can never really understand"—and prevents it from being utterly erased by subsequent historical consensus. This kind of history takes to heart Johann Wolfgang von Goethe's assertion that "Life can only be understood backwards; but it must be lived forwards."

I hope that this volume is such a work: a partial overview of the Undine War, compiled from the running recollections of key figures who served as eyewitnesses to the Federation's long conflict with that enigmatic species. History as remembered by those who experienced those turbulent times as headlines. This is an attempt to balance the Department of Peace's initial goal of revising and preserving that "first rough draft" of Undine War history with the need to *analyze* that history, walking that history backward from our still-unfolding twenty-fifth-century vantage point while trying to soften the sometimes unforgiving lens of accumulated hindsight.

Because there can be no better witnesses to history than those who were there—especially the relative few who were called upon to risk everything on behalf of the needs of the many.

—Jake Sisko
Terrebonne Parish, Louisiana
Thursday, February 16, 2423

Jake Sisko is the author of the Betar Prize–winning Collected Stories *and the acclaimed novel* Anslem.

"Peace demands the most heroic labor and the most difficult sacrifice. It demands greater heroism than war. It demands greater fidelity to the truth and a much more perfect purity of conscience."

—THOMAS MERTON

"The needs of the many outweigh the needs of the few."

—SURAK, ANALECTS

The Undine War

UP CLOSE AND PERSONAL

Commander Drake, the agent from Starfleet Intelligence, has spent the past two days conducting lengthy interviews with every member of the crew who might have witnessed any part of the . . . incident that resulted in the sudden arrest and removal of Captain T'Vix, First Officer Donovan, and Security Chief Patel at Draken during one of the *Cochrane*'s routine patrols of the Romulan Neutral Zone boundary. Even *I* got interviewed for a couple of hours, and I was nowhere near the bridge when whatever was supposed to have happened there happened. After all, I'm just a *cook*.

It didn't take long for me to size up this Drake character as an inherently untrustworthy bastard. Commander Donovan probably would have described him as "oleaginous," but I'll settle for smarmy, or maybe just oily. Adjectives aside, I don't trust him any more than I trust those . . . creatures that Ensign Farquar tells me he somehow unmasked impersonating the captain, Commander Donovan, and Chief Patel. Which is why I'm making this recording on my own personal tricorder rather than on the *Cochrane*'s computer system. Before he leaves us, Drake will no doubt purge the

---

[*] December 20, 2396.

main computer of any explicit reference to what's just happened to the top of the *Cochrane*'s chain of command. That is, if he hasn't got around to doing it already.

This afternoon, Drake called me in to the temporary Starfleet Intel HQ he's set up for himself in Captain T'Vix's ready room. He assured me that I'm above suspicion now, though he won't tell me exactly why that is. Has he managed to run some sort of medical scan on me without my noticing? He isn't telling. Still, it was a relief to hear that I'm no longer considered a serious risk of suddenly transforming into a vicious, three-meter-tall praying mantis.

Then the oily bastard told me what he expects me to do next—entirely in my capacity as chef for the officers' mess, of course. Apparently, Drake is convinced that T'Vix, Donovan, and Patel weren't the only disguised monsters still trying to blend in among the *Cochrane*'s senior staff. He suspects that there at least two others, and he hopes an experimental food additive that SI has just developed—to be dispensed discreetly by me—will flush out any remaining infiltrators.

I almost wouldn't put it past him to give me poison to spike the food with, so that anybody who *doesn't* have to rush to sickbay before dessert will stand revealed as an enemy infiltrator. . . .

JAKE SISKO, DATA ROD #S-13

Kaferia (Tau Ceti IV), just outside the spaceport city of Amber

A man of early middle age greets me at the seafront resort, where a strip of low, modern hospitality structures fronts a wide swatch of fine white sand that borders a preternaturally calm, cerulean ocean. A few families and small children stroll the beach and wade out into the peaceful waters. When I turn my gaze inland past the buildings, I see groves of slender Kaferian apple trees swaying gently in the warm breeze. Although this place is the stuff of holosuite fantasies, I have it on very good authority that it is indeed real. If I had lived this man's life—that of a soldier who had survived an attempt to beard the Undine/8472 monster in its lair—I suspect I'd be sorely tempted to retire to someplace as peaceful as this.

Speaking with a faint but unmistakable Texas twang, the man introduces himself as Paul Stiles, a former Starfleet ensign turned enlisted private in the MACO (Military Assault Command Organization) during the "hot" part of the Undine War. He tells me he's now a master sergeant, retired, though a MACO is always a MACO.

Stiles's handshake is as firm as duranium, and his eyes—or some of the memories lodged inextricably behind them—look every bit as gray and unyielding. His gaze, though superficially warm, only barely conceals a cold, distant cast that reminds me of the million-mile stare I've seen in the eyes of Jem'Hadar soldiers. I can't quite tell whether his smile indicates genuine appreciation for an opportunity to record his combat experiences for posterity, or whether he's merely eager to get this interview done so he can go back to the business of putting the horrors of the war behind him. After we've been speaking for a few minutes I notice that this man often straddles a line between what I call "military briefer mode"—an emotionally unconnected, stick-to-the-facts mode of communicating—and the strained, melancholic silences of a soldier afflicted with survivor's guilt, a man who believes that he somehow let his fallen comrades down by making it safely home from the field of battle. I've encountered a lot of people like this. No matter what their counselors may tell them, no matter how many Christopher Pike Medals of Valor such men and women may receive, they will never measure up in their own uncompromising eyes, simply because they failed to do the impossible.

I notice right away that Sergeant Stiles is quick to scowl at my freely admitted ignorance of military lore, and that he is plainly uncomfortable hearing anything that sounds remotely like hero worship. Recollections of combat sometimes make him shudder visibly, making *me wonder if the Undine stalk him in his dreams even now. But he doesn't quite fit the profile of a chronic post-traumatic stress case, since he frequently dons a warrior's bluster that fits him like a comfortable pair of running shoes. His boasts might impress a Klingon, though they sometimes make him sound as though he's really whistling—or perhaps shouting—past the graveyard. But he is also quick to chuckle, and I get the feeling that he does so in response to some private joke rather than to any of my questions. I find that strangely reassuring—it almost makes me overlook the sense of hypervigilance the man radiates.*

Almost, but not quite.

You were a junior officer on a path toward a solid Starfleet career when the Undine conflict entered its "hot war" phase.

I was an ensign. A junior tactical officer with pretty good prospects for promotion. I was expected to be career Starfleet. There's always been a Stiles or three in the service, going back to the Earth-Romulan War. And we were a clan of web-footed wet-navy sailors before that.

So with all that tradition behind you, why did you transfer over to the MACO?

I have relatives who'd disagree with me loudly for saying this, but serving in Starfleet was never an end in itself to the Stiles clan. At least it shouldn't have been. I always saw it as merely a means of keeping humanity safe from whatever Big Bad might be out there sharpening its claws, getting ready to snuff us out, be it paranoid Xindi or Romulans, or those giant three-legged stick bugs who call themselves the Undine.

But Starfleet was heavily involved in the Undine War from the very beginning, just as it was in those earlier wars with the Xindi and the Romulans.
Mister Sisko, there's "involved" and then there's "committed." Those two concepts don't overlap as much as you might think in times of war. The difference between them is the same thing that separates the chicken from the pig at an old-fashioned breakfast. You see, the chicken is "involved" with breakfast.

But the pig is "committed."
That's it exactly. I wanted to be closer to the real action. Not sitting on the bridge of a ship, launching torpedoes by tapping at some tactile interface.

So you wanted the pig's greater "commitment" to the cause. But if you play that metaphor out to its conclusion, you're talking about a level of commitment that nobody can survive. A suicide mission.
As a MACO infantryman, you have to make peace with a truth as old as the Trojan War: you might come back with your shield carrying *you* instead of the other way around. And that's assuming that you

were lucky enough to come back at all. I've lost count of how many of my buddies were either vaporized in space, or buried on some godforsaken nowhere-world after a slash from some Trike's claws left him full of cooties that ate him from the inside out.

Trike?
Trike. Kickstand. Three-legged Deano. You know, the Undine.

Every war generates a fair amount of shorthand nomenclature, mostly pejorative, intended for refer-encing enemies. The Undine War is no exception to the grand military tradition that allowed such monikers as "Jerry," "Fritz," and "Victor Charlie" to enter the general lexicon. I understand the impulse. Still, I have to wonder how the many tripeds who served as MACOs during the war—Triexians and Edosians, to name only two species—feel when they hear a slur like "Trike." But I sense that bringing that up might not endear me to the sergeant.

Of course. You've been in closer quarters with the Undine than most Starfleet officers have managed to get.
I suppose I got closer to Deano than even most MACOs did.

Even that might be a bit of an understatement. After all, you're one of the relatively few humans who's

actually been aboard an Undine starship and lived to talk about it.

I just did what anybody else with the same training would have done: I tried to keep my buddies alive.

I'd like to discuss the boarding operation, if you don't mind. Can you give me some of the details?

I was serving with a MACO detachment that the *U.S.S. Thunderchild* was ferrying toward a hot spot just outside of the old Romulan Neutral Zone boundary. The place we were headed for was an asteroid, an airless hunk of rock and metal that the Romulans left honeycombed with mining tunnels. I never learned the Romulan name for the place, but I know it was renamed Chiron Beta Prime after the Earth-Romulan War left it under Earth's jurisdiction.

So we were training hard throughout the voyage, running environment-suit combat drills in holographic mine simulations throughout every duty shift. Didn't want to get caught with our cammies down around our ankles, you know?

It's a good thing you were so vigilant. According to the mission logs, the *Thunderchild* was nearly a parsec away from its destination when it encountered the spatial anomaly.

That's right. I heard later that Lieutenant Andex was at tactical when the bogey appeared, and that he reported the anomaly as a graviton ellipse. Most of the guys in the *Thunderchild*'s MACO unit assumed that

Deano had to be hiding either inside the ellipse or right behind it. All the squids on the bridge thought so, too.

Squids?
It's shorthand for "Starfleet." From an old nautical term referring to sailors. Goes back to the days when wet navies landed jarheads on beaches for amphibious assaults. The guys who piloted the boats were the squids. The marines who leaped off the boats to storm the beach were sharks. You know, like in the language of the Maori, where the word for "shark" is *mako?*

Anyhow, "squid" was our sort of good-natured nickname for the Starfleeters, though it didn't always fit them all that well. Take Andex, for example. He was from Sauria, and it would have been a lot easier to think of him as a "squid" if his mouth wasn't a half meter across and bristling with about a hundred steak-knife-sized teeth.

I want to thank you for being so patient with my asking questions that nobody who'd served either in Starfleet or with the MACO would have to ask. And I hope you'll indulge me with another stupid question: What exactly is a graviton ellipse?
I'm not surprised you don't know about those. Nobody in the MACO does, and in Starfleet it's next to nobody. A graviton ellipse is a small volume of normal space—it can range from microscopic size up to the size of a small asteroid, or maybe even bigger—that's been kicked into high warp speed because it

somehow got tucked inside an envelope of gravimetric distortion. GEs mostly travel through subspace, only popping out when their trajectories take them close to an EM hot spot—like a Federation starship on its way to a throwdown with the Kickstands.

Anyway, most everybody aboard expected the Trikes to leap out of the ellipse and down our throats any second. Me, I wasn't so sure.

Why?

Because of something nobody else in my combat unit was thinking about, probably because none of them were part squid the way I was. As dangerous as GEs can be, I knew that they had one redeeming trait: the fact that they're about as rare as monasteries on Risa. Only a handful of GEs have been documented since a big bastard of one plucked the old *Aries IV* command module right out of the Martian sky way back in 2032. If Deano really *was* surfing into our universe on top of that anomaly, then he was damned lucky to have found the perfect wave by sheer accident. Either that, or he was damned smart to have figured out how to re-create the very subspace storm that nearly shut down all human space exploration beyond the Earth-Luna system forever and ever, amen.

Well, we always knew that Deano was a clever bastard. Maybe even a *very* clever bastard, having built all those elaborate simulation-environments they'd used to train their fake-human infiltrators. He was certainly clever enough to surf in on a convenient spatial anomaly he happened to notice heading toward us through fluidic space and subspace. But was he a clever enough bastard to build both his own board and the wave beneath his three big nasty-scary feet? I was still holding out some hope that he hadn't gotten quite *that* clever yet.

The after-action reports of Commander Marta Segusa, the *Thunderchild*'s senior science officer, say that the initial analysis of the spatial anomaly turned out to be wrong. The phenomenon turned out not to be a graviton ellipse at all.
That's what Major Shea told us once the bridge crew discovered that what we were really dealing with was just a garden-variety subspace rift. I would have been relieved to hear that, but there wasn't time for that because the rift opened up almost directly in the *T-child*'s flight path. And it spat out a honking huge Trike bioship so close to us that we almost traded paint jobs.

The Undine ship was hiding inside the anomaly, waiting to ambush the *Thunderchild*?
It sure as hell looked that way. I mean, what are the odds of our two ships crossing paths purely by accident? Look, the word "astronomical" was coined specifically for situations like that one. Space is really, really *big*, so a haircut's-breadth near-collision like that couldn't have been an accident. I figured they must have entered normal space at the exact location

−13−

and time that they did because they knew we were coming. They were *watching* us. Somehow they had learned to monitor our universe from safely inside their own, or from inside subspace. And that allowed them to engineer the superluminal almost-crash that collapsed our warp field and knocked out our shields, among other things, in the same slick maneuver. Like I said, Deano is a very clever bastard—for a three-legged alien grasshopper from the darkest pit of hell, that is.

Before you boarded the Undine ship, did you get a good look at it from the outside?
Hell yeah. I saw way more of it than I wanted to, as it turned out, inside and outside. Neither one are sights you ever forget, no matter how much you might want to. I got a good, long look at the thing's hide—you have to call it that when you see it up close, since it resembles crocodile skin a lot more than it does hull metal—because one of the systems that went down during the near-crash was the transporter. So beaming a combat team inside Deano's ship simply wasn't an option. Fortunately, Major Shea and Sergeant Ogilvy had worked out a plan for this very contingency with Captain Hoffman and Lieutenant Andex: we did an old-school boarding, using breach pods.

I've had some . . . unfortunate experiences with escape pods, so I'm familiar enough with those. Can you explain how a breach pod is different?

Sure. A breach pod is really just an escape pod that's been repurposed to run *toward* trouble instead of *away* from it. Instead of abandoning the *Thunderchild* and the ship that was getting ready to rip her to pieces like a lion dismantling a zebra, we aimed our pods straight at the enemy. That was when I got my closest view of the outside of Deano's ship—when our pods approached that weird, bumpy hull, latched on with the magneto-mechanical grapplers, and started cutting into the crocodile hide of Deano's ship.

What was your first impression of the enemy vessel?
That it was actually *alive.* I mean, it didn't have a machined look to it. You could tell it wasn't built in any shipyard. Its hull metal didn't come from some foundry. It looked more like it was hatched from some enormous alien seedpod, or grown out of a blob of jelly from some colossal beehive. And it sort of . . . *undulated* through space like an enormous three-tailed squid with rough, mottled green skin and a mass of writhing, very grabby-looking tendrils streaming from the tip of the bow section. Or maybe that part was the thing's mouth. I don't know how else to describe it.

Anyway, when we were making our approach in the breach pods, it was as though we were moving in slow motion. It seemed to take a year to get through the few minutes it took to reach their hull, clamp on, and start cutting our way inside. That part I remember really well, since I was in charge of the cutting phaser. It felt like I was slicing into an impossibly huge pumpkin. It's funny, because I can remember thinking at the time that there was stuff inside the hull that had to be a hell of a lot scarier than pumpkin seeds.

The worst part of cutting our way in was the way the hull felt when I touched it, even through the environment suit's gloves. You'd swear the thing had a pulse, or that the ship's hide was actually recoiling from the cutting beam, the way the tourists here do when the local pollinators start swarming. Of course, I suppose that sensation could have been just a rumbling power conduit or something. But it was damned spooky just the same.

How big would you estimate the Undine ship was?
It was goddamned *big*. Nearly two hundred meters along the long axis, and maybe forty meters at the beam—if the damned thing *had* a beam, which I suppose comes down to whether the thing really was a ship or a living creature. Either way, there was a real sense of menace about it. You could feel it in your marrow when you stared at it. It was . . . *malevolent*. Sinister, full of hate. That ship, or whatever it was, was an abomination. Wrong as a Vulcan *drad* band.

But you went inside the thing with the boarding team anyway.
Boo-yah. I was MACO to the bone. A marine. Still am,

'cause there's no such thing as an "ex-marine." *Semper Fi, Semper Invictus.** We had a job to do, and we went in and did it. When we finished cutting through the hull and our escape pod started to flood with the squishy warm goo the Trikes used for an atmosphere, we weren't gonna let it slow us down. We just adjusted the breach pods' force fields to cram the stuff back into the breach in Deano's hull—and to carry us inside with it.

What did the Undine ship look like on the inside?
Everything was sort of indistinct, since we were trying to move in full environmental suits while carrying our rifles and field packs through "air" that had a viscosity factor like orange marmalade. But I remember stepping into a narrow corridor with shiny, glistening walls and deck that made a wet *squish* that got you thinking about revisiting your breakfast whenever you moved. It was like we had just been injected out of a giant hypospray into the veins of some alien leviathan.

But mostly I remember the hard surge of adrenaline that struck me like a disruptor bolt when the firefight got started. And it was "game on" from the moment we finished pushing through into the corridor, where we were caught immediately in a

---

* *Semper Fidelis* was the official Latin motto of the United States Marine Corps, while *Semper Invictus* was the Latin phrase similarly adopted by its twenty-second-century successor, the MACO (Military Assault Command Organization), which is still extant today.

crossfire, which must have been coming from at least two groups of Trikes that I couldn't see yet. Of course, with all the confusion of the battle, and the trouble we had with visibility, we probably lost at least a few to friendly fire.

Why were you having visibility problems? Do the Undine use a different spectrum of visible light than we do?
Deano obviously likes his mood lighting, and the ship's internal atmosphere really scattered our helmet lights. But if there's enough light to carry off a romantic dinner, then there's enough light for a MACO squad to put down a column of Kickstands. No, a lot of our visibility problems came from the e-suits themselves. They're a necessary evil in a ship that's designed to keep Deano comfy, but those helmets really cut down on your peripheral vision, which is tough to take in a close-quarters combat situation. That alone can raise the "scary factor" of anything by at least tenfold. Running into Flotter T. Watter III while I was wearing one of those helmets, and under those conditions, would have scared the living piss out of me. And if you have to face something that's *already* scary in circumstances like that . . . well, then you're just about certain to decorate the inside of your suit with the Brown Cluster Award for Combat Incontinence.

You were lucky you had enough time to get your breach pods into position on the hull before the

Undine managed to charge up their ship's external weaponry and open fire on you.

Damn right, you know? We were already slicing into Deano's hide when the Trikes finally cleared their tubes. We were literally already on top of them, so they couldn't hit us with their bio-pulse cannons or particle beams or projectiles without damaging themselves more than we'd already done. *Thunderchild* wasn't quite so lucky, though. She took several direct hits before Chief Engineer Thomas could get her shield generators back on line. The *T-child* was crippled, and she would have been destroyed entirely unless Deano got real distracted, real fast.

Didn't the Undine have shields of some sort to fend off boarders?

It's true, Deano usually had some pretty powerful shields up his sleeves. But this one's shields were down when it came swooping into normal space, as was his weapons array. The squid engineers chalked this up to the cost of this particular type of ambush maneuver, which temporarily disabled both ships, at least to some extent. The Kickstands were evidently gambling that their systems would recover faster than the *T-child*'s could. The Trikes were right about that, at least in terms of defense.

You mean they hadn't taken a MACO offense into account.

Well, I wasn't counting on that at the time, just hoping, and with a pretty fair degree of confidence, even though we all knew already what a tough sonofabitch Deano was. I mean, there was good reason to hope that they'd have real trouble coping with the MACO. After all, we'd heard a lot of thirdhand intel and scuttlebutt about the great lengths the Trikes had gone to in trying to infiltrate Starfleet. But nobody's ever found any evidence that they'd so much as tried to do that with the MACO.

An absence of evidence isn't evidence of absence. Starfleet Command once thought they'd made their ranks infiltration-proof, only to find out the hard way that they were wrong about that. There's a first time for everything, to coin a cliché.

I guess we'll have to wait and see, then. But if you ask me, I think Deano might have decided he just couldn't quite pull off a convincing impersonation of a MACO. Not after receiving the stern talking-to that we delivered that day. Maybe from that time forward he decided to spend his time going after easier targets.

About the combat itself: what kind of tactics were effective against an enemy like the Undine?

The squids used to consider a lot of our tactical plans unorthodox—until they saw them working in the field when standard procedures failed. I'm talking about a number of engagements with the Borg, the first of which left us sadder but wiser. Like Major Shea used to say, good judgment comes from experience—and experience comes from bad judgment. So I guess we have the Borg to thank for the fact that every MACO trooper in our boarding party was carrying energy dampeners and modified TR-116s instead of standard phasers.

Would you mind describing the TR-116?
The TR-116. My sweetheart. It's a piece of old-school warfare technology. The TR-116 is a rifle that Starfleet developed for use in high-radiation environments that would cripple a phaser. Or against enemies like the Jem'Hadar, or the Borg—a foe with the ability to shield itself from directed-energy weapons. But instead of firing a collimated energy beam, the TR-116 uses an internal chemical explosion to launch metal projectiles, either one at a time or in rapid-fire mode. We called it the T-Rex for short because it was a technological dinosaur. And because it was loud, not to mention scary as hell.

I remember someone going on a killing spree decades ago aboard Deep Space 9 using one of those things.
So you know how effective a weapon like that can be, even in the age of the phaser. The TR-116 can shred nearly any solid enemy with a lethal hail of ballistic micromissiles. It can even fire through most material barriers without so much as scratch-

ing the paint on the walls, thanks to its computerized targeting system and the microtransporter built into the barrel.

When we boarded Deano's ship, we had to soften him up before our T-Rexes could answer his greeting in the manner that etiquette demanded. Major Shea and Sergeant Ogilvy took care of that by launching the energy dampeners down that squishy-soft corridor in both directions. Usually we'd throw the damps like old-style grenades, but the viscous air forced us to launch 'em like mortars, or old-style rocket-propelled ordnance. There was a blinding flash a couple of seconds later, and the energy beams coming at us from both ends of the curving hallway immediately stopped.

That's when Deano came in close, once he realized his bio-pulse disruptors were out of commission. So we locked, loaded, and split into two back-to-back firing formations as they approached.

We can take a break if you'd like.
No. I'm fine. I'll just try to avoid going into too many of the gory details about what can happen when Deano has the home-field advantage. Like what happens to the human body after a Trike's claws slash open his e-suit and lets it fill up with that warm goo they pump their ships full of.

I've seen the logs from *Voyager*'s early encounters with the Undine. Ensign Harry Kim nearly died

after one of the creatures injected him with some sort of enzyme that started consuming him from the inside.

Nearly died. Huh. Deano must have learned something from his scrimmages with the *Voyager* squids. If the Trikes *we* fought got their claws on you, you were toast. No "nearly" about it.

Didn't your TR-116s at least discourage them?

Hell, yeah, even though there was some worry that the goo we were wading through might get past the protective coating on our T-Rexes and foul their firing mechanisms. But they knew right away that we weren't sending them valentines. We started choppin' 'em up like confetti the moment we were in position.

The trouble is, Deano doesn't discourage easily. He kept coming. And coming. And coming. And when they got close enough, those claws would fly at you faster than anything had the right to move. Especially something that spent its life submerged in pressurized jelly.

They fought like demons for every centimeter, and a few of them kept right on gaining ground no matter how many of them we blew to pieces right in front of their eyes. They'd just climb over each other, and all while the corpses and pieces of their dead just seemed to . . . melt very slowly back into that pile of bread dough they used for a deck. One of them got close enough for me to smell his sweat—if those monsters had sweat glands. But thanks to my helmet, all I could smell was my own reek. To this day, the scent of sweat in a confined space takes me right back to that time and place. . . .

But you made it through that time and place, and made it back. That says something about you.
Sure. It either says I'm lucky, or that I've borrowed every scrap of luck I might have counted on for the rest of this life and the next. Or maybe it says that the universe has a perverse sense of humor. We lost a lot of good marines in that battle. Better men and women than me, and smarter ones, too. People with families at home waiting for them. The major and the sergeant both bought it on that Trike ship, minutes apart. Then O'Neill. Palmieri. Clark.

I'm sorry.
Not *your* fault. Snavely was the first to go down.

Were you and Snavely close?
No. Corporal Snavely was insufferable. He always seemed to hold it against me that I'd been through Starfleet Academy and had an officer's commission before deciding to go jarhead. Thought I was a poseur for insisting on entering the MACO as a noncom instead of an officer, which I could have done if I'd put in the paperwork. Snavely and I used to argue constantly. Not about anything important, you understand. Just . . . philosophical points. Stuff that seems kind of silly now, after the war.

What kind of philosophical points?
War and peace. Are any of the alien races out there really so different from us that we can never find a way to cope with them other than war? I tended to take the more optimistic Starfleet position in that particular recurring fight. Snavely always toed the more conservative line, which was really nothing more than MACO conventional wisdom, at least for the most part. Snavely was just a bit louder and more obnoxious in talking up that philosophy than most of our fellow MACOs tended to be. It's not that we MACOs don't like to talk, or even debate—I mean, I'm letting you talk to me, aren't I?—but most of us would rather spend our time training than thrashing out some cocktail-party controversy. Or better yet, fighting a real, concrete, flesh-and-blood enemy.

But whatever Snavely and I might have thought about each other didn't matter at the time. He was a brother in arms, and I hadn't stopped Deano from getting close enough to grab him. None of us had. We weren't even able to prevent Deano from carrying off his body. Not to mention some of the others they'd torn to pieces during the fight. . . .

I know that the MACO are committed to the ideal of never leaving a comrade behind. It must have been extremely difficult for you to be put in a position—
Of failure, you mean.

No. Of being forced to withdraw without being able to pick up any of your fallen comrades.
I suppose that's one way of looking at it.

Your assault on the Undine vessel can hardly be called a failure. The enemy clearly sustained the biggest losses. And you and others made it back alive, and were decorated for conspicuous bravery.
We just did whatever seemed to make the most sense under the circumstances. There were a few of us left after Deano finally saw the better part of valor and scattered. But we'd taken heavy losses—three quarters of us were already either dead or dying—and we were running low on ammo to boot. Then our corpsman's tricorder registered an onboard energy spike that could only mean that Deano had activated his autodestruct system. Since we were in no position to secure the Trike ship or prevent the explosion we all knew was coming, it wasn't hard to be persuaded to withdraw to the breach pods, which were about to become escape pods.

Judging from the after-action reports I've read, you were the one who had to do most of the persuading.
Even through those e-suit helmets, I could see a lot of blank, exhausted, and frightened faces. We'd just lost both the major and the sergeant, and everybody else at the top of the chain of command. Somebody had to take charge, or else we'd all have been blown

to quarks, just like all the Kickstands who'd managed to run from the teeth of our T-Rexes.

So you left in the same pods you'd arrived in.
Less than a minute before Deano's ship went up in the biggest fireworks display since the Hobus supernova. *Thunderchild,* or what was left of her, picked us up a few hours later.

Do you suppose any of the Undine managed to escape from their ship before it blew?
I sure as hell hope not. And not because I've let my commitment to fighting Deano lead me into becoming unhinged with hatred for an old foe in an old war that ended years ago—even though for some time afterward I still felt committed to ferreting out every last Kickstand and wringing his bony neck with my bare hands. . . .

I'm not here to judge your motivations, Sergeant. I'm not a Starfleet counselor.
I just don't want to leave anybody with the impression that we MACOs are nothing but bloodthirsty, chest-thumping killers. We're *warriors.* There's a big difference between those two things. If you don't already understand the difference, then I suggest you spend some time hanging around with Nausicaans. Assuming you survive that, move on to the Klingons next. There's no comparison.

But I'm wandering off, aren't I? Retirement must

finally be turning me into an old man. Now where was I?

I think you might have been about to drill down into your reasons for hoping that none of the Undine survived your engagement with them during the voyage to Chiron Beta Prime.

Right. The reason I still hope to this day that none of those Trikes got out of that ship alive is that I know all about how Deano pulls off his infiltrations. He can do it, and get away with it, because he has a talent for doing near-perfect impersonations. But he can only do *that* if he has access to the DNA of the person he's mimicking.

If Deano managed to sneak off that ship, he could have taken the DNA of a bunch of my dead buddies with him. And if that's what really happened, then there's no way to stop him from using that DNA to make doppelgängers—very close copies of human beings that are actually pure, distilled Deano, at least under the skin.

But I thought you said you considered the MACO to be infiltration-proof.

And *you* said there's a first time for everything. Well, you're probably right about that. I mean, just because something *hasn't* happened yet doesn't mean it *can't* happen.

Even now, so long after the end of the war?

When something can give so many people so many

nightmares this many years later, you have to ask yourself if the war's ever going to end—at least while any of us who saw it up close and personal are still on this side of the grass.

Suppose you *do* bump into one of your MACO buddies who was confirmed to have died in that battle all those years ago. That person would have to be a disguised Undine by definition. Do you think you're prepared for that?

I don't know if anybody can ever really be prepared for something like that, Mister Sisko. But if Deano really *does* try to use DNA from my MACO unit as cover for one of his spies, I'll rely on my training and do whatever has to be done. That's what commitment is all about, after all.

Anyhow, if Deano ever actually sends one of his spies-in-human-clothing my way, I only hope he sends me one that looks just like Snavely.

Still carrying a grudge against your old debating nemesis?

Nah. It's not that. It's just that I hate having to admit that the bastard seems to have won that running argument we used to have about war and peace. Sharks one, squids zero. It's a little disappointing, is all.

Maybe deep down you're really more squid than shark.

Maybe. But Deano taught me that the big bad ocean we all have to swim in is a lot safer for sharks than for squids. The problem is, some fish are so big and nasty that they can gulp 'em both down, squid or shark, in one shot.

I decide to wrap up the interview quickly after Stiles's final mention of Snavely's name. That's because a wicked-looking knife, apparently concealed in Stiles's sleeve, appears in the retired sergeant's hand as though conjured by magic. An almost predatory grin slowly spreads across his face as he speaks of the possibility of encountering an Undine replica of one of his fallen comrades. Needless to say, I feel intensely uncomfortable, though I do my level best not to let Stiles know it. I hope my experience writing fiction has made me a convincing enough actor.

Then Stiles thanks me for allowing him to tell his story, says his farewells, and leaves me standing alone except for a few quietly strolling tourists, listening to the distant keening of Kaferian seabirds. I spend an uncountable interval standing in the warm, faintly saline breeze, silently processing what I've seen and heard—until it becomes crystal clear to me just what the Long War has cost Paul Stiles.

This protracted twilight struggle has caused him to jettison the long-cherished belief, inculcated during his time in Starfleet and stomped to an ignominious death by his tenure among the MACO, that peace is an achievable goal.

JAKE SISKO, DATA ROD #H-4

Septimus Settlement Observation Tower,
Heronius IIc

Although none of the constellations that bejewel the black sky look at all familiar to me, I find myself tracing the gaps between the individual stars anyway, my finger brushing the panoramic transparent aluminum window as I connect the distant pinpoints of fire into ad hoc shapes composed of lines and curves. Below the alien starfield, the window reveals a battered, gray moonscape that looks a lot like the vast tracts of still relatively untouched vacuum wilderness that even today encompass most of the surface of Luna back home.

I am thankful for the artificial one-g environment that prevails in this visitors' center as I cast my eyes upon two other, similarly scarred gray worlds. These bodies are visible as narrow crescents floating just above the horizon, framing the blue-and-garnet planet that has just finished making its ascent above the jagged line of rugged scarps and crater rims in the distance. Heronius II is nearly at full phase, presenting a slightly oblate shape in the brilliance of the twin suns of the Heronius system. Though the planet looks superficially like Earth, its profusion of suns and satellites—not to mention the unfamiliar constellations in its night skies—ensures that there is little chance of confusing this place with the birthplace of humanity.

Despite the alienness of these skies, or perhaps because of it, this system is home to at least a million humans and humanoids. More than a few of Heronius II's settlers have used this world as a jumping-off point for further explorations of deep space. Exobiologists Magnus and Erin Hansen were two such adventurers, and they number among the few that never made it back to Heronius because of the manifold dangers that dwell in the unexplored reaches that lay beyond these cosmic shores. One of these dangers turned out to be the Borg collective, which forcibly assimilated the Hansens—along with their child, a six-year-old girl named Annika.

After two decades of enslavement by the Borg collective, during which time she lived under the designation of Seven of Nine, Tertiary Adjunct of Unimatrix One, Annika Hansen eventually found her way back—both to her humanity and to the world her parents had embraced a lifetime ago. Other than a certain rigidity in her bearing and the gleaming metal filigree that adorns her left brow, the tall, stern, and apparently middle-aged woman with whom I now share this stunning view of Heronius II displays no trace of her twenty-year cybernetic nightmare. Of course, not all scars are immediately visible on the outside. I haven't exactly *been the president of the Borg collective's fan club since the Battle of Wolf 359, so I'm thankful for that.*

We could have met on the planet itself, but Ms. Hansen asked me to speak with her here instead, where our viewpoint seems decidedly Olympian. Or perhaps "Borgian" would be more accurate. I find myself wondering which of the two adjectives is most applicable as our conversation begins.

Many years ago, you famously predicted a wave of new Borg attacks, even as Starfleet was disbanding its Borg Task Force.
I do not always enjoy being proved right. Particularly where the Borg collective is concerned.

Don't worry. I wasn't expecting you to gloat.
Gloating is inefficient, as well as inappropriate. However, I suppose an "I told you so" might have been in order.

You left Starfleet over their assessment of the threat posed by the Borg, didn't you?
Correct. With Starfleet's Borg Task Force disbanded, I believed I could accomplish more in terms of maintaining the Federation's readiness to repel Borg incursions by accepting a position at the Daystrom Institute.

During those years, you said very little to the media, either about the Borg or anything else. Did you

continue to offer advice to Starfleet concerning the Borg even after you took the Daystrom job?

I did, though the effort turned out to be wasted.

I see. "Assistance is futile."

How very droll, Mister Sisko. But you are correct. Clearly, Starfleet Command was uninterested at best—until it was very nearly too late. But I thought you had come to discuss the conflict with Species 8472.

Just setting the stage. After all, we wouldn't have encountered that species if not for the Borg. Let's go back to the beginning. You were present when *Voyager* made first contact with the Undine— Species 8472.

Other than Admiral Janeway, you're the only person I've interviewed who still refers to them by their Borg designation.

I was Borg for many years. The collective leaves a lasting imprint, even on those who manage to escape it.

The Borg and the Undine were deadly enemies from the time of their first meeting. You were still part of the collective then, weren't you?

Yes. First contact between the collective and Species 8472 occurred on Stardate 50762. I was still serving as the Tertiary Adjunct of Unimatrix One at that time.

That must surely give you a unique perspective on the Undine.

I was among the first to witness just how formidable Species 8472 can be against anyone they consider an adversary—even against an enemy as powerful and as determined as the Borg.

Weren't the Undine the only species ever to successfully resist Borg assimilation?

Species 8472 was the first such species.

You sound as though you expect there to be others.

I would argue that there already is at least one other such species. In my estimation, humanity qualifies as the second. That could change, of course, once the collective returns yet again to renew its efforts to assimilate us. The possibility always exists that they will overwhelm us eventually with sheer numbers, or volume of force.

Well, at least it's nice to hear that resistance may not be _entirely_ futile.

Only unpreparedness and complacency are futile, Mister Sisko. Any other measure, however difficult, is worth considering when confronted with implacable enemies such as the Borg—or Species 8472.

Humanity's so-called resistance to Borg assimilation—or even to outright destruction by the collective—was actually the cumulative effect of

a whole lot of hard-fought, bloody battles. But the Undine's resistance was another thing entirely. How were they able to thwart Borg assimilation so thoroughly, and so early in their . . . relationship with the collective?

Species 8472's natural immune response to Borg nanoprobes is formidable.

"Natural immune response" looks like an understatement to me. The Undine didn't simply beat the Borg back during that first clash. They wiped out whole fleets of Borg cubes. Millions of drones. Entire Borg planets.

Indeed. Species 8472 handed the collective its first serious defeat in the many millennia of its existence. In fact, they posed a serious existential challenge to the Borg as a race.

That gives us at least a rough idea of how serious the Undine threat was to the Federation. It seems that they posed an even bigger danger to us than the Borg did. Earth escaped Borg assimilation twice, and at a tremendous cost on both occasions. But during the first round of their fight with the Borg, the Undine delivered a near-knockout blow. And yet not even the Undine were able to wipe the Borg out entirely.

Of course not. However, Species 8472 might well have utterly exterminated the collective had the Borg not adopted a technological countermeasure developed aboard *Voyager*.

You're referring to Kathryn Janeway's decision to furnish specially modified nanoprobes to the Borg in exchange for *Voyager*'s safe passage through their space. Some have called Janeway's bargain a "deal with the devil" that was ultimately responsible for the Undine deciding to treat us as a Borg ally, and therefore as one of their enemies in our own right. They blame Janeway for the "blowback" that created the deadliest adversary that the Federation has ever faced.

That perspective is both incorrect and foolish. Kathryn Janeway made the best decision possible at the time, given both her responsibility for the safety of her crew and the incomplete nature of the information she possessed. She did not discover until later that the Borg had lied to us about Species 8472 being the instigators of their conflict, when the exact opposite was the truth. The admiral's critics ought to commend her for being the first human to obtain a truce of any sort with Species 8472. Even if the agreement she struck turned out to be with just a small faction of the 8472 civilization.

Forgive me for noticing, but the notion of Janeway being at fault for putting the Federation in harm's way vis-à-vis the Undine appears to make you . . . well, angry.

Anger is irrelevant. I simply do not appreciate the idea.

You also seem to take it personally.
Would it really be inappropriate for me to take such an insult personally? Kathryn Janeway saved me from a waking nightmare. Although it was often a difficult and painful process, she restored my humanity to me. She deserves respect, not ignorant criticism. And she most certainly does *not* deserve to be blamed for Species 8472's attacks against the Federation.

That's probably true. But your anger suggests that you think *somebody* deserves the blame that's been directed at Janeway, rightly or wrongly. Who do you think that might be?
I'm not certain I can see the relevance of your question. However, if I were to accept for the sake of argument that blame should be assigned for enabling Species 8472 to become an existential threat to us, then it would be most appropriately directed at the Borg collective.

Which you were still a part of when it started its war against the Undine—a war that eventually spilled over into the Federation's lap.
Your historical analysis is facile and lacking in detail. But it is also essentially correct.

At the risk of getting too personal, it seems to me that you would sooner blame yourself than your former captain for the escalation of the Undine threat.
Nonsense. "Blame" is irrelevant, Mister Sisko. The

universe and the circumstances that arise within it simply are what they are, and we must rise to face them *as* they are. It is just that simple.

Now, do you have any further *relevant* questions?

I hope so. I also hope I haven't offended you.
Offense is irrelevant. The chronometer, however, is not. I have a great deal of work to do, so please get on with your questions.

All right. The ease with which the Undine took down the Borg collective and nearly exterminated it right after the two societies made first contact has always bothered me—as has the Borg's ability to bounce back from that conflict, as they appear to have done from other "killing blows" they took subsequently.
I have devoted a great deal of study to those very subjects, particularly since the start of my tenure at the Daystrom Institute. However, you must remember that despite its impressive array of capabilities, not even Species 8472 is omnipotent. And neither is the Borg collective.

But the Undine were certainly powerful enough to teach the Borg a valuable lesson about survival. The Federation needs to find out precisely how the Borg managed the trick of not only enduring an Undine onslaught, but also recovering from it.
Be careful what you wish for, Mister Sisko. Humanity may yet have to learn those lessons the hard

way, directly from Species 8472 itself. Even Starfleet Command appears to concede that point now, their recent experiences with the Borg having left them sadder but wiser—and more amenable to listening.

Point taken. But what I meant was that maybe the Borg could teach humanity a thing or two about survival should the Undine ever mount another large-scale offensive.

When they mount another large-scale offensive. Not *if.* But you are otherwise correct. Knowing everything that the Borg collective knows about fighting off Species 8472 would be invaluable to the Federation. I would favor striking such a deal with them should the opportunity arise.

Even at the risk of making another "deal with the devil"?

It is true that there would be a significant risk of the collective reneging on any such deal. The Borg are not known for their willingness to negotiate deals or engage in trade, after all. On those rare occasions when the collective does consent to such agreements, it often as not subjects them to unilateral modification. Dealing with the Borg in any capacity requires extreme vigilance.

But it isn't out of the question.

Obviously, I cannot speak for the Federation's policymakers. However, I *can* say that many Starfleet officers of my acquaintance would certainly be capable of grasping such an opportunity under the appropriate circumstances.

I suppose you might even say that your standing here now speaking with me can be seen as living proof of that.
You might indeed, Mister Sisko. You might indeed.

A smile creases her still supple face as she leaves her final answer hanging in the air between us before bidding me adieu in order to return to her labors—the eternal, never-finished work of a professional watcher. After all, for everything else Annika Hansen may be or may have been—scientist, engineer, and tactical adviser both to Starfleet's admiralty and to the Federation's top civilian officials—she is a dedicated seeker after portents of imminent attacks by the most lethal imaginable enemies, as well as opportunities to use the other foes' tactics against them.

Her obvious sense of ex-drone's guilt over having helped, however peripherally, to stir up the Undine hornet's nest in the first place demands that she do no less.

As I mentioned earlier, Annika Hansen could have asked me to meet her for this interview beneath the mild, beneficent skies of Heronius II, rather than from a vantage point some four hundred thousand kilometers above the planet's surface. But that was not her preference. It's as though she wishes to keep the planet on which she lived and played as a small child at arm's length, emotionally speaking, even after the passage of all the intervening decades.

But after having conducted a fairly lengthy conversation with this bluntspoken woman (lengthy by her standards, at least), I decide that her choice of backdrops for this meeting is an artifact neither of Borg detachment nor Olympian arrogance. Her perspective is a perfectly understandable one, especially for someone who has demonstrated as much concern for humanity's safety and well-being as she has since her liberation from the collective. After all, it's hard to imagine anyone who'd literally grown up in the thrall of the Borg having anything other than an outsider's perspective on the human species—just as it is difficult not to look upon an inhabited, M-class world like Heronius II from such a lofty, isolated perch without also experiencing intensely the fragility and vulnerability of life in a cosmos so surfeited with inimical forces.

Whatever her watchfulness against both the Borg and the Undine may have cost Annika Hansen over the years, her unending vigilance still has yet to rob her—thankfully—of that lamentably rare perspective.

The Undine

A VIEW FROM AN IVORY TOWER

. . . My blooded warrior brethren, the Federation, and the *tera'ngan* [Earth humans], *vulqangan* [Vulcans], *tella'ngan* [Tellarites], and *andor'ngan* [Andorians] who were so instrumental in its misbegotten creation, have ever been enemies of the Empire, going back to the pestilence their Captain Archer visited upon our ancestors centuries ago! There can be no question that the time is ripe to invade their worlds, and to revel in the lamentations of their women and children! The time has come to scuttle their *'ejyo'* [Starfleet], to slay their so-called defenders in their tracks, to beard their craven so-called leaders in the very burrows that will become their ignominious, unmarked graves!

I understand those of you who may object to the timing, if not to the intent, of my appeal to the Council's warrior spirit this day. Yes, we are presently at war with the *romuluSngan*

---

[*] April 1, 2389—as if the gathering threat of the Undine wasn't causing the Federation enough trouble.

[Romulans], and with the *gorngan* [Gorn] as well. But we are a warrior people. When was it ever not thus? War does not enquire after our convenience. It is the only way of life that assures we remain fully, completely Klingon! I trust I need not remind this august body of a fundamental, bedrock truth: *tlhIngan maH!* [we are Klingons!] We are deterred neither by the quantity nor the number of our foes.

Yet still, some of you continue to ask your-selves, "Is today a good day to die?" That is a fair question, though it is one that I must answer with *another* question. Is it not better to confront and beat back an implacable foe? Or is it more desirable to allow that enemy to slowly annex our space, quietly choking off future avenues for Klingon conquest, all the while smiling and mouthing fanciful plati-tudes about peaceful coexistence?

"Is today a good day to die?" Perhaps the best answer I can supply to the question is this one: It is a good day for the *Federation* to die. Or, as the great Kahless said, "*QamvIS Hegh qaq law' torvIS yIn qaq puS.*" ["Better to die on one's feet than to live on one's knees."]

JAKE SISKO, DATA ROD #P-28

Amherst College, Amherst, Massachusetts, Earth

Professor Timothy T. Palmer is a tall, gangly man with an unruly mop of graying hair. His postdoctoral field-work in alien psychology and anthropology began half a century ago, when he was a junior member of a Federation exoanthropological team observing an Iron Age–level Vulcanoid culture on Mintaka III. Dr. Palmer learned early just how badly awry alien encounters can go (even when both sides have only the best of intentions) in 2366, when the highly rational yet fearful Mintakans tried to offer him to their gods as a human sacrifice. After that early near-disaster, Dr. Palmer's career has encompassed dozens of far more successful alien contacts, culminating in his current posting as chair of Amherst's Department of Exo-anthropology—from which he propounds a decidedly unconventional, if not downright contrarian, view of the Long War against the Undine.

Although Palmer speaks quickly and has a no-nonsense air about him, he smiles and laughs easily as he strikes an old-style sulfur match against the desk, leans forward across a heaving sea of books and padds and papers to transfer a tiny, guttering flame to a second anachronism, a very handmade-looking briar pipe. Having spent a fair amount of time with bohemian types over the years, I'm familiar with the not altogether unpleasant sweet-acrid aroma of high-quality synthacco that soon permeates the small office. As Dr. Palmer turns to toss his spent match into the waste disposal slot, I notice the patches sewn onto the elbows of his jacket.

In keeping with his contrarian reputation, Dr. Palmer doesn't wait for me to start asking questions.

Mister Sisko, it's common wisdom these days to look at the Undine War as another "good war," like the conflict with the Dominion, or even World War II. Even most academics have readily fallen into this "good war" trap.

"Trap," Professor? I mean no disrespect, but what other way is there to look at it? The Allies had to defeat the Axis powers back in the middle of the twentieth century, just as the Federation had to defeat the Borg, the Dominion, and the Undine. I'm no lover of war, but you have to admit that we wouldn't be having this conversation if the aggressors in any of those wars—including the Undine War—hadn't been defeated.

Of course, of course. Setting aside the Undine for the moment, all the other wars you mentioned were at least arguably inevitable. Perhaps even noble.

But the Undine civilization is not Nazi Germany, or Imperial Japan, or even the Borg collective. The ordinary dynamics of war that have motivated humans and humanoids for millennia simply do not apply to the Undine.

Which "dynamics of war" are you talking about specifically?
The need to acquire new resources and territory. Look, in the mid-twentieth century, the Axis powers of Germany and Japan stood in contention against the United States and the democracies of Europe on a finite globe. Territory and material wherewithal have sharply defined limits for nations bound to a single forty-thousand-kilometer-circumference globe. And perhaps more fundamentally, Earth's World War II represented a clear-cut choice between freedom and tyranny. The planet simply couldn't accommodate both the democratic ideology of the Allies and the authoritarian worldview of the Axis, since both had essentially the same need for expansion and growth. The same applies to the Borg collective, which had to engulf and devour whole worlds continuously in order to sustain the cancerous rate of growth to which it had become accustomed.

But the Undine are entirely different. They aren't playing the same game at all.

I'll give you that the Undine were a good deal more subtle than the Borg, with their preference for slow

infiltration over quick conquest. But they seemed no less aggressive than the Borg. How were the Undine any different, really, or less of a threat?

The Undine posed a very real threat, no question— but only because we confirmed their worst xenophobic fears by enabling the Borg to defeat them.

You seem to be saying that the Undine War was *our* fault.

In a manner of speaking, it was. Look at it this way: the Undine certainly didn't attack us because they needed to take anything we have. They have the run of an entire universe of their own, after all.[*] Like I said, war is usually about the need for expansion and resources. But not *this* war.

So the Undine wanted revenge?

Don't make the mistake of anthropomorphizing the Undine. They aren't human—or even humanoid, except when they morph themselves using extreme technological measures—and that means that their emotions and motivations might not be entirely congruent with our own, or even entirely fathomable. But they clearly didn't attack us merely to raid our resources. Look, twenty years ago the Undine established that they had all the resources they needed to

---

[*] The extradimensional realm that has become widely known as "fluidic space" since its discovery in 2373 by the crew of the *Starship Voyager*. As the name suggests, matter in this dimensional plane exists in a "fluidic" state, as does space itself.

resist the Borg, and perhaps even to eliminate them once and for all. Or at least they did until Kathryn Janeway traded technology to the Borg—technology that left the Undine vulnerable as never before to a devastating attack by the Borg collective.

The Borg gave the Undine the first name we humans ever knew them by: Species 8472.
That's right. "Undine" is Species 8472's own name for itself, rendered in their own language—or at least it's as close as any humanoid speech organ can come to pronouncing it. The word translates into Federation Standard, roughly, as "Groundskeepers," which would seem to imply that they feel a sense of stewardship toward their home realm of fluidic space.

That's ironic, considering all the destruction they've caused in *our* universe.
Perhaps not, at least from their own perspective. They see us as hungry coyotes who have threatened all life in *their* universe. They're merely acting as lookouts and watchmen—watchmen who aren't afraid to pick up their shotguns and open fire.

In spite of the nonaggression agreement Kathryn Janeway struck with them in 2375.
Janeway was dealing with only one small group of Undine, so that agreement was never binding on anyone *beyond* that small group. She never had the ear of the entire society, nor did she give us so much

as an inkling of how many factions might have had to come to the negotiating table in order to secure a substantive, enduring peace with all the various Undine groups.

Maybe we and the Undine are simply too different from each other to permit a real, permanent understanding to develop. Maybe force is the only way to answer them if they ever come back.

I don't think so. I truly believe that there's something of us in them, and vice versa, if only by dint of the fact that humanity and the Undine are both sentient species. I believe that they're connected to us on some deep if obscure level.

Judging from the vast biological differences between us and them, "obscure" might just be the mother of all understatements. For instance, the Undine DNA helix is a braid of three strands, compared to our two. They have at least five sexes. Their bodies produce enzymes that can literally eat human beings alive, from the inside out. And they're too cantankerous to be assimilated by the Borg collective.[*] If the Undine are "connected" to us, it's difficult for me to see how.

I'm not speaking strictly about biology, although it's an at least anecdotally documented fact that the

---

[*] For more insights into the Borg collective's failed attempt to conquer the Undine, I recommend my O. Henry tribute, "The Assimilation of Red Chief," from my *Collected Stories*. (J.S.)

Undine are capable of falling prey to a certain . . . fascination with human and humanoid cultures.

Any species that has placed such a large number of deep-cover spies on Federation worlds has to know that a certain small percentage of their "sleeper agents" are always bound to get a little bit too comfortable while living undercover and end up "going native," so to speak.

Perhaps, but the phenomenon of sleeper agents "going native" is real and documented. It stands as evidence that at least some small patch of common ground might exist upon which to build a bridge between the two cultures. Even their native collective name of "Undine" presents us with a curious cross-cultural connection. I refer, of course, to the Undine from Roman mythology.

The water elementals?

Exactly. Undine, from the Latin noun *unda*, which means "wave." And the Undine come from a place called "fluidic space." What better home for water elementals who call themselves Undine? Not to mention the fact that their efforts to integrate our DNA into their bodies resonate with the myths in which the mythical Undine could gain a soul only by giving birth to a human child.

Couldn't that be a simple coincidence?

We once believed that the plenitude of similar

humanoid societies across the galaxy was merely the work of coincidence, too. We now know better, Doctor Hodgkin's Laws notwithstanding.

But we're digressing. To the Borg, the Undine were simply another nameless, numerically designated species. Yet another potential assimilation, and a prospective new notch on the collective's belt. And to us—or rather to Janeway—the Undine were less than nothing. They were merely a means to an end. A bargaining chip that Janeway used to get her ship and her crew home from deep Delta Quadrant space a little more quickly than might have been possible otherwise. No wonder the Undine learned to fear and hate us as much as they have over the years since then.

Forgive me, Professor, but didn't you warn *me* not to anthropomorphize the Undine?
I acknowledge that there are limits to scientific objectivity. It's part of being human, I suppose. And remember, it's not as though the Undine know nothing about being human, given the number of times they've infiltrated Federation worlds over the past couple of decades.

By disguising themselves as humans and members of other humanoid races.
"Disguise" hardly does justice to what the Undine infiltrators do when they go under "deep cover" on a Federation world. They don't simply don a disguise,

or change their features cosmetically. They actually alter their DNA at the codon level in order to ensure that they can pass as human. That's no mean feat, this little understood retooling of their own densely packed, three-stranded DNA to make it compatible with the much simpler, two-stranded stuff we keep coiled in *our* cell nuclei. Despite all the difficulties involved, the imposture is usually so perfect as to be virtually undetectable.

Except when the faux-humanoid DNA breaks down, causing an Undine to spontaneously revert to its native form.

Which merely demonstrates that no plan, no matter how brilliantly conceived or executed, is perfect. But perfection was the goal of the Borg collective, which nobody seems to be all that frightened of these days. The Undine merely had to do a good enough job at infiltration to leave us wondering how many more of their operatives *weren't* accidentally revealing their presence because of some chance nucleic-acid-level cellular meltdown. In fact, the occasional sudden public "reversion" probably helped the Undine's cause more than it hurt it. Those periodic reversals, when they happened in plain sight, allowed the Undine to sow fear, nurture it with the passage of time and the fertilizer of the humanoid imagination, harvest it like a cash crop, and export it all over the galaxy. No wonder the Undine inspire such a unique level of fear among humanoid species, even now.

Not even the Klingons are immune to it, for all their bluster.

I have a few Klingon acquaintances who might take rather sharp exception to that, Professor.
Of course. Klingons will be Klingons, after all.

Humans, Klingons, and Romulans all faced shape-changers during the Dominion War. What do you think it is about Undine infiltration that's more terrifying than the masquerades the Founders used to perform in our midst? Or the mass identity thefts committed by the Borg, for that matter?
It's true, we have endured this sort of existential terror before, thanks to the Founders of the Dominion, and to the Borg collective as well. But those earlier assaults on personal human sovereignty were somehow less all-encompassing than what the Undine tried to do. True, the Founders created a lot of confusion on Earth during the years leading up to the Dominion War, which cost the lives of millions of Federation citizens and nearly a billion Cardassians before it was over. But a Borg assimilation bespoke such a profound loss of identity as to be tantamount to outright murder. And the few Founders that managed to infiltrate Earth could only copy a person's gross external characteristics. All it took was a simple blood test to uncover the ruse.

But Undine imposture is a very different thing. When the Undine steal a humanoid's identity, they take it all the way down to the genomic level, making the infiltration all but undetectable. If I were part of the philosophy department, I might describe it as an almost literal theft of the soul. Or maybe, to put it in law school terms, it's a kind of "copyright infringement" of the soul. This predilection with taking the only thing humans generally believe is indissoluble from existence itself—the notion of identity—is, I think, what makes the Undine so fundamentally frightening, even in a galaxy that's fraught with encounters with every other imaginable sort of terrifying adversary.

I couldn't help but notice that you often refer to the Undine in the present tense, even though there hasn't been a major incursion during the last several years.
You're a very astute and attentive interviewer.

I'm also one who's immune to flattery, Professor, but thank you anyway. It sounds as though you're saying that you don't believe the Undine War is really over.
Not for a Scalosian minute.

Life During Wartime

FEAR AND DISILLUSIONMENT VERSUS IDEALISM AND COURAGE

To: Martok, son of Urthog, Chancellor of the Klingon Empire and leader of the High Council
From: Quen, Klingon Intelligence
Re: After Action Report, *choS* Battle Group

Chancellor, I regret to inform you of the loss of the *choS* Battle Group. The crews fought with honor, sacrificing everything to send back to us intelligence about a new threat to the Empire.

The image included in this missive is of the ship that destroyed the battle group. We know little about this starship other than that, and what we do know is due to the heroic actions of Captain D'rakal and his crew. They died well, and I honor them.

In its continuing investigation into the events of the Ho'buS [Hobus] supernova, agents of Imperial Intelligence have been looking into reports of incredibly advanced starships appearing in Romulan space.

There must be some validity to these rumors. The *Narada* was a civilian ship captained by a common miner. Nero was no warrior, and yet he defeated a fleet of our finest starships! I cannot look in the faces of the mates and children of blooded Klingon warriors and tell them that these great men and women were killed by a miner! Even if all of the Fek'lhri had fought at his side, this should not have happened. I will not rest until I have uncovered the truth of all that occurred.

With the chaos enveloping the Romulan colony worlds, entering Romulan space has become a simple matter of engaging our cloaking devices. This is the perfect time to increase intelligence gathering, and I strongly recommend that the High Council authorizes more espionage missions. The more information we have, the more questions about the Ho'buS supernova and the destruction of the fleet we will be able to answer.

To this end, on the fifth day of the month of *Soo'jen*, in the Year of Kahless 1,015 [Stardate 66710.12*] the Klingon Defense Force ordered the *Qiv*, the *Tagak*, and the *Ki'tang* to find a space station known as the Forge.

Reconstruction of the *Narada*'s movements before Nero engaged the Klingon fleet has revealed that the *Narada* diverted to an area of deep space near Chorgh'etlh [Eta Crucis], where it stayed for several days. It may have been here that Nero acquired the advanced technology and weaponry that he used against our fleet.

Klingon Intelligence has known about the Forge for some time. There were many who considered the existence of a secret space station capable of equipping ships with the most advanced technology in the quadrant to be little

---

* September 17, 2389.

more than a child's story, but our experience with the *Narada* proved that it was possible.

After four days of searching, the *Ki'tang* found the Forge. The space station was empty. Its computer core had been wiped clean, but we did find information in the station that leads Klingon Intelligence to believe that the projects that the Forge had been home to were not abandoned.

In addition, Captain D'rakal reported that the Forge must have been working with Borg technology. The remains of a regeneration chamber were found in one of the laboratories, and the station itself had been outfitted with a central power matrix similar to those found on Borg cubes. It is reasonable to assume that if the Forge had been adapted to operate with Borg technology, then its creators have discovered a way to adapt that same technology to their ships as well. That could explain the incredible abilities of the *Narada*—General Worf reported that the ship appeared to not only have superior weaponry and cloaking ability, but that it also practically seemed to repair itself.

After consulting with Captain D'rakal, I ordered all three ships to expand their search to find the creators of the Forge. It was my hope that we would find definitive evidence that the *Narada* visited the Forge, and used the advanced weaponry it acquired there in its battle with General Worf's fleet.

It was during this search that the ships encountered an unknown vessel. It appears to be similar to a Romulan ship design, but was equipped with greatly advanced sensors. The unknown ship detected our vessels in cloak, fired, and destroyed the *Tagak* before any of our captains had a chance to react.

The *Qiv* and the *Ki'tang* fought valiantly, but normal disruptors had little effect. The ship's shields regenerated any damage within seconds, and it appeared to have no power drain when cloaking. In fact, the ship used rapid cloaking and decloaking as a combat maneuver.

Unfortunately, the outcome of the battle was, as the humans say, a foregone conclusion. D'rakal managed to deploy a beacon with his logs before the *Ki'tang* was destroyed, and that is how we have this image of the ship that annihilated three Klingon starships. May the crews of the *Qiv*, *Tagak*, and *Ki'tang* be welcomed in the halls of *Sto-Vo-Kor*.

Chancellor, I recommend further investigation of this mystery vessel. It may not be the only one of its kind, and our fleets in the Tran'omSar [Tranome Sar] and Neq'enSHov [Nequencia] systems should be briefed about this danger. It will require the efforts of many great warriors to defeat it.

Qapla'!

JAKE SISKO, DATA ROD #M-94

The Daystrom Institute of Technology Annex,
Galor IV

Captain Bruce Maddox looks as hard and lean as the sere, windswept desert landscape I can see through his panoramic office windows. His dark eyes have a watchful, vigilant cast, evidence of a highly disciplined mind. But that's not at all surprising—the man is one of the Federation's premier experts on artificial intelligence in general, and Soong-type androids in particular. But mystery dwells behind his eyes as well; although Maddox resumed his duties as the Daystrom Institute's chair of robotics several years ago, following his sudden and still-unexplained departure, he gives the impression of wishing he were someplace else. When he smiles, it seems forced, or perhaps rehearsed—almost the mannerism of an android who's had to be carefully coached through the niceties of human social interactions. During some of the more difficult phases of our conversation Maddox makes frequent pauses, during which he seems to study me in silence, his hands clasped before him as he leans forward across his immaculate desk.

Though his alert eyes are still during these conversational lacunae, I sense a great deal of activity behind them as he weighs his answers with obvious care.

Captain, I want to thank you for agreeing to speak with me.
Not at all, Mister Sisko. I think of it as my duty to posterity.

My first question probably won't be an easy one for you. You've never spoken much about your departure from the faculty of the Daystrom Institute. The same is true of your decision to return a few years later. Do you mind discussing either of those decisions now?
I suppose there's no getting around either question. What would you like to know?

When you left the Institute, Undine infiltrators were busy stirring up both the Klingon Empire and the Gorn Hegemony, and the Federation was getting caught in the crossfire. It has recently come to light that the project you were working on at that time might have enabled Starfleet to take a major step forward in ferreting out the Undine spies among our own people.
It would have. In fact, it *did,* once the project's new management finally got up to speed. I'm proud of whatever role my participation might have played in eventually beating back the Undine.

You certainly have a right to be proud, Captain. You and your team laid the groundwork for the pattern-recognition algorithms that made it possible to expose Undine infiltrators, despite the DNA alterations they'd been so successful in hiding behind. Not to mention the fact that your research allowed one of your oldest friends to return from the dead, in a manner of speaking.

I try not to think about that.

But wasn't Captain Data one of your closest friends? Of course he was. Despite my having tried to have him disassembled once. Fortunately for me, Data was never one to hold grudges. He's better than that.

I'm confused. Your research not only held the promise of shaving years off the duration of the Undine War, but it also had the potential to resurrect an android you had come to regard as both a sentient being and a close friend. Yet you walked away from the project before it could accomplish either objective. Why?

The price Data's return would have exacted from me was just too great. So I decided I simply couldn't afford to be a party to it.

Even though the solution to the "Data matrix" problem might have brought the Undine War to a much earlier end?

I think history has shown fairly conclusively that that

idea was oversold. Not that Data didn't make a significant contribution to the war effort, particularly after Starfleet decided to give him command of the *Enterprise.* It's just that the Undine ended up adapting more quickly than we had anticipated to the new detection algorithms that came out of the project.

Point conceded. But you didn't know any of that yet when you decided to leave the Daystrom Institute. What happened?
I suppose I changed more than I realized since I . . . since I tried to have Data dismantled for study, as if he were nothing more than some kind of technological curiosity.

Changed by the danger posed by the Undine infiltrators? As far as anybody knew back then, they might have been anywhere. Even inside the Daystrom Institute.
I think it was my initial encounter with Data that changed me, or at least put my feet on a certain path. My resolve that Data was a person rather than a chattel possession only got steadier after he volunteered to begin helping me study his positronic neural nets. All in spite of what I had tried to do to him.

No, the Undine didn't change me, at least not in any way I can detect. But I suppose the war *did* test my determination never again to cross certain ethical lines that I hadn't even been able to *see* twenty years earlier.

After you left the Daystrom Institute, one of its affiliate organizations—the Soong Foundation on Omicron Theta—offered to move some of your old research projects forward. How did you feel about that?

I had pretty mixed feelings. I suppose I was disappointed that my former staff had hit a research impasse so soon after my departure, and that others had had to then swoop in to "rescue" the work. And I was definitely concerned about what was going to become of B-4 after he left the Daystrom Institute to live out on Omicron Theta.

Was that because Noonien Soong built B-4 and his sibling androids at the Omicron Theta colony?

No. I'd never begrudge anybody the right to go home again—even if that home had been effectively wiped off the map years earlier by some murderous crystalline lifeform.

I think I understand now. You had come to regard B-4 as a sentient being, like Captain Data.

Frankly, I don't think there's any other way to see him. He had embarked on the very same voyage of discovery that Data had undertaken—a personal quest to become more human than he was. He'd just kept a lower profile along the way, which was to be expected since he wasn't serving aboard the Federation's flagship. And because everyone seemed to regard him as something . . . *less* than Data was. Data's cognitively impaired, emotionally stunted sibling. It just never occurred to us that his silences might have denoted something other than dullness or vacancy. Or that he might have been quietly pursuing his own unique path to humanity, all the while reading our databases in the hopes of someday becoming more like the man after whom the Soong Foundation had been named—the man who had created him and his silicon-based brethren. B-4 accomplished all this right under our noses because we dismissed his potential. We mistook the meditative for the moronic.

You make B-4 sound like a savant genius. But I'd never heard of him showing any sign of high cognitive achievement. At least nothing comparable to Data's scientific and technological skills, or, say, his ability to play the violin.
Certainly, B-4's programming was far less sophisticated than Data's, despite Data's entire library of internal files—what came to be called the "Data matrix"—having been uploaded into him a few years earlier. That so-called matrix was supposed to represent the essence of Data's intellect and personality, and perhaps even his emotions. But it would always just lay there, inert within B-4's more rudimentary positronic neural pathways.

But all of this was already moot as far as I was concerned. I was out of the loop at that point, and B-4 was no longer my responsibility. There was nothing more I could really do on B-4's behalf. Other than maybe filing yet another damned suit in a Federation court, accusing them of "insensitivity to the civil rights of artificial persons."

But you opted not to do that. Why?
It would have been pointless. First, I probably forfeited any legal standing I might have had on the matter when I left the Institute. And second, the Soong Foundation had already been hard at work for some time in trying to create a working mobile holo-emitter, ostensibly to emancipate holographic intelligences from the programs they'd been shackled to. That would have been hard to square with any accusation that they'd been suppressing the legal personhood of inorganic beings.

Do you regard holographic beings as deserving of legal personhood, as you do with B-4 and Captain Data?
Yes. If they can pass a Turing test, then they get to be in the club, so to speak. Now, if you're thinking about getting metaphysical and asking me whether holograms and androids have souls, you're wasting your time. I don't know whether organic humanoids, let alone synthetic life-forms, have souls. *Cogito, ergo sum—cogito.*

"I think, therefore I am—I think." I have just enough schoolboy Latin to appreciate the joke. So you were reasonably confident that you and the Soong

people were on the same page on the issue of synthetic rights.

The Soong Foundation's general counsel had already argued on behalf of the rights of sentient holograms, so I believed they were on the correct side of the issue with regard to androids. And I didn't want to burn my bridges permanently with either the Soong people or the Daystrom people by meddling. Now I wish to God that I *had* meddled. Maybe things would have turned out differently.

Are you saying that you wish Captain Data *hadn't* returned from the dead?

Of course not. Let's just say I was relieved when I heard that the Soong Foundation's research had run into the same initial impasse that my own people had encountered.

Meaning that their luck in cracking the "Data matrix" hadn't been any better than yours.

Exactly.

Until they called in another one of Captain Data's old friends to take a fresh look at the problem.

You'll have to ask the Soong people about that, Mister Sisko. All I know for certain is that they seemed to have had better luck than I did in restoring Data's personality. And while working on two fronts simultaneously, no less.

Can I assume that one of those fronts involved continued efforts to unlock the "Data matrix"?

Of course. And the other was their ability to use the Undine crisis to justify what they did next. And *that's* something I really don't care to talk about.

Standing unsmilingly behind his desk, Maddox crosses to the wide window's desert vista, signaling that he's done with the interview. The temperature on both sides of the transparent aluminum seems to have plunged by at least fifteen degrees Celsius in the space of so many seconds. I rise from my chair as well and begin awkwardly gathering up my recording padd and the small holoimager I had set down on Maddox's desk.

I briefly consider asking him whether he includes his old friend Data in whatever ethical indictments he might be thinking of leveling at the Soong Foundation. Thinking better of it, I thank him for the interview, finish packing up my gear, and exit the office. In the hallway outside, I make a mental note to get Captain Geordi La Forge's side of this story as soon as I possibly can.

JAKE SISKO, DATA ROD #Q-22

Quark's Bar, Federation Starbase Deep Space 9

Quark doesn't pour many of the drinks or wait tables himself these days, which accounts for his availability on this rather busy evening. Other than his ears being slightly larger than I remember, Quark hasn't changed much over the years: he's still a flashy dresser who enjoys flaunting his latinum, and who can make a great show of wounded pride when someone calls into question the veracity of his anecdotes. He continues to be a past president and member in good standing of the Federation Starbase Deep Space 9 Promenade Merchants' Association, not to mention the owner and sole proprietor of Quark's Bar, Grill, Gaming House, Holosuite Arcade, and Ferengi Embassy, which looks as prosperous now as I've ever seen it—more prosperous, in fact, since he's been allowed to expand his enterprise into some of the neighboring Promenade storefronts.

Quark leans back into the luxuriant upholstery of the booth we're sharing near one of the walls on the main level. The noise from the bar, the other booths and tables, and the gaming area beyond is considerable, but it works in tandem with the subdued lighting to assure our privacy—

along with the discretion of a number of shady-looking characters I glimpsed on my way to the booth. (Despite Quark's obvious success and frequently convincing veneer of legitimacy, some things clearly will never change.)

Quark and I ease into our conversation via small talk and shared reminiscences, and soon he seems to be getting comfortable relating to me as a journalist rather than as the son of one of the station's former commanding officers. As he warms to the interview process, it occurs to me that this man is a natural raconteur, which should come as no surprise considering his line of work. Still, I'm impressed by his ability to draw me into his narrative just as surely as I'm drawing it out of him. The realization makes me wonder how much trust I should invest in the tales he's telling. But at the moment, I am content merely to satisfy my very human need to know what happened next.

The Undine War, huh? Well, it just so happens I played a role in that. Probably a much bigger role than you'd expect.

Was that when Grand Nagus Rom tried to cut a deal with the Undine leadership—like you always thought the Federation should have done with the Dominion?

I think it was around that time. But I don't think the Undine would have come to any negotiating session. It should have been obvious by the time the fighting really got started that the Undine weren't like the

Dominion. We *might* have come to some sort of economic *modus vivendi* with them—the Dominion, I mean—if the Federation hadn't gotten so bent out of shape over those initial incursions from the Gamma Quadrant. No, the Undine weren't remotely like the Founders, or the Vorta, or even the Jem'Hadar. The Undine made the Borg look . . . *reasonable.* My brother should have seen *that* from the beginning. He might be the Nagus, but he's still an idiot.

As far as you know, did the Undine ever manage to put any of their spies on Ferenginar?
I've asked that same question myself more times than I can count over the years. I've never heard a satisfactory answer—in spite of all the pull I have with the Nagus. Bottom line? Nobody knows. But at least I know one thing for a fact: the Undine had definitely managed to compromise at least some of the Ferengi Alliance's major trade partners during the Long War years. And you happen to be looking at the very Ferengi who discovered that fact, let me tell you.

Tell me, tell me. That's why I'm here. I'm all ears.
Huh. Look who's talking.

Well, during the early phases of the war I had some dealings with a certain high-ranking member of the Orion Syndicate.

The Orion Syndicate? Are you sure you really want to talk about this on the record?

How do you know I wasn't working with Security Chief Ro as part of a covert—and entirely legitimate—sting operation?

Fair enough. Of course, I could check with her—
And get either a flat denial or a "no comment"—for security reasons, of course. Now where was I?

The Orion Syndicate.
Right. It all began around the time of that Hobus supernova business. Not long after a thoroughly unpleasant individual named Hassan pushed aside a minor crime boss named Raimus and took over his various enterprises, both legal and illicit.

Hassan the Undying? The Orion crime lord?
The very same—green, but not from any lack of experience. He earned that name by being bold enough to grasp any opportunity that came his way, yet cautious enough so as to appear practically unkillable. After all, it wasn't as though there was any shortage of Syndicate underbosses ready and willing to put Hassan's "Undying" sobriquet to the test, at least early in his career. I lost track of all the assassination attempts he survived. He had a kind of sixth sense, and that made him one of the biggest players in the Orion Syndicate. At the height of his power, most of the drug trade, prostitution, and weapons trafficking in three sectors went through his giant jade fingers.

But Hassan wasn't the biggest player in the Syndicate.

I wasn't exactly sure what Hassan's standing with the Syndicate was when I first started doing business with him, back in the day. I mean, it wasn't as though I was *trying* to associate myself with that organization. I've always been a legitimate Ferengi businessman, just trying to turn an honest profit—preferably a large one. But whenever the needs of *any* large organization operating anywhere in the sector create the potential for me to make a killing—so to speak— my lobes are bound to pick it up.

Of course. Rule of Acquisition Twenty-Two: "A wise man can hear profit in the wind."
Jake! You've really done your homework. I think I might cry, really.

Anyway, the Orion Syndicate had a complicated hierarchy with a lot of levels to it, even then, when the Orions were only beginning to seize direct control of all the top crime tiers. So it was no small achievement on Hassan's part that he answered directly to Melani D'ian herself, instead of one of her many underlings.

Melani D'ian. The Orion Syndicate's so-called Emerald Empress.
Not to mention the star of several exclusive and highly profitable holosuite programs crafted for . . . highly refined sensibilities. But I digress.

The long and short of it is that a played-out pergium mine at the Xoxa colony had recently come into my possession, thanks to my cousin Gaila having a run of bad luck at the tongo wheel. The mine was so worthless that it almost didn't merit the effort to get it on the market—and *off* my books.

How did a played-out pergium mine get you involved in deal-making with Hassan the Undying and Melani D'ian?
By turning out to be smack on top of a thick deposit of kelbonite that had hidden a huge vein of decalithium from all the previous deep scans of the mine. And it just so happened that Hassan and D'ian found themselves in great need of decalithium, in bulk and in a hurry, not long after I made that little discovery.

Wait a minute, Quark. Isn't decalithium a volatile material with a lot of weapons applications?
True enough, though it was a new enough discovery at the time so as not to have run afoul of a lot of fussy Federation laws and interstellar transport regulations yet. There's always a regulatory lag of a year or so, and an entrepreneur who's willing to trust in the Ninth Rule[*] and step into the gap at the right moment can make a fortune.

How? By developing decalithium weapons?
I thought you knew me better than that, Jake. After that

---

[*] The Ninth Ferengi Rule of Acquisition is stated in the form of an economic equation: "Opportunity plus instinct equals profit."

fiasco with Hagath back in 'seventy-three, I was done with the weapons trade for good. And I was only a broker then, mind you, not a full-fledged arms dealer.

Are you saying that the Orion Syndicate was interested in *peaceful* ways of using decalithium?
Rule Number Thirty-five: "Peace is good for business." Even those green glandular cases who were trying to take over the Syndicate back then knew *that*.

And I'm sure they were at least as aware of what the Thirty-*fourth* Rule said.
"War is good for business." Of course. That's what makes the Rules so beautiful, elegant, and versatile, not to mention so universally relevant: you can apply them to any given situation. But the Orions aren't one hundred percent about death and destruction, even though some of their, um, less savory ventures have shown the galaxy no shortage of either. Even the *Klingons* aren't all bloodlust; somebody has to grow food, build and repair things, and pilot the freighters and garbage scows.

So what exactly were the Orions using your decalithium for?
Interstellar transportation. Or more precisely, multi-parsec subspace *teleportation*.

Interstellar-range transporters? Like the technology the Dominion had?

A *lot* like that. Imagine the benefits. No more risky smuggling operations. No more chance of being boarded unexpectedly by Starfleet. No more cargoes or freighters being impounded. Merchandise would just disappear from one secure location and reappear in another one, light-years away.

The Orion Syndicate really had that kind of technological know-how?
Let's just say that there were more than a few highly competent scientists and engineers at the Syndicate's disposal. Some of them came from Starfleet, and ended up entangled in webs of gambling debt and blackmail that gave them no choice other than to quietly cooperate with Hassan. The Dominion had already proved that it was possible to beam across interstellar distances, though nobody else had managed it yet. Hassan's people must have figured that all they really lacked was a sufficient source of power.

Your decalithium.
Exactly.

You don't seem quite so proud of that now, Quark.
Did you come here to give me a counseling session, or to conduct an interview?

Sorry. Obviously, the first shipments of decalithium from your Xoxa mining operation to the Orion

Syndicate had to arrive the old-fashioned way, smuggled via freighter.
Shipped. Not smuggled. Shipped. Remember, the regulations curtailing decalithium transport hadn't been written yet.

So you weren't breaking any laws when you rode along with Hassan's lieutenant, Raka, to take that first decalithium delivery to Hassan's private shipping depot?
Not yet.

So how could you have been conducting a "sting" operation, if nothing technically illegal was going on?
Like I said, you'd have to ask Ro Laren or Starfleet Intelligence about that, if either of them are willing to talk to you about this, which I doubt. But I'm sure they felt as entitled to do surveillance on Raka and Hassan as Odo used to feel in keeping an eye on *me*.

So you had some time to generate a lot of quick profits before the new rules drove the decalithium trade underground.
I should have known it was too good to last. There were only so many paid-by-the-piece cargo runs I'd be able to supply before Starfleet closed the door on this opportunity—at least as a *legitimate* venture. And I certainly wasn't looking forward to the prospect of being arrested by my own nephew. So when Raka made me a lump-sum offer on the mine, I was sorely

tempted. I mean, I could have made more money over the long haul by hanging on to the deed to the mine and filling the Syndicate's orders as they came in. . . .

Assuming that Melani D'ian didn't decide to have Hassan or Raka kill you so she could just move in and annex the mine herself.
I'll admit, that possibility *had* crossed my mind once or twice, though I didn't think that even Melani D'ian wanted to risk getting sideways with the Grand Nagus of the Ferengi Alliance by murdering his brother. I mean, Rom might be an idiot, but he's as loyal as a Drathan puppy lig and he wields more power than anybody as ambitionless as he is has any right to. But as it turned out, fear of Orion assassins wasn't what made me decide to sell and get out of the decalithium-mining business while the getting was still good.

Maybe you'd gotten tired of dealing with gangsters and corruption.
Jake, have you ever tried keeping a bar and gaming establishment profitable *without* dealing with "gangsters and corruption"? No, I made my decision based on something else entirely, and I did it during that first flight from the Xoxa mine with Raka, after we'd picked up the cargo. We weren't halfway to Hassan's undisclosed location when it happened.

When what happened?
Raka and I were flying a two-man cargo ship, and

our course took us through an ion storm–infested region on the ragged edge of the Badlands. A plasma discharge opened up one of the decalithium canisters and catalyzed the material somehow—releasing some of it into the ventilation system, which sprayed it into the cockpit.

You're lucky you weren't killed.
Doctor Bashir treated me for radiation poisoning after I got back to Deep Space 9. But Raka wasn't so lucky.

Did the radiation kill him before you returned to DS9?
No. Raka wasn't killed by the radiation. In fact, he must have been dead before we left Xoxa. Maybe a long time before.

What do you mean?
I mean he wasn't . . . *Raka*. At least, not anymore. The radiation must have been the trigger. One moment, he was this huge, green humanoid sitting behind a control panel that was already too small for him. And then he started . . . changing into an even *huger* purple-gray thing. He was becoming something not even remotely humanoid, something that looked more like a giant predatory bug.

He was an Undine infiltrator, placed in the Orion Syndicate—until he underwent a sudden unintentional "reversion" to his natural form. I remember

one of Captain Janeway's Delta Quadrant logs recording an incident like that happening in *Voyager*'s sickbay.

It was the only answer that made any sense at the time. The radiation from the burst canister must have reversed whatever gene-surgery those aliens do on their deep-cover operatives. The accident turned "Raka" back into what he was really supposed to look like, and did it in a hurry. His Undine was undone, so to speak. But he wasn't showing any signs that he was about to die. Instead, he seemed angry that he'd blown his cover. And at the time I really wished he hadn't done it right in front of me, since I was all alone with him in a cramped freighter cockpit.

Now the timing of your decision to retire from the mining business makes perfect sense to me.

Unfortunately, "Raka" wasn't interested in leaving retirement on the table as one of my available options. He had claws the size of Talarian hook spiders, and they were at my throat in a heartbeat. I tried to get to the rear of the cabin, to get away from him, but he was just too fast.

That's all I remember, until I came to in that Starfleet infirmary, with Ro and Nog flanking my bed. It seems I'd been rescued in the proverbial nick. A crack Starfleet security team had dealt with the Undine monster with what you might call "extreme prejudice."

Getting back to the bar after that must have been a welcome change of pace.
It was. Eventually.

You didn't go home right away?
Starfleet Intelligence needed somebody to be aboard that freighter when it delivered its cargo to its destination at one of Hassan's distribution hubs. The trouble was, I really didn't see that as a viable option at the time.

Aside from your own healthy instinct for self-preservation, why not? Wasn't your original plan to deliver the freighter's cargo to Hassan?
Sure it was. But think about it, Jake. I hadn't planned on having to explain the sudden absence of one of Hassan's most trusted lieutenants. I mean, the man was bound to be pretty peeved when I turned up alone.

Even though you would have been bringing him the cargo of decalithium he was expecting?
Along with a dead Undine that used to be Raka until it somehow acquired a phaser hole in its chest. And a lame story about having had no choice but to kill the thing after it had revealed itself as a spy that had obviously killed and replaced the *real* Raka some time ago. I pointed out to Ro, Nog, and anybody else who might have listened that nobody was likely to get into the habit of calling me *"Quark* the Undying" if I were to try this stupid stunt.

I gather from the fact that you didn't go back to the bar right away that Starfleet Intelligence finally persuaded you.

The Starfleet spooks didn't persuade me. Ro did.

How?

She said that Hassan was liable to be in an even worse mood if he had to go searching for that freighter—and that he'd be angrier still if he found it adrift with a dead nightmare creature sprawled across the cockpit in place of both me and Raka. He'd no doubt come looking for me next, and if he were to find me alive and well at the bar, he'd be pretty insistent about getting a detailed explanation from me—probably after a lengthy interview in a soundproof chamber filled with sharp objects.

Excellent point.

Debate may be one of her lesser-known areas of expertise, but she's always been as good with a cutting comment as she is with a phaser. A lot like Kai Kira, in her way. So I decided it would be a lot better for me if I came to Hassan instead of making him come to DS9 looking for me.

As well as better for Lieutenant Ro, I'd imagine. She couldn't have been eager to have Orion assassins come aboard DS9. And I suppose Starfleet Intelligence would have wanted to keep you as close as possible to Hassan to help Starfleet assess the extent

**of the Undine's infiltration of the Orion Syndicate—
which I've heard turned out to be considerable.**

You're wasting your talents. You really ought to be writing more novels. Or preferably holonovels. Technothrillers. You could do one about how the Undine tried to use the Orion Syndicate to create a long-range subspace transporter as part of their Alpha Quadrant invasion—until their plans were foiled by the time-honored Ferengi values of pluck, haggling, and good old-fashioned greed.

Speaking of which, I have a business proposition that might be right in your wheelhouse. . . .

JAKE SISKO, DATA ROD #F-19

On the upper levels of Quark's Bar, Grill, Gaming House, Holosuite Arcade, and Ferengi Embassy lies another world. Or rather a near-infinitude of other worlds, realms of light and shadow and force fields that can simulate every sensory input to the point that fantasy can become all but indistinguishable from reality. In one of these technologically conjured worlds, a perpetual summer reigns, and dream teams whose members lived decades and even centuries apart engage in genteel combat amid the scent of newly mowed grass and cleat-turned earth. In another faux-reality, a mid-twentieth-century international super-spy, armed with only a Walther pistol and his wits, fights the enemies of freedom to an uneasy stalemate.

And in still another, Earth's entertainment-and-gambling capital, Las Vegas, remains as it was nearly four and a half centuries ago, frozen in the golden age of 1962. Despite the passage of so many years since the last time I saw him—and the fact that his program, Bashir Sixty-two, has been running more or less continuously in this holosuite for more than a quarter century—Vic Fontaine looks exactly as he always did, from the immaculate black tuxedo to the tidy salt-and-pepper haircut that gives him a perpetual aspect of both vital early middle age and the accumulated wisdom of centuries of keen human observation. Though Vic is occupied with the duties of an attentive host, working the holographic dinner crowd in his busy nightclub, he easily disengages himself from the clusters of conversation that surround him.

"You rescued me from a bunch of sharkskin-suited Madison Avenue admen," he says as he greets me just past the periphery of the fashionably dressed, cocktail-sipping crowd, which never wanders far from the stage where several jazz musicians are quietly setting up their instruments and equipment.

Vic's firm handshake and inimitable high-wattage smile immediately remind me that he is far more than a mere photonic construct. I notice his eyes briefly searching mine, silently sizing me up in his own unique way, reminding me that he was the one everyone always came to when they needed help with personal problems but didn't want to go through the formality of scheduling a meeting with a Starfleet counselor. I try to maintain my best poker face before deciding that it's useless to try to conceal anything from this self-described "student of the human heart."

Although I know the past quarter century has etched itself conspicuously into my face, Vic makes no mention of having noticed it. It's as though no time at all has passed since my last visit, for me as well as for him.

As I immerse myself in his milieu* after such a long absence—starting with a martini-fueled crash course in operating the ancient audio equipment that dominates one of the club's out-of-the-way corner tables— I remind myself not to be surprised by the fact that Vic hasn't changed a bit, even though for him 1962 has already lasted twenty-five years and will continue into eternity, or at least until the power fails. But then why should time change him, whether he's fastened to one particular year or not? After all, he's not subject to the entropy and decay to which all flesh is heir. He's an unreal thing, a human creation. Only a hologram.

Or is he?

Well, the microphone's tested out okay, pally. Now, is this thing on?

I can see the red light from here, Vic. And it looks like the wheels have finally started turning.

"Reels," kid. They're called reels. Don't look so worried about how this little recording session is gonna turn out. This baby's a transistorized, battery-powered TransFlyweight Series 312 portable field

---

* In order to record my interview with Vic Fontaine, I had to dispense with my usual complement of holographic recording equipment. Because Vic's 1962 Las Vegas holosuite program is strictly period specific, I had to use an ancient audio recorder that encoded our conversation in the form of magnetic particles embedded into reels of extremely flimsy-looking tape. I would have felt a lot safer using a pencil and paper.

recorder from the Amplifier Corporation of America. Top of the line. Cost me a bundle, too. It'll work just fine.

That thing's portable? It must weigh as much as your piano.
Hey, what do you want from me, kid? This is 1962. But you didn't come all this way just to chitchat with me about hi-fi systems. Am I right?

Hi-fi?
Forget it, pally. Let's catch up. Long time, no hear from.

I'm afraid work has been keeping me from visiting the station as often as I'd like, Vic.
Well, all work and no play can make Jake a dull boy. So what brings you back to the Strip after all this time?

Actually, Vic, work is what brought me here. I'm compiling an official history of the Undine War. Interviewing some of the key participants. I just finished a session with Quark, and I couldn't pass up an opportunity to visit you before I leave the sector.
So that's what you meant by "interview request." I oughtta warn you, though: I'm bound to be a disappointment, since my program is period specific. An Undine War diary would be as out of place here as a manatee on a unicycle.

Actually, Vic, you might be surprised by how relevant you are to what people will know about the Undine War. Well, maybe your experience isn't directly pertinent to the war itself, but there are some interesting parallels. For instance, the Federation experienced some important social changes during the Long War years.

I get it. Like those Rosie the Riveters who split from their kitchens for factory gigs back during Dubya Dubya Two. I guess I shouldn't be surprised. You futurefolk may have conquered the stars, but you're still just as human as anybody from *my* era. And the world's bound to have at least a little unfairness in it as long as human beings are running the show.

Exactly. Of course, the sociological experts will always argue about the details of the various cause-and-effect relationships, but the fact is that war always creates social upheaval.

And social upheaval creates social change. I dig. But what I don't get is exactly what kind of changes you're talking about here. Like I said, my program is period specific. For me, 1962 is as stable as all the gold bullion in Fort Knox. Of course, thanks to the historical files in Deep Space 9's computers, I know a lot about what's coming up *after* 1962: the Beatles are gonna take the stage away from guys like me. Civil rights aren't gonna stop at the front of the bus. There's women's liberation and the end of the Cold War. . . .

Some of these things are supposed to be in the very near future, at least from my 1962 pee-oh-vee. But thanks to the way Felix wrote my program, the very near future always turns out to be a mirage. New Year's Day 1963 sometimes gets almost close enough to spill your champagne on it, but in here—in my Las Vegas—it really might as well be as far away as the moon.

But you're more than four hundred years past any of that, Jake. So when I try to imagine whatever "social change" *your* world might be going through . . . well, I've gotta tell you, pally, you've lost me.

Appropriately enough, time seems to stand still, even though no one has called a halt to the program. Vic's words hang in the air, like the handiwork of one of this era's skywriting aircraft. During that elastic moment I'm tempted to ask him what actually does *happen here each and every New Year's Eve. Does the clock really just reset immediately to New Year's Day 1962, one infinitesimal nanotick past the stroke of midnight? How many times can he remember this same thing happening? With a shudder, I realize that I'm very glad indeed that I'm not in Vic's shoes; I decide that I far prefer my ever-advancing slow march toward entropy, and the oblivion beyond it, to Vic's stasis. I put this idle line of speculation aside, forcing myself back on-topic in order to deal with Vic's confusion.*

I'm talking about civil rights, Vic.
Like I said, a lot of that's sort of permanently over the

horizon, at least for me. You see, I'm stuck in what Felix called a "post-1962 Zeno's Paradox." Sorry, but if it happened after 'sixty-two, then I can't experience it.

That's not entirely true anymore, Vic. I'm talking about civil rights for synthetic persons.
Rights for synthetic persons? You mean . . . for light-bulbs like me?

"Lightbulb" sounds a little too much like a racial slur for my taste, Vic. How about using terms like "self-aware holograms" to describe people like you, or "sapient androids" for people like Captain Data. For years now, the Soong Foundation and other organizations have been lobbying the Federation Council to grant synthetics full rights under the UFP Constitution, including the right to vote, and all the other protections that organic citizens like me get to take for granted. The upheaval created by the Undine War may have given the synthetic rights movement all the impetus it needed to bring these changes about. What do you think?
What do I think? I think I'm glad I was already sitting down before you started talking about this.

I notice that Vic has begun to look unsteady, as though he's had too much to drink. I suddenly realize I've only seen him this distressed on one other occasion—when holographic gangsters took over his club and bodily threw him out of it—and I find myself regretting having barged into Vic's unchanging, comfortable world with such epoch-making news. Vic sits quietly, processing what I've told him. Looking away from his discomfiture, I turn my gaze toward the stage, where a period-appropriate jazz combo—a piano player, a stand-up bassist, a drummer, a guitarist, and a couple of brass players— has begun to tune up in preparation for Vic's next set. When I glance back at Vic I can see that he wants to speak, but remains at a rare loss for words for nearly a minute.

Crazy. Your Foundations and Councils are actually thinking about ending Jim Crow for us holograms. Some clever team of Starfleet legal eagles might even actually get it done. But I have to wonder how many of 'em would be comfortable with a hologram or an android marrying their sisters.

Progress usually comes as two steps forward and one step back.
I wouldn't know, pally. I'm stuck in the same year forever. And since it's one of those years that's west of 1968, I'll never get to experience any of the progress you're talking about. As long as I'm period specific, I'll just have to be content with experiencing it all through somebody else's eyes.

I'm sorry, Vic. I've been really insensitive. I had no idea you felt so . . . isolated from everything in here.
Hey, do I *look* isolated to you? Don't sweat it, Jake.

I've got a good life here, thanks to your father and his friends talking Quark into keeping my program running twenty-six/seven. I'm grateful for that. Sure, I wouldn't have known that the Beatles were coming if somebody from the outside world hadn't let me read about 'em in the station's computer banks. But on the flip side, I also know they're never gonna actually *get* here. As long as it's 1962, I'll never have to worry about going out of style.

That's what I always liked best about you, Vic: you're optimistic almost to a fault.
Guilty as charged. Now *I* have a question for *you*. Why would your war with—who is it again? The Undine? Jeez, it sounds like you've been fighting off a bunch of French lingerie models—why would *this* particular war push civil rights for androids and holograms onto the front burner? I mean, why didn't the Dominion War do it, or one of your big dustups with the Borg?

I've been wondering that a lot myself lately, Vic. I've interviewed grunt soldiers, ivory-tower academics, and everything in between. And I've asked a lot of them the same question you just asked me.

The best theory I can come up with is that the idea of being replaced by Undine infiltrators terrified human beings on a really deep and profound level. It's apparently had the same effect on Vulcans, Andorians, Tellarites, Klingons, Romulans,

and on and on down the list. It's such a fundamental, existential fear that it's made everyone question what it really means to be human, or Klingon, or whatever, in a way that even our scariest encounters with the Founders of the Dominion never did. The only thing that's become crystal clear to me is that I don't have a very good answer to your question. At least, I can't find an answer that justifies synthetic people being exploited as a . . . well, as a slave race.

We sit in contemplative silence and sip at the round of martinis that a convenient bar maid brought us while I was answering Vic's question. It's a long time before either of us speaks, and Vic beats me to it.

So how does it all end up, pally?

End up?
For us lightbulbs. Holograms, I mean. And for the androids, too.

I realize belatedly that Vic is now the one who's conducting this interview, not me. But that's Vic all over, isn't it? It's the way Vic quietly sizes his guests up so that he can always provide advice that they can really use—even if they don't always quite realize it at the time. I do my best to gather my thoughts to bring him up to speed on the latest developments on the synthetic civil rights front.

Well, let's look at some of the recent box scores. An android was officially declared a person in 2365, and Starfleet's JAG office upheld that decision twenty-one years later. That same android is now in command of the Federation's flagship. A hologram who served aboard the *U.S.S. Voyager* fought for eleven years to get the Federation Supreme Court to recognize his personhood, and finally prevailed. And the Soong Foundation is on the verge of creating a mobile holo-emitter that will allow self-aware holograms to live independently in the outside world.

You mean *outside* of the holosuites?

That's the plan. And the holoprogrammer who created *you*, Vic, has helped to create a new version of your program for Starfleet, under the supervision of Captain Deanna Troi, formerly of the *U.S.S. Titan.*

Crazy. Not that I think I'm perfect or anything, but why would Felix take a Mulligan on my program?

It's for the new ECH: the Emergency Counseling Hologram that some of Starfleet's new ships have started carrying as a supplement to the Emergency Medical Holograms that have been in use since back in the seventies. It's really just an extension of the service you've been providing to the crew of DS9 for years anyway.

I'm just a hardworking entertainer, pal. If a little crooning from a close relative of mine can bring some distraction to an overworked Starfleet officer's life, then all those hours rehearsing with the band seem a lot more worthwhile. But I think I dig where the Starfleet headshrinkers are coming from. Healthy body, healthy mind, right?

Exactly.
So what you're saying is . . . it hasn't really ended.

What hasn't ended?
The synthetic-rights struggle you've been telling me about. The Undine War might be behind us—knock on wood—but the other fight's still being slugged out. A complete lightbulb bill of rights might be headed in my direction, but it's still over the horizon—even from where _you're_ sitting.

Maybe that's true right now. But it won't be forever, and it's not as though you have any shortage of time. So for you, Vic, some of that change _will_ come. No matter what year Felix might have stuck your program in.
Not for me, pally. Maybe this Vic two-point-oh you just told me about will see the Promised Land. But me? I'm part and parcel of Felix's 1962, and I always will be. I might take one small step or two for a lightbulb, but it'll have to be a later model of me that finally takes that one giant leap for lightbulbkind.

As the interview winds down to its conclusion, I consider pointing out that Vic has made a number of anachro-

nistic references—the Beatles, late 1960s social unrest, and the first Apollo lunar landing—which might be considered hopeful signs of his untapped capacity to transcend his program, and perhaps even time and space itself. But for once, Vic—the man who gave my friend Nog so much encouragement after a Dominion War injury had nearly taken his will to live—doesn't appear to be in the mood for hope. I'm beginning to wish that I'd stayed away from the holosuite as Vic drains what's left of his martini, bids me a quiet farewell, and then mounts the stage upon which his jazz combo waits to begin his set.

To Vic's credit, he performs with all the ease and charm I remember from the time of the Dominion War. He jokes with the dinner crowd and trades good-natured barbs with the Madison Avenue advertising executives he mentioned earlier. Then he wows his audience with renditions of some familiar tunes from his standard set list: Russ Morgan's "You're Nobody 'til Somebody Loves You" comes first, followed by Arlen and Koehler's "I've Got the World on a String" and Coleman and Leigh's "The Best Is Yet to Come." With the steady support of the band, he seems to draw strength from the act of singing itself, almost as though it is a kind of therapy for him. It reminds me of the way I often take refuge from the world via the raw, creative act of writing.

While Vic performs, I down two more martinis—real ones, not synthehol—which is something I never do. Abashed at having dragged an old friend down into melancholy (not to mention being sorely tempted to follow him there myself), I decide I've done enough damage for one day. As Vic finishes up his regular set with Gershwin's "They Can't Take That Away from Me," I rise unsteadily and head for the holosuite door, remembering as I exit not to shut down Vic's program, which has been running continuously since the final months of the Dominion War. I wonder, however, whether Vic would think of a shutdown as a mercy.

Then I hear his encore, a long, slow melody that sounds out of place amid the swing-era standards that comprise Vic Fontaine's traditional musical fare. Out of place, but not inappropriate. After a few beats of Vic's a cappella crooning, the band, apparently as surprised as I am, finds its way into the tune, hesitantly at first, and then with enough brio to sweep the audience along with them, transforming confused scowls into winsome smiles and finally, enthusiastic applause.

I pause on the holosuite's threshold, knowing in a rush that I will leave feeling uplifted rather than downcast. For Vic is singing a nearly five-century-old anthem, an ode to the struggles of oppressed minorities everywhere. And I sing it with him.

"We Shall Overcome."

JAKE SISKO, DATA ROD #J-53

Federation *Starship Tucker*, near the Hobus Nebula

Although the Excalibur-*class starship that has carried me out to the ragged edge of the Romulan Neutral Zone has been in service for nearly twenty years, its design is of relatively recent vintage. Originally commissioned back in 'ninety-one, the simple, clean lines of this vessel evoke a simpler, more Romantic period in the Federation's nearly quarter-millennium-long history—a time when a mere dozen* Constitution-*class heavy cruisers plied a largely unexplored galaxy, doggedly expanding a volume of known space that the Federation's present territory now dwarfs.*

Being one of Starfleet's most versatile ships of the line, the U.S.S. Tucker *has drawn the job of performing the Federation Science Council's mandated annual survey of the Hobus Nebula—and the mysterious, still-active stellar remnant (now known as the Hobus Cinder) that pulsates at the center of the mysterious, parsecs-deep shell of expanding gas, plasma, and radiation that comprises the remains of the infamous Hobus supernova. I am fortunate to have timed my interview to coincide with this week's survey mission,* whose subject is of considerable historical and scientific significance; back in 2387, Hobus caused one of the worst catastrophes in Beta Quadrant history—the utter destruction of Romulus and Remus, the co-orbiting central worlds of the Romulan Star Empire. The repercussions of this event made the infighting that followed Shinzon's assassination of the Romulan Senate in 2379 look like a holiday on Risa by comparison.

Admiral Kathryn Janeway, in command of the Tucker *for the duration of the current scientific survey mission, greets me warmly in her ready room, rising from behind a surprisingly spartan desk to shake my hand. The holoimages I had seen of the admiral had me expecting someone with a much sterner manner; certain pictures of Janeway, evidently taken early in her command career, had shown her shoulder-length brown hair gathered into a bun so severe as to make me imagine her ship's barber and chief engineer working together frantically to adjust its tension to prevent it from injuring any innocent bystanders. I'd always thought she'd be taller as well, literally larger than life.*

But whatever Janeway might lack in physical stature she more than compensates for with the air of authority and sheer presence that surrounds her. Kathryn Janeway comes off as a tough, veteran flag officer, tempered by the U.S.S. Voyager*'s legendary seven-year sojourn in the Delta Quadrant. The passage of time since that voyage ended has made her a silver-haired Starfleet eminence—albeit one with an unmistakable glint of self-effacing humor in her questing and ever-curious scientist's eyes.*

During our discussion, Janeway pauses periodically to gaze toward the ready room's wide transparent aluminum window, through which we can both see the faint, rhythmic oscillations of the Hobus Cinder through the distortion of the surrounding nebula's amber haze. The supernova's gradually cooling corpse seems to twitch metronomically, pulsating like a distant, sinister heartbeat. The effect is both horrific and hypnotic.

Janeway seems to have to work as hard as I do to tear her gaze away from the apparition in the window. Then she focuses her full attention on the art of explaining this complex subject with simplicity and clarity. As I listen, I begin to understand why she excelled as a science officer during an early phase of her Starfleet career. But I also get a sense of how formidable a command officer she is when some of my more probing questions regarding war, peace, and the Undine appear to strike a nerve. Though she appears to have no problem keeping a deep, smoldering anger in check behind her enigmatic smiles, I have to wonder how many times she may have asked herself many of the same questions I'm raising today— and whether she privately blames herself for failing to enact an early and lasting peace with the Undine.

After all, history has given her most of the credit— some might say blame—for making humanity's first contact with the Undine.

Thank you for allowing me to observe your present mission, Admiral.
Delighted to have you aboard, Mister Sisko.

This isn't the first time you've investigated the remains of the Hobus supernova, is it, Admiral?

You might say that. I oversaw one of the first short-range surveys of the Hobus stellar remnant back in 'eighty-eight, nearly a year after the initial event. It took that long for the hard radiation and subspace effects to die down enough to let us risk getting any closer than two light-years from the Hobus Cinder itself. Prior to that, we had to settle for whatever data we could collect from the MIDAS* array.

Isn't it unusual for a supernova's effects to linger for such a long time?

Yes and no. I mean, the actual explosion of a star into a supernova usually peaks, tapers off, and then fades into the background after a fairly short time. But during the few weeks or months while the actual "kaboom" phase of the supernova lasts, the blast can emit as much energy as Earth's sun will produce over the course of its entire ten-billion-year lifespan. Which is why approaching an active supernova requires extreme caution. You shouldn't try this at home.

Aren't the chances fairly remote that a supernova like Hobus can endanger inhabited planets?

That's a tough one to answer, since before the Hobus

---

* Mutara Interdimensional Deep space transponder Array System. In 2376 this facility played a pivotal role in opening up long-range subspace communications with the *U.S.S. Voyager*, still stranded in the Delta Quadrant at the time.

disaster* nobody had ever seen a supernova behave the way this one did. But I can say that an inhabited world getting snuffed out by a regular, garden-variety supernova is very definitely a low-probability event. Hobus, though . . . Hobus was—*is*—an entirely different breed of cat.

Apart from what it did to Romulus, how, specifically, was the Hobus event different from the typical supernova explosion?
The problem with Hobus is that it's so unlike anything else known to science. So let's start by taking a look at some of the more typical stellar explosions. Our galaxy usually experiences one of those about twice every century.

I'm surprised to hear they're that rare. My layman's impression is that they occur a lot more frequently than that. I mean, a whole clutch of them happened during your time in the Delta Quadrant. And closer to home, there was the Beta Stromgren supernova about forty years ago, and the one that almost wiped out the Bynars at Beta Magellan a couple of years before that—
I can see you've done your homework, Mister Sisko. And yes, during recent decades we may have seen a few more supernovae than you'd normally expect to

---

* Admiral Janeway's choice of the word "disaster" in this context is an entirely appropriate one. The word comes to us, by way of Old Italian and Middle French, from Greek roots that mean, literally, "bad star."

see. But that overabundance turns out to be statistically insignificant when you factor in the intervention of the Q Continuum. The so-called collateral damage from their civil war back in the 2370s touched off a whole series of supernovae in pretty quick succession.

Did the Q cause all those supernovae deliberately, or was it an accident?
I was never able to settle that question. I think the best answer is to believe whichever answer costs you the least amount of sleep.

I start to experience the same queasy-in-the-pit-of-the-stomach feeling I always used to get whenever the wormhole aliens—the Prophets of Bajor—would monkey around with my father's so-called destiny. There's something about functionally omnipotent beings, whether they be Prophets who manipulate the lives of individuals, or Q superintellects who blow apart entire solar systems the way children tip over dominoes, that offends my fundamental sense of the fairness of the universe. I try to push the notion of mad or careless gods out of my mind even as I struggle to keep my gaze from drifting back to the Hobus Cinder. I renew my concentration on the admiral, who is continuing in Former Science Officer Lecture Mode.

Luckily for us, the Milky Way is a very big place, which means that most of the time life manages to dodge the bullet whenever a supernova occurs. And that bullet takes the form of intense bursts of highly energetic radiation, including gamma rays. Fortunately, class-M worlds typically have two significant layers of protection—their local stellar magnetosphere and their own planetary magnetic fields.

So the incoming supernova radiation just gets turned aside, the way a starship's deflector shields ward off incoming phaser beams.
Exactly. Unless, of course, the supernova happens close enough to a planet so that the radiation output simply overwhelms that planet's "shields."

How close would a supernova have to be, typically, in order to do that?
That depends on which type of supernova we're talking about. And *that,* in turn, depends upon its mass and composition. In general, the larger the stellar mass, the shorter the stellar lifespan—the time from birth to "boom"—and the bigger the explosion at the end of the star's life. Without going through the whole supernova bestiary, let's just say it's now common wisdom that the Ordovician mass extinction on Earth nearly half a billion years ago was the result of a supernova that occurred at about a one-hundred-light-year distance. That one stellar event wiped out almost sixty percent of Earth's ocean-dwelling species, and the effects of that extinction lingered for tens of millions of years afterward.

In spite of myself, I glance again across the desk at Hobus's glowing carcass. Suddenly I feel as though I'm sitting way, way too close to the thing. In my mind it's become a predator that merely lies injured rather than safely dead.

One hundred light-years away, and it still did that kind of damage. Is that fairly typical?
Again, that depends on the exact kind of supernova we're talking about here. A Type II specimen would have to be around a quarter of that distance from a class-M world to start doing really significant ecological damage to it. On the other hand, one of those dim, sneaky Type Ia supernovae could cause the same amount of havoc from over three thousand light-years away.

Hobus was something like five hundred light-years away from Romulus. Shouldn't that have been a wide enough separation to keep the Romulan Empire's twin homeworld safe?
Safe from anything except a Type Ia supernova—and Hobus, as we discovered the hard way twenty years ago.

And something else has just occurred to me: Even assuming that the Hobus supernova's effects were bound to cross the five hundred light-years or thereabouts that separated the explosion from Romulus and Remus, shouldn't those planets still have been safe for at least . . . another five hundred years? I mean, natural phenomena aren't supposed to be able to beat light in a foot race, right?

Mister Sisko, you just put your finger on the major difference between Hobus and every other supernova that's ever been observed. The first thing that bothered me about the Hobus Event was the fact that its effects were somehow propagating through space at multiwarp speeds. As a general rule, that's impossible. With the exception of certain spaceborn cosmozoa,* natural phenomena simply can't travel faster than the speed of light.

The Romulan Senate must have been counting on that general rule as well, since they rejected Ambassador Spock's analysis of the Hobus threat out of hand shortly before the supernova occurred. They even ignored warnings about Hobus from their own Romulan Mining Guild.

It was far easier for them to believe that the Federation was trying to fool them with some elaborate ruse than it was for them to take Ambassador Spock's warnings at face value. But let's be fair. Without the benefit of hindsight, their reaction is easy enough to understand. You have to take into account the isolationist psychology they've embraced for so long, almost since their ancient ancestors first migrated from Vulcan.

That also explains the accusations that Proconsul Sela made against us after the supernova wiped

---

* Organisms, like those discovered at Deneb IV by the crew of the *U.S.S. Enterprise*-D in 2364, that live in space and feed on the raw EM emissions of stars and other bodies in interstellar space.

out Romulus—that the disaster was really caused by some new Federation weapon. As it turned out, that charge was pure psychological projection. Sela blamed us for Hobus in order to cover up her own illegal weapons experiments—experiments that were probably the real cause of the Hobus explosion.

I wonder if the jury might still be out on that one.

I'm surprised to hear you say that, Admiral. From what I read in the logs from your original Hobus survey mission, it seems pretty clear that the Romulans were secretly working on new armaments at that time. You caught them trying to cover up a program aimed at adapting captured Borg technology into powerful subspace weaponry—in a program that blatantly violated several treaties the Romulans had signed.

Oh, I'm not disputing any of *that*. They *were* violating the weapons clauses of those treaties. I've just never been entirely convinced that whatever experiments the Romulans lost control of right before the Hobus Event were quite powerful enough to have touched off a supernova explosion of that kind. Something else might have been behind it.

Something else? Or some*one* else? Like maybe the Undine?

I wouldn't go quite that far, at least not yet. Not until I find some real proof.

You're speaking in the present tense, Admiral. Does that mean you're still looking for that evidence?

Let's just say I've always been inclined to keep an open mind about the subject.

You must have seen something on that first survey mission back in 'eighty-eight—perhaps something that made you suspect that the Undine may have played a role in setting off the Hobus supernova. Do you mind talking about that mission?

Certainly. We took a small vessel, a variant of the original *Delta Flyer* that Tom [Paris], B'Elanna [Torres], and Harry [Kim] designed when *Voyager* was stranded in the Delta Quadrant.

Wouldn't a small ship have been more vulnerable to the effects of the supernova than a larger vessel would have been?

It was a calculated risk, but it was one we were all willing to take given the advanced multiphasic shielding the shuttle was carrying. Besides, a larger vessel ran the risk of attracting unwanted Romulan attention, and our relations with what was left of the Romulan Star Empire at that time weren't exactly cozy. Starfleet needed precise measurements of the Hobus phenomenon, and our task was to gather them as quickly—and as discreetly—as possible.

A small ship means a small crew. Who did you take with you?

I brought along a small group of volunteers, all of them seasoned Starfleet veterans. They'd begun working with me shortly after the astrophysics people started analyzing the first long-range sensor scans of Hobus the previous year.

And after you ran an analysis of your own, I'd imagine. Without getting too technical, can you spell some of your tentative conclusions out for us?
Let's just say I had the misfortune of noticing that the sensor profile of the Hobus Event bore a strong resemblance to that of the McAllister C-5 Nebula, back when 8472 was using it as a portal from fluidic space to our own universe. It's ironic, really. Despite their superficial similarities to each other—both nebulae are essentially gas-and-dust clouds that surround a central mass—they're very different phenomena. The expanding Hobus Nebula is essentially a shroud around a corpse, while the collapsing McAllister Nebula is more like a blanket swaddling a stellar infant. They're at opposite ends of their respective life cycles, a burned-out cinder and a growing protostar. But either object was a plausible candidate for having developed a spatial rift that 8472 might be able to exploit.[*]

I'd like to talk for a moment about your crew on that first Hobus mission, Admiral—specifically, about their prior experience with the Undine.

[*] In fact, the Undine did indeed use a spatial rift in the McAllister C-5 Nebula as a point of passage into our universe.

Actually, none of them had ever had any direct contact with 8472. At least not at that point in their careers. But they had all read the unclassified portions of *Voyager*'s Delta Quadrant logs.

So they knew about the secret fake Starfleet training facilities that the Undine had set up throughout Delta Quadrant space back in the 2370s.

The terraspheres. Species 8472—the Undine—built and operated at least a dozen of them. They were deep-space habitats, each of which contained pretty damned convincing duplicates of San Francisco and Starfleet Headquarters—including a simulacrum of Starfleet Academy. This was where 8472 brought their infiltrators-in-training up to speed on how to live undetected in human form, even among trained Starfleet officers. Not even the Founders of the Dominion, with their own shape-changing abilities and their penchant for subterfuge, had ever tried to infiltrate us on such a massive scale.

I've read your reports about *Voyager*'s encounter with Terrasphere 8, at least the ones that are part of the public record. It looked as though you had reached some kind of agreement with the Undine back in 2375. You appear to have left them convinced that the Federation didn't pose a threat to them, and that they therefore didn't need to prepare for war against us.

I thought so, too, at least for a while. Obviously I only managed to convince one small segment of 8472 to leave us alone, if that. After all, there were at least eleven other terraspheres out there that we never encountered. At least 8472 proved that we human-oids don't have a monopoly on paranoia.

Your reports about the Terrasphere 8 encounter make it pretty clear why the members of your initial Hobus survey team volunteered for the mission— even if they hadn't yet had any direct contact with the Undine.

Because they had read the very same reports that you did, each member of my team knew that they had already been touched by 8472—despite their never having seen one in the flesh. Those reports motivated Captain Valerie Archer and Commander Kinis to volunteer to be my pilots. Lieutenant Commander O'Halloran, an astrophysics specialist, rode herd on the specialized sensor package we were carrying because of what he read in my reports. And Lieutenant Commander David Gentry volunteered to handle tactical, just in case we encountered any-thing that was in the mood for a fight.

That was because each and every member of that crew knew that an 8472 infiltrator had "borrowed" his or her identity on Terrasphere 8. Hell, even [Starfleet Academy groundskeeper Liam] Boothby told me that if he was thirty years younger he'd have asked me to bring him along, too.

Was every one of the Undine-in-human-form you encountered on Terrasphere 8 disguised as real, existing humans?

We never found that out for certain, but I have a strong suspicion that the answer to your question is yes. It's a safe, conservative assumption to make, but it's one that Starfleet Command and I shared. After all, why would 8472 waste time and energy learning how to live the lives of fictitious humans and humanoids when it wouldn't have been any more trouble to just morph themselves into doppelgängers of real ones?

Didn't Starfleet Security have some concerns about your personnel choices for that mission? You might expect them to worry that an Undine sleeper agent might really be lurking among them, since it was already an established fact that each member of your team had already been duplicated by an Undine agent.

As a matter of fact, I *did* get some flack from Admiral [Marta] Batanides at Starfleet Security. Some of her staff could have taught even 8472 a thing or two about paranoia. We were both admirals, of course, but she had seniority on me. She could have shut the mission down.

But she obviously didn't succeed. Why?

Marta didn't reckon with my secret weapon: Admiral [Gareth] Bullock. Like the members of my team, he had a personal stake in the outcome of our mission—

because he was also among those that we knew for certain 8472 had "doppelgängered" aboard Terrasphere 8 back in the 'seventies. Gareth backed me up, and even told Marta that by her logic, he ought to be clapped in irons and thrown in the brig. But unless he failed an identity scan, or started morphing like a cornered Founder, Starfleet Command wasn't about to consider allowing Admiral Batanides, or anybody else for that matter, to do that.

So you were off to Hobus, or what was left of it, for the first time. What did you find when you arrived?
We began by confirming a great deal of what the initial long-range scans turned up. First of all, the neutrino counts were way off. Traditional supernovae give off pretty heavy neutrino emissions, but this one was an order of magnitude light on that score. We determined early on that the bulk of the neutrinos we *should* have detected coming from the Hobus remnant were somehow being shunted directly into subspace.

Subspace. That must explain how all that hard radiation and all the other lethal effects of the supernova were able to cross the hundreds of light-years between here and Romulus in a matter of days.
I think so. Of course, we still don't fully understand the exact physical mechanism that allowed it to happen. Still, it's the only explanation I've seen so far that makes sense and squares with all the data.

But the low neutrino flux was only the beginning. Believe me, Mister Sisko, even a year after the "kaboom" part of the supernova event, what was left of Hobus wasn't deficient in much of anything else. We had a damned rough ride, even with so much of the supernova's initial energy output already dissipated. Hobus was still throwing off intense streams of X-rays, gamma rays, delta rays, epsilon radiation, and even Berthold rays and tetryon particles, and the combined effect strained our multiphasic shielding system to the limit. Standard deflector shields would have been completely useless so deep inside what we had already started calling the Hobus Nebula. Needless to say, subspace communication with Starfleet was a complete hash everywhere within a light-year of Hobus. We got to within two AUs of Hobus before the structural integrity field itself became a cause for worry. But we managed to get the highest-resolution scans of Hobus to date.

You ran a significant risk to life and limb, Admiral. But you also stood a fair chance of being detected and attacked by the Romulans—or by one of the warring Romulan factions in contention for control of the wreckage of a post-Hobus Star Empire.
Every member of my crew agreed to run those risks, Mister Sisko. It wasn't just me.

But the diplomatic dangers could have affected a lot more people than you and your crew. How do you answer those who accuse you of jeopardizing

the Federation's goodwill vis-à-vis the Romulans because of a personal vendetta against the Undine? I don't have any answer for that, because I've always found that accusation ridiculous on its face. After all, that mission proved to be a fare-thee-well that the Romulans never had any intention of reciprocating any of the olive branches we'd extended to them since Shinzon's mercifully brief time on the praetor's throne. Their plan had always been to thank us by quietly slipping an Honor Blade between our collective ribs.

I certainly can't argue with any of that, Admiral. But at the time—and without the benefit of historical hindsight—your reputation inside Starfleet suffered quite a bit. Admiral Bullock notwithstanding, more than a few of your peers in Starfleet Command were critical of some of the risks you were willing to take in ferreting out possible Undine infiltrators.

True enough. Ironic, isn't it? I mean given Starfleet Command's worries that 8472 might have infiltrated my first Hobus mission crew. But I had to go with my own assessment of the damage that a species as hostile, intractable, and patient as 8472 was capable of inflicting on us over the long haul. It wasn't a pretty picture. It was the Dominion War all over again, only amplified by an order of magnitude in both severity and duration.

In view of that, a reputation never seemed like such a big thing to sacrifice.

And then there was the risk posed by Hobus itself: the supernova remnant was still spraying out intense streams of lethal radiation. Even given the valuable nature of the data you collected, that first survey mission seems like a pretty risky venture on a purely human level.

Sure it was. But was it *excessively* risky? Obviously I didn't think so at the time, and I still don't now. Remember, Starfleet couldn't allow 8472 a chance to secretly consolidate an invasion force on this side of fluidic space. It would have been riskier *not* to check out any place that might have provided them with a concealed beachhead from which they could have launched a large-scale attack. When O'Halloran's sensors picked up the warp signature of an 8472 vessel, it looked like that was *exactly* what we'd found.

Your shuttle was obviously pretty well equipped in terms of sensors and shields. How well armed were you?

We had two type-4 phaser arrays, as well as a pair of photon torpedoes. It gave us a sharp enough bite for a quick hit-and-run attack, though our teeth obviously weren't sharp enough to do any sustained damage. In other words, if we were put in the position of having to use our weapons, we'd be doing so either to cover our escape—or to make one last defiant gesture before being blown to atoms by a much bigger, much better armed enemy.

Of course, history shows that the Undine vessel that appeared on your sensors was really something else entirely. Do you ever wonder whether the personal stake you had in repelling a possible Undine invasion—not just you, Admiral, but your entire crew of "doppelgänger templates"—had left you predisposed to seeing something that wasn't really there?

That might or might not be true, Mister Sisko. But it's also irrelevant, as my old friend Annika [Hansen] might say. I still believe that any dispassionate analysis of those sensor profiles could have led to only one conclusion: we were on the trail of at least one 8472 vessel. And where there's one, there's always another, and another. We had no choice but to remain in the vicinity long enough to find out whether the Hobus disaster had created a quantum singularity capable of bringing that ship—or potentially a whole invasion fleet—into our universe.

And there was still another possibility we needed to check out: whether 8472 had actually *caused* the Hobus supernova, either to create a portal from their realm into ours, or simply to sow conflict between the Romulans and their neighbors.

I suppose it would have made sense to assume that they'd try to do both—even though history hasn't borne out your team's findings about any large Undine incursion having come our way via Hobus.

So far. Never make the mistake of thinking that history is over, Mister Sisko. A lot of Earth's best academic minds made the same mistake about four centuries ago, after the conclusion of a long period of bitter, mostly stalemated geopolitical conflict known as the Cold War. As the great Gallamite historian O'd'taa wrote, "History is one damned thing after another."

Yes, we were wrong in interpreting that warp signature as belonging to an 8472 vessel. But we also weren't so blinded by our previous brushes with them that we weren't capable of figuring that out for ourselves. Starting with an unusual subspace echo in the other vessel's warp field, which is something we'd never seen an 8472 ship produce before. Once we started tugging on that particular string in the sensor tapestry, a lot of the team's assumptions began to unravel.

According to your own logs, the Undine warp signature you found turned out to be a deliberate creation of the Romulans.
To cover up their tests of a new subspace weapon. We learned later that they developed it from dormant Borg transwarp technology that somehow fell into their laps deep in Beta Quadrant space.[*]

Why would the Romulans create fake Undine warp footprints when they could have covered their tracks using their cloaking technology?

---

[*] Starfleet experts have theorized that this Borg technology may have come from the same source as the weaponry that the Romulan Mining Guild representative Nero tried to bring to bear against Vulcan in 2387.

Romulan cloaking devices don't work any better inside the Hobus Nebula than ordinary deflector shields do. So they needed another way to hide what they were really up to—especially in light of Starfleet's conclusion that the Romulans' own subspace weapons tests were the likely cause of the Hobus disaster.

It makes sense. A subspace weapon touches off an accidental stellar explosion whose effects are felt almost instantaneously across entire sectors of space—via the shortcut of subspace.

It *does* make perfect sense. Maybe even a certain amount of poetic justice, too, so long as you're willing to overlook the billions of innocent Romulan civilians who died as a consequence of the Hobus disaster. But all we really have to link the Romulans to the Hobus supernova is circumstantial evidence.

Once again, you seem to be saying you don't agree with Starfleet's official conclusion that the Undine played no role in the Hobus disaster.

As I said, I've kept an open mind about that. I'm still not convinced that the energy levels the Romulans were playing with were sufficient to have caused an ordinary supernova, let alone a one-off stellar oddball like the one Hobus became.

Does that mean that your current crew might be scanning the Hobus Cinder and vicinity for Undine footprints right now?

Let's just say I'm not prepared to dismiss any possibility prematurely.

I'm about to ask Admiral Janeway a follow-up question concerning her obvious, if usually well-concealed, preoccupation with the Undine, when a voice from her combadge interrupts us to report that the long-range sensors have picked up another strange warp signature. I am frozen in place, still seated before her desk as she gets to her feet and acknowledges this surprising development with a curt "On my way, Lieutenant." She apologizes and vanishes, leaving me alone in her small office.

Later on in this voyage I still hope to probe more deeply into a few issues that deserve closer scrutiny. Does she second-guess herself because the truce she'd thought she'd negotiated with the Undine came unraveled? Does that arguable failure make her feel responsible in any way for the Long War that some say continues even now in the dark wainscoting of the galaxy? And what about the fact that Janeway continually referred to the Undine by the designation given them by one of their deadliest enemies (the Borg collective), rather than using the name by which Species 8472 refers to itself (the Undine)? That wouldn't seem to bode well for the prospect of an eventual Federation-Undine rapprochement, following the precedents set by the First and Second Khitomer Accords.

And what about the apparent Undine warp signature that the Tucker *has just detected? Could Admiral*

Janeway's initial instincts about an Undine presence at Hobus turn out to have been right all along? I rise from my chair and exit the ready room, determined to find out.

Once I reach the bridge, my eyes are drawn to the enormous forward viewer, like iron filings to a magnet. Through the haze and distortion of the nebular material beyond the ship's hull, I can just barely make out a **[REMAINDER OF INTERVIEW AND COMMENTARY REDACTED BY STARFLEET INTELLIGENCE]**

Fragile Alliances

A WAR SPANNING TWO QUADRANTS

Intercepted from the Ferengi Commercial News, stardate 85365.2*

Dateline—Mol'Rihan [New Romulus, aka Roma Nova, the Romulan Star Empire's post-Hobus capital on Rator III]

Romulan military vessels released the Ferengi Commercial Hauler *Noble Avarice* from impoundment today, following three days of intensive interrogations and intrusive medical examinations of the vessel's commander, DaiMon Brog, and his twelve-man crew.

"Being arrested for doing nothing other than fulfilling our commercial commitments to the Romulan Star Empire is an outrage," Brog told FCG shortly after his release. "Ferengi ore haulers have been handling a thick percentage of the Romulans' resource-extraction and transport needs ever since the Hobus disaster wiped out Romulus—and the Romulan Mining Guild along with it. The treatment my crew and I received is a damned strange way for the Romulan government to show its gratitude for everything the Ferengi Alliance has done for them over the past twenty years."

The Romulan government has issued no official statement about the detention of the *Noble Avarice*, though it seems likely that the incident had something to do with the installation of Sela, the new empress

_____
* March 13, 2408.

of the Romulan Star Empire, whose official coronation is now under way in Mol'Rihan, where the most stringent imaginable security measures have been instituted. Unnamed sources have told the FCN that the Romulan authorities have reason to believe that alien assassins disguised as Romulans may attempt to infiltrate the proceedings. Government officials refused to comment on this possibility, or whether it had any bearing on the *Noble Avarice*'s impoundment.

The office of the Grand Nagus has demanded a complete explanation and a full apology, and is expected to make an announcement shortly regarding the status of the Ferengi Alliance's existing business contracts and diplomatic treaties. . . .

JAKE SISKO, DATA ROD #G-72

Lakarian City, Cardassia Prime

As I walk along a mostly empty downtown sidewalk following an early morning tour of one of Lakarian City's newest construction projects, I imagine I'm being surveilled by any number of armed agents of the Cardassian government. That's unfair, of course; after all, Cardassia has undergone fundamental reforms during its decades-long transition from the rigidly authoritarian ideology that nearly allowed the flames of the Dominion War to consume it.

Even though I am standing at the side of one of Lakarian City's larger vehicular thoroughfares, I have seen only relative handfuls of Cardassian passersby so far this morning. Did my host arrange this for the benefit of his human guests, or is this apparent dearth of people normal for this time of day, or day of the week? Because my host has been oddly evasive about this, I force myself to go only by the evidence of my eyes, which tell me I've been noticed so far only by the two men who now flank me as I walk along the boulevard's broad sidewalk: Elim Garak, who has become a Cardassian official of no fixed title and seemingly limitless influence, a sort of diplomatic jack-of-all-trades; and Federation Council liaison Franklin Drake, whose dossier reveals a long career in Starfleet Intelligence, a fact that might explain the apparent ease with which Franklin appears to relate to Garak.

A forest of slender, thorn-studded duranium towers looms over us in every direction as Garak leads us ever more deeply into the downtown district, which appears to be the home of government, commerce, and art all at once. The dour beauty of Lakarian City's skyline—which the Jem'Hadar reduced to ashes during the Dominion War's waning hours—appears to have been restored to its former glory, right down to the street-level religious murals I've seen before only in archived prewar photographs and holoimages.

Unsurprisingly, our peripatetic conversation is largely a monologue on the part of our host, Garak, who has probably forgotten more about this place and its unique culture than I'll ever learn. Drake remains mostly silent during Garak's lecture, apparently as interested as I am in absorbing our tour guide's good-natured pedagogy.

The man who is doing most of the talking is a walking contradiction, a potent mixture of refinement and danger. He has become far more than the exiled former-spy-cum-tailor that he was when I first encountered him during our respective tenures on DS9. Although he was instrumental in Legate Corat Damar's revolt against the Dominion, he has repeatedly described himself as a mere apparatchik in the political machine of the new Cardassia, an edifice that remains perpetually under construction.

Garak is certainly that, but he is also a great deal more; following the devastation that this city and so many others suffered at the Dominion's hands, Garak helped to lay much of the groundwork for the progressive, democratic postwar governance that followed, from the Cardassian Union's first great democratically elected castellan, the late Alon Ghemor, down through Natima Lang, the current holder of that high office. And with a long and storied career in the shadowy world of Cardassia's intelligence networks behind him—he was once a highly effective agent of the late, unlamented Obsidian Order—Elim Garak is at least as well placed as anyone on the planet to understand the extent to which the Undine may have succeeded in infiltrating not only his own government institutions but also those of the Federation, the Klingon and Romulan Empires, and other Alpha and Beta Quadrant powers.

As he shares his knowledge of the Undine with Mr. Drake and me, Garak's pleasant, personable manner falters only briefly. From somewhere behind the facade of refined Cardassian civility, I hear a slightly bitter timbre enter his voice whenever his narrative wanders too close to the topic of the earlier war with the Dominion. Though the change in his manner is both brief and subtle, it hits me like a bucket of cold water, delivering a forceful reminder of the two-million-plus innocent people who died in Lakarian City during the Dominion War's twilight. I try not to wince at Garak's occasional bouts of gallows humor, which have no doubt often served as his only buffer against the soul-devouring despair that can afflict anyone whose people have been as thoroughly defeated as the Cardassians. Though they come and go in the space of heartbeats, those subtly pain-wracked moments in our dialogue surround him with an almost palpable shroud of grief that only serves to increase his author- ity and credibility on virtually any topic. That air of credibility extends even to his otherwise highly dubious tale of a recent life-or-death struggle with an Undine agent, years after the conclusion of the Long War.

However, I must add a word of caution, based upon my time of observing Garak back on DS9: it can be dif- ficult to verify his stories, wherein the whole truth as often as not can live comfortably alongside a verita- ble painter's palette of improvised omissions, ad hoc distortions, and highly creative half-truths—not to mention the finely crafted whole-cloth lies of a master prevaricator and confabulator. Therefore, a warning here is in order: Caveat lector *(Let the reader beware).*

I've heard quite a few reports lately—not all of them confirmed by the Federation News Service or other mainstream media outlets—that Undine infiltra- tion of the Alpha and Beta Quadrants during the war years may have been a lot more extensive than most people have been led to believe.

GARAK: Unquestionably. The documents that the

Federation Council recently declassified speak for themselves. A picture of the Undine conflict is finally emerging that shows it as very much like the Dominion War that preceded it. Only *this* picture is painted across a much larger canvas. Undine agents can be literally *anywhere*—and are far more difficult to detect than were the shape-shifting Founders of the Dominion.

You're speaking about the Undine War in the present tense, even though the common wisdom is that the Long War is now behind us—years behind us, in fact. Most people think of it as a thing of the past, like the Dominion War, or the Borg collective's attempt to alter Earth's history.

GARAK: You just used a rather intriguing turn of phrase, Mister Sisko: "common wisdom." What a semantically twisted idiom. I suspect, however, that it is as much an oxymoron as its elocutionary cousin, "common sense." That's certainly true with regard to the Long War, a name that has proved to be far more appropriately descriptive of its subject than most people would prefer to believe. I'm sure that Mister Drake agrees with me on that point.

So you *don't* think that the war is behind us?

DRAKE: My career in diplomacy has taught me a few inviolable rules, Mister Sisko. And one of those is never to assume that an enemy you've defeated is necessarily going to *remain* defeated simply because you'd like to put the unpleasantness of the fight behind you.

GARAK: I tend to agree, Liaison Drake. That must be the reason you and I get along so well. In fact, it is often those things that are "behind" you that can be the most dangerous. I give you some of the recent activities of the changeling Laas as a case in point. I trust you've heard of him.

Of course. Laas was one of Odo's "siblings." One of the hundred infant changelings that the Founders sent out into the universe maybe centuries ago.
GARAK: Then you may also be aware that Laas and some of his confederates who comprise the so-called Missing Ninety-seven are discussing the creation of a new Dominion.

I've heard, though I'm not sure what to make of it yet. It could amount to nothing more than a pile of rumors. I suppose we'll just have to wait and see what happens.
DRAKE: Merely watching and waiting isn't always the smartest course of action, Mister Sisko—whether we're talking about changelings from the Gamma Quadrant or even more powerful shape-shifters from fluidic space.

I don't know anybody who seriously believes that the Dominion will ever cause us any trouble ever

again. So let's talk about the Undine: Are either of you actually arguing that they still pose a real danger, even now?

GARAK: Much as I would prefer that it were otherwise, I can't rule out the possibility that Undine infiltrators are moving about freely across the Alpha and Beta Quadrants even now. Perhaps even here on Cardassia Prime itself.

I'm surprised to hear you say something like that on the record.

GARAK: I've said a good deal more than that on the subject, addressing your Federation Security Council directly. Not to mention your new president and his cabinet. Unfortunately, no one in your government seems eager to give sufficient credit to the highly likely possibility that I am right—despite my having presented them with my own eyewitness reports on the matter. I'll also level the same charge at your news services.

Well, Mister Garak, I'm more than happy to put your own eyewitness account of recent Undine activity on the record, for whatever it's worth. But first I have a question: Aren't you concerned that you might encourage a level of paranoia that could do a lot of the enemy's work for them?

GARAK: Mister Sisko, paranoia is the only truly rational response when someone really *is* out to get you.

Are you saying that you had an individual, personal encounter with an Undine?

GARAK: I am indeed, Mister Sisko. And it happened not too terribly long ago, right here on Cardassia Prime, though it was some time after the so-called end of the multifront war that the Undine started—and have never entirely stopped trying to prosecute, so far as I can tell.

What happened?

GARAK: It was during the temporary breakdown of Cardassia's planetary climate-control grid, not quite two years ago. The weather-generation systems were being recalibrated and fine-tuned as part of our long-term climate remediation program—a program that the Federation helped Alon Ghemor's government institute many years earlier, during the immediate aftermath of the Dominion War. We're still coping with many of the attendant problems today, in fact.

I hadn't realized that the Dominion had inflicted such extensive environmental damage on Cardassia Prime.

GARAK: Well, to be completely fair to the Dominion, the Allies can share some of the credit for that. Certainly, the majority of the particulate matter that blocked out the sun for months—and, not incidentally, caused crop failures on a previously unheard-of scale—entered the upper atmosphere after the

Jem'Hadar vaporized Lakarian and several other densely populated cities. But the dust kicked up by the Allied fleet's subsequent invasion of Cardassia Prime, to say nothing of the many inadvertent additions our liberators made to our civilian casualty lists, also helped to exacerbate the problem.

DRAKE: With all due respect, Mister Garak, you're not being fair to the Federation. During war, we have always done everything possible to keep civilian casualties to an absolute minimum. That was one of the Federation's guiding principles as part of the Allied invasion force, even during the darkest hours of the Dominion War.

GARAK: I have never disputed that, Liaison Drake. However, neither of the non-Federation components of the Allied invasion force have ever pretended to possess any such scruples. In fact, the Klingons appeared willing to go well out of their way to offer public demonstrations of that lack. The Romulans, by contrast, at least displayed the virtue of treating us with arrogant indifference.

However, it wasn't my intention to wander into a minefield of pointless recrimination and finger-pointing. The simple fact is this: when pulverized, cities tend to loft rather large plumes of smoke, soot, and debris skyward. This effect can blot out the sun for months, even years, disrupting photosynthesis and cooling the planet to the point where natural climatic feedback loops fail and the prospect of a runaway "icehouse effect" can become a very real danger. In the short term, however, the bulk of the atmospheric chaos—which included such charming features as crop-destroying acid rain—fell across the broad, strong backs of Cardassia's small but increasingly indispensable population of agriculturists.

DRAKE: Those climate effects constitute a phenomenon that one of Earth's great atomic-age thinkers called "nuclear winter." The Klingon homeworld experienced something a lot like it more than a century ago, after Qo'noS's moon Praxis exploded.

GARAK: "Nuclear winter." With the human propensity for such elegant turns of phrase, one would expect Earth to have produced a great deal more interesting literature than it has. Forgive me—I'm digressing again.

As I was saying, unless certain drastic early steps are taken to counter such a catastrophe—the onset of a so-called nuclear winter, as you humans describe it—then famine will inevitably follow, marching arm in arm with disease. And no civilization can long survive such a double-pronged assault—even a civilization as old and sophisticated as Cardassia's.

Fortunately for your homeworld, the aid sent by the Federation seemed to have blunted the worst of the

environmental effects. We sent doctors, medicine, food, industrial replicators—even atmosphere processors aimed at repairing at least a good portion of the global climate damage.

GARAK: All of which proved essential, and earned the undying gratitude of both the Ghemor government and the Cardassian people. But the wounds we sustained during the Dominion War were so deep that even the Federation's best efforts were only barely adequate to stanch the worst of our collective bleeding.

Cardassia truly passed through the eye of a needle that initial postwar year, particularly during that especially unforgiving first southern winter. Many couldn't cope with the constant, grinding hardship, particularly the very young and the very old. Of course, the Jem'Hadar's parting gesture had been to reduce the number of mouths we had to feed by nearly a billion. So I suppose we owe them a debt of gratitude for the help they so generously provided in resolving certain aspects of our resource allocation issues.

Restoring Cardassia's climate and atmosphere to normal was obviously a much bigger problem than I'd realized.

GARAK: It's a decades-long process, at the very least. And as I said, it isn't over even now. Our climate engineers are still making minute adjustments from day to day and week to week. Atmosphere remediation and management is an extremely delicate and difficult-to-anticipate business. A malfunction in, say, a key temperature-regulation node can alter the weather locally, and the climate as a whole, in fundamental ways—in addition to entirely predictable ones. It was just such a global climate-control malfunction that brought my transport pod down over South Forbella's Great Desert, only a few hundred *decas** from this very city.

Where were you going at the time?
GARAK: I was conducting Castellan Lang to a joint session of the Detapa Council when a rather powerful—and entirely unscheduled, I might add—bolt of lightning struck our craft. We were under attack, but there was precious little I could do about that after we were hit, even though I did everything I could from the copilot's chair. The blast disabled several key systems, and we would have dropped into the desert like a meteor were it not for the flying expertise of a member of the castellan's security detail, the man who was serving that day as our main pilot. The ship avoided utter destruction as a consequence, though only just; she made an extremely hard landing on a stretch of radioactive wasteland that had been declared unfit for habitation since the Dominion War.

Was anybody hurt?
GARAK: Oh, yes. The pilot died in the impact. But fortunately there were no other fatalities.

---

* A Cardassian *deca* is roughly equivalent to a kilometer.

You said this lightning strike that brought your transport down was "unscheduled." But you also characterize it as an attack. Isn't it possible that your craft just happened to wander into a desert squall and got hit by an entirely natural electrical discharge?

GARAK: That's possible, certainly. But not in any way credible. One would have to maintain an entirely unhealthy belief in coincidence, and I have never been accused of harboring such an irrational faith. Considering the degree of weather control we've had to exercise as part of the ongoing climate normalization program, a random lightning strike is rarer than a nine-legged riding beast. And a stray bolt of atmospheric electricity is orders of magnitude less likely to hit anything consequential than would have been the case in the old days, when we used to let the climate "run wild." Therefore a random lightning strike capable of finding the transport ship carrying the castellan of the Cardassian Union is essentially an impossibility—orders of magnitude less likely than finding, say, a Klingon capable of chewing with his mouth closed.

Good point—about the odds surrounding the lightning strike, not about the chewing. So you were attacked and forced to make a hard landing. What happened next?

GARAK: I probably should amend my description of our craft's touchdown. The term "hard landing" paints entirely too cheery a picture of what had just happened to us. "Crash landing," or perhaps even simply "crash," would be far more accurate. The transport was a total loss, right down to the comm system. I suffered a broken arm in the impact, but at least I was able to remain conscious. Castellan Lang was out cold, a consequence of the rather alarming, though happily nonfatal, head injury she had sustained (of course, at the time we had no way to be certain that the castellan would survive).

Only one member of the castellan's two-man security detail survived, and somehow he managed to do so without suffering so much as a scratch. He was a young military officer named Krota. I should have taken his apparent invulnerability as the first sign that something wasn't right—something other than the fact of the lightning strike itself, that is. But, as you humans are so fond of saying, hindsight is always twenty-twenty.

You and Krota were in a pretty serious situation. What did you do?
GARAK: Why, Krota and I did the only thing we *could* do: we tended to the castellan's injuries as best we could using the transport's first aid supplies, saw that she was resting comfortably and that the transport was secure, and then set out for the nearest sign of civilization.

A nearby city or town?
GARAK: No. That would have been far too conve-

nient. Unfortunately, the only sapient-created artifact within a day's walk of our crash site—besides our
wrecked transport, of course—was one of Cardassia
Prime's weather-remediation stations. It was part of
the climate-regulation network that the Ghemor government had begun building immediately after the
end of our Dominion occupation.

**A weather station. Did it have a crew, or was it
automated?**
GARAK: Many such facilities were, and still are,
completely automated, with staff visits occurring
at regular intervals to address basic maintenance
issues and to execute periodic equipment upgrades.
As luck would have it, this particular weather station
did indeed have a live caretaker, according to Krota,
who managed to raise him briefly on his personal
comm device. Unfortunately, a magnetic storm
came up and interrupted our transmission before
Krota could get much past the "hello" phase of the
conversation.

**You weren't able to tell this caretaker how serious
your situation was?**
GARAK: Nor were we able to explain that we had the
castellan with us—or that she was in urgent need of
medical attention.

**Was this storm another "unscheduled" weather
event, like the lightning that caused the crash?**

GARAK: It was most certainly unplanned, at least by anyone in authority. And it left us with only one real option: to leave the transport. Unfortunately, both the castellan's injuries and the storm conditions outside the transport made it unsafe to bring her along.

You left Castellan Lang unattended?
GARAK: But also safe and in relatively stable condition, considering the circumstances. There was really nothing further we could do for her—other than do whatever we could to expedite the arrival of help, which we as yet had no assurance was on its way.

But you say you were under attack. If that's so, weren't you leaving the castellan at the mercy of whatever enemy might have brought the transport down?
GARAK: It certainly could appear that way—unless one takes into account the fact of the storm itself. The ferrous metal content of the sand particles being lifted by the storm's winds generated a great deal of static electricity. All that flying grit not only provided a barrier to locating the crashed transport visually, it also set up a highly effective sensor screen. An enemy using tricorders, or even orbital scans, would have been confounded for several of your hours—potentially a long enough interval to allow me and Krota to summon help. So we set out on foot for the weather station, across one of the nastiest stretches of irradiated desolation you can imagine. If you need a visual

reference, think of some of the landscapes that characterized your own world's postatomic horror.

Were you confident you could make it, even with the storm?
GARAK: Well, as I said, I knew we were within a day's walk from the facility, though the storm had made it all but impossible to get and keep our bearings visually, let alone to zero in on the place with handheld scanning devices. So I took the point as we pushed forward in what we hoped was the right direction while Krota continued trying to make contact, using his mobile comm unit.

Weren't you carrying any communications gear of your own?
GARAK: We had only one other mobile comm unit with us—the one that had belonged to the castellan's dead pilot/bodyguard—but we had decided to leave it aboard the transport. If the castellan were to awaken before we returned, and if the storm were to subside sooner rather than later, she might have needed it. As it turned out, we needn't have bothered; the storm raged on for most of the remainder of the day, erecting what amounted to a solid wall of flying magnetic particles that no comm signal could penetrate.

Well, since you and Castellan Lang both survived the incident, can I presume that you made it to the station?

GARAK: That certainly would have made for a more pleasing narrative than what *actually* occurred, at least from my perspective. I'm still not entirely sure what precipitated it—perhaps it was the ionization in the air, or some other effect of the persistent and intensifying storm—but as Krota hiked into the storm he began to . . . *change*. Right before my eyes he became one of those . . . three-legged *things* that the Federation seems so delighted not to be actively fighting at the moment.

You're saying that an Undine infiltrator had somehow managed to worm its way onto Castellan Lang's security detail—even though the Undine were no longer at war with any of the Alpha or Beta Quadrant powers?
GARAK: No longer *formally* at war, perhaps. But at war nevertheless. And there I was, all alone but for him—or rather *it*—in one of the most inhospitable places on Cardassia Prime, and under some of the worst weather conditions imaginable. Needless to say, it was a highly inconvenient situation.

Do you think Krota had intended to reveal his Undine identity to you then and there?
GARAK: I'm almost certain that he didn't. His "unmasking," as it were, had to be inadvertent. Really, can you think of a less commodious place for a thing like that to happen? I can't. So I must have been witnessing that accidental "reversion" process

that Undine spies have been known to undergo on occasion—especially during times of stress or injury, according to certain Federation intelligence reports on the subject that had . . . come into my possession.

I almost feel foolish for asking this, Mister Garak, but how did you get hold of Federation intelligence reports about the Undine?

GARAK: It's never foolish for you to do your journalistic duty, Mister Sisko. But it would definitely be foolish of me to furnish you with a forthright answer. Besides, I don't want to waste your time with material that Starfleet Intelligence is almost certain to redact from your project anyway.

All right, then. Let's go back to Krota. Do you think his plan was to assassinate the castellan?

GARAK: He must have had a much longer-term agenda than that, though if killing Natima Lang had suited his purposes I'm sure he wouldn't have hesitated to do so. After all, if his principal goal had been to assassinate the castellan, he had already gotten close enough to her to have had many previous opportunities—none of which he'd acted upon as yet. Of course, if he wanted to preserve such opportunities for the future, he would have had to prevent me from revealing his secret to anyone else.

Then I take it the next thing he did was to try to kill *you*.

GARAK: You may find this surprising, but that isn't at all what happened. Instead, his body changed again; after expending considerable effort, he transformed back into the likeness of Krota. The entire metamorphosis, from man into monster and back again, took only one or two of your minutes. It also appeared to be exceedingly painful for him. Despite their occasional slipups—most notably and spectacularly their so-called reversions to their natural forms—Undine operatives are obviously highly dedicated professionals, devoted to maintaining their cover identities at all costs.

So he didn't try to kill you. What did he do instead?
GARAK: Believe it or not, Krota—or whoever he really was—actually took a far more audacious tack than violence: he tried to deny the evidence of my eyes. He knew as well as I did what I had seen, no doubt because my injuries had compromised my ability to conceal my surprise at his transformations. Expecting an immediate attack, I wasted no time drawing my disruptor and training it straight at his head. Understandably, this put him into a fairly cautious frame of mind.

I didn't realize anybody outside the security contingent was allowed to carry arms in the castellan's presence. I thought you were a diplomatic adviser.
GARAK: That's correct, Mister Sisko. But since my advice frequently concerns matters of state security,

I'd been granted a certain amount of leeway regarding the official sidearms policy. This was merely one of a distressingly large number of occasions when this leeway proved invaluable.

So you confronted Krota at disruptor-point and accused him of being an Undine spy.

GARAK: Indeed I did, since there was no way he could believe I hadn't seen his metamorphoses. It's probably at this point you'd expect him to risk everything by lunging at me in a desperate bid to silence the only living witness to his ongoing crimes. Instead, he flatly denied that anything had happened. He said that my eyes must have been playing tricks on me. I was hallucinating because of the combined effects of injury, fatigue, and dehydration. We'd been out in the raging elements for several hours by then, so what he was saying actually had a certain . . . credibility about it.

As you said, you were injured, tired, and dehydrated. Were you beginning to doubt what you'd seen—or what you _thought_ you'd seen?

GARAK: I knew what he was telling me wasn't true, Mister Sisko. I know what I saw.

As confident as you are by nature, Mister Garak, even _you_ have to admit that you can't be one hundred percent certain of that. After all, you've already conceded that you weren't at your best at that time.

"Compromised" is the word I believe you used. And add to that your history—please pardon my being indelicate here, but I feel my duty requires me to bring up certain facts. Your history of psychiatric conditions. Your chronic claustrophobia. Your psychological issues related to years of exposure to the artificial endorphins generated by a device implanted in your body by the Obsidian Order. The post-traumatic stress of your protracted years of exile, which ended at the same time your homeworld was being laid waste by the Dominion. . . . Taking all of these things into consideration, isn't it at least *possible* that you really *did* imagine this alleged Undine encounter?

GARAK: Certainly, I acknowledge the possibility, though I utterly reject its likelihood, just as I do the notion of the castellan's transport sustaining an "accidental" lightning strike. After all, isn't it also technically possible that *you* are hallucinating our exchange, Mister Sisko, and that neither Mister Drake nor myself are even here? As I said, I know what I saw.

I'm sorry, Mister Garak. I didn't mean to offend you.

GARAK: I'm not offended in the least, Mister Sisko. As you said, you are merely doing your duty to history. Just as I am doing my duty to Cardassia by trying to get my recollection embedded in the wet concrete of galactic history—before that concrete cures and hardens into something impermeable and static. Now, where was I?

You were in a standoff with Krota, or whoever he was.

GARAK: Oh, yes. A rescue party interrupted our little tableau, picked us up, and finally rescued the castellan. My debriefers asked me many of the very same questions after I leveled espionage charges at the alien creature that had called itself Krota.

Regarding your rescue, did your debriefers believe what you told them about Krota?

GARAK: Not to the extent that they were willing to risk allowing Krota to be shot down in cold blood. Therefore, they disarmed me during the rescue. However, they also took my word that Krota needed to be restrained, at least until the matter of his identity could be sorted out once and for all. Krota, or whatever the thing that wore his form really called itself, was intelligent enough to keep up his charade of innocence while the matter was still subject to some justifiable doubt in the minds of those who hadn't seen his transformations with their own eyes.

It was only then that I realized how very, very dangerous these Undine could really be. These were no mere shape-shifting monsters to be sniffed out and destroyed, like the Founders of the Dominion. No, the Undine were something far more clever and sophisticated than that. For under the right circumstances, they can maintain their cover even *after* they've been sniffed out, merely by remaining calm and appearing reasonable—and by casting a mere dusting of doubt over the sanity of any lone accuser. Their most fearsome attribute is not their physical strength, their ability to infuse an adversary with parasitic life-forms, or even their talent for making themselves into DNA-perfect doppelgängers of their enemies.

No. Their most frightening talent is their *persuasiveness.* From behind the barrier of their disguises, they exude the slickness of master politicians. They can insinuate themselves inextricably into our civilizations. And no amount of vigilance can completely safeguard even the topmost levels of our leadership hierarchies.

DRAKE: If you don't mind my saying so, Mister Garak, you're starting to sound paranoid again.

GARAK: But appropriately so, I should think, under the present circumstances.

I have to agree with Liaison Drake, Mister Garak. Cardassia is the civilization that produced the Obsidian Order, one of the most feared intelligence bureaus in two quadrants. Even granted that the Undine were formidable adversaries, how could a civilization like yours be such easy pickings for them—especially so long after the Long War's generally agreed-upon end?

GARAK: I can point to two main reasons. For one, the Undine study each of their target societies with painstaking care before they begin their infiltration ops. For another, the Obsidian Order—which might have stood as a sentinel against Undine incursions—was never reconstituted under any of Cardassia's post–Dominion War governments. Not even the best efforts of such hard-line reactionaries as Gul Madred, not to mention the rump Parliament his so-called True Way party now represents, were sufficient to get the late Enabran Tain's old spy bureau restored and operational again.

The True Way. What are their main objectives?
GARAK: What you probably imagine them to be. They started with an only barely failed attempt to quash Cardassia's nascent democracy. Now they're all about the restoration of Cardassia's former "greatness," which presumably includes reconstituting the intelligence bureau that everyone feared so deeply.

The very same Obsidian Order that you served for so many years.
GARAK: Which is perhaps why I now channel so much of my energies into atoning for my misspent youth.

You played a major role in the Ghemor government's decision to kill and bury the Obsidian Order. It's not always easy to slough off the past.

Do you ever have any regrets about leaving behind your former life as a spy—especially in light of the Undine War?

GARAK: I'm afraid that much has changed since the carefree days of my service as an intelligence operative. And regrets serve little purpose, especially given the limited palette of choices the Ghemor government had in founding a viable democratic system on post–Dominion War Cardassia. For most people, the Obsidian Order was too painful a reminder of the bad old days of Dukat's sellout to the Dominion and all the indignities that followed. Do I regret Ghemor's decision not to exhume the Obsidian Order once he was in power? Only when I imagine the bureau being used to protect Cardassia from alien infiltration. But the practical reality is that Ghemor would never have been allowed to govern had he decided not to leave the Order moldering in its grave, so to speak.

Of course, even a fully operational Obsidian Order might well have failed to stop a foe as wily as the Undine.

I'm surprised to hear you speak that way about the Obsidian Order. In years past, you've described their reach and abilities as almost limitless.

GARAK: If I ever left you with that impression, please allow me to disabuse you of it now. *Nothing* is limitless. Take the example of our only peers in the intelligence business, the Romulans. I mean to offer no offense to the many fine intelligence professionals who protect your Federation, Mister Liaison.

DRAKE: None taken. Besides, what would *I* know about the intelligence business?

What about the Romulans, Mister Garak?
GARAK: Although their Tal Shiar spy organization has weathered the storms of Romulan politics for decades, and has survived relatively intact, even the Romulans have suffered Undine infiltration. And I'm told that much of it has occurred recently, though only a few Romulan intel veterans are inclined to speak of it, even in the gentlest of whispers. Mind you, that's an example of Undine relations with only one non-Cardassian power. If you had access to as many of my outworlder colleagues as I do—and I'm talking about members of species that aren't commonly regarded as prone to panic, like the Klingons and even the Gorn—then you'd hear substantially similar stories. The Undine may be keeping a low profile in comparison to the time of the Long War, but they're busy—and they're gradually getting *busier*.

DRAKE: I've heard such things as well, on Earth. Just stories, mind you. Nothing to panic about. It all could amount to nothing more than tall tales of mermaids and sea monsters.

GARAK: We'll see, I suppose.

Let's go back to your standoff in the desert for a moment, Mister Garak. Didn't your rescuers try to test your story against Krota's, right then and there? Didn't they at least scan him to try to get at the truth?

GARAK: They did indeed, Mister Sisko. Our rescuers were soldiers of the New Cardassia, which means that they were methodical, careful people. Unfortunately, they were limited both by the resolution of their instruments and by the DNA-duplication talents of the Undine.

So either Krota was an Undine capable of fooling a tricorder, or his story was on the level.

GARAK: I have never been one to place more faith in a scanning device than I will in my own instincts. That predilection has saved my life on any number of occasions.

I know that you and the castellan quickly resumed your duties once you were both released from your doctors' care a short time after the crash. What became of Krota?

GARAK: Why, he disappeared shortly after our post-crash debriefings. It happened a day or two after the scans I had asked to be performed on him had proved inconclusive. I regard his disappearance as at least circumstantial corroboration of my story; it seems that in accusing him, I had indeed compromised his usefulness as an Undine spy.

Was Krota ever found?

GARAK: If by "Krota" you're referring to his Undine doppelgänger, that creature was gone without a trace, and has remained that way ever since. If you mean the genuine Cardassian article, his body turned up a few weeks later, in a badly decomposed state. This discovery tends to support my contention that an Undine operative had murdered and replaced the real Krota several months prior to our desert sojourn.

Or it might just mean that Krota had fallen victim to a terrible but completely ordinary crime of violence. According to the public records my padd has just accessed, the Detapa Council's special investigative panel seemed satisfied with that explanation.

GARAK: You are more than welcome to believe their findings as well, if you find them as comforting as the Detapa Council did. But I stand by my story, Mister Sisko. I know what I saw out in the desert.

DRAKE: I hate to admit it, but the Federation Council seems no more eager to consider the possibility of renewed Undine hostilities than the Cardassian government has been. I suppose we'll have to leave it to history to make the final judgment on the matter.

Before history can do that, it will have to tie up a few loose ends about that desert crash landing. Mister Garak, you insist that both the lightning

that caused the crash and the subsequent magnetic storm stemmed from deliberate acts of sabotage.

GARAK: Even the Detapa Council had to concede that as the likeliest explanation, given the astronomical odds against such weather anomalies occurring by pure chance. However, the Council's investigative panel was somewhat less categorical in identifying the likely perpetrator or perpetrators.

Do you think this weather manipulation was an attempt by the Undine to assassinate Castellan Lang?

GARAK: I don't. The Undine already had one of their operatives positioned a mere knife-thrust away from the castellan. Why should they go to all the trouble of hijacking the weather—risking the life of a difficult-to-replace operative in the process—when they already had a far simpler alternative placed within easy striking distance?

DRAKE: The saboteurs could have been allied with Gul Madred and his True Way movement. Madred and his followers have been dead set against every progressive leader in recent Cardassian history, going back to Castellan Alon Ghemor.

GARAK: But they're also hopeless narcissists who would have insisted on issuing announcements, delivering speeches, and taking credit—even for an assassination attempt that ultimately failed. No, it seems likelier that the responsible party was actually a Cardassian patriot who had somehow gotten wind of the Undine penetration of the chancellor's office. This person, or group of persons, seized control of the weather station remotely and used it as a weapon to take down the infiltrator.

But they would have sacrificed the castellan in the process.
GARAK: An unfortunate choice on the perpetrator's part, and one with which I must vehemently disagree, since I worked so hard on behalf of the castellan on the campaign that ultimately put her in office. Perhaps the perpetrator had been an equally vehement supporter of one of Castellan Lang's electoral opponents.

Or maybe this perpetrator was actually gunning for *you*, Garak, and wasn't all that concerned about causing a little additional mayhem.
GARAK: Mister Sisko, you flatter me! Some of Doctor Bashir's vivid imagination must have rubbed off on you during all those years aboard Deep Space 9. No. I feel confident that I was beneath the notice of any self-respecting assassin then, just as I am now. The short answer is that I simply don't know who was responsible for using that weather station to attack our transport. At least I haven't determined the perpetrator's identity *yet*.

What about whoever was supposed to be running the weather station you and Krota were trying to reach?

GARAK: The station turned out to be one of the fully automated ones after all. There hadn't been a living soul in that facility for more than a year. It seems that the Undine simulacrum of Krota lied to me about having reached anyone there on his com unit. Isn't that strange?

But why would he make something like that up?

GARAK: Perhaps to lure me out of the transport with him. To convince me that the weather station had a comm system with which he might summon help— but only if he could obtain some technical assistance from me.

And you think his plan might have been to steal your identity next.

GARAK: Or perhaps, eventually, that of the castellan herself. The storm could have covered up any act of murder and replacement well enough to satisfy anyone else who might have happened by. But whatever the creature's real agenda may have been, its apparently accidental "reversion" disrupted it.

I'm confident that I'll figure its plan out. Someday.

In search of a midday meal, we enter a venerable-looking example of Cardassian architecture that in actual fact can't be more than three decades old, give or take. As we wait, the three of us seated at one of the tables in the all-but-empty dining area, Garak's interests gravitate toward a discussion of food and the decline in the art of waiting tables during recent years. But whenever Garak isn't holding forth on such weighty cultural matters, he tends to trail off onto increasingly speculative ground while somehow never wandering far from his desert confrontation with a suspected Undine operative.

As we peruse the menu, Liaison Drake sips at a tall flute of kanar that the waiter brings out, along with the glasses of plain, cold water that Garak and I are having. Drake listens to Garak with an attitude that I can only interpret as silent pity. The Federation Council liaison looks as uncomfortable as I feel at the prospect of someone as disciplined as Garak succumbing to the siren call of obsession. I know I've heard that call, or at least its tantalizing echoes, myself. I've felt it tugging on my soul like the pitiless attraction of a neutron star. Therefore I tell myself, There but for the grace of God, the Prophets, or blind luck go I.

Whether the Undine still are, as Garak warns, a menace capable of penetrating the spy shops of the most influential empires of two galactic quadrants is almost beside the point. What's important is that the earlier, incontrovertibly tangible Undine War appears to have cost Elim Garak much of his sense of self-possession and competence. There was a time when Garak seemed relatively at ease with himself— at least as at ease as an exile in a hostile foreign land can be. Back aboard DS9, a veneer of equanimity had usually countered his natural baseline state of semi-justifiable paranoia. That veneer had enabled him to endure previous conflicts and move on afterward. His accomplishments rebuilding his homeworld after the Dominion War—which had nearly broken him psychologically after his realization that his assistance to the Federation had cost innumerable Cardassian lives—still stand as a testament to that psychological resiliency.

But Garak strikes me as subtly different *now*. For the first time since the death of Enabran Tain, former leader of the Obsidian Order, Garak has had to come to grips with the very real possibility that somebody else—and an inscrutably alien and hostile somebody else, at that—might be better at cloak-and-dagger operations than even he *is*. It must be intensely humbling for a man like Garak, to say nothing of frustrating. It's almost as though he has allowed his fight-or-flight response to be triggered continuously, heedless of the fact that neither fight nor flight will avail him in any way in the struggle against the Undine. It's a chilling thought.

After I give the waiter my order (some kind of Cardassian fish that I hope I won't regret), an even more chilling thought occurs to me: What if Garak's view of the universe is the only accurate one—the only one that hasn't been distorted beyond all recognition by wishful thinking?

JAKE SISKO, DATA ROD #R-29

Dahar Master Kor Monument, Donatu V

To describe Worf, son of Mogh (commander in Starfleet, retired; Federation diplomat, retired; general in the Klingon Defense Force, presently inactive) as intimidating is to make a gross understatement. Even when he is kneeling respectfully before a gleaming, bat'leth-*wielding statue erected in honor of a fallen comrade-in-arms, Worf seems larger than life, not to mention ageless. Addressing him as anything other than "General" seems out of the question, since neither "Commander" nor "Ambassador" seems quite adequate to entirely encompass this remarkable individual.*

I had always hoped that the passage of time would cause Worf to mellow a bit, but it seems to have had the opposite effect—due largely, I'm sure, to the unique trials he experienced as a consequence of the many incursions and sneak attacks carried out by the Undine during the war years and before. But those traumas, along with the duties incumbent upon the patriarch of a noble Klingon House, appear to have honed Worf's hypervigilance to its keenest possible edge.

Of course, Worf's long transition from warrior-diplomat to family man probably accounts for some of that. Worf first expressed an interest in his current wife, the Lady Grilka of Mekro'vak (a province of the Klingon homeworld Qo'noS), way back in 2373, but she rejected him then for reasons of Klingon politics. The following year saw Worf marry his Starfleet colleague Jadzia Dax, who subsequently died at the hands of Gul Dukat about halfway through the Dominion War. But time and circumstance brought Worf and the Lady Grilka together again in 2385; two years later they were wed and their union produced their first child in 2388. Having so much to protect has no doubt made Worf particularly sensitive to the stealthy threat of Undine infiltration.

Although one might think that longstanding animosities for and conflicts with the Romulan Star Empire (to say nothing of the Dominion) would have inoculated the Klingon Empire against Undine-style treachery long ago, the Klingon people's strong preference for straightforward combat between warriors left them peculiarly vulnerable to infiltration during the Long War. That vulnerability might have left the Empire permanently splintered along the numerous political fault lines that ran through the High Council—but for the willingness of Worf and a relative handful of others to act decisively when it mattered the most.

My challenge today, beneath the gentle yellow glow that Donatu casts across the loose crowd of heroically posed Klingon statues known as the Field of Heroes (and the smattering of other admirers with whom the general and I share the grounds today), is to persuade a man who is modest to a fault—and taciturn even by Klingon standards—to discuss his unique contribution to, and perspective on, the Undine War. When he speaks of those times, I occasionally see something cross Worf's face that I have never seen before—and can only describe as either fear or fear's pale ghost.

Before we begin, I remind myself one last time to avoid asking Worf questions that can be answered with a monosyllable; he is, after all, the exact opposite of Elim Garak in terms of verbosity.

Thank you for agreeing to speak with me today, General.

Not at all. I could do no less for the son of Benjamin Sisko—or for the young journalist who had the courage to seek me out on Qo'noS for an interview without first obtaining official permission to travel to the homeworld.[*]

I'm not sure I still qualify as a "young journalist," General, but thank you anyway. I suppose I'll never live that first interview down. Now that decades have passed since that time, what can you tell me about your experiences during the Undine War years?

---

[*] Federation News Service, 2388.

I am not certain how much I can add to what has already been said about the war against the *qa'meH quv.*[*] By the time the true extent of their infiltration began to come to light,[†] I had little direct involvement with the Empire's response.

But you had encountered the Undine on several occasions during the years leading up to that time.
It was a period of my life I would have preferred to have devoted to matters of home and family, rather than to war.

You're referring to your involvement with the Lady Grilka.
I am. As I said, I had wanted to devote myself to matters of family during those years. So much so that I was willing to resign my commission in Starfleet and return to the diplomatic service in order to be closer to she whom I was determined to make my wife. But whether a warrior has an active commission or not, his time is no longer his own when a new enemy decides to strike. At such times, a warrior's duty is clear.

It occurs to me that my wife, Rena, has often accused me of seeing the craft of writing through a similarly single-minded lens. Fortunately, I have the good

---

[*] The Undine, or literally "replacers-of-honor-with-dishonor."

[†] Circa 2395.

sense not to mention this to General Worf, just as I resist a strong but ill-advised desire to ask him so many other questions. What was it like to find happiness at long last with Grilka and the family they raised together, so many years after his beloved Jadzia's death? Was he torn during those times in the Undine War when tensions escalated between the Federation, where he was raised, and the Klingon Empire, where his new family had taken root? Did he worry about jeopardizing his future with Starfleet in order to defend his new family's home on Qo'noS, which the Undine threatened as gravely as they did Earth? Klingons, I remind myself, tend not to be very big on introspection, and they enjoy talking about their feelings even less, particularly for publication. Discussing their battles is nearly always a far better way to draw them out, and to keep them talking.

The planet Vulcan owes its survival to you, General. If you hadn't persuaded Chancellor Martok to send a fleet to protect Vulcan and help with its evacuation, the attack by the late Romulan miner Nero could have devastated that world and decimated its population.

I learned long ago never to be surprised at such treacherous behavior coming from Romulans.

Of course, Nero's motivations were slightly more complex than simple treachery. He was traumatized by the Hobus supernova that destroyed

Romulus and killed his wife and unborn child. His actions were certainly inexcusable, but he was a man lashing out in pain.

I understand all of that. But his motivations were never relevant to me. He chose to make a craven attempt to commit murder on a planetary scale, and it had to be stopped at all costs. Chancellor Martok and I dealt with it as such.

Saving billions of lives in the process. Not to mention the fact that Nero came very close to killing you when you confronted him aboard his vessel, the *Narada*.

Klingons are . . . difficult to kill. Besides, I was highly motivated not to die. Grilka was carrying our child. I was determined not to make the final journey to *Sto-Vo-Kor* before the birth.[*]

The last time I spoke with you, General, you indicated that your first brush with the Undine occurred while you were recovering from the injuries you received during the fight against Nero.

Yes.

According to the records of that battle, you were stabbed through the midsection from behind by one of Nero's remote-controlled mechanical

---

[*] Worf and Grilka's son, K'Dhan, was born in 2388 (stardate 65548.43), more than six standard months after Nero's 2387 attack on Vulcan.

mining implements. What other details can you recall about the encounter?

Very little that you haven't already mentioned. After Nero's cowardly attack, I was taken to a hospital facility on Vulcan. I regained consciousness within a day, and much of my mobility a day after that.

That's remarkable, considering the extent of your injuries.

Perhaps it is not as remarkable as you think. Klingon physiology incorporates many systemic redundancies. Those redundancies enabled me to resist the Undine agent who subsequently attacked me, just as they enabled me to resist succumbing to the injuries that Nero first inflicted upon me.

Do you think the Undine had planned all along to go after you, specifically? Or was the Undine attack on you just a crime of opportunity because of the happenstance of your being on Vulcan at that particular time?

I still do not know. After the attack, I presumed that the creature targeted me in order to gain a toehold inside both Starfleet and the Klingon Defense Force, since I was known to have attachments to both. I did not understand until later that the creatures had already placed a surprisingly large number of covert operators inside Starfleet.

Maybe the Undine were looking to replace someone who could move back and forth between the

Federation and the Klingon Empire without being scrutinized too carefully.
Perhaps. The *qa'meH quv* had to have known by then that Starfleet Security was watching the Federation and Klingon diplomatic corps with the eyes of Norpin falcons. Since I was a Klingon general at the time rather than an ambassador, I might have been an object of lesser scrutiny.

As I understand it, the Undine infiltrator you encountered came after you right there in the Vulcan hospital where you were recuperating.
Early on the third day, one of the medical assistants informed me that the physician in charge of my case needed to run certain specific tests on me. She escorted me out of my recovery chamber and into a turbolift that took us into one of the hospital's sub-basements.

I hope that the Vulcans are logical enough to make hospital gowns that close up in the back.
They are not. I prefer not to speak about it.

I see . . . well, then marching you off to the basement sounds pretty odd, especially given the condition you were in. And Vulcan medicine is supposed to be the Federation's absolute state of the art. So I wonder what test they needed to conduct that they couldn't have done just as easily in your room, using portable equipment.

I made a similar observation, and I obtained an unsatisfactorily vague answer when I asked about it. But there was as yet no reason to suspect the medic of having any sinister purpose. Despite their outward resemblance to Romulans, such behavior is nearly unheard-of among Vulcans.

Which was obviously what made them such attractive targets for Undine infiltrators.
Precisely. And it wasn't until the medic escorted me into a large chamber that was nearly empty of equipment that I began to realize what was happening. Not only was no recognizable diagnostic equipment visible, but I could see only two devices of any kind: the small, tricorder-sized mechanism that seemed to appear out of thin air in the medic's hand, and a large medical-waste disposal unit that was built into one of the walls. I was already on my guard, if not overtly suspicious, before we entered the basement. But it was only when the medic suddenly pointed her handheld device at me and began to . . . transform before my eyes . . . that I became absolutely certain that something was very wrong.

The Vulcan medic was really an Undine in disguise.
It was the first such impersonation I was to witness during the conflict. And it was the first time I had seen anything of the kind since the Founders of the Dominion had employed similar tactics against both

the Federation and the Klingon Empire more than a decade earlier.

Not many people have witnessed an actual Undine transformation and lived to tell about it. What did the process look like?
I considered it . . . an affront to nature. I still do. And if I believed in any deity, these creatures would be an affront to *that*.

Can you elaborate?
It was simply . . . *wrong*. Joints suddenly bent at unnatural angles. The creature appeared to be in agony as its assumed Vulcan identity melted away in the space of a few seconds, leaving in its place a creature of pure malevolence. A . . . *thing* with the capacity for neither mercy nor sympathy. Its eyes were bottomless pools of loathing, and its pupils looked like targeting crosshairs designed to direct that hatred like a tactical weapon. It is not something you would ever wish to see. It is something even *I* hope never to see again.

The sepulchral quality of Worf's voice sends a chill, like the tiny feet of an Andorian polar millipede, on a slow ascent along the length of my spine. I look up, half expecting some mysterious force to have suddenly extinguished brilliant Donatu. But the local sun continues to shine on the orchard of statues and the other visitors to this place. I begin to wonder if

Worf intends to write a detailed memoir of his own, or maybe take up writing horror novels as a hobby. I decide instead to be thankful not to have him as a literary competitor. Then I realize that something even more fundamental is bothering me.

If you'll allow me to play devil's advocate for a moment, General, what you're saying sounds somewhat . . . xenophobic. I mean no offense, but doesn't that go counter to your Starfleet training?
You would not say that had you seen what the creature did next.

Please go on.
No sooner had the creature's initial transformation settled down than it began to change form a second time. It was the same process as the first, only this time it ran in reverse as the creature once again began to impose a humanoid likeness over its natural appearance.

Only this time it had used *me* as its template.

Which must be why she—or it—led you to a medical-waste disposal unit. The Undine must have planned to use it to disintegrate your body after taking your place.
Yes. I knew I had only seconds left to act before the *qa'meH quv* murdered me and disposed of my remains.

So the Undine waited until after it had taken humanoid form—specifically your form—before it made its move and attacked you? I know that Undine in their natural state are much larger and stronger than most humanoids. Why didn't it try to take you out of the picture when it still had that advantage over you?

Perhaps it could not. It may be that a successful impersonation requires a continuous molecular-level scan of a victim's DNA throughout the transformation process. If that is so, then I would theorize that they cannot risk killing their target until after they've matched their own DNA profiles precisely to those of their victims.

If that's true, then you may have had a critical advantage over your attacker.

Perhaps. However, the injuries I sustained aboard the *Narada* had left me in an extremely depleted condition. The creature may have assumed that I was too weakened to put up an adequate fight. Perhaps it was not far wrong in that assumption.

Worf falls silent and I see a look in his eye and a cast in his jaw I haven't seen before, even in the heat of battle against odds that probably shouldn't have been surmountable. That look prompts my next question—a question that would probably earn me a quick death were I to ask it of any Klingon other than Worf.

Were you . . . afraid?

Worf's eyes narrow perilously and blaze with cold fire before he replies. Though he's always been physically imposing, he seems to have grown both broader and taller in the space of a few heartbeats. As I await his reply, I wonder if I've gotten carried away and pushed him too far.

I have stood toe to toe against some of the strongest, swiftest, and most belligerent warriors from all four quadrants of this galaxy and beyond. My fellow Klingons. Romulans. Jem'Hadar. Nausicaans. Hirogen. Even Kelvans twice my size. I recognized the eager nearness of death during each of those clashes. However, I do not believe I have ever experienced what you humans would call fear.

Until that day on Vulcan.

Was that because the outcome of the fight was more in doubt than in those earlier battles you mentioned?
No. That is not to say that I ever felt any certainty that I would prevail. One never does when going into combat. All a warrior can really do is optimize the odds in his own favor as best he can, and then . . . *fight*. Allow his body and his weapon to become one, and press his every advantage forward. Begin improvising and continue to improvise in one unending, fluid motion, according to

the ebb and flow of combat, until his enemies lie dead at his feet.

So you let your warrior's training take over. Since you're here telling me the tale, you obviously prevailed.
Obviously. However, I have no recollection of the fight itself. I can remember only its aftermath. It was as though I had blacked out during the battle, and recovered consciousness moments after finishing it. I remember the creature completing its transformation into a perfect duplicate of me, right down to my hospital attire and the bandages wrapped around my chest. And I remember the thing lunging toward where I stood, near the middle of the room.

The next thing I recall was standing before the medical-waste disposal unit, my hands locked around the creature's neck—around *my* neck—just as I finished forcing it backward into the open chute, where it lost its grip on the chute's edge and fell into the teeth of the disintegration beams.

You shoved a creature as big as you are into a medical-waste disposal unit? That sounds like one big machine. Why would a Vulcan hospital keep something like that around?
I wondered that myself, until a hospital administrator explained it to me. With few exceptions, what Vulcans choose to entomb after death is largely intangible.

Vulcan's tendency toward a purist Syrrannite way of life has become a lot stronger over the past few decades. Maybe the stress of war has forced them to work harder to maintain their logic.

Perhaps. Regardless, once they have preserved a deceased person's thoughts, their attitude toward the disposal of corpses is almost . . . Klingon.

So after they save the *katra*, they just dump the rest of the body down a disintegration chute?

Or they employ more traditional cremation techniques. Like we Klingons, most Vulcans regard the bodies of their dead as mere empty shells, and they treat them as such. The circumstances forced me to use the hospital's corpse-disposal system as an expedient weapon. My first recollection following my struggle with the *qa'meH quv* was the sight of its body—which appeared identical to *my* body—flash-disintegrating in the crossfire created by the disposal beams. Recalling that sight has always been nearly as disturbing as the memory gap that preceded it.

Isn't it unusual for Klingons to have blackouts like that during combat?

The Vulcan doctors did not believe it to be a cause for concern, especially considering the extent of the injuries from which I was recovering. Besides, such lapses are not entirely unheard-of among uninjured Klingon warriors, though I had never had one before and have not had one since. Like many warriors,

I *have* experienced occasional episodes of what a human might describe as "berserker fury" during the heat of battle.

Regardless of whatever tricks a warrior's mind might play in the midst of a battle, his spirit is never absent from the fight—not even when the combat is particularly strenuous. We merely store our more inopportune emotions—especially the one you humans describe as fear—into small and unobtrusive packages. These we relegate to the farthest corners of our minds in order to keep them out from underfoot.

We do not banish *memory*, however. We Klingons relish honorable victory too much to do that. After all, who would sing of a victory that neither the vanquished nor the victor can remember?

So why do you think you have no recollection of overcoming the Undine who tried to replace you on Vulcan?
I do not know. But it does not matter. It is merely a distraction, one that I let go nearly twenty years ago, just as I have always put aside any other distraction whenever it becomes necessary to do so. Besides, the actions I took immediately after the fight should have laid the entire matter to rest.

What actions were those?
I insisted that the Vulcan medical staff run a thorough analysis of any biological residue my attacker might have left behind inside the disposal unit. And

I asked both the Klingon Defense Force and Starfleet to double-check the Vulcans' initial DNA analysis, just to be on the safe side.

On the safe side of what? Were you afraid . . . were you _concerned_ that the creature you'd pushed into the disposal unit had survived somehow?
Not exactly. It was just that what I _did_ remember of the fight had begun to trouble me.

But you said that all you remember was the sight of the creature tumbling into the waste chute.
And the fact that the honorless _qa'meH quv_ had been trying to duplicate me _exactly_, right down to my injuries and bandages.

But doesn't it stand to reason that the creature would do that? Wouldn't it have roused the suspicions of a highly logical group of Vulcan doctors if they had seen an injured but convalescing General Worf replaced with a General Worf who was suddenly, miraculously unscathed?
I thought that as well, at least at first. But then I began to wonder why the creature had failed to give itself a clear advantage over me in the fight. Why didn't the thing use a weapon?

Maybe he—maybe _it_ had gotten overconfident. Maybe it just assumed that you were still too weak after your ordeal aboard the _Narada_ to pose much of a threat.

But that does not explain why the creature would place itself in exactly the same weakened state as my own. It seemed to me that the *qa'meH quv* had made the odds between us precisely even, which makes no sense. Either of us might have ended up in that waste disposal chute. Add to that the brief gap in memory, which conveniently prevented me from recalling any details from the fight itself . . .

Worf trails off. I think I finally understand where he's going. Despite his denials, he does indeed know fear. In fact, over the last few decades he's become one of its most intimate companions.

You weren't completely sure which one of you actually won the fight. You couldn't be certain that *you* weren't the one who'd been reduced to carbon ash in the chute.

No. I was Worf, son of Mogh, just as I had always been. Just as I still am *now*.

But there was obviously some doubt in your mind. I mean, if the process that the Undine used to change themselves into humanoid doppelgängers was so perfect as to enable them to escape detection most of the time, then it had to be possible for it to work *too* well from time to time.

I know of a number of . . . incidents that tend to support that notion. But I will not speak of them here for security reasons.

All right. Putting the notion of "unconscious Undine sleeper agents" aside for the moment, can you tell me if either the Federation or the Klingons learned anything critical about the Undine from your encounter?

The KDF* engineers took possession of the scanning device the creature had discarded during the fight, and subjected it to a thorough analysis, as Starfleet did a short time later. The data kept the analysts busy for years. Both the Federation and the Empire learned a great deal about the mechanics of the creatures' transformation process. That proved invaluable throughout the war in developing new methods of uncovering *qa'meH quv* infiltrators.

Including Undine infiltrators whose disguises are so perfect that they don't know that they're Undine infiltrators?

I continue to consult with engineers from both the Federation and the Empire on such matters even now.

A brief but unmistakable frisson of doubt clouds Worf's gaze, but he covers it swiftly with a heavy spackling of Klingon stoicism. As the interview ends and I return to my lodgings to make my preparations for departure from Donatu V, I wonder how many unsuccessful scans for Undine DNA Worf will force

---

* The Klingon Defense Force.

himself to endure until he's finally able to convince himself that the right person won the fight that fateful day on Vulcan.

Only then does the nature of the sacrifice that the Undine forced upon Worf come sharply into focus for me. And that cost seems inestimable, particularly when reckoned in the only currency that has any real, enduring value to a Klingon. After all, the one thing that any Klingon warrior prizes more highly than anything else is the exultation that can only come from a victory in battle, honorably won.

Now, thanks to the Undine, Worf can never again trust such a victory, or risk taking it at face value.

EXCERPTED FROM AN OFFICIAL FEDERATION
COMMUNIQUÉ, TRANSMITTED
STARDATE 76422.5[*]

To: J'mpok, son of Q'thoq, Chancellor of the
Klingon Empire and leader of the High Council
FROM: Grebav of Tellar, Secretary General of the
Federation Security Council

. . . The Council protests, in the strongest possible
terms, yesterday's incursion by the Klingon Defense Force into the sovereign space of the Gorn
Hegemony. The Federation has worked in good
faith for many years to forge a workable peace
between the governments of the Klingon Empire
and the Gorn Hegemony, and can only regard the
Empire's present action as both ill-considered
and counterproductive. The Council appeals to
Chancellor J'mpok and the Klingon High Council
to reverse this rash action before forces become
fully engaged on both sides of the conflict. The
Council further recommends a cease-fire, con-
current with an immediate return to the nego-
tiation tables at Khitomer for high-level talks between Chancellor J'mpok of the Klingon Empire
and King Slathis of the Gorn Hegemony. . . .

---

[*] June 4, 2399.

JAKE SISKO, DATA ROD #Y-11

Press Room, Nanietta Bacco Stadium,[*] Pike City, Cestus III

Captain Kasidy Danielle Yates[†] walks to the wide window that overlooks the playing field, which the groundskeepers are grooming this afternoon in preparation for an evening game between the Pike City Pioneers and the Prairieview Greensox. One of the ballpark workmen is hoisting a banner up the flagpole just behind the center-field fence. The breeze spreads the canvas out, proudly displaying the stylized covered-wagon-and-baseball logo of the Pike City Pioneers.

Judging from Kasidy's easy smile and ubiquitous laughter, motherhood and grandmotherhood have

---

[*] Also known as Bacco Field (originally Ruth Field), Bacco Stadium was named after Nanietta Bacco, over her own strenuous objections. Bacco served as president of the United Federation of Planets from 2379 until 2389, after serving eleven years as governor of the Federation colony world Cestus III, where she had previously served as representative for Pike City's Fifth District.

[†] Full disclosure: Captain Yates is my stepmother, the second woman (after Jennifer Felecia Sisko, my late mother) to exchange vows with my father, Benjamin Lafayette Sisko. (J.S.)

agreed with her at least as much as her decades-long career as a freighter captain ever did. And despite everything she's been through—the disappearance of her husband (my father, Benjamin Sisko) into the Bajoran wormhole following the allied invasion of Cardassia; the perpetual uncertainty of trying to raise a family in the long shadow of uncertainties cast by Bajor's enigmatic Prophets; and the nerve-wracking Undine War years—she looks much as she did when she lived with my dad aboard Deep Space 9. Here, at historic Bacco Field, the cradle of a special kind of human renaissance, where bleachers ring the manicured expanse of aquamarine native grass beneath a vault of cerulean blue, it is easy to understand the reason for Kasidy's agelessness.

The ancient pastime of baseball, it seems, has a way of keeping a person young.

I suppose you can guess why I wanted to speak to you here as opposed to anywhere else.
Ruth Field. There's certainly a lot of history here.

It's Bacco Stadium now, Kasidy. Try and keep up.
Jake, I'll start calling this place Bacco Stadium after President Bacco finally stops grousing about the name change, and not before.

Fair enough.
Well, Jake, whatever you call this place, you obviously chose it because the home-team dugout here was the

closest I ever came to actually having anything to do with the Undine War.

I thought that coming back here might jog your memories about the Big Game a little bit.
I take it you're referring to the game you wrote about in your *Collected Stories.* "The Gorns of Summer," I think you called it.

"The Gorns of Summer" was only a piece of fiction, Kas. I based it on the Big Game of 'Eighty-Nine, but only very loosely. What you and Uncle Kornelius[*] actually did that day, on the other hand—well, that was something very real and valuable. If not for the two of you, the Federation would have lost out on a major diplomatic opportunity. If that had happened, who knows how the war might have turned out.
Nobody can say. Which is why I've tried not to get into the habit of bragging about it.

All modesty aside, Kas, that game really ought to earn both you and Kornelius Yates a solid place in history. At least if there's any justice.
A place in history. Ouch. I don't think I'm quite ready to go into a glass display case just yet, Jake. Isn't it

---

[*] Kornelius "Junior" Yates is one of the most celebrated baseball players in the history of the Cestus Baseball League, which he helped to establish in 2371. Although Yates was widely considered to be past his prime by 2380, he played shortstop for the Pike City Pioneers for another decade before becoming the team's manager.

enough that my brother's baseball jersey is up on a wall at the Pioneer Pub?

Nope. Because they also serve who never swing a bat or shag a fly ball.
All right. I'll talk to you. Just remember one thing, Jake: there's no "I" in team. Whatever the Pioneers accomplished that day was a group effort.

Hey, I know the game as well as you do, Kas. I'm a Sisko. Let's start at the beginning. Where did the idea for playing such an unorthodox game come from?
It was definitely a Kornelius idea. My brother missed his calling—he should have been a diplomat. Hell, after helping put the league[*] together and then *running* the Pioneers for as long as he did—not to mention playing alongside them all those years—he had all the right qualifications to serve as a Federation special envoy.

Anyway, the Klingon Empire and the Gorn Hegemony were at each other's throats in those days. The situation hadn't grown into a full-blown war yet, but out here this close to the core of Gorn territory[†] we could see the writing on the wall pretty clearly.

As I recall, Ambassador Worf managed to convince

---

[*] The Cestus Baseball League of Cestus III was the first professional baseball association to form in Federation history.

[†] Located deep in Beta Quadrant space, Cestus III has been an object of contention between the Federation and the Gorn Hegemony on several occasions over the past two centuries.

Chancellor Martok to agree to let the Federation mediate the Empire's dispute with the Gorn.

That's right. But the Gorn weren't such an easy sell. After all, Martok considered Worf a member of his family.

While the Gorn didn't even belong to the same phylum.

Let's just say that young King Slathis wasn't the cuddliest adversary Worf had ever encountered—even for a reptiloid. "The Lizard King" had ascended to the throne less than three years earlier, after old King Xrathis died of old age. Slathis was aggressive and ambitious, and he wasn't old enough to have any clear firsthand recollection of the blood his people had spilled in prior battles, even as recently as the time of the Dominion War. Worst of all, he seemed to feel he had something to prove. Daddy issues, maybe.

Anyway, he was perfectly happy to get sideways with the Klingons at every opportunity. And to spark a quadrant-spanning Klingon-Gorn war that the Federation would have had to get into up to its neck because of our Khitomer Accords commitments. And this was all going on at the same time that Starfleet was encountering its first real trouble with the Undine.

So Worf had convinced Martok to allow the Federation to mediate a truce with the Gorn. But the new Gorn leader didn't see Worf as an honest broker because of his relationship to the House of Martok.

Exactly, which was why King Slathis wouldn't agree to any Federation mediation conducted by Worf. In fact, the only Klingon diplomat who ever seemed to get any traction with King Slathis was Ambassador B'vat, who offered his services as mediator between Martok and Slathis.

But B'vat didn't represent the Federation, or any other third party. How could the Gorn have thought of him as an unbiased negotiator? After all, B'vat was a loyal Klingon.

I think that's still open to debate, Mister Historian. Of course, a lot depends on one's definition of "loyalty." Sure, B'vat was loyal to the Klingon warrior ethic, at least as he defined it, which was pretty much in old-school terms—he thought that the Klingon Empire should try a lot harder to live up to its imperial reputation by doing a lot more conquering and a lot less negotiating. In B'vat's mind, only a perpetual state of war could keep the Klingon Empire sharp. He was a hard-line Duras supporter back during the Klingon Civil War of 'sixty-eight, though he also somehow managed to worm his way into Chancellor Gowron's good graces once he realized he'd been backing the wrong side.

That's an impressive accomplishment. Most Klingon chancellors don't get to that office by being overly forgiving. Or trusting.

B'vat was a rare bird. Very charismatic, as Klingons

go, and that enabled him to find a way to convince Gowron of his loyalty. B'vat was a born salesman. He could have sold a Risan *horga'hn* to a Vorta. But he was also a very sneaky sonofabitch. I remember overhearing Worf describe him as having the heart of a Romulan and the soul of a Ferengi. And Martok once said the man was "slick as *targ*-snot."

Yet after replacing Gowron as chancellor, Martok never saw fit to do anything to break up B'vat's growing power and influence on the Klingon High Council.

Even though the Klingon Empire was on the winning side of the Dominion War, the Empire was pretty badly beat up after the invasion of Cardassia. Martok had to get busy with the job of rebuilding, and that meant walking a fine line between honoring Klingon tradition and doing a few things differently going forward. And there might have been an element of "keep your friends close and your enemies closer" going on there as well. So Martok still had some poisonous snakes living in his garden when the troubles between the Klingons and the Gorn began.

From what little I know about the Gorn, I find it hard to believe that either charisma or salesmanship could have convinced King Slathis that B'vat would be an honest broker for peace.

You're right. Because the idea of a mediated peace wasn't what B'vat actually wanted to sell. And it wasn't what Slathis wanted to buy, either. Slathis *wanted* a war between the Gorn Hegemony and the Klingon Empire. And because B'vat had an old-school take on Klingon foreign relations, that was exactly what *he* wanted as well.

So there you were, visiting your brother, Kornelius on Cestus III on the eve of what looked to be a very nasty Gorn-Klingon conflict—a war within a war, really, because the Federation was already quietly locking horns with the Undine all across Federation space and beyond. And the two of you suddenly decide to propose that the Gorn and the Klingons resolve their dispute with . . . a baseball game? Seriously?

Well, when you put it that way it sounds kind of crazy, doesn't it? But the truth is, it didn't look like we had anything to lose by running strange ideas up the flagpole. Cestus III would have to face the prospect of mass evacuation once the Gorn and the Klingons officially went to war.

And then Worf—*Ambassador* Worf, I mean—came to town.

What was Worf doing on Cestus III?

Cestus III wasn't just a backwater Federation planet in those days, or a prime strategic target for both the Gorn and the Klingons. And it wasn't just home to my brother and his family, or one of the hubs of my freight business. It had also become a diplomatic way station. So when Worf passed through the Pike City spaceport on his way to an emergency session of the High Council, he had some layover time that took him to the Pioneer Pub. Kornelius and I had a few drinks with him and pumped him for information from the Gorn diplomatic front.

You "pumped" *Worf* for information about his job? And he talked? You must be talking about some other Worf.
No. Ambassador Worf Rozhenko.

What did you use on him, Romulan mind probes? Worf has got to be the least talkative person ever to have accepted a diplomatic post.
He might not be very talkative, but he's absolutely *terrible* at telling convincing lies of the "don't worry, everything's going to be all right" variety. Worf was evidently on his way back from a meeting with King Slathis and his new ad hoc "mediator," B'vat. From what I was able to gather, Slathis had not only refused Ambassador Jean-Luc Picard's offer to mediate, but he had also just shot down what amounted to Martok's final truce offer. So except for a bit of official paperwork, the war was already just about a done deal. That was when Kornelius floated the idea of resolving the conflict via a single game of baseball—a contest between King Slathis's own handpicked team of Gorn players and Kornelius's Pike City Pioneers.

Your idea sounded crazy when I summarized it a minute ago. And it still sounds insane when you talk about it now, even after all these years.

Crazy ideas were all we had left, Jake. Cestus III was about to be caught in the Klingon-Gorn crossfire. Kornelius wasn't about to just sit back and let that happen, and neither was I. Part of being a pioneer, I suppose, is standing your ground and fighting to protect your homestead when you have to, using whatever weapons are available—even when your only weapon is a baseball bat. I guess that's also part of being associated with the Pike City Pioneers. Like I said, we didn't appear to have anything to lose, so there was no reason not to swing for the fences, so to speak.

You and Kornelius must have had a lot of confidence in the Pike City Pioneers.

Sure. And why not? They were the cream of professional baseball on Cestus III. They'd taken the Cestus Series in 'eighty-two, 'eighty-six, and 'eighty-eight, and had just pulled out in front of the Northern Division in the 'eighty-nine season, which was already well under way. Besides, what could a bunch of awkward, shambling lizard-men know about fielding, hitting, pitching, or baserunning? Baseball is a game of finesse. And judging from the holoimages we'd seen—you know, the stuff that came from the transmissions the Metrons transmitted to James T. Kirk's *Enterprise* over a century earlier—the Gorn moved like they were under water.

So you ran your idea past Worf. He must have liked it. After all, he knew the game; he played with us against Captain Solok's Vulcan team in one of Quark's holosuites back in 'seventy-five.

You know Worf. It's hard to tell right away whether he likes an idea or not. All I know is that he presented our challenge to the Council, in person, while Kornelius and I made the exact same sales pitch to King Slathis, using Ambassador B'vat's new diplomatic aide, Ja'rod, who would later end up in the KDF serving aboard the *I.K.S. Kang,* as a go-between.

Ja'rod. Wasn't that the name of the man who helped the Romulans launch their sneak attack on Khitomer when Worf was a boy?

It was, though I didn't know that at the time. The Ja'rod *I'm* talking about was the grandson of the man who sold out his people at Khitomer. He was really just a kid—but a kid with ambitions as big as his forehead, and an ego to match. Honorable, in an old-school Klingon way, but also a real schemer, as we'd discover later on.

That's not surprising, considering Ja'rod's pedigree. His uncle, Duras, was the assassin who poisoned Chancellor K'mpec in 'sixty-seven and tried to take his place as leader of the Klingon High Council. Ja'rod's mother was a woman named Lursa, who fought on the wrong side of the Klingon Civil War in 'sixty-eight. A year or two later, Lursa and her sister,

B'Etor, started selling weapons to Bajoran terror- ists. And not long after Ja'rod was born, both sisters were killed after they'd sabotaged the *Enterprise.*

That family history is probably why Ja'rod's life was what Kornelius described as "snakebit." Ja'rod was working as a junior diplomat under B'vat—a job that must have looked like a good path toward redeeming some portion of his family's badly blemished honor, or at least toward jump-starting an otherwise stalled career—while we were working out what the press eventually dubbed the Cestus Accords.

The Cestus Accords. Peace through baseball. The trusty ash wood bat as an instrument of diplomacy.
Baseball *does* have a way of inspiring cooperation, Jake. Our proposal to settle the conflict with a ball game somehow managed to get Martok, B'vat, and Ja'rod all on the same page, after all.

How did that come about?
Worf convinced the Klingon High Council to delay its planned invasion of Gorn space until after our chal- lenge was either officially rejected or accepted by both sides, and—if accepted—played out to its conclusion. I heard that Martok initially pooh-poohed the whole idea, but decided to take advantage of it as a chance to gain extra time to get his forces deployed properly for the coming Gorn War. He sold the "baseball truce" to a majority of the High Council on that basis. Of course, Martok had seen the same images of that slow,

clumsy Gorn captain that we had. So he expected an easy victory for the Pioneers, just as we did.

And what exactly were the stakes that both sides agreed to?
First, Slathis agreed to send a team of Gorn to play one game against the Pike City Pioneers. The winner was to gain a few specifically defined concessions from the loser, just as though he was signing the surrender documents that the loser always ends up having to ink after the end of a long, bloody war. The game just let both sides leapfrog over the really messy parts of the war.

That sounds extremely civilized. But not very Klingon.
Only because the Klingons didn't think that the Gorn had any real chance of beating the Pioneers—and because a Pioneers victory would force the Gorn to accept a very Klingon-friendly border-revision treaty drawn up by Ambassador Jean-Luc Picard himself. On the other hand, a Gorn victory would have cost the Klingon Empire a half dozen border worlds that the Gorn Hegemony had been itching to annex for decades, and Slathis wouldn't have to fire a shot to get them—assuming his team won, that is.

If King Slathis never had any real intention of making peace with the Klingons, then why did he agree to this charade?

Taking up our challenge was a public relations coup for Slathis. It made him look a lot more fair-minded than he really was. It helped him bolster the lie that he'd been negotiating in good faith all along, even though he was really just using the additional time the agreement had generated in exactly the same way that Martok was—that is, Slathis was preparing for a war that both leaders now saw as inevitable. And B'vat was happy to help the Gorn prepare their team—very quietly and discreetly, of course.

I know that B'vat never had any love for Chancellor Martok. But why would he actively work to undermine an outcome that would have benefited the Klingon Empire?
Because B'vat saw the game as an opportunity to deal Chancellor Martok a humiliating political defeat, without actually having to get his own hands dirty bringing it about.

Did B'vat really think that a bunch of awkward reptilian bipeds who'd never played baseball before had a serious chance against a professional franchise like the Pioneers?
Let's just say that B'vat had discovered a few things about the Gorn that *we* hadn't yet. Even though the Federation had had a few encounters with the Gorn over the years—I remember reading about the *Enterprise* dealing with an uprising on the Gorn homeworld during the Dominion War—we still didn't

know much more about them then than we did when Captain Kirk had to use improvised field artillery to survive his own Gorn first contact back in the twenty-third century, after the lizards had wiped out the original Cestus III outpost.

It can take years to get good at playing baseball—and I'm talking about humanoids who _don't_ move like they're under water. How much pregame training time did the Gorn team ask for?
They only spent a few weeks preparing once we'd struck the agreement-in-principle. I had to scramble to delegate some of my upcoming freight runs so I could clear my schedule for Game Day and the few days leading up to it.

The Gorns' willingness to play sooner rather than later probably should have been our first clue that something wasn't right.

Do you think the Pioneers let themselves get complacent?
That's what Kornelius said afterward, even though he and I both knew how hard the team had worked over the years to stay at the top of the league standings—and how hard they _kept_ working during the weeks leading up to Game Day. On the other hand, I can also remember Hughes Baptiste[*] telling the

---

[*] Hughes Baptiste's broken bat, splintered when he hit the home run that clinched the Pioneers' victory in the series against the Port Shangri-La Seagulls, is on display in Pike City's Pioneer Pub.

press that the Gorn couldn't possibly touch us in "the Cross-Phylum Challenge," and calling baseball "a mammal's game." And then there was Nancy Addison,[*] drinking gallons of that nasty-sweet blue drink that they brew on the Gorn homeworld. We got a case of it, thanks to a convenient "logistics error" committed by Ja'rod, who evidently *wanted* the team to be complacent, not to mention hungover. What was that horrible, syrupy stuff called?[†] Anyway, word had gotten around that the Gorn found it intoxicating, but Nancy discovered that it acted on humans like a stimulant. Maybe she and a few of the other players did get complacent after that, at least a little.

But that changed pretty damned fast once Game Day finally arrived.

When did you and Uncle Kornelius first realize that a victory over the Gorn team might not be quite the cakewalk that the Pioneers had imagined?
Well, I can't speak for Korny, but I knew the Pioneers were in for real trouble the second I caught my first real glimpse of the Gorn team from my seat in the Pioneers' dugout. The Gorn had just arrived on

---

[*] Nancy Addison was one of the Pike City Pioneers' greatest power hitters during the 2370s and 2380s, despite her diminutive size.

[†] Meridor is a fermented beverage, usually a deep blue in color, that is brewed on several Beta Quadrant worlds, including the Gorn homeworld. Although the Gorn recipe is a closely guarded secret, Starfleet chemists have theorized that the active ingredient is a digestive enzyme that originates in the lower intestinal tracts of laborer-caste Gorn.

Cestus on Game Day itself, after doing all their training off-world. Their Gorn team was quite a sight.

The S'Yahazah City Talons.[*]
Great name. It made them sound as though they meant business, which they obviously did. And the black-and-red uniforms were a nice touch, too, even if they weren't uniforms in the traditional sense. More like big belts and sashes. Very impressive, even compared with the Pioneers when they were fully decked out in their green-and-orange home colors.

I've seen holos of the game. The Gorn players were dressed like the native Britons who fought the occupying Roman Legions over two thousand years ago.
The Talons uniforms, sparse as they were, had to have been designed for psychological impact as well as for the players' freedom of movement. The Gorn managed to look "uniform" without covering up too much of their skin—those iridescent green scales of natural body armor that must have intimidated as much as they protected. Even their caps were cut away until they were just bills attached to extended straps pulled tightly around their huge, leathery

---

[*] S'Yahazah is the name of the Great Egg Bringer from Gorn mythology, roughly analogous to the Eve or Earth Goddess figure from many human myths. S'Yahazah's name has become attached to one of the largest cities on Tau Lacertae IX, the Gorn homeworld.

heads. I suppose they did that so as not to cover up those scaly red crests that ran along both sides and down the middle of their skulls.

Other than the head crests, what specifically was it about these Gorn that had you so worried?

What *wasn't* there to worry about with these guys? First of all, they didn't bear much resemblance to the big, clumsy Gorn that Captain Kirk had tangled with. They didn't move much like the Gorn we've all seen in the holos. Hell, with their bony, blood-colored head crests, they didn't even *look* like any Gorn anybody in the Federation had ever seen. Sure, they had the big crocodile jaws full of razor-sharp teeth, just as you'd expect, but that was pretty much where the resemblance ended. And they didn't have the silver compound eyes that had made Kirk's Gorn such a weird, alien sight. Instead, their eyes were almost golden, and they had single pupils, arranged vertically, like a cat's eye. They had only three fingers on each of their hands and feet, none of which were stuffed into baseball cleats, by the way. Those three fingers were a lot longer and more dexterous than the five we'd all seen in the old first-contact holos. With hands like that, gloves were redundant, not to mention impractical for players equipped with claws as sharp as old-time surgical scalpels.

I suppose the Talons didn't bother with batting helmets, either.

They didn't see the point. If you hit any of them with a pitch, they probably wouldn't even have noticed.

So it wasn't until Game Day itself that you had your first serious exposure to the Gorn caste system.

We learned a lot about that the hard way. But don't get the wrong idea, Jake. We weren't *complete* idiots. We already knew that *some* sort of caste system was operating in the Gorn Hegemony, since we were already better acquainted with the warrior caste than we'd ever wanted to be. And thanks to the reports we'd read about political upheavals on the Gorn homeworld during the Dominion War, we also knew about the political caste that ran the Gorn government. Most of us assumed that Gorn castes were just a way to deny special privileges to a majority so that a lucky few could enjoy them—you know, the way things were done in a lot of Earth's ancient societies, only with lizard lords and lizard serfs.

But the truth turned out to be a lot more complicated than that, didn't it? More like, say, the system of *D'jarra* castes that was in use on Bajor before the Cardassian Occupation.

Even Bajor's *D'jarra*s don't really do justice to the Gorn caste system, even though both have very complex hierarchies based on profession—which adds up to lots and lots of highly specialized castes. And I think everyone imagined that however unequal the power relationships might have been between the castes, the highborn and the lowborn had to be identical apart from their status. I mean, whatever limits Bajor's *D'jarra* system might have set on an individual's social mobility, those things didn't extend to the genes.

Not so with the Gorn.
No. We didn't realize that some of the Gorn castes—or maybe *all* of the Gorn castes—had specialized physical characteristics. At least not before Game Day.

I learned later that the Talons had all been drawn from the Gorn technological caste. But at the time, we had expected the opposing team to consist of a bunch of dangerous but sluggish and relatively slow-witted lizard-men.

A team of snapping turtles was something the Pioneers could have handled. Instead, they found themselves going toe to toe against a squad of very clever, very sharp-clawed . . . velociraptors.

How much of the game itself do you remember?
Every damned pitch, Jake. I have a photographic memory for baseball, especially for the really *important* games. Maybe that's one of the qualities of mine that drew your father and I together. Just don't ask me to try to pronounce the names of any

of the Gorn players. That's a good way to give yourself laryngitis.

Will you give us some game highlights?
Well, the Pioneers recovered their composure pretty quickly after they'd all taken their first good, long look at the Talons. The Pioneers were professionals, after all. They represented the best the Cestus Baseball League had to offer, which at the time was the same as saying the best that *baseball* had to offer. And everybody on Cestus knew there were holocams present that would transmit this game all across the Alpha and Beta Quadrants.

So the Pioneers and the nineteen thousand or so spectators who'd come to Ruth Field that day—it was still Ruth Field back then, Jake, so don't correct me—doffed their caps for the singing of the UFP national anthem, which was performed that day by a Sinnravian *drad* musician named J'Nat Cton. Even the Talons seemed to be trying to be good guests, putting their claws over their chests, if only for the benefit of the ranks of cameras that were trained on them. Besides, it was a beautiful, cloudless day. Perfect for baseball, despite the weird, surreal circumstances.

Since they were the home team, the Pioneers took the field at the top of the first inning. Blaithin Lipinski was on the mound. She'd been pitching for a lot of years by then, but her arm was strong and she could still throw nearly fast enough to beat an impulse engine at full throttle. She'd built up a hell of a reputation by then, with a career total of five perfect games[*] under her belt.

I wonder if she thought she might be about to pitch perfect game number six.

I'm sure that thought crossed her mind—especially after she threw three innings' worth of pitches without letting any of the Talons reach a base. But the Gorn batters weren't failing to connect completely. They were hitting more than their fair share of foul balls. And every one of those turned yet another bat into a shower of hickorash[†] slivers. Halfway through the game the officials had to call a time-out to replicate more bats.

Anyway, it became obvious to everyone right away that even the smallest player on the Talons' roster could hit a hell of a lot harder than the strongest Pioneer could. They just hadn't managed to hit the ball in the right direction—yet. Of course, that left

---

[*] This is a remarkable achievement for a single player, considering that from 1880 until the cessation of Major League play on Earth in 2042, only twenty-seven perfect games (defined as nine-inning or longer victories during which no opposing players managed to get on base) were pitched.

[†] Hickorash (*Caryafraxinus cestana*) is a species of fast-growing hybrid tree, developed specifically to prosper in the mineralogically unique soils of Cestus III. Developed from hardy strains of ash and hickory, it is famous for yielding exceptionally strong wooden baseball bats. The abundance of hickorash on Cestus III probably played a key role in the emergence of that world as the cradle of the modern baseball renaissance.

everybody wondering just how much speed the Gorn baserunners would be able to get out of those scaly, velociraptor legs and the shoeless, clawed feet that were attached to them.

Didn't you get to see how fast they could move when they took the field?
Not during the early part of their game, and that was probably deliberate on their part, to keep everybody wondering about the extent of their capabilities. They did all their prep and training on a Federation-inaccessible Gorn planet, probably for the very same reason. So the Gorn players always took their time walking out onto the field. They literally *strolled* to their field positions, even though their minimalist uniforms showed off reptilian muscles that looked like duritanium springs coiled up tight just beneath their scaly hides.

They were obviously holding back. Of course, we might have seen the Talons in real field action sooner if their pitcher had let any of the Pioneers actually *hit* anything during those first three innings. All we knew for sure by then was that their pitcher had the accuracy of a MACO sharpshooter, and had speed to match.

But they didn't leave us wondering what they could do for long. When they went to bat at the top of the fourth, we got our first real sense of how much damage technology-caste Gorns could really do. I hoped at the time that that first Gorn home run would turn out to be just a lucky fluke, but somehow I could already tell that I was indulging in pure wishful thinking. Maybe the Gorn had only been toying with us at the start of the game, testing us even though that cost them five base hits and two batted-in runs. Or maybe Lipinski was already starting to get tired up on the mound. Whatever the reason, that first solid Gorn hit put the Pioneers squarely on notice—along with several of the spectators in the right-field bleachers, who nearly got mowed down by that first ballistic home run. Fortunately, the only injury was to another Gorn bat, which was just about vaporized in the hitter's claws—along with Blaithin Lipinski's prospect of earning her sixth perfect game that day.

According to the holobroadcasts of this game, and even some of the more speculative holoprograms it has inspired over the years, that Gorn home run marks the moment when all hell began to break loose for the Pike City Pioneers.

That's not far from the truth. The Talons immediately went into overdrive. Either they'd decided to quit toying with us at last, or their game had finally begun to click. Either way, they started scoring one railgun-fast hit after another. Nearly all of their swings were not only connecting, they were staying well out of foul territory. A few hits went on long, high arcs that were easy pickings for the Pioneers' fielding staff. But most of them were legitimate doubles and triples, in-the-park home runs, or out-of-the-ballpark, damned-near-escape-velocity homers.

Of course, the Talons didn't chalk up so many triples and in-the-park homers because their baserunners couldn't get around the diamond quickly.

You should forget all about the slowpoke warrior-caste Gorn. The Talons' baserunners made Talarian whippets look like paraplegic voles. These guys were *fast.* By the time the Pioneers got another turn at the plate, the Gorn had evened the score, passed the home team, and left 'em six runs behind. And that was only the beginning of the Pioneers' humiliations, even after Kornelius rotated Lipinski off the mound and replaced her with Hank Gordimer, the relief pitcher.

And the Pioneers' secret weapon, as it turned out.

Let's not get ahead of ourselves, Jake. Anyway, by the seventh-inning stretch, the score stood at seventeen to four, in the Talons' favor. And the Gorn were poised to go right on widening their lead once they picked up their bats again for the eighth inning. Even though Gordimer, with his at least theoretically fresh arm, was on the mound, the Talons' hitting had swept over the Pioneers like a force of nature. No organic creature, let alone a reptilian one, had any right to have such lightning-quick reflexes, or such perfect hand-eye . . . er, *claw*-eye coordination.

A lot of games would have been effectively finished long before this point. The trailing team would have been just too demoralized to do anything but go through the motions—until a last death-blow pitch finally put them out of their misery.

That's not the Pioneers. Too much of the blood of Cestus III's original settlers flows through their veins.

As bad as the game was going for them, the Pioneers did manage to score two more runs during the middle third of the game—right in the midst of receiving what Pioneers third baseman Yusef Farouk used to call a "clobberation" from the Gorn batting rotation. Was the Talons' pitching starting to get soft?

That's the likeliest scenario, given what happened in the bottom of the eighth. I suppose that's why this particular game has become such a popular jumping-off point for holoprogrammers over the years. What would have happened if the game had been played right through to the end? If the circumstances had worked out just a little differently, would the Pioneers have found a way to exploit the weakness on the mound that Kornelius told me he'd seen as early as inning five? Would the Pioneers have somehow got their second wind and evened up the score? Would they have pulled ahead of the Talons after that surprise eighth-inning meltdown? Like your father always said, you can never overestimate the role of contingency in the outcome of a baseball game.

Let's talk about that "meltdown on the mound" the Talons suffered during inning eight. How much of it were you able to see?

At least as much as anybody who was there and paying close attention to the field, instead of slipping out early to try to beat the hovercar traffic, or running to the concession stands for one last beer. As a matter of fact, what happened on the mound at the bottom of the eighth made me wonder if *I'd* had one too many. At least at first.

Can you describe what you saw?

It was the creepiest thing I'd seen since the Dominion's Founders were at our throats. The Talons' pitcher started to look unsteady, weaving on his big, clawed feet. Then his uniform and his skin began to ripple, as though I was watching him through the haze that rises off spaceport tarmacs during the hottest weeks of Cestus III's northern summer.

But it wasn't the air that was distorting my vision. The Gorn pitcher's body was . . . *changing*, right before my eyes. His head lengthened and his limbs were extending, as though his entire body had just transformed into so much taffy, and an invisible giant had started pulling on it from both ends. He even sprouted a third leg while I was watching. He seemed to be in agony.

He must have been undergoing the process called "reversion." The Gorn had just learned the hard way

that they had an Undine infiltrator in their midst. And it was quite a diplomatic embarrassment for the Gorn, believe me. That little revelation happened right before the watchful eyes of two entire quadrants.

Most of the holos taken after that point in the game don't shed much light on what happened immediately after the S'Yahazah City Talons' pitcher reverted to his natural form. I know that Cestus III's Starfleet garrison and the planet's civil defense authorities dispatched first responders to help with the spectator evacuation, and with the effort to keep the creature contained inside the stadium.
You can still see the scorch marks from the disruptors the Talons used to bring the creature down, way out there on the left-field fence.

So the Gorn didn't wait for Starfleet or the local fire department to handle the problem.
Well, a lot of us thought the way the Gorn handled it was better than possibly giving an Undine agent an opportunity to rampage across Pike City, where the thing might have assumed a new *human* identity. Or it might have tried to sneak off the planet disguised as a member of the Klingon diplomatic team. Looking back, I think that would have served Ja'rod right. Or Ambassador B'vat, depending on the creature's preference.

The Cestus Baseball League officials initially handed the game to the Pike City Pioneers, since the Talons had disqualified themselves.

They had deviated from the approved team roster they'd laid out in the pregame agreement, which specified that the Talons were to play with an all-Gorn squad. And even if they hadn't, the genetic treatments that the Undine pitcher had to undergo in order to pass as a Gorn were the functional equivalent of a violation of the long-standing rule against performance-enhancing drugs.

That official ruling never seemed very sporting to me. I mean, the Gorn didn't violate the roster rule *intentionally*. They were deceived by an Undine infiltrator, just like what happened to so many others throughout the Long War.

That's true. But sneaking disruptor weapons into Ruth Field was no innocent mistake on the Gorns' part. That offense alone would have got the Talons booted from the park, and the Pioneers would have been handed a default victory that way.

But none of that mattered to the Gorn. All King Slathis cared about was that the Talons were ahead when the game ended, through no fault of his team. He was treating the game's outcome as the Gorn victory regardless of the officials, and wanted the victor's due per the formal diplomatic agreement governing the game. He threatened to declare all-out war against the Klingon Empire if Chancellor Martok refused to cede all the disputed border worlds to the Gorn Hegemony immediately. If some of the Gorn Hegemony's most powerful allies and trading partners—the Romulans, the Tholians, the Breen, the Tzenkethi, and the Kinshaya—hadn't pressured Slathis to calm down and accept Federation mediation of his Klingon disputes, Cestus III would have become ground zero in the biggest Gorn-Klingon conflict anybody had ever seen up to that point. And it all would have hit the fan immediately after the Big Game.

And it all would have been _because_ of the Big Game, at least arguably.
If that had happened, it would have been a hell of a blotch on the sport's reputation. Worse than any betting scandal, or the nanotech doping incident of 2035.

Why were the Romulans, the Breen, and the Gorn Hegemony's other allies suddenly so averse to a Gorn-Klingon war?
I'm no expert, but I imagine it has to do with one of our diplomats—I think it might have been Jean-Luc Picard—pointing out to them that they all had mutual defense pacts with the Gorn Hegemony. And that that would have made King Slathis's costly vanity war _their_ costly vanity war.

Having the Gorn crowing that they'd won couldn't have pleased Martok very much. The entire episode

must have been something of an embarrassment to him.

Well, I don't have any inside knowledge about that, but you're probably right. But at least Martok could take his frustrations out on Ambassador B'vat, the man he'd assigned to oversee the whole affair.

Let's put galactic politics and diplomacy aside for a moment. The Big Game of 'Eighty-Nine officially entered the history books as a heavily asterisked draw rather than as a clear-cut victory for the Pioneers. Nobody would say why officialdom decided to log the game that way—until very recently.

Ah. You must have heard about [the late Pike City Pioneers relief pitcher] Hank Gordimer's funeral three weeks ago.

I have a copy of the letter he'd asked to be read aloud at his eulogy. The letter that finally cleared up the mystery surrounding the outcome of the Big Game of 'Eighty-Nine.

Well, I suppose Hank wasn't telling tales out of school when he read that letter out loud. The league officials only asked us—Kornelius, me, the Pioneers themselves, and anybody else who happened to be in the know—not to talk about the real reasoning behind the league's decision. They wanted us all to keep quiet about it for the rest of our lives. But they couldn't very well stop Hank from talking after he was dead. Of course, if you'd known Hank you'd know how hard it could be to stop him from doing *anything* once his mind was made up.

Then just to keep you from getting sideways with the Cestus Baseball League, *I'll* tell the rest of the story, for the record. Gordimer had that case of Gorn-brewed, syrupy blue booze that you mentioned earlier (Meridor is what they call the stuff, by the way). And he'd heard that some of the Talons had a real weakness for it—perhaps even their starting pitcher. So he had one of the water boys keep bringing the stuff to the Gorn dugout throughout the game. By the fifth inning, the Talons' hurler was already so tipsy that Uncle Kornelius had noticed it from the Pioneers' dugout. By the seventh-inning stretch, that pitcher was probably seeing double.

You'd think a life-form that hails from a place called "fluidic space" would be able to handle its liquor better than that.

Yeah, you'd think. But by inning eight, he was inebriated enough to start having trouble maintaining his molecular cohesion—and that's no alcohol-fueled metaphor. This is the kind of thing that can only happen in baseball.

Is this a wonderful sport, or what?

Let's return to the subject of the Klingons for a moment: You hinted earlier that Chancellor

Martok might have taken his Gorn frustrations out on Ambassador B'vat.

I don't know all the details, of course, but it's pretty clear that all the Gorn saber-rattling that followed the Big Game marked B'vat as a huge failure in Martok's eyes. B'vat was summarily recalled to Qo'noS the day after the game, and I'm sure Martok called him on the carpet loudly once he arrived.

But fortunately for B'vat, the ambassador had somebody handy he could take *his* frustrations out on before he left Cestus III.

Who was that?

Ja'rod, son of Lursa, of course. He soon found the only way he could regain the honor he'd lost because of the Gorn debacle was to serve for a few years in the Klingon Defense Force. And rumor has it that Ja'rod's finest tour of duty aboard the *I.K.S. Kang* involved a lengthy assignment doing something that every Klingon alive dreads.

Okay, I give up, Kas. What was Ja'rod's assignment?

Tribble eradication duty. It seems those fuzzy little things have been proliferating across the Alpha and Beta Quadrants ever since your father returned from an excursion to the twenty-third century he took a few decades back.

Do you think the Pioneers might be up for a rematch with the Gorns someday—provided, of course, they

can keep the mound free of alcoholic saboteurs from fluidic space?

Kornelius is still one of the team owners, and he's even more cantankerous now than he was back then. If the Gorn ever issued a challenge like that, you can be sure that Korny would take it up. In fact, you can ask him about that tonight at dinner. He might even ask you why he should insist on keeping the Undine out of the game this time. After all, those alien doppelgängers would have a pretty tough time handling nine determined Cestans. Like your father always said, baseball is all about heart.

And if the Undine didn't have the heart to beat us in the Long War, why should we worry about what they might do to us out on the diamond, right?

Let the other team worry, whether they've got scales, claws, or three legs. Bring 'em on. After all, lots of things in life are worse than losing a baseball game.

Kasidy and I have dinner that evening with her brother—my uncle Kornelius—and my younger half-sister, Rebecca. Unfortunately, my travel schedule won't let me linger over coffee and dessert after the meal. As my transport ship departs from Pike City's Robbins Spaceport, my mind starts replaying some of the observations Dad made about baseball over the years. The first to spring to mind is, "Baseball is a lot like life, because in baseball, anything can happen."

That includes, I assume, a human victory over terrifying and determined adversaries like the Undine.

My ship reaches orbit, providing me with a spectacular vista of the ocher-and-blue world that has nurtured baseball's rebirth and renewed growth for so many years. I look out to the sun-dappled horizon, across vast swaths of cobalt ocean, golden desert, and olive-and-emerald hickorash forests.

And I breathe a silent prayer of thanks that the game of baseball was not among the many things humanity had to sacrifice during the Long War against the Undine.

Excerpted from an official Klingon
communiqué, received Stardate 76429.4[*]

From: J'mpok, son of Q'thoq, Chancellor of
the Klingon Empire and leader of the High
Council
To: The Federation Security Council

... On multiple occasions, Empire has officially
requested the Federation's aid in seeking out
qa'meH quv [Undine] infiltrators. The Federation has refused us such assistance each time,
demonstrating that the Khitomer Accords are
not worth the replicated papers that carry
their outmoded text.

Therefore, in the furtherance of the Klingon
Empire's security, as well as its self-evident
right to expand its boundaries, I hereby con-
sign those papers to the flames that forge our
*bat'leth*s. ...

_____
[*] June 6, 2399.

Earth

THE HOME FRONT

Federation News Service
DATELINE—LYNNWOOD, WASHINGTON STATE,
EARTH STARDATE 76815.8[*]

Julietta Harter turned herself in to local police yesterday morning, in connection with the murder of Kenneth Lawrence Shore, whom family members discovered in his apartment last Thursday, dead as a result of multiple stab wounds.

Until this morning, the police had assumed that Shore had struggled with a burglar, who had fled with a number of valuables from the apartment. But the police will probably revise that working theory in light of Ms. Harter's public statement, in which she claimed to have taken the missing items from Shore's apartment to disguise what she herself has called "an act of premeditated murder" as the result of a burglary.

An anonymous police source has admitted that detectives considered Harter a "person of interest" from the outset of their investigation, but that they had failed to locate her for several days after Shore's death. The reliability of Harter's confession may be in doubt, however, since she reportedly has a history of making "wild claims" about her neighbors, including Shore.

"I told the police exactly who and what Ken really was," Harter said in her public statement. "But they didn't want to believe one of those giant Undine bugs was living

---

[*] October 25, 2399.

across the street from me, right under everybody's noses, in disguise."

When asked whether she could produce any evidence that might corroborate her assertion that Shore was a clandestine Undine agent, she said only, "Can you prove to me that he *wasn't*?"

JAKE SISKO, DATA ROD #P-26

Paris, France, Earth

The silver-haired woman who greets me in the shadow of the Palais de la Concorde, the sleekly vertical nerve center of the Federation government, has to be in her seventies by now. But Esperanza Piñiero appears ageless, her effervescent smile revealing the boundless energy and enthusiasm that made her such an asset to Nanietta Bacco during her many years of service as Bacco's chief of staff, both during Bacco's tenure as Cestus III's governor and as the Federation's thirty-eighth president. As we exchange handshakes and pleasantries in the broad public courtyard that fronts the Palais, I wonder if Ms. Piñiero's infectiously upbeat manner stems from having a first name that translates into Federation Standard as "hope."

Or could it be because the dark days of the Undine War are now many long years behind her?

You served in Starfleet for thirty-five years before you began the government career from which you've only recently retired. Your perspective on the Undine War may be a unique one, Ms. Piñiero.

Possibly. But it's a perspective that's limited to a lot of meeting rooms in places like the Palais. And mostly on Earth, at that.

But it was time spent in the company of some of the most pivotal decision makers in the Federation, and during the most dangerous phases of the conflict. What was life like for you here on Earth's front porch in those days?

For *me?* I didn't really have any time for *me,* so it would be hard to tell you. It was meetings, meetings, and more meetings. Schedules, notes, minutes, and reports. But I had it dead easy. For President Bacco, it was acute duodenal ulcers and chronic insomnia. As much as I love Nan, I wouldn't have traded places with her for anything.

For the world beyond the security screens of the Palais, I imagine life during the war years was pretty much like whatever you experienced in . . . where were you living then? New Orleans?

Close. Terrebonne Parish, Louisiana. But most humans on Earth weren't living on the bayou, so I don't consider my experience typical.

I spoke with a lot of people from just about every imaginable walk of life during those years. It didn't matter where you were living. Everybody was tense. Nobody had experienced anything like it since the early seventies, when a handful of Dominion shapeshifters brought our communal sense of paranoia

Checkout Receipt

Albany Public Library Main Branch
08/20/14 02 04PM

The needs of the many /
31182019084432   09/17/14

Peaceable kingdoms /
31182020869607   09/17/14

The folded world / The Folded World
31182020507801   09/17/14

Losing the Peace /
31182018686484   09/17/14

The shocks of adversity /
31182020508247   09/17/14

OTAL: 5

to a rolling boil. Some people reacted to that stress pretty badly—including some highly trained, powerful people who really should have known better.

People like Admiral James Leyton, who tried to stage a military coup against President Jaresh-Inyo when he decided that the Palais had gone soft on enemy infiltrators during the years leading up to the Dominion War.
Leyton's Coup of 'Seventy-two. Leyton's actions had such far-reaching implications that it's already become part of a nursery rhyme, the way the Black Death and Guy Fawkes's Gunpowder Plot did.

Historians already seem to be pretty much of one mind on Leyton. They regard him as a traitor, no matter how noble his intentions might have been. Who knows, a hundred years or so from now "James Leyton" might replace "Benedict Arnold" as a synonym for traitor. But ever since the Long War ended, I've been thinking that maybe history ought to amend its judgment about Leyton.

I'm surprised to hear you say that, Ms. Piñiero.
Ugh. Please, you can call me Esperanza, as long as you let me call you Jake. "Ms. Piñiero" is what they call my mother.

It's a deal.
Jake, I think what surprises you is that I don't automatically spit when I speak Jim Leyton's name.

I know there's a minority school of political thought that considers Leyton a legitimate hero, and I don't want to start a debate about that. Or offend you if that's the way *you* see Leyton—
Jake, I'm the loyal former chief of staff to Governor Bacco, and later President Bacco, a reformer who took over after the almost two-term maladministration of Min Zife. So please, never make the mistake of confusing me with one of those reactionary neobirch[*] "the-ends-justify-the-means" culture warriors who seem to exist only to test the sincerity of the Federation Charter's free-speech guarantees.

Of course not. It's just that I thought that you'd have no truck with a traitor like Leyton.
Believe me, Jake, I don't. Please don't misunderstand me. What Leyton did was unconscionable, not to mention utterly incompatible with the Federation's democratic ideals.

But I also think that history will conclude—someday—that Jim Leyton did us all a tremendous favor back in 'seventy-two.

By trying to seize power forcibly from a duly elected president?

---

[*] So-called neobircher political action groups have popped up throughout Federation history, mainly as a reaction to perceived Federation decadence and indolence. The term "neobircher" is derived from John Birch (1918–1945), a missionary and military intelligence officer who became the namesake of a fringe right-wing twentieth-century political movement on Earth.

By calling our attention to one of our society's worst vulnerabilities: our own complacency. Our unexamined assumption that the Federation can only be dragged down to destruction by a sufficiently powerful external enemy, like the Dominion or the Borg.

When circumstances forced us to add the Undine to the Federation's rogues' gallery of would-be conquerors, the memory of our own behavior while we were under siege from our two worst previous adversaries was still fresh in the minds of everyone old enough to remember. Sometimes people revisited their own behavior during that time and said to themselves, "I'd do the same thing all over again." Others looked back and had to confess, if only to themselves, that they weren't exactly proud of the way they'd acted during a time of real crisis.

I think that we—the people of the Federation in general, but also the people of Earth in particular—handled ourselves much better during the worst parts of the Undine War than we had during some of the preceding crises. The vast majority of us made a conscious decision to listen to the better angels of our nature. And I think we owe part of the credit for that to Jim Leyton, for giving us a good, close look at the wages of fear.

So you still see Leyton's act as a crime—but you also see it as a kind of cultural inoculation against our repeating some of our earlier mistakes during the Undine conflict.

An inoculation—that's a perfect metaphor! I think I'm going to steal it.

Feel free. Which mistakes are you referring to, specifically?
Acting almost entirely out of fear was our principal mistake. I'll give you an example: The Founder crisis of 'seventy-two started off with a Dominion bombing of a Federation-Romulan diplomatic conference in Belgium. The blast took twenty-seven lives in less than a second. But it also robbed us of something we weren't even aware that we citizens of Earth had: our sense of invulnerability. Our belief that whatever dangers might lurk out there in the depths of space, we could be safe so long as we stayed *here,* on good ol' terra firma.

I remember those times all too well. A lot of people wanted to climb into deep holes and pull them in after themselves.
The only problem was that there was no way to dig a hole deep enough. Fear can only take you so far. Even a fear-monger like Pascal Fullerton knew it, or he wouldn't have said, "The gulf of interstellar space can no longer protect us."

Even though it was wrong, Leyton's Coup of 'Seventy-two was a completely understandable—and maybe even natural—reaction to that fear.
Understandable, sure. Natural? That I'm not so sure

about. Calling Leyton's actions "natural" is tantamount to calling Jaresh-Inyo's much more measured approach "*un*natural."

And Jaresh-Inyo turned out to be right. He understood that turning Earth and the Federation into armed and armored police states wouldn't make us any safer in the long run. He knew that a strategy like that would only do the Founders' dirty work for them by forcing the Federation to change itself into something it was never intended to be: a collection of frightened souls motivated by suspicion, fearful that their neighbors and loved ones might really be monsters in disguise. Jaresh-Inyo understood how vulnerable we were to becoming so preoccupied with whispering campaigns and fear that we'd forget our birthright of civil liberties. We barely avoided becoming a planetwide warren of frightened rabbits who were willing to spend the bulk of their time spying on one another.

Correct me if I'm wrong, Esperanza, but you must have written at least a few of President Bacco's more memorable speeches.
I may have helped her through one or two of the bumpier passages. I'm prepared to let her have credit for all the rest.

I agree with you that President Jaresh-Inyo was right to err on the side of civil liberties, even when that wasn't popular in more hawkish quarters. But

the electorate evidently didn't see it that way—not even after the collapse of Leyton's coup and the Dominion's failure to trick Earth into effectively destroying itself.

And so it goes with inoculations—sometimes a vaccine can cause the very disease it's supposed to stave off. It's a calculated risk.

And don't forget, we didn't have the benefit of hindsight back in 'seventy-two. The bombing in Antwerp grabbed us by the throat and shook us. It forced us to face the fact that there was no way to avoid engaging with the rest of the galaxy. The only question was how to go about it, with a sense of hope or an attitude of fear. Earth spent the next few years staggering in a drunkard's walk around the right answer, taking three steps toward it and two steps away each time.

Meanwhile Min Zife's eight-year reign of error got under way—and nearly provoked the Klingon Empire into going to full-scale war against us before it was through. But even though we both seem to differ quite a bit from Zife politically, we ought to be fair to him. During his time in office we learned that there really were some very good reasons to be afraid. There are always good reasons to be afraid, Jake. The only question is whether you'll rule your fear or allow your fear to rule you.

That sounds a lot like something President Bacco said.

Another Profile in Plagiarism on my part. I hope it means that at least a little of Nan has rubbed off on me over the years. But we were talking about fear. Often entirely justifiable fear. Such as the fear that spread out across the planet like seismic waves after the Breen attack on Starfleet Headquarters in 'seventy-five.

The Breen had just joined the Dominion a short time before the attack.
And they seemed very eager to please their new shape-shifting overlords. The objective of their raid on San Francisco was to create fear, and lots of it, on the Dominion's behalf. And they succeeded.

Of course, the fear the Breen brought us wasn't quite the same as the general, unfocused dread that the Founders had created a few years earlier. It didn't quite measure up to the fear that the person sitting right next to you on the hoverbus might be a shape-changing alien monster just under the skin. But it was pretty damned effective nonetheless; the image of Starfleet HQ and the Golden Gate Bridge both reduced to charred, twisted piles of rubble had a pro-found effect on everybody who was living on Earth at the time. Or anywhere else in the Federation, for that matter.

A lot of people living on Earth then were talking openly about moving off-world.
Sure they were. But surprisingly few actually followed

through and relocated. I mean, despite what the Breen did to us, how could anyone be sure they'd be any safer anywhere else in the Federation while the Dominion War was still raging on across dozens of other systems in and around Federation space? We were vulnerable *everywhere,* or at least we felt that way.

And that brings me all the way back to your vaccine metaphor, Jake. The Breen attack was kind of a booster shot for the inoculation that Jim Leyton unwittingly gave us three years earlier. And it all added up to humanity's eventual readiness for the coming of the Undine.

As I recall, the Dominion War left the Federation in pretty rough shape, and our Klingon and Romulan allies had pretty much the same experience, or worse. If anything, the Founders and their allies left us depleted.

But only materially, Jake. I'm not talking about cities and starships and infrastructure. I'm talking about the condition of humanity's *spirit.* Our willingness to reach out to one another during times of upheaval and crisis. Our ability to work together toward a common goal—particularly when the stakes are high.

We're damned lucky that the Borg didn't launch a major assault while we were still sweeping up and binding our wounds after the Dominion War.

Amen to that. But even if that had happened, I think we would have gotten through it. Maybe. Somehow.

During the Undine War, Federation Council often didn't bear much resemblance to the rosy picture of human nature that you've been painting today. The Undine had so many Federation representatives spooked that they wasted weeks of valuable time debating useless measures, like declaring the Undine to be unlawful combatants.

The Security Council got itself worked into a particularly vicious bureaucratic lather over the Undine's many alleged violations of the Jankata Accord, specifically the section that reads, "No species shall enter another quadrant for the purpose of territorial expansion."

But the Undine had never signed the Jankata Accord. That was a pact between the Federation and Cardassia, if I remember correctly. The closest the Undine ever came to inking a treaty with us was the informal cease-fire that Kathryn Janeway arranged with one small Undine faction back in 2375.

It was nuts, I agree. Like a Ferengi trying to pass a law against rain. Fortunately, Councilor Lynda Foley of Deneva managed to convince a slim majority to vote the measure down by pointing out that the Undine didn't seem as interested in seizing territory as they were in preemptively wiping out humanity—along with all the other humanoid races in the Federation and beyond.

But I really hope you don't expect that sort of stuff to make any sense, Jake. After all, we're talking about the machinations of frightened politicians and political apparatchiks. What *I* was talking about was the human race, and its kindred species throughout two quadrants. The *real,* nonpolitical humanity that lay beyond the Council chambers.

Wait a minute. *You* were a politician once. Or at least a "political apparatchik."
I was a lot of things, Jake. But I hope I was always a human being, first and foremost. And it was ordinary humans and humanoids—regular folk who raise families and build things, not those who are drawn to power and influence as ends unto themselves—who made the difference in the fight against the Undine invaders.

The Federation Council didn't seem to think so back in the day. They were so worried about humanity cutting and running from the Undine that they actually drafted conscription legislation.
Legislation that turned out to be just more wasted time and misapplied energy. The Council badly misjudged humanity. It underestimated our capacity to trust one another, to rely on one another, to shoulder not only our own burdens, but the next guy's, too. The way people did during the rebuilding of Merak II and Catualla after the Undine left those worlds mostly in ruins. Humanity had to summon the strength to soldier on from some deep inner wellspring, in spite of everything the Undine had tried to take from us.

The Undine must have been nearly as surprised as the Federation Council when ordinary people turned out to be the ones who rose to the occasion to drive them out. Never underestimate the power of pitchforks and torches, Jake.

It almost sounds like you're saying that we owe a debt of gratitude to the Undine for helping us cultivate our better natures.
Not at all. I think of the Undine almost as a force of nature. You don't thank a force of nature. You don't thank the Black Death of a thousand years ago for reshuffling medieval Europe's economic deck enough to finance the Renaissance and all the advancements it ushered in. You don't thank the asteroid that smacked into the Yucatán sixty-five million years ago for wiping out the dinosaurs so that we primates could have a crack at walking upright, ruling the world, and building the fleets of starships that have enabled us to explore the galaxy.

Nevertheless, I suspect you'd agree with the notion that a little adversity, taken in just the right dose, can greatly sharpen a person. Or even a species.
We definitely owe something to adversity, no question. It tests us and keeps us strong. Science has known for centuries that people actually tend to grow healthier, physically, during tough times—even in times as tough as the Great Depression of Earth's twentieth century. The people of that generation

knew how to throw overboard any nonessentials that might distract them from the essential business of surviving and prospering. When push comes to shove, our generation can learn to live without its replicators and holodecks when the need arises. And we're usually better for the experience—not that those are experiences anybody's eager to repeat unnecessarily, myself included.

Anything that doesn't kill us makes us stronger?
I'm not a big fan of Nietzsche, Jake, but maybe he had a point when he originated that thought. After all, with all the power and technology the Federation has had at its disposal for so long, it would be easy for us to devolve into a civilization of indolent lotus-eaters. But as long as we're willing to keep challenging ourselves, that'll never happen to us. Particularly if we always remain willing to help out our fellow humans and humanoids, the way so many did all those years ago on Merak II and Catualla.

Maybe what Nietzsche should have written was, "Anything that *almost* kills you just might make you a bit nobler."

At least until the Next Great Big Scary War.
Yeah, at least until the Next Great Big Scary War.

JAKE SISKO, DATA ROD #F-36

Nowhere in particular

Before I agreed to embark on this assignment, I decided to institute only one rule vis-à-vis any prospective participant: an insistence on fair play.

That didn't mean that everybody was obligated to adopt whatever notion of truth I might find most appealing. Truth, after all, is highly subjective and elastic, particularly when one is dealing with such an emotionally charged subject as the Undine War, and so many years after the fact. Any attempt on my part to "steer" an interviewee toward or away from any particular "truth" would have been completely counterproductive, since what I wanted were the unvarnished accounts of some of those upon whom the war had had the most profound effects.

But that rule also applied to any participant who might have seen my work as an opportunity to etch his or her pet political talking points into the long-term emergent consensus of history. These were the ones who demanded to vet every question in advance—a demand that I always stood firm in declining as part of my commitment to keeping these chronicles honest and as free as possible of individual attempts to push history in any particular ideological direction. (Those prospective interviewees who either declined or ignored my meeting requests represented self-correcting problems, at least in terms of my aforementioned commitment to the integrity of the growing tapestry of personal stories I had begun weaving.) By enforcing this simple "fair play" rule strictly, I had hoped to assemble a wide range of personal stories from across the Federation's ideological spectrum and beyond.

And yet something was missing. While it was true that I needed to protect this project from being polluted by what I will charitably describe as "misinformation"—this translates roughly as "lies" to any reader less inclined than I am to afford the bearers of misinformation every reasonable benefit of the doubt—my emerging skein of narratives was largely bereft of some of the Federation's more conservative political perspectives. So I contacted a number of individuals and interest groups across the Federation that I thought might best represent the ideological perspectives most contrary—or is that complementary?—to my own.

I heard back from only three of these respondents. Of these three, two steadfastly refused to let the conversation advance past the not-entirely-unexpected demand to vet my questions in advance. While I'm happy to discuss the broad outlines of the conversation in advance, I will not submit detailed lists of questions for advance approval. Nor will I rule out, a priori, any area of discussion that may appear relevant as the interview unfolds. Nonfiction interviews, like the fictional characters I develop for my stories and novels, have lives of their own.

The third response, which came from the offices of a culturally conservative political action group known as the New Essentialists, likewise insisted on trying to control the proceedings. This is why the meeting I had hoped to set up with the New Essentialists' founder, leader, spokesman, and ideological soul, Pascal Fullerton—a man who achieved notoriety (if not much of a following) in 2373 by sabotaging Risa's weather-control grid as a cautionary object lesson about the perils of Federation complacency and decadence—never happened.

But Fullerton's office was kind enough to supply a press release (in both text and holo formats) about his organization and its beliefs. I have chosen to reproduce the text of that press release, perhaps bending my own rules in the process, for two reasons: because of its relevance to my assignment, and in the interests of simple fairness to an ideological opposite—one who nearly persuaded Worf to join him about thirty years ago.

I will allow Pascal Fullerton's own words about the state of the Federation before, during, and after the Long War to speak for themselves.

For Immediate Release
NEW CENTURY BEGINS WITH UFP SECURITY AT LOWEST EBB SINCE UNDINE WAR

Phoenix, Arizona, 2 January 2401—The Rally for Human Greatness will be held at 2:00 p.m. on

Saturday, January 6, at the Phoenix Municipal Stadium. Join the New Essentialist movement in protesting the morally lax and inhuman policies of (Saurian) President Okeg!

"The Federation was already in an advanced state of cultural decline long before the Undine appeared," New Essentialist founder Pascal Fullerton said during a rare recent appearance on the public affairs holoprogram *Illuminating the City of Light.* "The rot had set in even before the Dominion and their Cardassian and Breen allies were at our throats. Far too many of our people simply wanted to escape in those days, fueling Earth's skyrocketing rates of holo-addiction and an alarming upsurge in retreats to so-called vacation paradises like Risa and Argelius and Pacifica.

"After our relatively humanoid Dominion War adversaries were replaced by utterly unsympathetic, inhuman monsters—monsters whose talent for stealing our identities exceeded even that of the Dominion's Founders—we became even weaker and more morally bankrupt than ever before. We've even begun to manifest a new psychosis during recent years, a disorder that manifests itself as the delusion of *being* one of those demons from fluidic space, disguised as a human being. . . .

"What's the remedy for our decadence, for our collective lack of will? The answer lies with a deliberate disconnection from the quasi-magical technologies-of-abundance upon which we have allowed ourselves to become overly dependent. We need to recover our moral roots, giving our primary allegiance to all things human, or at least humanoid. How far we've allowed ourselves to drift from those eternal verities. I cite as an example the creature who currently dwells in the Palias [*sic*] and runs the Federation government. President Aennik Okeg is not only inhuman, he's not even mammalian. The vast majority of the populace of Earth, the Federation's primary founding world, has nothing in common with the UFP's current president—not even a common phylum.

"Could Okeg's decidedly nonhuman perspective and influence have anything to do with some of the most dangerous interstellar policy decisions the Federation Council has made over the past several years? I number among these Starfleet's many fruitless attempts to reason with foes like the Undine, creatures so alien and antithetical to our way of life that the only truly safe recourse is to deal with them decisively, using the deadliest imaginable force. One can neither reason with, nor make peace with, fiends who have already demonstrated that they cannot be trusted to hold up their end of any treaty."

The issues Mr. Fullerton raised on *Illuminating the City of Light,* along with many others, will be raised at the Saturday rally, which will be followed by panel discussions and/or a public Q&A.

The New Essentialists for a New Federation is a nonprofit enterprise devoted to reclaiming the lost moral and ethical greatness of the United Federation of Planets and its human founders.

Contact:
Kopyc K'narf, Director of Public Relations
The New Essentialists for a New Federation
2 Goldwater Square, Paxton Annex
Phoenix, Arizona, Earth

Past and Future

WORLDS IN COLLISION

Charles Ryerson disappeared almost twenty years ago, along with his small warp-drive-capable skiff—or so the crew of the U.S.S. *Zife* discovered last week when they picked him up near Barnard's star. According to Ryerson, time essentially stood still for him during most of his lengthy voyage, even though his vessel's computers confirmed that he and his ship had indeed been in space continuously for more than nineteen years.

"He appears to have coasted without engine power once his impulse engines had accelerated his vessel to a speed of just under warp one," said one of the *Zife*'s officers, on condition of anonymity. "Newtonian momentum and Einsteinian time dilation took care of the rest." Though contemporary interstellar travelers rarely experience it today, time dilation is a relativistic phenomenon, predicted by the theories of Albert Einstein, that greatly slows down shipboard time for those traveling in normal space at a significant fraction of the speed of light. The closer one approaches light speed, the more pronounced the effect of time dilation becomes. "From Mr. Ryerson's perspec-

[*] January 2, 2409.

tive," the *Zife* officer explained, "he's only been out here for a little over two weeks."

Leapfrogging over two entire decades of history would probably be more than enough to satisfy anyone's appetite for strangeness and adventure. But Mr. Ryerson's time displacement turned out to be only the *start* of the strangeness he was to experience, a truth that he discovered only after one of the *Zife*'s communications officers made contact with Ryerson's family on Alpha Centauri III. Ryerson's relatives greeted the news of their missing patriarch's unexpected reappearance not with joy, but with disbelief. Ryerson's wife, Eileen, seemed to react with particularly intense incredulity, and not because she had remarried and moved on since her husband's disappearance.

Her reaction was spurred instead by the bizarre fact that Charles Ryerson had never left home, and remained at her side even now, though he appeared to be some two decades older than the man who was calling her from the *Zife*. "It's a little like Einstein's twin paradox," the renowned science popularizer known as Doctor Jack explained when asked to comment on the story. "Except that we can't account for the prodigal twin that left home."

According to an unconfirmed report, Starfleet Intelligence took both Charles Ryersons into custody early yesterday, presumably to ascertain whether either man might be an Undine sleeper agent. No agency in Starfleet or the Federation government will make an official comment on the matter, and the local authorities governing the Barnard system and vicinity are maintaining a like silence. . . .

JAKE SISKO, DATA ROD #DTI-1

The Federation Rehabilitation Center at **[LOCATION REDACTED BY STARFLEET INTELLIGENCE]**

Despite their penchant for maintaining a low profile, the participation of special agents Adam Lucsly and Wolf Dulmer in the fight against the Undine made headlines across the Alpha Quadrant. As career investigators for the Federation's notoriously clandestine Department of Temporal Investigations, both Lucsly and Dulmer examined dozens of so-called temporal incursions—trips through time, often but not always taken inadvertently—during their many decades of service in the ranks of the Federation's most accomplished "time cops." Of necessity, such investigations have always been conducted quietly, in the figurative shadows. But the Undine effectively dragged the DTI's activities at least partly into broad daylight, even as the aliens' attempts to destroy all sentient life in our galaxy changed the course of history itself.

Though the spotlight of public attention had caught Lucsly and Dulmer squarely in its unblinking glare during the Long War, no one ever would have described either man as talkative. Therefore it shouldn't come as a shock that this was not an easy interview for me to obtain. Even years after the conflict had ostensibly wound down, and Wolf Dulmer had at long last agreed in principle to grant the Federation News Service's request for a "public debriefing session" regarding his career as a temporal investigator, two significant stumbling blocks stood in the way. The first of these was Agent Dulmer's eight-year-long-and-counting inpatient residency at a psychological rehab center (a place whose coordinates I couldn't disclose even if I wanted to, since our destination was kept from me during my carefully stage-managed transportation to this secret facility). And the second came in the person of Adam Lucsly, Dulmer's former partner at the DTI.

Over the years, Lucsly became the closest thing Dulmer now has to a family member, and he is understandably protective of his longtime DTI mentor and colleague—particularly after the temporal incident that precipitated his long-term rehab in the first place. But because of the services my father rendered to the DTI long ago—for security reasons, Lucsly is close-mouthed about the exact nature of the temporal crisis that Ben Sisko helped him resolve—I have become the first representative of the media to quiz both former DTI agents together since the height of the Long War.

I somehow manage not to fidget nervously in the rehab institution's sterile reception-area-cum-conference-room while Lucsly presents his credentials to one of the orderlies, a tall but otherwise nondescript *human male who promptly vanishes behind the door of an adjacent antechamber. As Lucsly and I take our seats at the pastel-blue table whose circular expanse dominates the sparsely appointed room, I feel a gnawing apprehension that belies the intended calming effect of the color scheme.*

Do you mind answering a few preliminary questions while we wait for Agent . . . for former agent Dulmer?
LUCSLY: Mister Sisko, I only agreed to do this as part of a . . . tag-team effort.

And thank you again for that, Mister Lucsly. However, your perspective is bound to be a bit different from that of former agent Dulmer, in view of his . . . present circumstances. And you may be able to shed some additional light on the DTI's involvement in the Undine War.
LUCSLY: Regardless of what the news-holos were saying at the time, we never played a truly pivotal role in the war. In fact, I can only think of one particular Undine-related incident that involved the DTI even peripherally.

At the time, the Undine were supposedly trying to use time travel against us, the way the Borg did. Are you saying that that isn't true?
LUCSLY: I'm not sure it's such a good idea for me to talk about any of this.

For what it's worth, whatever you say for the record will be thoroughly vetted by Starfleet Intelligence before it's released to the public.

LUCSLY: All right. Go ahead and ask your questions.

After it came to light that Undine operatives had infiltrated at least one of the department's key temporal monitoring stations—that's undoubtedly the lone incident you just referred to—you and Mister Dulmer suddenly found yourselves drawn into the heart of the conflict, at least according to the media reports of the time.

LUCSLY: We'd been in the "heart" of other wars, too, Mister Sisko. The Undine were just the first enemy that managed to get us onto people's morning news-padds.

But why would the Undine want to "out" DTI agents? What was in it for them?

The door to the anteroom opens again before I've finished asking my question, interrupting the flow of conversation. Wolf Dulmer, clad in a light blue hospital coverall that closely matches the color of both the table and the walls, enters the room, followed by the same orderly who had left a few minutes earlier. A tall, dark-haired, middle-aged human male, he now looks much more nondescript than he did before, perhaps even passingly familiar. He identifies himself only as Quelle as we finally get around to exchanging perfunctory greetings. The orderly doesn't leave the room this time, but rather fades into the background, remaining as a watchful yet otherwise mostly unobtrusive presence as Dulmer takes a seat at the round table, roughly equidistant from both Lucsly and myself.

LUCSLY: The answer to your last question should be obvious, Mister Sisko. The Undine wanted to sow confusion throughout the Federation and beyond.

No doubt. But the Undine already had far more efficient ways of doing *that*, wouldn't you agree?
DULMER: You're talking about their impersonations of various Starfleet officers, Earth politicos, and even Klingon warriors.

LUCSLY: Not to mention Romulan military officers and senators. You may not be aware of this, Mister Sisko, but they even succeeded in placing some of their infiltrators inside the Gorn royal family.

My point exactly. The Undine were obsessed with wiping out every sentient race in the galaxy, but they went about it very patiently. Sometimes they'd attack directly. At other times they'd use fear to play people against their own public institutions, or to pit one government against another. *Those* were

the places where they sowed confusion, and pretty damned successfully—because they made us begin to doubt that the best and brightest of us really *were* us. They made us wonder if even our best-protected leaders might not really be alien monsters under the skin.

DULMER: And some fears are even more funda-mental than those the Undine invested so much of their energies into stirring up. Being afraid to trust the admiralty at Starfleet, or even the UFP president, is one thing. But being afraid to trust reality itself—that's something else entirely.

I have always suspected that the Department of Temporal Investigations—or at least the two of you—played a much more significant role in the Undine War than the bureau's previous public statements ever let on. Do either of you care to comment on that?

LUCSLY: If we were to confirm that kind of specu-lation, we'd just look like a couple of former minor bureaucrats trying to polish their own reputations.

DULMER: Come on, Adam. That's just tail-covering Department boilerplate. The Undine made the DTI at least as big a front in their war against humanity as they did any of their more public targets. We just happened to have been the only ones who knew it at the time.

Except, of course, for the Undine.

LUCSLY: Don't you think you might be overstating your point a bit, Wolf?

DULMER: Not in the least. The Borg weren't the only adversary we've faced that had the ability to engage in deliberate, directed temporal displacement. The Undine knew how to do it, too. Maybe it was a function of their ability to navigate back and forth between our universe and their own. We were never quite sure about that.

To put this in plain, non-DTI English, you're talking about time travel, right? Deliberate, on-purpose time travel. You're saying that the Undine used that ability as a weapon against us, even though the DTI has publicly denied that ever since the war ended.

DULMER: Exactly. And with a few notable exceptions, DTI agents like us were the Undine's only serious obstacles—at least in terms of their temporal operations.

Agent Lucsly, did an Undine temporal operation ever force you to travel into the past to correct some injury the enemy had inflicted on the timeline?

LUCSLY: I can recall only one major temporal incursion committed by the Undine—and we managed to nip that one in the bud. We canceled out everything they had done, or tried to do, to the timeline.

You say that you had to stop an Undine time-travel attack only once. Did you have to respond to a lot of other similar incidents perpetrated by others?

LUCSLY: I'll admit, there were a number of occasions—and I'll refrain from going into any of the details here—when we had to perform a bit of "emergency surgery" on the timeline here and there, to undo something that some Federation time traveler or other had done.

Time crime, so to speak?

DULMER: At least half the incidents Adam is referring to were just innocent accidents.

You mean like when a ship loses its warp drive and has to travel under high impulse long enough to get seriously out of sync with the calendar?

LUCSLY: That's simple time dilation—fly long enough at a high enough percentage of c, and subjective shipboard time can slow enough to put you in the wrong century. The DTI considers those sorts of accidents natural phenomena, and doesn't get involved. Trying to undo that breed of time travel runs too big a risk of getting the universe tangled in one of the worst possible crosstime cat's cradles.

DULMER: It's called a "predestination paradox." Maybe that hypothetical subwarp, time-dilated starship was *supposed* to displace itself in time.

I get it. If the DTI were to send that ship back to the time it came from, somebody's grandfather might die at the wrong time, and history comes unstitched. My God. Thinking about these things can give you a real headache.

DULMER: Or worse.

LUCSLY: The DTI concerned itself with the more exotic types of time-travel accidents. A merchant ship getting retrodisplaced by an unexpected gravimetric slingshot effect, say.

DULMER: Or a vessel getting flung back in time by the space-time lensing that can happen near the event horizon of a black hole. Those sorts of things aren't as unusual as you might think. Enough Starfleet officers have been temporally displaced over the years to force the DTI to create an entire office just to handle those incidents.[*]

LUCSLY: The rest of the temporal incidents that the DTI would act on generally involved some deliberate action on the time traveler's part. But only a handful of those actions were motivated by actual malice. For instance, there was the musicologist who tried to prevent the late-twentieth-century assassination of John Lennon; he sincerely believed

---

[*] The Temporal Displacement Division, which functions both as a Federation civilian authority and as a Starfleet administrative office, known alternatively as the Starfleet Department for Temporally Displaced Officers.

that he was increasing the universe's net content of peace and love.

DULMER: And then there was the disgraced Klingon agent[*] who returned to the twenty-third century with a plan to assassinate James Kirk. He was a totally different story.

   As were the Undine. When they came, everything changed.

LUCSLY: I remember all of those incidents clearly enough. Except for that last part . . . I'm sorry, Wolf, but the idea that the DTI was somehow maintaining the thin line between order and chaos during the Long War . . . well, it's just—it's more than a little paranoid.

I notice that both Lucsly and Quelle—the latter still hanging back near one of the walls—have tensed as though expecting Dulmer to react explosively.

   Instead, the elder time cop merely sits quietly, nodding as he absorbs his old friend's words, still diamond-hard despite their almost apologetic delivery. Then Dulmer chuckles gently, as if enjoying a private joke at everyone else's expense.

DULMER: Don't worry about offending me, Adam. I wouldn't expect you to remember the bigger

---

[*] Gralmek, aka Arne Darvin, aka Barry Waddle, was surgically altered to pass as human as part of a failed plot by Klingon Intelligence to sabotage Federation efforts to colonize Sherman's Planet in 2267.

temporal picture in quite the same way *I* do. Even though you saw it all, right alongside me. Before everything that happened that day—or *almost* everything that happened that day—got . . . canceled out.

Lucsly says nothing as he releases a sad sigh. Quelle approaches and addresses me in a tone that seems calculated not to provoke his patient.

QUELLE: I'm afraid what you're hearing is one of the classic markers of temporal psychosis.

I regard Quelle for a moment. For the first time since his arrival in the room, his face is becoming familiar to me. I'm almost certain I've seen it somewhere before, though I'll be damned if I can say where.

Temporal psychosis. Can you define that for me?
QUELLE: Well, I'm certainly no expert on the subject, but temporal psychosis is a disorder of the central nervous system that sometimes results from multiple incidents of time displacement. One of the disorder's most common manifestations is the emergence of persistent memories of events that can be verified as never having occurred.

DULMER: There's a couple of major problems with that diagnosis, Quelle. For one, it doesn't square with my complete lack of sensory aphasia symptoms, which nearly always accompany temporal psychosis. And for another, it doesn't take into account the fact that there's no way to tell the difference between events that never occurred and events that *did* occur, but were subsequently canceled out of the timeline because of the corrective action of a time traveler. The best temp-ops always cover their tracks.

QUELLE: Only not quite completely enough to erase the memories of everyone involved.

DULMER: Exactly.

QUELLE: As convenient as that may be for you, Mister Dulmer, I suppose I have to grant you that. After all, you're absolutely right about the fact that I can't prove that some temporal incursion didn't erase all the events you claim to remember. On the other hand, I can't prove that you're not at this moment sitting beside an invisible two-meter-tall white rabbit cloaked in a tricorder-proof force field.

DULMER: I know. I know. The fact that everything neatly cancels out is all part of the delusion. Or so Doctor Wykoff keeps telling me.

I take a few moments to study Dulmer carefully. He seems anything but crazy. In fact, he seems preternaturally calm, almost priestly. I wonder if he's had to go out of his way to cultivate that quality as part of whatever therapy regime he's undergoing here—wherever "here" is. What's more, his words resonate with me, evoking ghost images of my future—including my eventual death as an old, old man—that I've somehow retained in bits and pieces, like the fragments of half-remembered dreams.

Or are these images really something more substantial than that?

Mister Dulmer, are you talking about events that were "canceled out" because of actions that you took—you, personally—as a time traveler?
DULMER: Yes. Actions that I—that a lot of us—*had* to take, in order to correct the horrendous damage the Undine had done to humanity's history.

So you weren't working alone when you took these . . . actions.
DULMER: Sometimes I was on my own. At other times I had Lucsly or other agents working closely with me, depending on the specific circumstances, personnel deployment situations, and the degree of danger the timeline might be facing from a particular Undine incursion.

When some sort of temporal crisis occurs, how do you assess the degree of danger to the timeline?
LUCSLY: It's not an easy thing to measure, even for a trained professional.

DULMER: There's an element of instinct involved, in addition to all the empirical measures.

Is "fixing" broken timelines a big part of a typical DTI agent's training?
LUCSLY: Let's just say that DTI field agents never know when they might have to perform "surgery" on the time stream—without having any assurance in advance how it's all going to turn out.

DULMER: Even if the circumstances of the "surgery" might prevent the agent from remembering anything about whatever temporal crisis he had to fix.

It all sounds really risky. How do you know when it's appropriate to do something like that?
LUCSLY: It's all about weighing causes and consequences, Mister Sisko. Making a prospective appraisal of not just the repercussions that will emanate from actions you may be about to take, but also whatever consequences might flow from your *in*action. That's a complicated process, because the "timeline" isn't really a line at all. It's actually more like a bush. A network of branching and twisting consequences that has a nearly infinite capacity to confuse.

QUELLE: I've always preferred to think of the timeline as more of a tapestry. Pull on one thread, and others beside it can become unraveled. If you pull too hard on too many threads, the entire weave could begin to collapse.

LUCSLY: Unless you take a needle and thread to it on occasion, and make some rough-and-dirty repairs when it becomes necessary.

DULMER: Sometimes the scalpel has to come first. And *then* the needle and thread.

So it really *is* time surgery, in an almost literal sense. But isn't cutting and sewing the timeline nearly as risky a business as letting it try to heal itself?
DULMER: There are some who say it's unnecessary to try to intervene to preserve the timeline. They say that no temporal incursion can ever really erase any of us from history, because all a time traveler can ever really do—even a malevolent time traveler—is add a new "track" to reality, running parallel to our own. And forever inaccessible to us.

LUCSLY: Everett's gamble. The "many worlds" hypothesis.*

Several decades ago, the crew of the *Enterprise* briefly came into contact with thousands of their counterparts from parallel universes. Doesn't that

---

* Hugh Everett III (1930–1982) was the physicist who pioneered the "many worlds interpretation" of quantum mechanics—the view that all conceivable chance events, even mutually exclusive ones, will occur in other, otherwise identical parallel universes. His views remain controversial today, despite the documented existence of both alternate quantum universes and the time displacement events that might serve to create them.

pretty much prove the "many worlds" idea and render the DTI unnecessary?

DULMER: It's hard to argue with Everett when you have several of his "many worlds" living right inside your head with you, keeping you company all the time. If Everett were still alive, I imagine the DTI would have sent him here to study me.

LUCSLY: I don't know about that. But I *do* know that there's no hard proof that any of those parallel universes the *Enterprise* discovered bore any relationship to time travel or its consequences. Time carries with it a lot of unknowns. The only thing that the DTI knew to an operational certainty was that we could never afford to sit back and do nothing when somebody altered the timeline, either deliberately or by accident.

Did our fixes pose some risks of their own? Sure they did. That's why DTI agents receive as much training as they do. You might not realize this, Mister Sisko, but both Agent Dulmer and myself hold advanced degrees in probability-matrix calculus and psychohistory. We've both been through extensive field training, including multiple passages through the time portal at **[CONTENT REDACTED BY STARFLEET INTELLIGENCE]**. So when circumstances forced one or the other of us to perform a "temporal surgery," the risks were roughly comparable to when a competent surgeon performs a procedure on a patient.

But patients have been known to die during surgery from time to time—so to speak.
LUCSLY: Since the universe is still here, I'd have to characterize our "surgeries" as one hundred percent successful. Or at least close enough to one hundred percent so that the difference isn't worth mentioning.

DULMER: No comment.

Agent Lucsly's point appears to be a valid one, Agent Dulmer. We wouldn't be having this conversation if the patient had died on the table, as it were.
DULMER: True. But there's a big difference between "one hundred percent successful" and "close enough for DTI work." Even after an imperfect-but-good-enough battlefield surgery, a patient might live on for the remainder of a normal lifespan. But he might also have to hide a nasty scar or two, or learn to live with a permanent limp.

I'm not sure I understand.
DULMER: How should I put it? Whenever history undergoes a major repair—or sometimes even a minor one—there's always the potential for leaving behind a little continuity glitch of some sort.

"Continuity glitch"?
LUCSLY: Sorry, Mister Sisko. It's DTI field jargon. A continuity glitch is a small anachronism. Some

minor detail in the fabric of history that doesn't really belong where it is, but also doesn't quite rise to the level of requiring additional corrective temporal action. Like the official picture of Gabriel Bell, taken in the twenty-first century.

Gabriel Bell. The antipoverty activist after whom the Bell Riots of 2024 were named.
LUCSLY: The same. Back in the year 2024, Bell's official identification photograph somehow got replaced with an image of your father.

Yeah, I've seen it. Weird.
LUCSLY: Very. After the DTI discovered this small anachronism, we officially classified it as only a continuity glitch associated with an accidental temporal displacement experienced by your father and several members of his crew. It posed no real danger. Therefore we didn't have to take any further action in dealing with it.

Because taking action might have made a small-to-negligible "glitch" into a much bigger one. And would have risked pulling more threads than you'd intended from the weave of the "time tapestry," to borrow Mister Quelle's metaphor.
DULMER: Exactly.

QUELLE: Since you're borrowing one of my metaphors, I hope you don't mind me embroidering it a bit.

Please go right ahead, Mister Quelle.

QUELLE: Thank you. Imagine you've accidentally started a small fire in the living room of your home. After you put the fire out, you discover that your replicators are down, so you can't use them to simply replace the carpeting. So you might have to make do with a little emergency stitching and some throw rugs to cover up the worst of the damage.

DULMER: And to hide the *really* bad scars in the carpet, you might even have to rearrange the furniture a bit.

So you're saying that the DTI's repair work may have left some fairly big scars and rips hidden under the universe's sofa?

LUCSLY: I suppose that's been common knowledge ever since Friedman[*] wrote up his visit to the time portal at **[CONTENT REDACTED BY STARFLEET INTELLIGENCE].** The DTI has always done its best to keep all temporal inconsistencies and discontinuities to a minimum. But no matter how carefully the DTI conducts its business, this sort of thing is still bound to come up occasionally.

DULMER: Some of the temporal discontinuities we're talking about can even take the form of spatial

---

[*] Friedman, Michael Jan. *New Worlds, New Civilizations.* New York: Federation News Service and Simon & Schuster, stardate 52954 (2375).

phenomena. Like the eruption of anti-time particles that appeared about forty years ago in the Devron system. Or that Borg temporal anomaly that turned out to be instrumental in saving Vega from an all-out invasion by the collective. Others can center around certain people, who can become the focal point of temporal forces. Something like that happened to Jean-Luc Picard, during the very same Devron incident I just mentioned.

Dulmer's mention of people becoming temporal focal points makes me wonder if something like that might not have happened to him as well. Because unless the universe has transformed him into some sort of temporal lightning rod, a nexus at which multiple timestreams intersect, he's just a burned-out wretch caught in the grip of a time-travel-generated psychosis. I'd much rather believe the former to be true than the latter, and the sad, pleading look on Lucsly's face makes it obvious to me that he feels the same way.

LUCSLY: Wolf, I don't remember any "anti-time eruption" ever happening in the Devron system. Or anywhere else, for that matter.

DULMER: Then I suppose we can chalk it up to yet another continuity glitch. Or maybe an even *larger* temporal discontinuity, like the alternate Gorn timeline I can remember, the one that started back in 'eighty-one. That was when Captain Riker and *Titan*'s crew gathered the Federation's first detailed intel about the Gorn civilization's nonwarrior castes.

The technological and religious castes. I thought the Federation hadn't discovered those until years later, when the Cestus Accords between the Gorn Hegemony and the Klingon Empire were being settled.

Dulmer's lips tighten into a bitter, humorless smile that does nothing to relieve the haunted look I see in his eyes.

So does everybody else, Mister Sisko. But that's the nature of self-canceling temporal discontinuities— at least when they don't quite cancel themselves out completely. After all, it's not as though the DTI hasn't encountered and identified things like that before. Some very large TDs popped up when the Undine tried to reach back into humanity's past. When they made their first preemptive attempt to exterminate us.

LUCSLY: Only it doesn't count as a temporal discontinuity if nobody can remember it.

DULMER: Or even if *almost* nobody remembers it, evidently.

Mister Dulmer, doesn't this memory discrepancy itself—that is, your ability to recall events that your former partner can't—constitute a pretty significant continuity glitch in its own right?

Dulmer aims an accusing stare at Lucsly.

DULMER: It would, I suppose. Unless you've chosen to misclassify it as a sign of temporal psychosis.

Mister Quelle, *has* Mister Dulmer been misclassified in your opinion? Or misdiagnosed?
QUELLE: It's not my place to say, Mister Sisko. I'm not a doctor. When it comes to temporal disorders, I'm strictly an amateur.

Do you have any proof, Mister Dulmer, that any of your disputed memories are—or were—real?
DULMER: Proof? Other than the sworn affidavits of three Vulcan mind-meld specialists, four Betazoid telepaths, and a Ullian memory engram expert? Not a shred.

I'm appalled by this revelation, and I can tell from Lucsly's defensive body language that I haven't done a very good job of concealing my reaction.

Is that true, Mister Lucsly? Mister Quelle?
LUCSLY: It's true. But as much as I personally might want to believe Wolf, I have to be objective about this.

QUELLE: I'd like to think that Mister Dulmer's alleged "canceled-out experiences" constitute something other than an unusually self-consistent delusion. But I'm only a caregiver, not a psychiatrist. I'm afraid I simply don't have the credentials to circle this particular square.

DULMER: Mister Sisko, in all fairness to Adam and Quelle, the only thing those telepaths really proved to the DTI was that I'm sincere—that I believe in the contents of my own . . . orphan memories.

LUCSLY: But they couldn't vouch for the veracity of the memories themselves, since the timelines that would have produced them don't appear to exist.

DULMER: At least not anymore.

QUELLE: If you don't mind my saying it, Mister Dulmer, that's a far too binary way of looking at the world. Existence or nonexistence. One or zero. On or off.

LUCSLY: Didn't you just get done explaining that you have to believe that my old friend's memories are just self-constructed delusions? Or have you finally decided that he's really *not* delusional after all?

QUELLE: I was merely trying to explain Doctor Wykoff's diagnosis. Like I said, I'm not qualified to have an opinion on the matter. I'm just a therapy provider.

LUCSLY: And a part-time philosopher, too, apparently. Look, Quelle, things either exist or they don't. What other way is there to look at the world?

Quelle regards Lucsly for a long, silent moment. A look of sadness crosses the orderly's face, and I'm now more certain than ever that I've seen him before. But where? And when?

QUELLE: There may be an infinitude of other ways, Mister Lucsly. Unfortunately, most humans—and most humanoids, for that matter—aren't evolved enough to grasp that one simple truth about the cosmos.

DULMER: You're right, Quelle. What I should have said was that the timelines that produced my orphan memories aren't accessible from *this* timeline, at least not directly. Regardless, a lot of what's in here in my head—the dead-end memories I've been trying for years to integrate with what all the psych specialists call "timeline prime"—is what the DTI would classify as "counterfactual."

Meaning "contrary to fact." Will you share some of your "counterfactual" memories with us?
DULMER: Where should I start? There are so many

small details, little things. There was a boy named Noah Powell, whose mother served as the first head nurse in the *Starship Titan*'s sickbay. Only Noah was also a girl named Suzi.

Couldn't that just be some record-keeper's clerical error? It hardly sounds like a sign that the universe is in any danger of unraveling.

DULMER: All right. Let's look at the bigger picture, then. Let's see, I have a vivid recollection of the Borg completely devastating Deneva and Risa around twenty-five years ago. The Borg sent about seven thousand cubes into the heart of Federation space. They wanted to wipe out the human species, and they set about the task with an efficiency that would have terrified even the Undine. They did a lot of collateral damage as well, with their attacks on Qo'noS, Andor, and even Vulcan, before Starfleet finally put them down, somehow. Chancellor Martok's son Drex sacrificed his life to try to stop the assault, but the collective just rolled right over his fleet. And they destroyed Pluto on their way to their big assault against Earth itself.

Starfleet lost a lot of good people during the Big Borg War. Admiral Janeway was one of the earliest casualties. They got Admiral Paris a little later. And thousands of other Starfleet officers. There's one thing I can't quite figure out, though: how the Borg managed to attack Vulcan over a century after the planet had already been blown to smithereens. . . .

Lucsly listens resignedly until his old partner trails off into anguished silence. He's obviously heard it all before. I say nothing as the older man speaks, since the act of putting his recollections into words appears to be making Dulmer uncharacteristically emotional, sending a single tear running down his craggy cheek until he wipes it away with his palm. I don't want to risk upsetting him further by mentioning my complete unfamiliarity with any of the events he just recounted.

But facts are facts. As far as I know, Pluto is still right where it's been for umpteen billion years, and neither Risa nor Deneva have ever suffered a Borg attack of any kind, much less the global devastation that haunts Dulmer's memories. And I'm sure that Dulmer's obituaries for Admiral Kathryn Janeway, Admiral Owen Paris, and Captain Drex would come as complete surprises to their subjects, all of whom are still very much alive as far as I know.

DULMER: I'm okay. I think it actually gets a little easier every time I run through the worst of the memories. Especially the really inconsistent ones, like Vulcan.

QUELLE: Maybe it's all finally starting to integrate, the way Doctor Wykoff hoped it would one day.

Since Dulmer no longer seems to be teetering on the edge of an emotional meltdown, I decide to press on. I really want to believe that he isn't crazy, and I want to give him the chance to prove it, if not to his caregiver's satisfaction, then to that of history.

Given the possibility that a time traveler might succeed in bringing about some of the very "counterfactual" catastrophes you just mentioned, why is the DTI so adamant in insisting that you must be suffering from temporal psychosis? Why won't they concede the possibility that you're actually learning to cope with memories of real but aborted timelines?

DULMER: I've wondered about that myself for years, and I think I finally have an answer. Their attitude is perfectly understandable, if you stop and think about it. If I'm really crazy or delusional, then the DTI isn't obligated to follow up on what's in my head. That means they don't have to face the possibility that the Undine aren't finished trying to snuff out the human race using temporal means. And neither does Starfleet, or the Federation Council, or the Dragon [UFP President Aennik Okeg] in the Palais.*

Or the half trillion Federation citizens who aren't eager to go to war again any time soon, whether it's against the Undine or anyone else.

DULMER: Eager or not, they'll have to deal with it eventually. The universe isn't some holodeck designed to tailor reality until it's more to your liking. It doesn't have safety protocols to protect you from

---

* This description of the Federation's chief executive as "the dragon in the Palais" is an unfortunate anti-Saurian ethnic slur that originated during Aennik Okeg's first successful campaign for the UFP presidency. Unfortunately, the sobriquet is still used by some of President Okeg's detractors even today.

your own recklessness. And it absolutely won't let you get away with arbitrarily deciding which parts of it are real and which parts aren't.

But how do you tell the difference between the real and the unreal—especially in circumstances like yours?

Quelle approaches Dulmer, who checks his wrist chronometer to confirm that the time allotted for this interview has more than fully elapsed. Dulmer acknowledges this with a nod, rises, and moves toward the door with the orderly. Then Dulmer pauses on the threshold and faces me and Lucsly.

DULMER: It took me years to realize it, Mister Sisko, but it's actually pretty simple: the things that can kill you if you ignore them are the things that are real. Anything else is a phantom.

With that, Dulmer disappears through the door. Quelle lingers on the threshold and faces the table for a moment before following his charge into the adjacent chamber.

QUELLE: Of course, even the phantoms can be more real than you might think.

It's only after I'm once again alone with Lucsly in the reception room that I realize where I've seen the orderly's face before. Some of the images I recall now are about forty years old, drawn from the declassified portions of Jean-Luc Picard's logs. My mind's eye sees the enigmatic creature whose species had once considered excising humanity from the universe just as the Undine would later on. These beings had decided instead to stay their hand, but only after a starship captain demonstrated the human ability to think beyond the prosaic limitations of everyday reality.

Suddenly it becomes crystal clear to me why a man like Dulmer—a man who stands astride multiple realities—has become such an object of fascination for a man like Quelle.

Or rather, for a multidimensional superbeing like Q.

The Undine War

LIFE AND DEATH . . .
. . . AND LIFE

To: T'Vanik of Vulcan, Secretary General of the
Federation Security Council
From: Otera Tul, President of Trillius Prime
[Trill]

. . . The Trill government categorically denies the
spurious rumors that have circulated lately alleg-
ing security breaches in the caverns of Mak'ala.
Absolutely no such security breaches have occurred. Because Mak'ala nurtures a habitat that
is critical to the survival of our symbiont population—and by extension Trill civilization as we
have come to know it—it is one of the most carefully guarded regions in the entire Trillius system.
It is inconceivable that Mak'ala could be used by
the Undine, as the rumors allege, as a staging post
for new military incursions from fluidic space, or
as a beachhead for clandestine acts of impersonation and infiltration. . . . The Security Council's
offer of Starfleet troops, facilities, and equipment
to preempt such developments is, of course, ap-
preciated, but wholly unnecessary. Therefore
the offer has been officially declined by the Trill

---

[*] September 8, 2406.

government. . . . Mak'ala's symbiont pools are ecologically fragile places, and the presence of large numbers of outsiders would pose a significant threat to the ongoing health and well-being of our symbiont population, which has already been badly stressed by other matters during recent decades. . . .

JAKE SISKO, DATA ROD # L-52

Cochrane Institute, New Samarkand,
Alpha Centauri III

The former chief engineer of two successive Starfleet flagships, Captain Geordi La Forge has a surprisingly easygoing manner for someone about to receive his first command, the Galaxy-*class Starship* Challenger. *The man exudes an energy and enthusiasm that peel several decades from his true age. I feel an immediate bond with him, which makes perfect sense since we're both Starfleet brats. Like La Forge, my father was a Starfleet officer (as was his mother), and both of our mothers died aboard starships.*

La Forge's expansive office at the Cochrane Institute's Starship Design Lab suggests an almost art-gallery-like sense of order and aesthetics, despite being filled with images of starships real and imagined, ranging from flat images on padds and wall screens and paintings to holographic miniatures to three-dimensional, hand-built models.

Although the ocular implants that compensate for Captain La Forge's congenital blindness are all but indistinguishable from natural, fully organic eyes, the windows to his soul hint at mysterious sights that those of us possessed of ordinary vision can scarcely imagine—and perfectly normal things as well. For example, in the center of his desk are several small framed holophotos of hearth and home, among which are images of La Forge standing in a lush garden beside a smiling young woman; three children at play; and several shots, both candid and posed, of adolescents and young adults that I assume to be later images of those very same children.

We exchange greetings and handshakes and take seats on opposite sides of Captain La Forge's photograph-festooned desk. He seems very open and eager to talk.

Just as we're about to begin the interview in earnest, he catches me staring at his family photos.

That one's my first wife, Leah. Just to the right of it are some shots of our kids, Alandra, Bret, and Sidney.

And that one, at the top, is Mikaela, who's about to become my chief engineer aboard the *Challenger*. And the next Mrs. La Forge.

Congratulations, and on more than just the captaincy. It's obvious from your photo gallery that family is at least as important to you as Starfleet is.
I'm Starfleet on both sides of the family, and my parents moved me around a lot when I was a kid. Since we're talking about the Long War, it's probably worth mentioning that the pictures remind me of what we

were fighting for, back in the day. Whether the enemy was the Borg, the Dominion, or the Undine.

How many times did you encounter the Undine during the hot part of the conflict?
Not as many times as you might think, what with the Federation News Service trying to turn us all into superheroes. Contrary to popular belief, neither of the *Enterprise*s that I served on were always right there in the thick of things. The Undine War was a really wide conflict that covered a lot of ground, and it would have been incredibly coincidental for us to have been in every major battle, or even most of them. That kind of thing might happen in fictional holonovel scenarios like *Battlecruiser Vengeance,* but not in real life.

But surely you can't mean to minimize your contribution to driving the Undine back into fluidic space. According to Starfleet's official public reports, you—you, personally—were instrumental in keeping the Federation's alliance with the Klingon Empire from falling apart at a critical juncture.
I suppose you can give me credit for knowing which buttons to press when the time came to execute the plan. But I wasn't the one who did the really hard work. There was no way I *could* have. It was Data who made all the real-time calculations that had to be performed in order to seal the portal to fluidic space at the proper time.

But you were one of the few who were prescient enough to foresee the possibility of emergencies that only Data might be able to cope with.

Believe me, I'd be more than happy to have been wrong about that. Being right on that sort of thing is more of a curse than a blessing. Just ask Cassandra.

Point taken. But surely Data couldn't *really* have been your only hope—especially since he'd already been dead for several years by the time the fluidic-space rift affair began. At that point, the *Enterprise*-E had just undergone an extensive series of refits. Why wasn't her revamped main computer up to handling the crisis?

Actually, the fluidic-space rift started to turn critical—not to mention the Federation-Klingon diplomatic crisis that was looming at the time—before the refit was completely finished. The *Enterprise* had to leave Utopia Planitia months before she was really ready. That probably had a lot to do with why the main computer wasn't up to speed on crunching the necessary numbers in real time.

Setting aside your personal modesty for the moment, Starfleet Command decided that you were indispensable for the duration of the emergency. Didn't they pull you out of this very office by invoking the reserve activation clause from your commission?

Actually, I was in a slightly smaller office at the end of the hall at the time. All they had to do was ask, though I wasn't sure going into it what I could really do about the crisis. Again, that's one of the problems with the media turning you into a superhero. As one of my predecessors who served aboard an earlier *Enterprise* once taught me, engineers should do whatever they can to keep their COs' expectations realistic. And since I had no way to predict the outcome of the emergency, I was relieved to have Data as an ace in the hole.

If I recall correctly, Data was supervising the refit of the *Enterprise*-E at the time—his first Starfleet assignment after his "return from the dead."
Not only did he supervise the finish of the refit—including the extensive repairs that had to be done following the fluidic-space rift crisis—but Starfleet also officially put him in the captain's chair just before the *Enterprise* left spacedock again.

Regarding the so-called rift crisis itself: just how serious a threat was it?
What we had to contend with was an interdimensional rift that was already the size of a small moon and expanding visibly by the hour. Without Data's help, we probably not only would have failed to seal it, but could easily have ripped it into a light-years-long spatial gash capable of flooding an entire sector of Klingon territory with the gunk that fills fluidic space—an "ocean" that only Undine ships can navigate safely. If that had happened, the Klingons would

almost certainly have blamed us, and we would have had *two* bloodthirsty enemies to contend with for the price of one. So if anybody ought to be singled out for praise, it's Data, not me.

Wasn't this Captain Data's first significant crisis since his . . . resurrection?
I think so. At least it was the first time I saw Data since immediately after he . . . came back to us.

You haven't talked much about this before, but I gather that you were on the scene when Data's "resurrection" occurred.

La Forge suddenly begins to look uncharacteristically uncomfortable. I suppress a shudder as I notice the tiny biomechanical components embedded in his pupils rotating almost a full clockwise turn and back again as he studies me, apparently considering how best to an-swer my question. Knowing that Captain La Forge's ocular implants are merely stirring up my own unresolved Borg anxieties does nothing to put me at ease. I force aside my thoughts of the Borg, the killers of my mother, but it does little good; the biomechanical louvers obscuring the windows to Captain La Forge's soul merely conjure a decades-old image of my old friend Nog, whose Dominion War service earned him a biosynthetic leg. As I await La Forge's answer, I marvel briefly that I have somehow managed to retain all my own original equipment after the passage of so much time and danger.

I was spending some time on Omicron Theta helping out the Soong Foundation's researchers at the time of Data's . . . recovery. The team hit a serious snag on a . . . project they were working on.

Captain Maddox told me that the Daystrom Institute's Soong Foundation team was working with the early prototype Soong-type android known as B-4. They were trying to unlock the so-called Data matrix—the suite of files that Data had copied from his own positronic brain onto B-4's.

At the time I was already skeptical about whether what they were calling the "Data matrix" even still existed.

Why? I can remember more than one occasion when my own father returned from what looked like irretrievable doom.

And I can say the same thing about Data. But luck isn't an inexhaustible resource. Once your luck runs out, it's all over. And hope can start looking a lot like denial.

But I would have thought that your having access to so many of the Soong Foundation's cybernetics experts would have given you very real hopes of recovering Data. Especially since that's the way things eventually worked out.

Engineers are conservative creatures by nature. We wear belts and suspenders both, just in case. And the disappearance of my mother and her ship taught me some very hard lessons about being conservative about hope. Hope is a fine thing, and it's a worthy motivator. But wishful thinking can be an engineer's worst enemy. It can even get people killed.

But a man's reach should exceed his grasp—
"Or else what's a heaven for?" Don't look so shocked. Engineers sometimes read things other than technical papers.

Now, I don't want you to get the wrong idea. I never really entirely lost hope that Data might return. At least not completely. Data was my best friend for fifteen years, so I *always* held out at least *some* hope. Look, nobody could have served aboard the *Enterprise* on as many exploration missions as I did without being basically hopeful by nature.

But I also knew the difference between hope and delusion. I knew that I would have given anything to bring Data back, and I suppose I distrusted my own motivations because of that. I knew I would have died in his place if I'd been given the choice. Hell, there were times when I wished I had. After all, Data was supposed to outlive all of us. It's one of the universe's nasty little ironies. . . . But all hoping aside, I still had an engineer's duty to face the world as it was, rather than how I might have preferred it to be. After all, it had been almost *six years* since Data had been vaporized in the Battle at the Bassen Rift. . . .

But as it turned out, the Data matrix was still lurking somewhere in B-4's positronic brain, otherwise Data never could have been restored. Hope, rather than delusion, won out in the end.

I hope you're right about that. I really do.

I don't understand. Wasn't Data's return a good thing?

Of course it was. The problem is that none of us ever stopped to consider the ethical ramifications of bringing Data back. But we understood the expectations of Starfleet and the Federation Council well enough, so we just bulled ahead without really thinking anything through—and more often than not ended up with egg on our faces for our trouble.

Can you describe what you were doing—preferably using layman's language?

Of course. I've spent years learning how to translate engineerspeak into something understandable by senior command officers.

Right after Data died, I did essentially the same thing the Daystrom people would keep trying for years, without any success—I used all of Data's files in the hopes that B-4's head would suddenly contain Data's mind. But the files would always just lie there like so many old tech manuals. You see, Data's personality and intellect weren't simply the sum total of a pile of disassembled parts. They were emergent properties that arose jointly from the information in his systems and the cybernetic material substrate of his consciousness, as well as who knows how many other immeasurable, irreproducible quantum-mechanical effects.

In other words, you failed to track down Data's soul.
I'm an engineer, not a philosopher. All I can say is that whatever "spark" made Data a unique individual appeared to have been snuffed out and wasn't showing any signs of coming back—at least not in response to any of the techniques I'd been applying up to that point, while B-4 was still living aboard the *Enterprise*.

Then the Soong people took custody of B-4, and they worked with him for nearly a solid year before Captain Maddox finally made the breakthrough that made Data's return even remotely possible. That was right before Maddox left the Soong team to return to his old job at the Daystrom Institute.

Maddox was also one of Data's old friends. It seems strange that he would choose to leave the "Data's resurrection" project just as it was about to bear fruit.
That's what I thought at the time, when the Soong team asked me to come aboard and help them apply the discoveries Maddox had made just before his departure. I suppose I was allowing my lingering hope of recovering Data to keep me from thinking too critically about what we were doing. I was trying to keep my focus on the practical application of Maddox's theory.

Can you walk me through some of Maddox's main ideas?

Sure. Maddox thought that [Data's creator] Doctor [Noonien] Soong must have embedded a special command string among Data's files for the express purpose of allowing him to "back up" his personality onto a second positronic brain, where it would run just as the original had. Maddox believed that this command string existed, but had somehow gotten fragmented during the process of being uploaded into B-4 because of all the damage that Data's emotion chip had sustained during the last several years before his death. Fortunately, Data had left his emotion chip behind aboard the *Enterprise,* which allowed the research team to take custody of the chip along with B-4.

So after a false start or two, we confirmed that Maddox was right—there really *was* an accessible Data matrix. Once we succeeded in repairing Data's emotion chip and used it in tandem with the complementary heuristic pathways from which B-4's brain ran its ethical subroutines, we discovered that we really did know how to unlock Data's personality matrix.

Which means that we'd discovered that we had the means to bring back Data whenever we wanted to.

When I tried to get Captain Maddox to speak to me about the particulars of Data's return, he referred

me to you. But you don't seem any more comfortable discussing this topic than he did. If you'd prefer, we could move on to some subject more directly related to the Undine War, like—

No. I think this is a story that needs to be told. Because if the story had turned out differently, Data wouldn't have been available to us when we needed him most. And Federation historians would be talking about something called the Undine-Klingon War now—if anybody in the Federation was even still in the business of writing histories, that is. So Data was a key player in the war that was actually fought. The story of how that happened deserves to be preserved for posterity.

So let's set it up: You went to Omicron Theta, Data's birthplace, to join the Soong Foundation research team to replace Captain Maddox and carry on with the work he started but didn't finish. Then you discovered you could restore Data to life within B-4's body any time you wanted to. What happened next?

At first, a whole lot of nothing happened, even with Maddox's new holographic-heuristic positronic initialization protocols in place. The team started celebrating when B-4 suddenly started singing an old Irving Berlin song. "Blue Skies." It was one of Data's favorites; he sang it at Will Riker and Deanna Troi's wedding.

Was this one of those early "false starts" you mentioned?

It was, but I think I might have been the only one to recognize it for what it was at the time because I'd seen the exact same thing happen before. A short time after Data's death, B-4 started singing the very same song he sang that day for the Soong team—"Blue Skies." All it proved was that he knew how to access some of the files Data had uploaded to him. But he was still accessing those files as B-4, not as Data.

It was beginning to look like we had another failure on our hands—until Stardate 62762.91.* I'll never forget it. That was the day we finally discovered how to unlock the "Data matrix." It was also the day that Data spoke to me—for the first time in nearly six years.

And it was also the day I finally understood why Maddox had decided that he couldn't go on with the project, even though Starfleet and the Federation Council had placed such a high priority on Data's return.

Because you finally realized that Data's return could only come at B-4's expense?
None of us had really paused to consider that, even for a moment. We were all just too caught up in all the endless minutiae of this incredibly complex, challenging task that had been laid in front of us.

---

* That's October 6, 2385, 19:05:29 GMT, on the Gregorian calendar.

But you got to know B-4 in the process. You started relating to him as a person, the way Maddox did.

I wondered for years afterward why that process didn't start right after Data's death in the Bassen Rift. Back when I was spending a lot of time working with B-4 aboard the *Enterprise*.

Have you come to any conclusions about why that might be?

I suppose I didn't want to think of B-4 as a person back then, because looking at him just slapped me across the face with the fact that Data was gone, probably forever. And the more time that passed without B-4 demonstrating any possibility that Data might return through him, the harder it became to even look at him. Which is why the main emotion I can remember experiencing after B-4 transferred over to the Daystrom Institute was relief.

But what failed to happen aboard the *Enterprise* finally came to pass—and on Data's "birthworld" of Omicron Theta, appropriately enough. So what can you tell me about what happened next?

I could hardly believe it at first. Data was back! It was still B-4 speaking, of course—his basic vocal apparatus was identical to Data's, after all—but his voice suddenly carried authority and experience, without any of the tentativeness that I'd gotten accustomed to hearing whenever B-4 spoke. I could hear Data's intellect in that voice. I could see Data's presence in

B-4's eyes, even though they were the same eyes that B-4 had always had, standard equipment for Soong-type androids. It all happened in the space of a few heartbeats, right after we activated the revised Data matrix protocols.

You knew that quickly that Data had returned?
There was no mistaking it. It was a pretty extreme contrast, even though Data and B-4 were virtually identical at the hardware level in many respects. But B-4 wasn't exactly—I guess there's no kind way to say this—he wasn't the most finely calibrated hydrospanner in the toolbox. He never came any-where near to exhibiting any of Data's potentials, despite having been made in the same mold, so to speak. So the moment Data came back to us, I knew it.

But that's obviously not the end of this story.
No. In fact, it was the beginning of another one. Data—B-4—stood up from the chair he'd always sit in whenever any of us were actively working on his isolinear circuitry, or his cybernetic subroutines. Then he turned in a slow circle, his eyes searching the faces of each member of the research team who was present at the time.

Then he saw me, called my name, and asked me where he was. I told him that we were on Omicron Theta, and asked him to tell me the last thing he remembered.

Did he have any recollection of what happened aboard Shinzon's flagship?

He remembered the *Scimitar*, of course. Only he didn't recall being vaporized along with the ship after sending Captain Picard back to the *Enterprise*.

Of course. He'd copied his files onto B-4's positronic brain before that happened. I suppose the last thing he remembered was plugging his system into B-4's.

That's just about right. Which was why his knowledge of his own death came to him second-hand, in the form of a personnel file that B-4 had left open in Data's memory buffer.

B-4 must have wanted to bring his . . . brother up to speed on current events.

Apparently so.

Most people would react pretty emotionally after getting news about their own death and resurrection. How did Data take it?

His reaction was a lot stronger than I expected, though looking back I'm not sure why I was surprised.

I know that Data's—I mean B-4's—emotion chip wasn't installed. Data had left the chip aboard the *Enterprise* before the last time he'd left the ship, and I had brought it with me as part of my engineering toolkit. Without that chip, his range of human emotions should have been pretty limited, at least beyond the ethical core Doctor Soong had given him—that part of him that always tried to behave decently and constantly struggled to be more human. But chip or no chip, I saw *suspicion* beginning to dawn in those yellow eyes.

Thanks to the Soong Foundation's extensive tricorder records of the events in question, Captain La Forge is able to provide a nearly verbatim account of much of what occurred next:

"All the information available to me indicates that a span of five years, eleven months, two days, three hours, thirteen minutes, and twenty-one seconds have passed since my final experiences aboard the *Scimitar*," Data said. "Since it is unlikely that you discovered a means of beaming me to safety—let alone a method that required such a lengthy interval to complete—I must conclude that you have employed other means."

I could only nod. It was difficult to know how he might react to the truth, even without his emotion chip. As I said, Data was an inherently ethical being. If he weren't, then why would he have cared so intensely about the human race and want to be a part of it?

"That's right, Data," I said finally. "Your original body was . . . vaporized when the *Scimitar* exploded."

"Ah," he said. He had ceased studying my face, or any of my colleagues' faces. Instead, he was taking a good, close look at the fingers of his left hand, as though he'd never seen them up close before. In a way, he hadn't. "You somehow . . . restored me to existence from the backup files I uploaded into my brother, B-4."

"It's good to have you back, Data," I told him.

Data's fingers moved in a high-speed blur as he tested his dexterity for a few moments before he stopped and looked at me with an almost glum expression. "It *would* be good to be back, Geordi. It is unfortunate that I cannot remain among you. My ethical subroutines prohibit my preserving my existence at the direct expense of another's."

I told Data that I didn't understand. After all, why had he bothered to upload all of his files into B-4's positronic neural network if not as a means of "backing himself up"? I challenged him on this, but he turned my objections aside. He said he had never intended to displace anyone else from existence, and that the Laws of Robotics applied to his dealings with other synthetic life-forms as much as they did to his interactions with organic persons.

I find that surprising. Not that Data would put another's life ahead of his own—he'd already proved conclusively that he was willing and able to do that—but because he couldn't exactly claim to have been a pacifist. During his fifteen years as the *Enterprise*'s second officer, he'd been in combat situations any number of times.

I raised the very same point, but Data brushed it aside. "My actions on those occasions were intended to prevent death or injury to the people around me," he said.

But I wasn't satisfied with that. "What about the way you handled Lore?"

"Lore posed a grave danger, Geordi," Data said. "His influence nearly caused me to take your life."

"That's true enough, Data. But how big a danger was Lore after he was deactivated? Was he still so dangerous after he was unconscious that you and I had to tear him down to his basic components?"

Something that probably should have been beyond his emotional scope moved across his face while he was thinking that one through. I could tell he was bothered by his own inconsistency.

Then he looked me in the eye. With a sad half-smile he shouldn't have been able to make, he said, "To quote the human poet Walt Whitman, 'Do I contradict myself? Very well, then I contradict myself. I am large, I contain multitudes.'" He tapped himself on the temple as he spoke, and I suddenly realized what he was talking about.

"I contain multitudes." The personal logs of all the Omicron Theta colonists who died because Lore had lured the crystalline entity there to destroy them.

Yes. I suppose it was his way of emphasizing what he was going to say next: "My elder brother, Lore, was unethical, immoral. A psychiatrist would almost certainly have diagnosed him with numerous psychoses, including borderline personality disorder, narcissistic personality disorder, and sociopathy. A philosopher would probably describe him as a power-hungry solipsist. I believe that Lore was *evil* as well, Geordi. Insane, certainly, but also malevolent. And he posed a terrible danger so long as any chance remained that he might be reactivated.

"But my other sibling is an innocent. I cannot deprive B-4 of life, not even to save my own. If I did, would I not negate everything I have always believed about the rights of synthetic persons? Would I not deny B-4's *own* personhood?

"Would I not be as bad as Lore?"

"Lore did more horrible things than I can count, Data," I said. "And he did them for one reason: because he could. If you really think you're the least little bit like Lore, then ask yourself this: If he were in *your* shoes right now, how much time would he have spent wrestling with *his* conscience?"

"You appear to be arguing my point for me, Geordi," Data said. "If I am to avoid repeating the crimes of my wayward brother, then I must not follow the same impulses that Lore would follow."

"Data, we *need* you," I said. I would have added, *"I need you,"* but I knew this shouldn't be about what I needed—or thought I needed. Besides, we were having this discussion in a room full of our colleagues.

"I am sorry, Geordi," Data said. "But I simply cannot do this. Good-bye, my friend."

Then he sat down again in B-4's chair, ramrod straight. His body remained rigid even as his face went slack, the way B-4's always was.

And a heartbeat later, Data was . . . *gone,* just like that.

And B-4 returned?
In an instant, as though somebody had just thrown a switch. I knew that those yellow eyes were just the same as they had always been. But they were somehow duller, less . . . *present.* Of course, that was just the way I perceived him—the way we *all* perceived him. Everybody tended to underestimate him. I suppose we all treated him as though he were a little kid. We looked out for him, but we always assumed that he didn't have a very good grasp of what was going on around him.

Of course, there was a huge problem with that perception: it simply wasn't true.

Did B-4 understand what had just happened to him?
I guessed at the time that B-4 knew that something unusual was going on, because he immediately asked us how long he had "been away." I told him that only a few minutes had passed, and reminded him about the files we'd uploaded into him from Data. He said that he remembered that. Then I told him that those

files had just become active, somehow allowing Data to "awaken."

That was when B-4 really surprised me. "I know," he said. "Data told me about that when he sent me back to talk to you."

So Data was not only still active inside B-4's positronic brain, he was also able to have an internal conversation with him?
Evidently, although it was news to us at the time. But the situation apparently wasn't going to stay that way for long. According to B-4, Data had just told him that he—Data—was already busy writing a subroutine intended to purge all traces of himself from the neural net that he and B-4 were sharing at the moment.

But why would Data have to do that? They were both living inside the same cortenide-duranium skull. Why couldn't they have just continued doing that indefinitely?
We wondered about that ourselves at the time. As near as we could determine, it was because of the software-firmware-hardware architecture of the Data matrix itself, specifically its synergistic and holographic nature.

What I mean is, in order to complete his "return to the living," Data's neural network had to begin an exponential expansion throughout B-4's positronic substrate. The unfolding of that process would have utterly overwhelmed and wiped out B-4's personality and memory engrams within a matter of hours. So we immediately took the precaution of copying all of B-4's files and memory engrams into the biggest computer buffer we had on hand, the one we used to create holographic design simulations.

But couldn't Data simply have made a conscious effort to set aside enough "head space" to accommodate B-4? After all, B-4 seemed to be much less sophisticated than Data. He shouldn't have taken up nearly as much room as Data needed.

Maybe some of the new heuristic neural nets are able to work that way, but not the Soong-type positronic brain. First, there would have been a serious risk of a psychotic break, possibly leading to an irresolvable multiple personality disorder that easily could have scrambled both B-4 and Data beyond any hope of recovery. Data might have been able to keep his cybernetic finger in the dike for a few hours—maybe even for a day or two, if he had B-4 actively helping him—but it would have been useless in the end. Data's program was—*is*—far more complex than B-4's was, as you say. And because of that very complexity, it simply would have had to spread out and take over the entire positronic substrate it inhabited. Unless, of course, Data took an extraordinary measure to prevent that.

You mean unless Data completely removed his program from B-4's body.

Yes. This stunned the entire team. As for me, all the grief I'd been stuffing down for nearly six years just came erupting straight to the surface. It's pretty hard to describe the disappointment we all felt. We were crushed. After all that work, all those dead ends and blind alleys, we'd finally succeeded. And Data's first act after rising from the cybernetic grave was to try to throw away the new lease on life we'd given him.

Was he really throwing his life away, Captain? Or was he just making another noble sacrifice?
Noble sacrifice. That concept must have run in Data's family—putting his "brother" Lore to one side, of course, along with his "grandpa," Ira Graves. Anyway, I knew I had some time to prevent what Data was trying to do. He needed at least a few minutes to write the subroutine that would remove his matrix from B-4's head. Maybe even an hour or more, so he could craft a deletion program that would be failsafe, erasing every trace of Data while leaving all of B-4's unique files and memory engrams undisturbed.

I know there had to be more to this than Data proverbially slashing his wrists, but did he *really* need that much time to write this sort of program? I thought he was capable of performing, I don't know, trillions of operations per second. Shouldn't he have been able to deactivate himself almost instantly?
Normally, that would be true. But Data was trying to perform an extremely delicate positronic brain-

surgery procedure. He was looking out for B-4's well-being. And the fact that his matrix was still confined to a relatively small portion of B-4's positronic brain was working in our favor. Remember, B-4's cerebral hardware was less sophisticated than that of the original Data's brain, so the Soong team had to compensate for that on the firmware and software level. And there's also the fact that the matrix of Data's consciousness hadn't yet had time to fully spread out and establish permanent control over B-4's brain and body. All of that meant that Data only had access to a fraction of the resources he normally had available to him. Think of him as running in "slow mode."

So I asked B-4 to speak to Data, to try to convince him to continue our conversation. At the very least, I hoped that if I could just keep Data talking, I'd have a shot at convincing him that Starfleet and the Federation really did need him. That the human race that he had always tried to emulate needed him, maybe for its very survival.

Because of the gathering threat posed by the Undine.
It was a valid enough reason, even if it wasn't generally known at the time for reasons of Federation security. Back then, those of us with a high enough clearance to have been briefed about the Undine already knew how dangerous they were. Of course, I would have said anything to convince Data not to . . .

decompile himself. I suppose I should be embarrassed to admit that, but I'm not.

So my next step was to gather every classified report about the Undine threat I could access and upload them into B-4 for integration with his existing memory engrams. I asked him to share those files with Data, who I hoped would finally understand the urgency of the situation in the outside world, and look at the bigger picture beyond the limitations created by his hardwired ethical constraints.

That was an extremely weird afternoon, even for veteran members of the Soong team. Whenever B-4 would have what you've described as an "internal conversation" with Data—bringing him the team's arguments in favor of his taking over B-4's body—B-4 would apparently vanish from the android body the same way Data had disappeared. B-4 would go rigid in the chair, and his eyes would go completely glassy. Vacant, like a mannequin, with nobody behind the wheel. Whatever was going on inside that android body was confined entirely to the deep recesses of its positronic brain.

Several of us stood around or sat nearby, anxiously watching B-4's motionless, lifeless-looking body. Doctor Kasdan compared it to sitting shiva with a corpse. I felt like a Klingon performing the *ak'voh* ritual for a slain warrior, keeping B-4's body safe from predators while his soul made the journey to the afterlife. When we all sat in a circle around the apparently dead android body, I thought of it almost as a kind of cybernetic séance, as though we were trying to conjure one or the other of the two personalities back by sheer force of will.

Your later attempts to persuade Data must have worked better than the first.
Not right away, they didn't. Maybe if Data were already up and running on all cylinders, I could have gotten through to him—made him see the absolute necessity of his being flexible.

Flexible with regard to his ethical subroutine, you mean. And B-4's life.
To most people, the stars may look white and space might look black. But I learned a long time ago that the dominant color in the universe is gray, no matter what other wavelengths my optical implants might contribute to the discussion.

Ironically, the limited computational resources Data had at his disposal then were also making his ethical subroutine less flexible than I'd seen it since the time Lore took over his mind. There was simply no way anybody was going to convince him to accept that B-4's death was a necessary evil, no matter how many classified reports about imminent danger I had B-4 lob at him. The Federation could sustain casualties in the millions or higher if Data were not around to help us prevent them. But he was caught in an ethical trap that no amount of logic or persuasion could break. I had no way of knowing if Data had even read the material I'd sent him, since he was still refusing to talk to us. B-4 told us that Data didn't want to discuss it anymore, and that he wasn't even talking to *him* all that much. All Data seemed to be interested in was completing and running the new subroutine he was working on.

The subroutine that would erase himself from B-4's brain forever.

His suicide capsule, so to speak. Leave it to Data to find a way to be totally right and totally wrong, all at the same time. I didn't agree with his decision, but I suppose I had to respect it for its purity, no matter how wrongheaded I might have thought it was. It wasn't that I *wanted* B-4 to die, you understand. But as the Vulcans say, "The needs of the many outweigh the needs of the few."

Right?

Regardless, I knew I had to put aside my own selfish agenda, no matter how nicely it might dovetail with the priorities of Starfleet and the Federation Council. So I started to make my peace with losing Data. Again.

But that's not what happened.

No. What happened next was completely unexpected. Nobody saw it coming. Not even Data, who'd been working so single-mindedly on making his own final exit. It never occurred to any of us that B-4 might have been reading all the documents he'd been passing along to Data, much less understanding them. Just as it never occurred to us that he knew more about Data's "suicide subroutine" than we had given him credit for.

Tell me.
Well, B-4 returned while there was very little time left on the clock. We were still in the midst of our "cybernetic séance," waiting and hoping for Data to announce that he'd had a last-picosecond change of heart.

What we got instead was B-4 reporting that he had made sure Data had received all the documents I had sent. It hadn't made any difference, though; Data had not only not changed his mind about leaving us, he had also just finished writing his erasure subroutine.

Now he was getting ready to actually *use* it.

We had one small ray of hope, though, despite all the gloom. B-4 might not have succeeded in changing Data's mind about ending his life, but at least he'd managed to convince Data to speak to me one last time. As a friend.

To say good-bye.
Yeah. He said good-bye to each of us, one by one. He spoke to me last, and I made a final attempt to talk him out of what he was about to do.

"I am sorry, Geordi," he said. "But I cannot reclaim my life at the direct expense of another being's life."

Then he said a last good-bye, and his yellow eyes

—313—

turned glassy and vacant for a moment as he "went inside" for the last time.

Then his eyes brightened. Once again, somebody was home.

"Hello, B-4," I said.

He looked puzzled, an expression I'd seen on B-4's face any number of times before. And that's when B-4 surprised me for the second time that day—because he *wasn't* B-4.

Had something gone wrong with Data's "suicide subroutine"?

That was the first thing Data and I checked, but it was still in place. In fact, it had run once already, flawlessly.

It looks as though Data must have underestimated B-4 as much as the research team had.

It didn't take us long to figure out what must have happened. B-4 had evidently read all the documents he'd been delivering to Data, so he knew all about the Undine threat—and how important Data was likely to be in dealing with it.

B-4 must also have been paying a lot closer attention to Data's "suicide program" than any of you realized.

Like I said, everyone underestimated him. While the research teams were studying him all those years, he must have been studying *them* right back. And that

—314—

enabled him to figure out how to edit and activate the erasure program, since Data's internal logs clearly showed that B-4 had detached it from Data's personality matrix and attached it to his own instead. He apparently hadn't figured out how to cover his tracks by making the program delete itself after he'd run it. But I suppose saying that is like watching a dog play the violin and then quibbling about his intonation. Anyway, B-4 had run the entire subroutine sequence all the way through to the end before anyone realized what had just happened.

B-4 hijacked Data's "suicide capsule" and swallowed it himself—for "the needs of the many."

In retrospect, it makes perfect sense, doesn't it? B-4 had Data's complete service record at his disposal, so he knew what kind of man his brother was. He knew all about Data's sacrifice at the Bassen Rift. Then, suddenly, he was face-to-face with his brother, cybernetically speaking; he could sense Data's anguish, along with the hope and disappointment and grief of the entire research team. Even if he didn't completely understand the emotions involved, he knew he had to do *something* to help resolve them. B-4 knew that his brother didn't want to die again. But he saw that Data was willing to do it anyway rather than take responsibility for causing another being's death.

So he resolved the problem by relieving his brother of that responsibility.

B-4 came up with the one solution that only he could supply.

I suppose that makes this story less about Data's return from the dead and more about B-4's sacrifice.

Of the two brothers, Data was destined to be the one who would go on to deal directly with the Undine in ways that no one else could. But that wouldn't have been possible without B-4's sacrifice. That's why I want his story to be told. I know that a lot of good people died driving the Undine back into fluidic space. And those people deserve to be remembered.

But I don't want B-4 to be forgotten either. I don't want him to be just another nameless nonentity lost to the chaos of the war.

How did Data take B-4's death?

Better than I did, frankly, but that shouldn't really be a surprise. Remember, Data didn't have his emotion chip installed at that time. If he had, I might have been seriously worried about the fact that his "suicide subroutine" was still in place.

You think he might have . . . followed in B-4's footsteps if he'd allowed himself to be overcome by grief? Thrown himself onto B-4's funeral pyre, as it were?

I wasn't worried about that at the time B-4 died. Data regretted B-4's death, but he wasn't overwrought with emotion because his chip wasn't in place. He was dispassionate, but not uncaring. He could see that his circumstances had changed, and that there was no reason now not to see his new lease on life as anything other than what it really was—a gift from his late brother.

But Doctor Kasdan, the Soong Foundation's counselor, worried that Data might enter a "delayed grieving phase" later on, when the team was finishing the upgrades we were doing on Data's emotion chip and getting ready to install it.

And did anything like that happen?
Probably the hardest part of having emotions is learning how to cope with them. Ask any Vulcan—or any android who's had years of practice integrating cybernetically generated feelings into his daily existence.

Now, I'm not going to presume to speak for Data about his personal, subjective emotional experiences. All I can say is this: I think grief must be just as rough on him as it is on any of the rest of us. That might have been true even long before he had the emotion chip, back when Tasha Yar[*] died on Vagra II.

Did Data ever discuss his feelings about B-4's death with you after his emotion chip was reinstalled?
He did, but I'd prefer to keep most of that to myself. But Data *did* say something to me that kept me from worrying too much about his grieving process.

---

[*] Lieutenant Natasha Yar (2337–2364).

Please, go on.

Data told me what B-4's last words had been. Actually, it was more like a note he'd left attached to Data's "suicide subroutine" than a last utterance from his deathbed. Apparently, B-4 had been paying attention to more than just our official files, service records, and programming techniques. He'd evidently begun making a serious study of the human sense of humor. And he must have been concerned about the possibility that Data still might use the "suicide subroutine" to erase himself.

What were B-4's last words?

According to Data, B-4 said, "I love you, brother."

Wow. According to Data's mission records, "I love you, brother," was exactly what *Lore* said at the moment Data deactivated him.

It was. Of course, B-4 wasn't anything like Lore. Because right after he said that—right before he disappeared into whatever afterlife androids have to look forward to—he gave Data a quote from an ancient Earth actor[*]: "Dying is easy. Comedy is hard."

We both pause for a good laugh, which seems to exorcise whatever old ghosts La Forge's sometimes difficult reminiscences may have disturbed.

---

[*] Sir Donald Wolfit (1902–1968).

That must have been B-4's way of encouraging Data to take full advantage of his second chance at life. As well as his way of encouraging Data to keep trying to become more fully human.

Since this has become B-4's story more than it is yours or even Data's, do you mind if I ask you to talk a little bit more about B-4?
Go right ahead.

You said a while ago that you had copied out the entire contents of B-4's head into one of the Soong Foundation's holographic imaging computers.
That's right. Once the team was satisfied that Data was restored—albeit in B-4's body—Data and I took a look at B-4's backups. At Data's insistence, the research team started investigating the possibility of unlocking a "B-4 matrix." We started looking for a way to resurrect B-4's consciousness and personality using duplicate information—just as we had done to recover Data.

But there was no body for B-4 to inhabit, other than the one that Data was using. If you had succeeded, wouldn't Data have had to surrender that body to its original owner?
We had scanned that body down to the Planck level. I was pretty confident we'd be able to create a holographic replica of both B-4's body *and* his positronic neural nets. And I was equally confident that

B-4 wouldn't mind being confined to the holodeck for the duration of the Undine War. After all, he'd stepped aside to give Data the use of his body for the very purpose of fighting that war.

But that's all moot now, of course. The Soong people stopped devoting any serious effort to the problem of bringing back B-4 pretty soon after that.

Please forgive me for saying this, Captain, but you sound bitter about it.
That's because I *am* goddamned bitter about it. And not just because of the way the Soong people decided to ignore B-4's dilemma. The Daystrom Institute, the Starfleet Corps of Engineers, and all of Starfleet's other technical branches reacted the same way the Soong people did.

The consensus, evidently, is that it's a waste of time and resources to try to rescue B-4. Maybe it would be different if Starfleet could see some utility in B-4. If they thought they'd be getting another Data in exchange for restoring him. But all they ever saw when they looked at B-4 was a simpleton. A low-level intellect barely fit to push a broom.

A profound sadness sweeps over me. Even though I've never met B-4, after this interview I know I will never again be able to think of him as "simple." Following our conversation, B-4 will be forever linked in my mind to some of the bravest souls ever to appear in my homeworld's literary canon: He was Lennie from John

Steinbeck's Of Mice and Men—*if Lennie had had the perspicacity and the courage to shoot himself before the angry mob could reach him. He was Sydney Carton, bound for the guillotine in place of Charles Darnay, determined to shield his beloved Lucie Manette from heartbreak in Charles Dickens's* A Tale of Two Cities.

This story begs the obvious question, Captain, even if it's one you can't answer right now: Whither B-4? Well, these days I obviously can't devote as much time as I'd like to B-4's . . . problem. But I'm not going to let him languish forever as nothing more than patterns of archived information—no matter how busy my new job as the *Challenger*'s captain might keep me. I know that Data and Captain Maddox feel the same way. So we'll keep at it, however long it may take, until we find a way to bring him back.

I think it's the least we can do for one of the greatest unsung heroes of the Undine War.

Lurkers in the Shadows

WAR WITHOUT END?

Members of a religious group that calls itself "the Children of Fluidic Light" left Earth last month in a chartered private ore freighter, bound for the spectacular McAllister C-5 Nebula, which has become a sacred place to the fledgling order. Prior to embarking on their pilgrimage, the group's founder, an elderly human woman who goes by the name of "Grandmother Neduni" issued a statement articulating her group's intention to take up station at the turbulent nebula's periphery in order "to bring the Children of Fluidic Light's ceaseless prayers for peace as close as possible to the perfect gods that dwell within" the McAllister cloud.

Only today did it become apparent that "as close as possible" meant taking a suicidal plunge into the nebula's violently chaotic heart, whose countless hazards include unpredictable and potentially deadly natural phenomena such as developing protostars, and such decidedly unnatural effects as wormholes that open up into fluidic space. Echoing the comments of members of the cultists' families, a source at Starfleet Headquar-

---

* June 30, 2408.

ters said that reaching fluidic space (the origin point of the Undine) had probably been the cult's real goal all along, given that the name of the order's leader (Neduni) was simply an anagram for "Undine."

Even if the "Children of Fluidic Light" fail to find their "perfect gods," the natural cosmic violence at the center of the McAllister C-5 Nebula makes it highly unlikely that the cultists will ever be heard from again. . . .

JAKE SISKO, DATA ROD #J-41

Arik Soong Institute, Keniclius Province, Udarburgh,
Trialas IV

*I hold my tricorder in my left hand and my holoim-
ager in my right, since I don't want to set either one
on the bare floor and risk creating a tripping hazard.
Although the office is clean and modern, every wall
liberally decorated by framed diplomas and academic
awards, the place is completely bereft of furniture. It
is almost as though the eight-meter-square chamber's
only other occupant—a wire-thin, preternaturally
young-looking man with a dark, neatly trimmed
goatee—regards things like desks, chairs, and sofas as
irrelevancies, or perhaps even distractions.*

*I observe the man's habit of pacing quickly back
and forth across what I've been told is his primary
workspace, all the while talking at breakneck speed
(frequently interrupting both me and himself). It
becomes obvious immediately that any body in such
constant motion would need an environment as free
of physical roadblocks as possible. The notion tickles
my irony bump when I consider the many far more
substantial obstacles he's had to overcome on the*

way to becoming one of the Federation's preeminent research physicians and teachers, a leading pioneer in the burgeoning field of savant developmental psychiatry, and a tireless advocate for the rights of the genetically enhanced.

After he pauses momentarily at the wall-mounted replicator, I breathe a silent prayer of thanks that he's drinking water rather than raktajino. *He offers me a beverage as well, but I decline politely because both my hands are still occupied by my recording equipment.*

The last time I caught a glimpse of this man was when I was still living aboard DS9. Except for his lingering habit of speaking almost too quickly for anyone other than a fellow genengineered genius to follow, he was very different in those days, when he and three others very much like him struggled to overcome the debilitating aftereffects of their illegal gene resequencings, procedures undertaken early in their lives by well-intentioned but misguided parents who'd hoped to raise wunderkinder. *But for the efforts of Dr. Julian Bashir, Dr. Karen Loews, and a legion of other specialists in psychiatry and therapeutic genetics, those aftereffects might have led ineluctably to lifetimes spent in sterile institutions—in effect, endless prison sentences served by innocents because of the sins of their parents.*

But the man who paces before me now has somehow managed to escape the fate that had befallen so many of his fellow "genetic augments." Today, he is known across the Federation as a dedicated researcher, university professor, and widely read popular author. In defiance of all odds, he's overcome his earlier antisocial tendencies to such a degree that he's essentially become what another era would have dubbed a "celebrity doctor." Always preferring to focus on the sunlit future rather than on his night-shrouded past, he has spent decades studying the children of many of Starfleet's best and brightest in his ongoing quest to identify, quantify, and nurture the seeds of greatness. The list of the subjects of his many inquiries into the "making of exceptional persons" includes: Miral Paris (born in the Delta Quadrant to Tom Paris and B'Elanna Torres aboard the U.S.S. Voyager, Ms. Paris is a recent Starfleet Academy grad and at this writing is an ensign serving as a junior tactical officer aboard the U.S.S. James T. Kirk); Naomi Wildman (Voyager's first Delta-Quadrant baby, she is also an experienced Starfleet officer, and has confessed to being more at home in space than anywhere else); Noah Powell, Totyarguil Bolaji, and Natasha Miana Riker-Troi (all of whom spent much of their childhoods aboard the exploration-dedicated U.S.S. Titan, commanded by Natasha's father, Captain William T. Riker); Molly and Kirayoshi O'Brien, who spent nearly as much of their respective childhoods aboard DS9 as I did before their parents relocated them to Earth (Molly and Yoshi have since moved on to prosperous careers both in and out of Starfleet); and even René Jacques Robert François Picard, the notoriously free-thinking and outspoken son of Dr. Beverly Crusher and Captain (now Ambassador) Jean-Luc Picard.

This man does the kind of work that draws his

audience's gaze toward the horizon, to the leading edge of what is to come. His work is usually a font of hope and promise, reassurance that the Federation's best times are still yet to come. But no one, however brilliant, can elude the darkness of his personal history entirely. Not even this ever-youthful genius whose clipped, staccato speech patterns and hyperactive, peripatetic manner make him such an exhausting interview subject—and whose vehement insistence on being addressed only as "Doctor Jack" reveals, if only inadvertently, that he embraces both the dark past and the bright future in nearly equal measure.

Those who've been following your career might be surprised that you have so much to say about the Undine War.

I wonder when the Federation will finally reach its saturation point for surprise, hmm? After all, Jake, my whole career came as something of a surprise, wouldn't you say? Hmm? Hmm?

I only meant that the Undine War never seemed to be your main area of expertise, Doctor. Your work usually centered either on therapies for complications arising from genetic augmentations, or the special abilities of naturally "gifted" people.

Which only goes to show that it pays to cultivate more than one main area of expertise. I've always been good at handling multiple projects simultaneously, even before [Doctor] Karen [Loews] finally certified me as fully recovered from the side-effects of my childhood genetic . . . alterations. If anything, I've been a whole lot less distracted since the bad old days before my . . . rehabilitation. I'm much more focused now. Therefore I'm much better able to split my attention across several subjects than I once was. Remember, even back in the day they used to call me a polymath genius, hmm, hmm?

But you don't appear to have written extensively about the conflict with the Undine.
It certainly appears that way, doesn't it? But there's only one problem with appearances: sometimes they're just not accurate.

I'm pretty sure I've read—or at least skimmed—your entire output while I was preparing for this interview. But as far as the Undine War is concerned, I've found almost noth—
You've read or skimmed everything I've written? I'm afraid that's not possible—unless you're the greatest espionage expert the Federation has ever produced. Because that's what you would have to be just to get hold of everything I've written. Of course, it's entirely possible that you've managed to read everything I've ever succeeded in having *published*, hmm? You see, the list of books, papers, articles, and comnet postings I've *written* and the list of what I've had *published* aren't even *close* to being the same. The latter is entirely a minor subset of the former, hmm, hmm?

You mean you've held some material back from release?
No. Nonononono. No. Absolutely not. I've released every paper I've ever written. Or at least I've *tried* to. Why be miserly with it? After all, you can't keep knowledge locked up in a cage forever.

I suppose you're right. So how do you explain these gaps in your bibliography?
Starfleet Intelligence has suppressed nearly everything I've ever had to say about the Undine War. Or at least they've suppressed everything really *important* I've ever written about it.

Suppressed? Were they trying to prevent you from revealing classified information?
If that was the problem, then I think Starfleet would have taken stronger measures against me. But I'm not turning big rocks up into little ones in some penal colony in New Zealand right now, am I, hmm? So I'd have to answer your question with a "no." It appears that I haven't violated any laws, or broken any confidences.

So why would Starfleet want to suppress your writings about the Undine War if not in the name of the Federation's security?
I've never sussed that out completely myself. As far as I can tell, Starfleet was just a little . . . uncomfortable with some of the things I've tried to publish regarding the Undine. And I have it on pretty good

authority that some key members of the Federation Council were a little uncomfortable, too. No, actually make that a *lot* uncomfortable.

What you're telling me is *huge*. You're saying there's some sort of conspiracy against you, not only at Starfleet, but also in the Federation's civilian government. A conspiracy to bury your work— and possibly without a legal basis that would pass muster under the Federation Security Act.

Yes. Right. Yes. Yepyepyep. That's *exactly* what I'm saying. Not only did they suppress the papers, they hinted that it would be unhealthy for my career if I were to continue pursuing the matter. And that included crying "foul" to the media about the suppression of my work. Can you believe it, hmm, hmm?

So you were censored, and then threatened with reprisals if you complained about it publicly?

That's one way of describing the situation. Another would be that my body of work was to be redacted, in effect—and then my *protests* about the redactions would be redacted, hmm, hmm?

But why?

Nobody ever told me why explicitly.

How much research on the Undine did you do during the years when the conflict was hot?

My research was extensive. They're a fascinating

species, you know. Absolutely fascinating. And studying them was a natural sideline to the area of research I'm best known for: savant developmental psychiatry, a field that emphasizes the identification and nurturing of exceptional abilities, particularly in the field of tactical studies. The Undine War certainly made it a much more urgent priority than ever before.

I can't argue with that.
After all, the Undine have the ability to copy us, to turn themselves into perfect human and humanoid simulacra, right? Hmm?

I'm no expert, but that's about the gist of it, at least as I understand it.
And their copying process—or, more precisely, their "doppelgängering" process—goes right down to the last base-pair sequence of the human genome, correct?

So I've been told. So why would the Federation Council and Starfleet want work that vital to be suppressed? Were they worried you might have tipped our hand to the enemy somehow?
If Starfleet really thought that my work might have somehow helped the enemy, they could have just accused me of trying to leak sensitive information. They could have had me tried as a traitor, hmm? But all they ever did was issue vague warnings. They must have known that they could never convince a Feder-

ation magistrate that I was a traitor—maybe not even one of those hardcore "hanging judges" that Min Zife used to like to put on the bench back in the bad old days of the Dominion War.

But to be fair to all the frightened brass hats, not to mention the ranks of intel people who *got* them so frightened, at least *some* of my Undine work was allowed to circulate.

You're talking about your medical analyses.
"The Physiological Effects of Undine Unarmed Combat Upon Humanoids." If you've read as much of my stuff as you say you have, then you must be familiar with that one.

I am. Pretty horrific stuff.
Merely accurate. I saw some of the victims of Undine attacks up close, and did extensive scans and holoimaging of the damage. What those creatures can do to human flesh in hand-to-hand situations isn't pretty. They're one of the few species known to be capable of using their immune systems as offensive weapons—that is, in addition to protecting the Undine's own bodies from disease agents or other antigens, the creatures can release their own antibodies into an enemy's bloodstream, where those antibodies become weapons. They spread immediately through every system in a victim's body, and within minutes start converting it into Undine-compatible protein structures.

Sort of the reverse of what Undine infiltrators do to their own bodies in order to assume a humanoid identity.

That's one way of looking at it. But it always seemed to me more like being devoured from the inside out, system by system. It's a directed microbial attack that works with all the efficiency of weaponized nanites, with none of the hit-or-miss inefficiency that even billions of years of natural selection ordinarily produces. As far as diseases go, only the Symbalene blood burn can bring about a swifter, more certain death.

I remember how . . . vividly you described what happened to the victims—those who weren't lucky enough to have the process stopped and reversed, the way Harry Kim did during *Voyager*'s first encounter with the Undine, out in the Delta Quadrant.

Unfortunately for many of their later victims, the Undine have been very successful at . . . adjusting their immune molecules over the years. Refining them. They seem able to manipulate them on the nanomolecular level. It's a lot like the way the Borg can "tweak" their nanoprobes for particular, specialized purposes. Or maybe the Undine are simply capable of evolving at a much faster rate than we'd ever thought possible for any life-form more complex than a virus, hmm, hmm?

Starfleet evidently had no problem with letting you speculate publicly about the underlying chemical and biological nuts and bolts of the Undine.

You're right. But that was just chemistry and biology. Engineering problems that you could solve by building little models. That wasn't the most interesting stuff about the Undine. Not by a long shot.

So what was it about the rest of your work on the Undine that the powers that be found so . . . objectionable?
Like I said, nobody ever told me explicitly. But I have to assume it's mostly about my tactical recommendation.

You made a recommendation about how Starfleet ought to handle the Undine militarily?
Militarily? Diplomatically? I'm not sure my recommendation really fell neatly into either category. Or maybe it fell into both, or between them. Or maybe I discovered an entirely new modality for intersapient relations.

Sounds like you suggested something unorthodox.
That's how Starfleet Command described my ideas as well—just before an ossified little jury of ancient admirals thanked me, sent me home, and dismissed everything I had to say out of hand.

Maybe Starfleet wasn't interested in hearing your tactical ideas regarding the Undine because of the recommendation you made about resolving the Dominion War. According to your autobiogra-

phy, you and your genetically engineered friends, Lauren and Patrick, concluded that the Federation couldn't win that war. Therefore you tried to advise Starfleet Command to surrender to the Dominion.

I'm not above admitting to my past mistakes. I'm a scientist, and science is an entirely self-correcting endeavor, maybe the only one the human species has ever devised.

What would you say went wrong with your Dominion War plan?

We simply didn't take all the variables into account before making our forecasts.

I'd say we're all pretty lucky that Starfleet and the Federation's allies never stopped looking for ways to win that war.

Just as Lauren, Patrick, and I are lucky that the public forgave us a long time ago for letting our genetically enhanced zeal get the best of us back then.

I'm sorry. I'm not here to crucify you about the past. The Dominion War is ancient history. And the truth is, my father never even handed your recommendation up the chain of command for consideration.

If he had, Starfleet Command probably would have written me off forever as a crackpot, hmm? They could even have turned all of us into public enemies by publicizing our recommendation at a time when Starfleet and MACO personnel were still bleeding and dying from Chin'toka to Betazed. But the public never rose in wrath against any of us—not even after I wrote about the incident in my memoir, years afterward. So during the Undine War years, I seemed to have Starfleet's ear—even though that ear didn't seem very inclined to listen a lot of the time.

Starfleet must have been listening with at least *one* ear, Doctor Jack. They can't suppress what they don't notice.
Good point.

Besides, I know you can be very persuasive. Even when whatever plan you might be trying to sell to Starfleet has a fatal flaw, you're capable of convincing some very smart people to go along with it.
You're still talking about our Dominion War plan, aren't you? About how Doctor Bashir believed in it, too?

You persuaded him after taking him step by step through all of your various mathematical calculations.
Julian always listened, even though he often had that insufferable air of *I-can-pass-for-normal-and-you-can't* smugness about him, whether he realized it or not. But he was genetically enhanced just like the rest of us, so he could actually *follow* our math. He took

the time to listen, and he understood. In fact, he was the one who presented our plan to your father.

I know. I remember seeing those stacks of padds teetering on Dad's desk, right next to his baseball. Your surrender plan.
A surrender plan that might have prevented the needless slaughter of billions of Federation citizens.

But only if your data hadn't been as incomplete as you've since admitted it was. Your key assumption going in was that the Federation couldn't win the war. That assumption was the bedrock on which you built the entire plan. But it turned out to be wrong.
Which was why I was so very, very careful before making my tactical recommendation regarding the Undine. I used much finer-grained mathematics than ever before when I set my psychohistorical parameters and began making the many necessary forecasts.
    None of that mattered to Starfleet, though.

I imagine it wouldn't—if they saw it as just another surrender plan, that is.
What I came up with was radically different than that. Starfleet should have seen that right away. But they chose not to.

Exactly what did you recommend that Starfleet do?
I'm getting to that. First, let's back up to what the Undine have been expending so much energy on

over the past few decades—inserting disguised infiltrators everywhere they can. I had been compiling case studies of "infiltration incidents" for years, and I had noticed a number of commonalities linking them together.

What sort of commonalities?
First, let's consider the method the Undine use to disguise themselves *as* us in order to live undetected *among* us.

Well, they . . . morph themselves somehow.
Yes, yes, of course they do. But they don't do it in the same superficial, cosmetic way that the Dominion's Founders did. The Undine use a much more subtle method. Much less skin deep, hmm, hmm? An Undine doppelgänger actually duplicates his victim all the way down to the DNA level. Down to the last nucleotide sequence. Right down to the neuropeptides that house memory in the brains of humans and most other humanoid species. And on top of that, their bodies generate a scan-obscuring biogenic field that's capable of covering up whatever all-but-undetectable tracks the mechanics of the transformation process might have left behind.

I know. That's what makes Undine infiltrators so difficult to ferret out.
Sure it does. Their genetic mimicry makes them the most pernicious enemy the Federation has ever

faced. But it's also the source of the Undine's greatest weakness, if you think about it.

I'm afraid I don't understand.
Think about it. You must have read "Instances of Metamorphic Dementia Among Known Undine Infiltrators," hmm, hmm?

I think so. Wasn't that the paper dealing with the tendency of certain disguised Undine agents to lose their sense of individual identity while operating under deep cover? You cited instances in which Undine infiltrators had become so comfortable in their cover identities that they actually forgot the whole "Undine agenda" they had been sent out to pursue in the first place.
Yes! Yesyesyes. You understand, then.

I'm not sure. Forgive me, Doctor Jack, but the phenomenon you wrote about in that paper wasn't anything new. Deep-cover spies have been "going native" out in the field for centuries. It's always been a simple function of how long a spy has to live under an assumed identity. Over extended periods, humans in situations like that will tend to form attachments to the people around them—and might even end up caring more about those relationships than they ever did about their original mission.
That's true, but for the Undine there's an additional

dimension to the problem. When they infiltrate us, they aren't just actors in danger of burying themselves too deeply in a role, hmm? They each carry within their bodies a precise copy of the genome and the memory engrams of a particular given victim. Therefore the Undine have to be far more intensively vigilant against the possibility of their operatives "going native" than any human spy bureau ever did.

It's not as though there aren't precedents. Consider the Kelvans. You've heard of them, haven't you?

I remember Commander Worf once talking about fighting off a bunch of Kelvans. James Kirk made first contact with them, right?
Yes, right after their arrival from Andromeda about a century and a half ago, when they began an invasion of our galaxy. But their attack didn't go according to plan because of their decision to adopt human form. That transformation was their big blunder, their Achilles' heel. Despite their advanced intellects and their superior physical prowess, they succumbed to humanity's vices and emotional weaknesses.

I've read about that. That took some inspired improvisation on the part of Kirk and his senior officers.
That's the kind of creativity Starfleet needs to nurture if the Federation is ever going to stand a chance against an enemy like the Undine. Going up against them on a purely head-to-head military level is a bad idea. Just ask the Borg.

**You seem to be saying that mimicking human-
ity may transmit some of our greatest weaknesses
to the Undine. But if that's true, then those very
human weaknesses—**

—could become our greatest strengths, yes.

**It almost sounds as if you recommended that
Starfleet exploit the gluttony and drunkenness of
the Undine, using food and booze against them
instead of phasers and photon torpedoes.**

No. My plan was both simpler than that, as well
as being far larger in scope. I concluded that the
Undine had gone to considerable trouble by trying
to replace so many of us with indistinguishable doppelgängers—alien agents who were so indistinguishable from their victims that they actually *were* their
victims in every way that truly mattered. And they
were straining their resources to the breaking point
in their struggle to maintain, on some deep, interior
level, the identities and agendas of each and every
agent they had placed among us. The Undine were
prepared for Starfleet to resist their incursions. But
what they *weren't* ready for was judo.

**Judo . . . ? You recommended that Starfleet use some
sort of metaphorical judo against the Undine?**

Only barely metaphorical, hmm, hmm? After I
told Starfleet everything I've just told *you*, I recommended that they use the Undine's own impetus
against them. Like I said, the aliens were devoting

a huge proportion of their resources to maintaining their existing operatives' disguises. At the same time, they were putting everything they could muster into their latest waves of new attacks and infiltrations.

That's where the idea of judo comes in. The concept of pulling your opponent in the direction he's already headed, as opposed to trying to put a barrier up in his path—a barrier he's just going to find a way to break through, or climb over eventually anyway.

I'm afraid you're losing me.
Don't you see? Starfleet was handling the Undine incursions as though they were defending an isolated home from an invading horde. I mean, they knew how to board up the doors and the windows, and they were even capable of taking a few good potshots from the roof. But that's not a good long-term tactical plan against an enemy as relentless as the Undine, hmm, hmm? So I advised Starfleet to do the one thing that the Undine could never anticipate or deal with adequately.

And what was that?
Let them replace us. In fact, we should have *encouraged* them to replace as many of us as possible.

Wait a minute. You told me that what you presented to Starfleet *wasn't* like your recommendation for ending the Dominion War. You said it *wasn't* a surrender plan.

So I did. And so it wasn't.

Ah, that look on your face. I've seen it before, at Starfleet Headquarters. You're having the same visceral reaction the brass hats did, every gray-haired one of them. I'm surprised at you, Mister Sisko. I thought you'd be more enlightened. I thought you'd have a broader mind than that.

Somebody once said that old age is the time when one's broad mind and narrow waist finally change places. But honestly, broad-minded or not, who wouldn't be horrified by what you've just told me? Maybe you have a point. After all, fear is an instinctive human reaction. It's fundamental and completely understandable. But human beings have learned to overcome a lot of the neurophysiological baggage we all still carry around in our limbic systems, not to mention in the more reptilian parts of our brains, hmm, hmm?

If you would take a minute to think the idea through, you'll see that it has serious merit, given everything we've discovered about Undine tactics, psychology, and physiology.

I'm trying very hard to think the idea through, Doctor Jack. But I can see why Starfleet Command would have seen it as a bridge too far. Try to be dispassionate for a moment. Think about it. When the Undine replace one of us, they leave behind a living genetic duplicate that's indistinguishable from the original—so much so that the duplicate tends to forget its original identity as an Undine.

But only in rare cases, when the Undine spy suffers some sort of stress or—
Those cases are rare only because we've always tried so hard to ferret out Undine doppelgängers. But *every* one of my studies on this subject concluded that nearly all new Undine impostors would "go native" once we employed my metaphorical judo—that is, once we began *encouraging* the Undine replacements rather than fighting so hard to stop them.

I take back what I said earlier about this plan being like your Dominion surrender proposal. What you've advocated is far, far worse. It's tantamount to just lying down and letting a lethal enemy slaughter us all. It's like putting our collective neck right into the mouth of a hungry tiger.
How?

How could it *not* be? Or did I misunderstand you? You *did* just give your blessing to humanity's collective replacement by Undine doppelgängers, didn't you?
Doppelgängers so perfect that they actually *become* us, and thereby forget all about their own agendas. Doppelgängers that would immediately lose their will to fight entirely, because their plans for conquest would be utterly swamped by *our* plans and schemes

and dreams. Not to mention the distractions from all those new, unfamiliar human sensory inputs— which by themselves were enough to abort a Kelvan invasion.

Even assuming that your studies and analyses were more accurate than your Dominion War calculus was, if Starfleet had followed your recommendation we'd all still have been . . . replaced.

But by duplicates so perfect that no one could tell the difference, hmm, hmm? Least of all the billions upon billions of beneficiaries of the plan. The entire human species. Maybe even the entire population of the Federation and its wartime allies, hmm, hmm?

But there *would* be a difference.

Only to a hardcore Lockean empiricist, Mister Sisko. Remember what the philosopher William James said: "A difference that *makes* no difference *is* no difference."

But there *would* be a difference.

Only the difference between you and the Undine duplicate who *believes* that he is you. And that's essentially the same as the difference between you— you as you are right now—and the version of you that gets assembled out of local particles the next time a transporter transforms you from a pattern made of energy to a pattern made of matter.

What's important is the pattern—the information

that makes you uniquely *you*—not the provenance of whatever material substrate it's using, hmm, hmm?

As I pause to digest what Doctor Jack has told me, I find myself wishing hard for someplace to sit besides the floor. It's difficult to get my head around what he's just told me. The unease that I'm experiencing at this moment catapults me back into mercifully long-forgotten recollections of some of the Pennington School's more head-spinning philosophy courses.

The worst part of it is this: despite the visceral revulsion that Jack's idea has placed in my belly, I have to concede that his logic is difficult to shoot down—at least without recourse to that very revulsion. I know that his plan was wrong, but I can't explain why it's wrong in anything other than a purely gut-level way.

Starfleet Command must have received Jack's recommendation in much the same way. That would certainly account for their decision to suppress any writing he may have done on the subject. After all, suppose the Vulcans, who pride themselves on logic, had decided to go along with Jack's reasoning? I try to tear myself from these ruminations, determined to square this philosophical circle somehow, with or without recourse to logic.

Until another thought, not quite as dark but very nearly so, occurs to me.

I'm surprised that you decided to share your . . . Undine proposal with me after Starfleet suppressed it.

It was an idea that was never given a fair hearing. But Starfleet Command dismissed it without giving it any considerations whatsoever. They never even tried to refute my logic.

Some things might be bigger than logic.
Maybe. And maybe history is one of those things, hmm, hmm?

And you think your "Undine judo" plan deserves its place in history.
It's one of history's great missed opportunities. It would have spared the Federation untold suffering and death, but it was never even considered. It ought to at least be preserved for posterity, should similar circumstances ever arise. And what better venue is there for posterity than *your* official assignment, Mister Sisko?

But if Starfleet has suppressed your every written reference to that plan over the years, what makes you think anything different will happen this time?
Recently, Starfleet has begun to give me . . . reason to believe that I've become a real thorn in its side. Or maybe it's just that they've finally gotten tired of keeping tabs on me, waiting for the next time I, ah, misbehave. You know, they claim they've actually been "protecting me from my own rash actions" all these years by working so diligently to keep so much of my work out of the public eye.

There's probably some real truth to that. The public was willing not to hold your Dominion War surrender plan against you because of all the . . . emotional difficulties you and your friends were experiencing at the time. But your recommendation for resolving the Undine War . . . well, the public is going to see that differently.

Maybe. But I certainly don't want to be beholden to Starfleet for doing me any favors.

Think about it, Doctor Jack. I'm reasonably certain that a thick percentage of your audience would drop you like a flaming chunk of trilithium if your plan for resolving the Undine War ever became common knowledge.

Maybe. Maybe not. Regardless, it ought to be in the historical record. Keeping it suppressed would be dishonest.

Even though keeping it suppressed may be the only hope you have of continuing your career?

Yes.

I don't know if I feel right about letting my assignment become the vehicle for wrecking your professional life.

You really shouldn't worry about that. Besides, if Starfleet decides to handle this interview the same way they've dealt with some of my earlier work, then no one will be the wiser, hmm, hmm?

You mean that Starfleet Intelligence will just quietly redact anything in this interview that they decide is too . . . sensitive.

Exactly. Yes. They're enlightened up to a point, but they're also paternal to a fault.

But if you've really become as big an annoyance to Starfleet as you say you have, then they could just use this interview as a convenient way to destroy you.

You mean by just leaving all this material *in* the interview. Releasing it as is, with no redactions.

They certainly could, even if they'd prefer to suppress the whole idea of surrender. Assuming they haven't already classified the entire matter.

As far as I know, they haven't. Like I said, I haven't violated any laws, or broken any confidences. But in a civilization that's as victory-oriented as this one, I may have violated something even more fundamental than a mere law, hmm, hmm?

And what's that?

One of the bedrock taboos of the tribe. It's one we share with a lot of other aggressive species, like the Klingons, the Romulans, and even the Jem'Hadar.

Which taboo would that be?

The one that makes surrender unthinkable—and very often makes wars last a lot longer than they really need to.

The interview trails off into disconnected academic small talk, and concludes entirely as I deactivate the recording equipment. As we exchange farewells and I take my leave of him, Doctor Jack strikes me as a man carrying a burden. A soul with a need to atone for past sins. Whether this is because he failed to convince Starfleet to embrace his heretical ideas, or because he committed the crime of presenting them in the first place, I can't say.

All I can do is speculate about his prospects for atonement and absolution—and whether those prospects depend upon this interview reaching anybody's eyes and ears other than my own.

And, of course, those of Starfleet Intelligence.

Whether or not the entirety of this interview manages to get out into the public eye, I, too, will carry a burden. Should Jack's "Undine judo" plan become known via my efforts, thereby wrecking him personally and professionally, I will share some of the responsibility for whatever consequences may follow.

And if the powers that be decide to suppress Doctor Jack's frightening recommendation yet again, I will carry the not inconsiderable burden of knowing about that as well.

THE TRANSFEDERATION EXAMINER
Dateline—Lae, Papua New Guinea, Earth,
Stardate 85893.2*

. . . Following her surprise "reversion" from her human guise to her natural Undine form, the enemy agent had yet another surprise for the representatives of local law enforcement and the Starfleet officers who were on the scene: she was actually a humaniform hologram who had intentionally altered her programming until she believed she was an Undine sleeper agent—thus becoming the harbinger of a new AI neurosis that might one day prove as lethal to humanity as are the Undine themselves. . . . †

_____
* November 22, 2408.

† It must be noted here that neither of this book's authors nor its editor could verify any aspect of the above story, which was published by a thoroughly disreputable news periodical that is a wholly owned subsidiary of Broht & Forrester, the equally disreputable holopublisher that once made a failed attempt to cheat the _U.S.S. Voyager_'s Emergency Medical Hologram out of his right to control the publication of his own original holonovel (an imbroglio that probably accounts for the publisher's evident antipathy toward holograms). This excerpt is included only to give the reader a small taste of the disinformation that the Undine War inspired. Ardon Broht, the architect of so much malfeasance of this sort, was given a five-year sentence at the New Zealand Penal Colony on Stardate 97267.3 (April 7, 2420), following his conviction on charges of laundering Orion Syndicate money for the Ferengi gangster Nava. What goes around, apparently, really does come around eventually, if one lives long enough and is willing to be patient. (J.S.)

Moving Forward

STARFLEET BRATS

(Or: How I Learned to Love
War Preparedness and Stop
Worrying About the Undine)

This correspondence is reproduced here with the permission of both the sender and the recipient, and with the approval of Starfleet's Public Affairs Office.

FROM THE COMLOGS OF DEEP SPACE STATION
K-7, STARDATE 85563.8[*]

To: Samantha Wildman, M.D. (Lieutenant
Commander, Starfleet, ret.)
FROM: Naomi Wildman (Commander,
Starfleet)

Dear Mom;

I hope this note finds you well (and Dad, too, because I expect you to pass this along to him the next time you two get in touch). First, let me apologize for not having contacted either of you via a live subspace feed (or at least sending you a holo) instead of this block of electronic text. But with the heightened security and encryption protocols we have to use out here on the edge of Klingon space—not to mention the lack of subspace bandwidth available to us because of all the outdated equipment here— text is my only option at the moment. I should also apologize for not having transmitted this letter a few weeks sooner than I have, but the security situation is sensitive enough to warrant the delay; after all,

[*] July 25, 2408.

we don't want the Klingons taking advantage of any time-sensitive information if they should happen to intercept this. I know how eager the both of you are to see that third gold pip on my collar—especially now that my promotion to full commander has been a done deal for a while now.

I have to confess that my first command isn't quite what I'd hoped for. This place has been in continuous operation for about 150 years now, and it looks like the last major systems upgrade here dates back to the middle of the 2350s. Ensign Esheli in engineering has been twisting her antennae into knots trying to remedy that situation ever since she got here three weeks ago, but she's been running the Red Queen's race just keeping this ancient station spaceworthy and on an even keel, so to speak. Fortunately, my new first officer knows a thing or two about solving thorny engineering problems on the fly, and because of him I expect this place to be entirely shipshape before mid-month—and, with luck, before any angry Klingons come a-calling. Icheb got promoted to lieutenant commander just before they sent us out to the Klingon Shore to run this hoary old outpost. He's become exactly the sort of Starfleet officer we'd always both imagined he'd one day grow up to be: competent, trustworthy, cool under pressure, and almost invariably the smartest person in the room, even when he's conferring with the Borg Task Force (though he probably could be a little more restrained about displaying that last characteristic, particularly around Commander Silel, who sometimes shows his typically Vulcan aversion to being out-thunk by anybody who looks as human as Icheb does).

I know everything I've just told you probably hasn't made you any less nervous about my having accepted this assignment. Yes, I'm posted almost right on the front lawn of Qo'noS. Yes, if and when the Klingons come here, it won't be to play *kadis-kot*. Yes, Deep Space Station K-7, as inadequate as it may be at the moment, is the only thing standing between a newly expansionist and bloodthirsty Klingon Empire and far too many more-or-less defenseless inhabited planets (Ajilon Prime, the Delta Outposts, Donatu V, Sherman's Planet, etc.), none of which can count on the Organians for help this time. On the other hand, I have a crew of Starfleet's finest pulling this place together, and in record time. And while I'll always hope for the best regarding the Klingons (the Federation has made friends with the Empire before, after all, and probably will do it again, someday), we'll be preparing for the worst as we get the station ready for what could be a long and brutal siege.

If you receive this belated note when I expect to send it, you can at least take that as a hopeful sign: it means we've managed to survive out here long enough to get the last of the hatches battened down—and *that* means we're finally ready to put up a fight that the Klingons won't forget any time soon.

More later. I can see sparks from the corridor

outside my office door. Lieutenant Tal and Lieutenant Gabriel need some help right now getting the new bioneural power relays installed, and everybody else is tied up putting out other fires (both figurative and literal) around here. Gotta run.

Love always,
Naomi

JAKE SISKO, DATA ROD #P-63

Champagnifer Planum (in Margaritifer Terra, just outside New Chicago), Mars

The ground beneath the vast overhead vault of pink-stippled atmosphere is thin and dry—not to mention cold enough to elicit a shiver, as though my dark thermal windbreaker were no more substantial than rice paper. Still, the chill afternoon wind carries a not altogether unpleasant bite, even though it's moving fast enough to kick up a small but noticeable amount of dust. The airborne particles broadcast the familiar baseline smell of the Martian regolith, its bleachlike aroma intermixed liberally with the gentler scents of growing plants and turned, living earth. I inhale deeply, though never quite deeply enough to suit a pair of lungs long since spoiled by the warm, humid breezes of Terrebonne Parish, Louisiana.

This world is the closest in proximity to Earth that merits description by the word "planet." Not surprisingly, humanity has treated Mars almost as an extension of its blue birthworld, leaving our unmistakable mark everywhere during the three centuries or so we've been here. With the exception of the polar regions, the skyward reaches of Olympus Mons, Ascraeus Mons, the Tharsis Bulge, and a few other plateaus and peaks in the southern highlands, the entire surface of Mars now constitutes a more or less continuous shirtsleeve environment. So the ruins toward which I walk, which consist mostly of an old, corroded section of a long-obsolete twenty-first-century pressure dome (complete with what appears to be the original outer airlock door!) is merely an ornament now—or perhaps a monument to the far less temperate climate that this world's twenty-first- and twenty-second-century pioneers subdued and tamed at such great human cost.

I lived here briefly as a boy, long after the life-and-death struggles of the pioneers, the political and economic storms of the War of Martian Independence, the sunrise of hope marked by the Fundamental Declarations of the Martian Colonies, and the marsquake-inducing Kuiper comet-bombardments of the great terraforming projects all had passed into history. Bradbury Township had by then become more a cozy bedroom suburb than a jumping-off place for those bound for the final frontier. About as exotic as the outskirts of Toronto, it had devolved into a place of tedium and ennui; it was a huge disappointment to a boy whose expectations had been primed by dozens of fictional (and often mutually exclusive) portraits of the Red Planet that had been written over the last few centuries.

The adventure I had always craved came at last when my parents and I shipped out on the Saratoga—

which became one of the thirty-nine Starfleet vessels that the Borg destroyed at Wolf 359. My father and I returned to Mars afterward, where he resumed his work for Starfleet at the Utopia Planitia Fleet Yards—and where I returned to my endless hours of reading and daydreaming.

And fought my first real battle against regret.

Today, as I trudge through the rusty, red-brown soil toward the ancient, ruined dome, leaving my shoeprints in a mix of artificially cultivated agricultural products and rehabilitated native regolith, I wonder how many times I've quietly wished that my family had simply stayed put here on Mars, sitting out the Borg attack that took my mother from me when I was only eleven. Perhaps a part of me—the part that still daydreams about Barsoom and all the other versions of Mars that never were but perhaps should have been—never left this place the first time.

With its salmon-streaked skies, Mars even now remains a quintessentially alien place, humanity's aggressive presence notwithstanding. Despite the purely decorative nature of the few fragmentary airlocks and dome sections that remain standing here and there, and the proliferation of much newer conifers I can see arrayed all along the western horizon, this place is still recognizably Other when compared with humanity's cradle, Earth. For starters, that tree-lined western horizon is much closer than it would be on an Earth-sized globe. The sun that illuminates the dust-pinked ceiling of sky is wan and pale and far too small to rule the *heavens properly. And Mars's point-three-eight g puts a spring in my step that sets my feet moving out ahead of my body whenever I'm less than completely careful; since the interplanetary transport first delivered me to Lowell Spaceport, I've landed flat-on-fundament twice already, and may do so yet again here at New Chicago. Despite my having been acclimatized to Martian standard gravity during my childhood, years of living on Earth—to say nothing of constant exposure to shipboard artificial grav plating—appears to have spoiled me permanently for any radical departure from an Earth-normal sense of up and down.*

Generations of terraformers have wrought uncountable environmental modifications on Mars over the past quarter-millennium, effectively remaking it almost into another Earth. Regardless, Mars has never entirely lost its air of strangeness and wonder, at least for me. When I gaze at any Martian landscape, whether it's festooned with recent-growth forests like the ones I see creeping up on New Chicago's margins, or sere with the ocher-and-brown grasslands, the seltzer lakes, or the carbon-fizz-and-brine seas that predominate elsewhere on this world, I still see a place where a four-armed Thark warrior straight out of the pages of Edgar Rice Burroughs might ride into battle, his eight-legged thoat leaping from crater-rim to crater-rim at full gallop; I still see a possible dwelling place for Percival Lowell's desperate, thirsty canal builders; or H.G. Wells' relentless conquerors; or Ray Bradbury's fearful, astronaut-murdering shape-shifters; or the human-

swallowing plants and prolific Martian flatcats that Robert Heinlein wrote about centuries ago. . . .

Of course, who really needs any of those things when you've got the Borg collective to worry about, or the Dominion?

Or the Undine?

I put aside my ruminations as a trim, wiry man of perhaps thirty emerges from the shadow of the ruined dome section and extends his hand toward me. He grasps my hand firmly as he introduces himself in a resonant, mellifluous voice. As we walk together past the crumbling dome section, our designated meeting place, I note that he smiles easily, and that his features are already familiar to me even though I know I've never met him before. Much of the familiarity no doubt comes from his more-than-passing resemblance to his famous father, from whom he acquired his European-inflected speech patterns, an impressive Roman nose, and an emerging pattern baldness that already appears to be driving his close-cropped, copper-hued hair into a slow but inevitable retreat toward the back of his head.

Despite the significant gap in our ages, I know I have something fundamental in common with this young man: like him, I have a parent who has acquired some renown, both in and out of Starfleet (he can boast two such famous parents, in fact). The interview begins in earnest after I activate my mobile recording gear, and we walk as we converse, leaving the pressure-dome ruins behind us as we head at a

brisk, body-warming pace toward the stand of coni-
fers that beckons us toward the horizon.

And I begin to discover what else I might have in
common with René Jacques Robert François Picard,
son of Jean-Luc Picard and Beverly Crusher.

**Your generation's perspective on the Undine War
years just might be a unique one, Mister Picard.**
How do you mean? And before you answer that, let's
agree right now to get ourselves on a first-name basis
with one another. There's always been far too much
protocol in the Picard family for my taste. Please just
call me René.

**René it is, but only if you agree to call me Jake. And
what I meant is that every Federation national your
age and younger has never really known a time
when humanity hasn't been either under threat or
direct attack by the Undine.**
I suppose you're right, Jake. You might even say that
for my generation the Undine simply became a part
of the cultural wallpaper, as it were. I suppose they're
still there, lurking in the shadows, at least sociologi-
cally speaking.

You don't believe they're still a real threat?
Quite the contrary, Jake. Anything that can influence an entire society so profoundly as to give it a
general tendency to jump at its own shadow poses a
considerable threat.

You don't seem all that jumpy to me, René. But then I suppose the apple doesn't fall very far from the tree.

My parents always placed a premium on rationality and coolness during times of crisis. On the other hand, perhaps the reason I don't fly into a panic whenever somebody utters the word "Undine" has less to do with that and more to do with the fact that I'm not in charge of any aspect of the Federation's response to such things. There must be a lot of fairly sobering information about the Undine that I'm simply not privy to.

If you don't mind my asking, René, why *aren't* you in charge of such things?

I suspect you already know the answer, Jake. Or at least a big part of it.

You're saying that the reason you came here to Mars instead of shipping out with Starfleet to the ends of the known universe might be the same reason I opted to pick up a pen instead of a tricorder?

It only stands to reason, Jake. Look at us. Either of us would have been given an extraordinary degree of consideration at Starfleet Academy.

But you know as well as I do that a pedigree can take you only so far in Starfleet, René. It's a true meritocracy.

Of course it is.

And you didn't find that just the least little bit . . . daunting?

Of course. Who wouldn't? After all, a surname like "Picard" doesn't guarantee anything—except, perhaps, a certain heightened degree of expectation on the part of others. I imagine it's much the same for anyone named "Sisko."

It's not something I enjoy thinking about, but I suppose it's true. Did those expectations cause you to doubt yourself?

Not really. I don't believe I've ever lacked for faith in my own merit, and I'd imagine that you're much the same as I am on that score.

Why would you assume that?

Because it's obvious from your choice of occupation. Now, I don't claim to be an expert about writing. In fact, you could probably fill several libraries with everything I *don't* know about the subject. Nevertheless, I'm reasonably certain that a writer must maintain a certain sense of hubris to believe his work is sufficiently worthwhile for anyone else to read. Since I know you've been writing since you were a boy, I have to assume you've been well acquainted with this hubris for at least that long.

That's . . . very insightful, René. You've just reminded me that the "family business" wouldn't necessarily have led you to the bridge of a starship. You could

just as easily have followed in your mother's footsteps, and become a medical doctor. You'd have made an outstanding psychiatrist.
I actually considered doing something like that. Just as I considered entering Starfleet.

But you would have carried quite a burden of expectation in either of those occupations.
A *double* burden of expection, considering who my mother is. And that's why I began looking for a . . . third way.

But I'd say you've done a lot more than just "consider" following in your parents' footsteps, René. You took a lot of advanced medical training during your undergrad years. And when you applied to Starfleet Academy they accepted you on the spot. Your Starfleet career might even have surpassed your father's. After all, his first application to the Academy was rejected—
I know. But getting accepted on the first try only made the burden of expectations *worse*. It seemed to make the comparisons between me and my father even more inescapable.

Is that why you made the last-minute decision not to enter the Academy?
Partly.

You needed to establish your own identity, distinct from those of your parents. Just like me—except

that while I was growing up I never had to worry that I might really be an Undine "sleeper agent" living under deep cover.

I suppose so. But the idea of personal identity—an identity that I'll always choose to believe belongs to René Picard, regardless of the Undine threat, by the way—is only part of the reasoning behind my choice in careers. The reality is actually a bit more complicated. You see, I came to realize that the Federation's relationship to the rest of the galaxy has . . . *changed* over the past several decades. That change was well under way before I was born, only Starfleet and the Federation Council hadn't realized it yet. Maybe they still don't.

That seems to be one of the great leitmotifs of history, especially with regard to large-scale conflicts. We always enter the next war by preparing to re-fight the last one.

Precisely. For most of the Federation's history, we've faced adversaries that were essentially nation-states that were, at least broadly speaking, constituted much as we were. Putting aside differences in ideology, economics, and so forth. In fact, our adversaries have nearly always been similar enough to us to instill a kind of empathy in us. This often led to alliances eventually, or even real partnerships and interstellar friendship.

But that began to change with the Dominion War.

Yes, but the change was almost too subtle to be generally recognized for what it was. The Dominion War brought us into contact with a nation-state that was not only hostile and paranoid, but also capable of infiltrating Federation society on a massive scale—or at least making us fear mass-infiltration to the point that we very nearly lost everything the Federation stood for.

The later Undine infiltrations and attacks carried the pattern further along than the Dominion ever managed—and the Undine managed to do it while keeping their profile so low that the nation-state vs. nation-state war paradigm ceased to work for us. Worst of all, the Undine delivered a fear factor that the Founders of the Dominion had never approached, not even on their best day.

But a lot of that fear is more than justified.
Certainly. But one has to keep things in perspective, especially when one is frightened. Fear or no fear, the sun will still rise in the east tomorrow—even here in the backwoods, on Mars. Fear or no fear, babies will keep being born, children will continue to grow up, and the wheel of life will go right on turning.

Maybe I'm just as blinkered and shortsighted as the leaders who always seem to fall into the trap of re-fighting the last war.
How do you mean, Jake?

Well, it's always been difficult for me to understand how your generation has been able to

tolerate having so much . . . tension and uncertainty in your lives. The threat of the Undine has dangled over you like some interdimensional Sword of Damocles for your entire lives. But your generation seems to have a very different take on the universe than mine does. You have more of a sense of serenity.

Mine isn't the first generation that's had to learn to live with some omnipresent Big Bad looming in the background. Look back through human history. In the middle of the twentieth century, the United States became the first of Earth's nation-states to use atomic bombs against an adversary. Two whole cities, both full of innocent civilians, were razed by nuclear fire in a matter of moments. And for several decades afterward, every child on the planet had to become accustomed to the specter of nuclear annihilation, which might have come at any moment.

I'm not sure that the comparison of your generation to that one is entirely fair, René. Humanity still possessed a lot of ugly characteristics that we've since managed to shed. Racism and sexism, just to name two.

But are we really all that different now than people were four or five hundred years ago, Jake? You and I might agree that we've changed for the better as a species, at least broadly speaking. But a Zimmerman EMH hologram that's spent years doing continuous waste-reclamation duty for Starfleet might have a considerably different perspective on the matter.

I see your point, René. But I still have to applaud your generation for having dealt so successfully with a threat as large and all-encompassing as the Undine.

I'm not sure thanks are in order, Jake. I think of most of my peers as merely doing whatever the circumstances demand of them. Rising to the occasion as much as they possibly can, just like any generation does. After all, human beings have always been amazingly adaptable, otherwise we never would have made it down from the trees. But it isn't easy to deal with a reality in which any friend, parent, child, or authority figure in someone's life might turn out to be an Undine spy transformed into human form via quasi-magical means. A bloodthirsty alien might lurk just beneath the skin of even a lover or a spouse, only a subtle twist of a DNA helix away from striking. And that lover or spouse might not even realize it! That knowledge has had a profound effect on everyone. So you should never make the mistake of thinking that everybody in my age cohort has managed to take this Undine business in stride.

I suppose not everyone can cover themselves in glory in an age of unbridled paranoia.

People are just *people*, Jake. They're not saints, but they're not demons either. I've seen classmates sequester themselves away in pixel-perfect holosuite simulations until they've lost all track of objective reality. People have starved to death that way. On another part of the spectrum, I've watched people routinely overindulge in whatever they decide to conjure out of their bottomless replicators in order to self-medicate their anxieties away. And I've seen people I'd believed to be rock-solid emotionally take up a phaser and dematerialize themselves because they believed they were really Undine "sleepers."

I suppose I can understand how people can succumb to a constant, unrelenting background of stress, so I don't want to be judgmental. After all, I have no more patience for those New Essentialist idiots who believe the Undine to be divine retribution for the Federation's decadence than I do for the lotus-eaters who think denial is a viable weapon against the Undine. But I have to point out that most of these . . . emotional meltdowns constitute "fleeing behavior," no doubt generated by the Undine's capacity to force an excessive "fight or flight" response from far too many of us over long periods of time.

I've never believed in flight, my decision to stay out of Starfleet notwithstanding. Life is something that has to be faced head-on. All the holodecks and replicators in the quadrant can't help you hide from it.

Interesting. You've just articulated a very go-getter attitude, René. It's the kind of worldview that's kept

pushing Starfleet out into the Deep Dark Unknown for centuries now. And yet you've decided to make your life here instead.

On exotic, faraway Mars, you mean?

Don't get me wrong. Mars certainly has an attractive literary and historical mystique about it. Once it even represented the pinnacle of human progress and expansion. But you have to admit that Mars isn't exactly the tip of the spear in terms of present-day deep-space exploration.

True. But neither is Terrebonne Parish, Louisiana.

Touché. Still, the comparison isn't entirely fair.

Isn't it? We both prefer the reliable comforts of hearth and home to the constantly shifting dangers of the final frontier, even though we're both sons of famous Starfleet captains.

My **dad commanded a space station that stayed put for the most part.** *Yours* **spent years commanding starships dedicated to pure exploration all across the galaxy, and even beyond.**

All right, Jake. I suppose I'll have to give you that one.

So why the preference for home and hearth?

Again, I suppose my response would overlap quite a bit with any answer *you* would give to the same question. There were, of course, all those issues of other people's expectations that we've already touched on. I suppose I didn't want to find myself going down a blind alley, the way my half-brother Wesley did.

It always comes back to those complicated "identity issues" again, doesn't it?
And maybe also to something even more fundamental than that. I think as I began really wrestling with the career issues—the idea of my personal destiny, for lack of a better word—I began considering the entire arc of human progress itself.

That's pretty daunting. It's a hell of a lot more complicated than any one man's career choices.
But it isn't really, at least not at the "big picture" level.

I'm afraid you've lost me, René. When you say "arc of human progress," I see an incredibly complicated tapestry woven from millions of threads that crisscross at every imaginable angle.
Then you're standing too close to the tapestry, Jake. Back up a bit, so that every little purl and snag in the weave doesn't distract you. Then squint, metaphorically speaking. You'll see that the human species has *never* advanced in an orderly way. Not even the coming of Zefram Cochrane changed that, no matter how many miracles followed as direct consequences of First Contact. Human progress has always taken three steps forward and two back for as long as we've been sentient creatures, and probably for a

fair chunk of deep time before *that*. And if we're honest, we have to acknowledge that the same historical pattern applies today.

So you see human history as an alternating series of advances and consolidations.
I think that's a succinct but fair way of putting it, yes. I was afraid for a moment that you were going to say "greatness always skips a generation" instead.

I'd never say that. I have the writer's hubris, remember? So . . . your life here on Mars, and your career . . . those constitute a period of consolidation, as opposed to the advancement represented by your parents' exploits as Starfleet officers?
I suppose that's so, in a manner of speaking. But the life I lead here also signifies that I recognize tradition. And tradition was one of the things my parents' generation always fought to preserve, no matter how far out into unexplored space their duties took them.

When humanity goes where no one has gone before, it's to preserve everything we are and everything we've been.
You understand. Perhaps my decision to live on Mars is a tribute to the history of the Picard family. After all, some of my ancestors helped to settle this world when it was far less agreeable than it is now. One of them even built the replica of the Millennium Gate that's still towering over the Endurance Crater today.

I suppose those ancestors accomplished what they did in between earlier periods of . . . retrenchment.
That's right, more or less. Look, not every generation can be lucky enough to usher in a whole new epoch.

And the generations that are probably look "lucky" only in retrospect.
Yes. The ancient Chinese had good reasons to consider "may you live in interesting times" a curse rather than a benediction.

Because it's a lot more fun to read about other people's "interesting times" than it is to be dragged through them yourself.
Exactly. But whether humans are charging beyond the current boundaries, or catching our collective breath while we try to make sense out of everything we've learned over the last generation or so, our traditions continue, just as they always have. Because if they don't, then what's the point in voyaging out into the unknown to wrestle all those far frontiers into submission in the first place? What's the point of forging all those new interspecies relationships out among the stars?

And why bother fighting off hostiles like the Undine if we never stop to honor and appreciate what we're fighting for?

As we finally reach the distant rows of conifers, I decide I really can't disagree with anything René has said for the past few minutes. We find ourselves quickly sur-

rounded by the slowly lengthening shadows of the elongated Martian pines and cypresses as the wan sun continues to settle ever lower in the carmine sky. The air temperature plummets under the cover of the spreading boughs, making our crossing of this narrow swatch of new-growth forest seem to take much longer than it actually does. Still, my eyes need a moment to readjust to the vista that awaits us as we emerge less than half a kilometer from our destination.

Beyond the ancient alluvial channel—typical terrain for the Margaritifer Terra region, it's now the site of a gently meandering stream transited by a short pontoon bridge that takes us only moments to cross—lies an almost completely treeless zone that nevertheless supports a profusion of green. Just past the stream's far bank lies the edge of a vineyard that extends to the newly revealed horizon, and a dusty red dirt road neatly bisects the innumerable tidy, manicured rows of grapevines. Bizarrely tall because of this small world's low prevailing gravity, the plants stand like sentinels on the slender stakes that support them, viridian-green sentries guarding the rustic mansion I can see in the distance. On the gazebo beside the house hangs a freshly painted sign:

THE PICARD WINERY, EST. 2407.

Tradition.

Or rather, as René tells me, the resumption of an interrupted tradition. Specifically, a centuries-old institution of viniculture that had faltered decades earlier, following the untimely death of Robert Picard—a *steadfastly traditional uncle whom René was far too young ever to have met.*

As we pass beneath the gazebo and mount the steps to the house's wide, wraparound porch, René says that the hard work of convincing the local authorities to allow him to change the name of this section of the Margaritifer Terra to "Champagnifer Planum" has already paid off. Once we're in the kitchen, he decants a recent vintage of Chateau Picard and goes on to explain that despite the overall Earthlike conditions that centuries of terraforming have brought to Mars, the groundwater here remains heavily influenced by the atmospheric carbon dioxide that has suffused the Martian soils for aeons. Therefore all the water here has a fizzy, bubbly quality—which means that just about everything that this new Picard family vineyard produces will sparkle with carbonation.

"If we're going to be in the business of making sparkling wine," he explains, "then we might as well find a legitimate way to call it champagne."

We clink glasses and discuss the future—specifically, the three children that he and his wife, Natasha Miana Riker-Troi, have had so far. I watch their dark-eyed images floating over the kitchen table's holocube as René explains that his wife is out right now, picking the kids up from the school they attend in New Chicago.

Growing up here among the grapes, will those children grow restive and depart one day for the beckoning stars? Although René offers only an ambivalent shrug in answer to that unanswerable question, I feel certain that this next generation can hardly do other-

wise, given the expectations that their extraordinary pedigrees will certainly thrust upon them (imagine being a grandchild of William Riker, Deanna Troi, Beverly Crusher, and Jean-Luc Picard).

I offer a toast to family and tradition, and I find myself in an almost celebratory mood as we finish our glasses, and then refill them. The amber liquid chases away the chill of the approaching evening, and I can almost make myself believe that the Undine are as ancient and harmless as dry dinosaur bones, something from the deep past that we've chosen to commemorate with a ceremonial libation. But that's not good enough. I move on to imagine the Undine as a vanquished foe whose recent decisive defeat has given us permission to drink our fill and howl our triumph out to the cold Martian moons.

Of course, I know better than to be so presumptuous. After everything I have seen and heard since I began this project, I believe that I labor under no illusions. The Undine will be back. For all I know, I'm in the company of one right now.

Or perhaps René Picard is.

I push that unpleasant thought into a dark, soon-to-be-champagne-saturated corner of my mind. And I toast the next generation in the hopes that they'll be the ones who finally bring the Undine menace to an end. Because it has to end someday. It has to.

Doesn't it?

APPENDIX
STAR TREK ONLINE

THE PATH TO 2409

2379–2380

- Cardassia Prime plunges into an economic crisis following the Dominion War.
- The Female Changeling is sentenced to prison in Federation custody for war crimes committed during the Dominion War.
- Tal'aura declares herself Praetor of the Romulan Empire.
- Tal'aura clashes with Commander Donatra, who is in control of the Romulan military.
- Remans demand self-sufficiency, asking for control of a continent on Romulus or a planet with sufficient natural resources to maintain settlements. In response, Tal'aura cuts shipments to Remus.
- Ro Laren surrenders to Starfleet and stands trial on charges related to her desertion and defection to the Maquis.

2381

- Construction starts on the *U.S.S. Stargazer*-A at the San Francisco Fleet Yards.

- Remans and Romulans skirmish in the space between the two planets.
- The Unification movement allies with the Remans, seeing them as another exploited population. Leaders of the movement request aid from the Federation Council.
- Donatra leads a military uprising against Tal'aura, taking over several farming worlds and declaring herself Empress of the Imperial Romulan State, with its capital as Achernar Prime.
- A coalition of planets led by Bajor demands that members of the Cardassian government and military stand trial for war crimes committed during the occupation of Bajor and the Dominion War. The Cardassians refuse, and the coalition appeals to the Federation to join them in seeking justice.

2382

- The Klingons take advantage of the civil war in the Romulan Star Empire and stage lightning strikes into Romulan space, retaking Khitomer and the region surrounding it. The Federation Council criticizes the act, but the Klingons respond that they are simply reclaiming territory that was theirs by right.
- Admiral Owen Paris of Starfleet Research and Development orders that the *Voyager* EMH's mobile emitter be taken to its facility on Galor IV for study.
- The Doctor files suit to block the transfer of the mobile emitter, arguing that he is a sentient being who

acted as a member of Starfleet during *Voyager*'s time in the Delta Quadrant, and that the mobile emitter is necessary to his existence.

- Tal'aura reforms the Romulan Senate. The Senate promptly votes her powers to appoint senators and veto bills. Tal'aura packs the Senate with her supporters, bringing her into conflict with the Empire's noble houses.

- Loss of farming planets to Donatra and the Imperial Romulan State threatens Romulus with famine.

- Tal'aura charges her proconsul, Fleet Commander Tomalak, with retaking the planets held by Donatra. Tomalak appoints Admiral Taris as his second-in-command and orders her to reorganize and mobilize Romulus's remaining military forces.

- The Federation Council takes up Ambassador Spock's request that it formally support Romulan-Vulcan unification. The council chooses not to vote on the matter, not wishing to take sides in an internal conflict. They are heavily influenced by T'Los of Vulcan, who argues that the result of the unification of the two races cannot be predetermined, while the probable course of the races remaining separate can be reasonably predicted. Therefore, her only logical choice is to protect the Vulcan way of life by opposing unification.

- Over the course of four months, 472 Cardassians on the Bajor coalition's war crimes list disappear from Cardassia Prime.

- Released from Federation custody, Ro Laren returns to Bajor and accepts a position in the Bajorian militia. She is appointed head of security for Deep Space 9.

2383

- Spock returns to Romulus to lead the Unification movement there.
- Riots protesting food rationing and limits on replicator use in the Romulan capital are brutally put down. Tal'aura says that the rationing of food and energy is necessary to support the military's campaign against Donatra and the breakaway Imperial Romulan State.
- In a narrow vote, the Federation Council decides not to formally censure the Klingon Empire for the invasion of Khitomer.
- The Romulan Senate votes to expand Tal'aura's powers, giving her the ability to grant or remove noble titles and the right to declare war without Senate approval.
- Tal'aura's forces, led by Fleet Commander Tomalak, attack Donatra's Imperial Romulan State fleet at Xanitla. Tomalak's forces are soundly defeated, and are dealt a further blow with Admiral Taris and the crews of the twelve ships under her command defecting to the Imperial side.
- A resurgence in support for religion and spirituality sweeps the population of Cardassia Prime.
- Rear Admiral Bennett of the Starfleet Judge

Advocate General's office rules that the "Data decision," referenced in the Doctor's legal arguments to keep the mobile emitter, is too narrow to be used in this question, and that it could only be applied to prove that the Doctor is not the property of Starfleet, and not to decide whether or not he is a sentient being.

- The Soong Foundation, a group affiliated with the Daystrom Institute and dedicated to promoting the rights of artificial life-forms, announces that it is beginning work to create a mobile holographic emitter of its own.

2384

- Sela replaces Tomalak as Tal'aura's proconsul. Tal'aura grants Tomalak the right to "retire" to his rural estates in return for his decades of service to the Empire.
- Donatra agrees to send negotiators to Romulus to attempt to reach a peaceful agreement with Tal'aura. She appoints Taris to lead the delegation.
- Tal'aura is assassinated in her private chambers. Various fingers point at a coalition of the noble houses, the Tal Shiar or agents working for the Imperial Romulan State.
- Donatra recalls Taris from Romulus and orders her to prepare to defend their holdings.
- At Tal'aura's funeral, Sela publicly blames the Remans and the Unification movement for the attack.

Public opinion swings against the Unification movement.

- A Bird-of-Prey conducting exercises in the space between the Klingon Empire and the Gorn Hegemony is attacked by a Gorn ship. The Gorns claim that the captain was acting against orders.
- Martok orders additional ships to the border with the Gorn Hegemony.
- Odo, acting as the Great Link's ambassador to the solids, meets with Laas on Koralis III and invites him to return with him. Laas refuses, choosing instead to continue to search for the missing ninety-seven of the Hundred.
- The android B-4 is transferred into Soong Foundation custody, and work begins on restoring his full positronic functioning.
- The Ferengi Alliance establishes an embassy on Deep Space 9.
- Bajor renews its application for admission to the Federation.

2385

- Sela moves to consolidate Tal'aura's remaining forces under her control. She replaces more than two dozen "populist" Senators with representatives from noble houses that had opposed Tal'aura. The backing of the nobles gives her the power she needs to take control of the government, but she lacks the support of the military or the Tal Shiar.

- Rehaek, leader of the Tal Shiar, announces that he is personally investigating the circumstances surrounding Tal'aura's death.
- Donatra and the Imperial forces win support among Romulan civilians by offering food shipments to nonmilitary settlements.
- Donatra, Sela, and Rehaek agree to share power, reforming the Continuing Committee. The worlds of Donatra's Imperial Romulan State are once again part of the Romulan Star Empire.
- Donatra visits Remus and meets with Xiomek. She offers the Remans citizenship and representation in the Romulan Senate in exchange for their support. Sela objects but Rehaek refuses to back her and Donatra proceeds with the plan.
- The Remans agree to back Donatra. Their physical strength adds to her formidable military force, and the supplies of dilithium and heavy metals allows her to increase production of ships and weapons.
- The Romulan Senate reluctantly endorses Donatra's deal with the Remans, but most Romulans continue to treat the Remans as second-class citizens at best.
- The Bajor coalition demands the Cardassians surrender colonies granted to them in the Federation-Cardassian Treaty of 2370. The Federation Council and Cardassians both support leaving the boundaries as drawn.
- All non-Klingons are expelled from Khitomer as a "safety measure." The refugees are allowed to

resettle on a nearby planet after they agree to recognize Klingon authority.

- The *U.S.S. Enterprise*-E returns to the shipyards at Utopia Planitia for an extensive refit. The Starfleet Corps of Engineers says the refit will take at least a year to complete because they are going to use the ship as a testing ground for new technology and weaponry.
- After more than two years with no sign of Borg activity in Federation space, Starfleet dismantles its Borg task force. Task force codirector Seven of Nine resigns in protest, and later joins the Daystrom Institute to continue her research.
- Jean-Luc Picard resigns his commission in Starfleet and is appointed ambassador to Vulcan.
- Beverly Crusher is promoted to captain and takes command of the *U.S.S. Pasteur*, which is assigned to support efforts to rebuild hospitals and medical facilities on Cardassia.
- Worf resigns his commission in Starfleet and is named an ambassador on Qo'noS. He reestablishes relationship with Grilka.
- The advanced sensor array first tested on *Luna*-class starships is deemed suitable for retrofitting onto other starships.
- Daystrom Institute scientists succeed in unlocking the "Data matrix" in B-4. With the Data personality and intellect dominant, the android assists the team to upgrade his positronic brain and re-create his emotion chip.

- The Romulan Mining Guild presents a long-term study of Remus to the Romulan Senate. The study finds that Remus has been seriously overmined, and suggests that to prevent a Praxis situation the Reman operations should be shut down and moved to more distant regions of Romulan space.

- Xiomek uses his new position in the Romulan Senate to argue that if the Remans must move that they be given control of a continent on Romulus. The Senate rejects that, but with the backing of Donatra and Rehaek instead offers the Remans the planet Crateris in the Gamma Crateris system. Site of a failed Romulan colony, the planet has a harsh climate and is beset with almost constant electrical storms, but is rich in dilithium and other natural resources. Thousands of Remans move to Crateris.

- Rehaek announces that he has proof that Tal'aura was assassinated by agents loyal to the noble houses. He begins an open campaign of attacks on noble assets in retaliation for Tal'aura's death.

- Sela pushes back against Rehaek's persecution of the nobles who support her. She uses her control of the government to cut funding for the Tal Shiar, and in a speech before the Romulan Senate, she accuses elements inside the Tal Shiar of knowing that Praetor Tal'aura was in danger but not acting to stop her assassination.

- Fighting between Sela's forces and supporters of

Rehaek erupts in Ki Baratan. Hundreds die in the uprising, and violence spreads to surrounding cities.

- Donatra refuses to take sides in the conflict between Sela and Rehaek, concentrating instead on mitigating the conflict's impact on the Romulan people. She orders the military to provide ships to take Romulans who wish to leave combat zones to colony worlds, and commands General Tebok to send troops to try to quell the violence.

- Rehaek's estate in Ki Baratan is destroyed by an explosive device. The remains of several servants and Rehaek's wife and daughter are recovered, but investigators believe that the initial blast was intense enough to have vaporized anyone close to the explosive device.

- Tal Shiar forces storm Sela's estate outside Ki Baratan and take her and her personal guard into custody for the murder of Rehaek. Sela is sentenced to death in a secret trial but Donatra intervenes, allowing Sela and her supporters to accept permanent exile.

- Taris travels to Levaeri V to investigate claims that the Sword of the Raptor Star has been recovered. The blade is reputed to be one of the swords created by the Vulcan swordsmith S'harien and taken into exile by S'task, the first leader of the Romulans.

- King Xrathis of the Gorn dies of old age. Prince Slathis ascends to the throne.

- Klingon forces take over the Gorn colony at Gila VI.

- Worf, son of Mogh, weds Grilka, leader of the House of Grilka, on Qo'noS.
- The Federation and Cardassians sign a new treaty. In it the Cardassians agree not to field a military or wage war, and the Federation agrees to provide additional security in the event of invasion of Cardassian space. Bajor drops its request to prosecute Cardassians for war crimes.
- Odo visits with the Alpha Jem'Hadar, and asks them to return with him to the Gamma Quadrant. Lamat'Ukan, First of the Alphas, rejects Odo as a false god.
- Grand Nagus Rom uses tax proceeds to start free schools on Ferenginar. Protests rock the capital for two days until Rom charges all of the protesters five slips of latinum each for mass assembly without a properly purchased permit.
- Data requests that his Starfleet commission be reactivated. Upon review, the Judge Advocate General's office rules that Data's use of B-4's body is no different than an officer returning to duty with an artificial limb and grants the request. Data supervises the completion of the *Enterprise*-E's refit, and takes command of the vessel when it relaunches in 2387.
- Starfleet updates its duty uniforms for all personnel.

2387

- Donatra accepts Xiomek's invitation to visit Crateris and inspect the new Reman colony. The two leaders meet privately for several hours. Donatra offers Xiomek passage on her flagship, the *Valdore*, so he can return to Romulus in time for the opening of the Romulan Senate.

- Donatra sends a transmission to Taris, ordering her to return to Romulus and submit to a full review of her actions. Taris deletes all evidence of the message from her ship's systems and relieves her communications officer of duty. Her ship does not change course.

- On the way back to Romulus, Donatra's fleet reports unusual stellar activity, including a disturbance equivalent to a force-seven ion storm. Romulus loses contact with the *Valdore*, and sends ships to search for the fleet.

- Ambassador Spock of the Federation appears before the Romulan Senate to warn them about the dangers of the Hobus star. Nero, a representative of the Romulan Mining Guild, corroborates Spock's claims that the star is experiencing eruptions powerful enough to destroy nearby planets, and is converting the mass of those planets into additional energy. If the sun goes supernova, it could create a chain reaction that would destroy much of the Empire. Some senators support Spock's plan to coordinate with Vulcan to find a solution to the problem, but the majority of the Senate believes that the threat is a plot to gain access to Romulan resources and Spock's request is rejected.

- Sela's fleet passes the Beta Stromgren supernova remnant and continues into unexplored space, looking for a suitable planet for colonization.

- In late 2387, the Hobus star goes supernova, creating a chain-reaction explosion that destroys dozens of planets, including Romulus and Remus. Billions of Romulans are killed.
- Ambassadors Spock and Jean-Luc Picard appeal to the Vulcan Science Academy to assist the Romulans with the Hobus supernova. The academy refuses.
- Hassan the Undying assassinates Raimus and takes over his slice of the Orion Syndicate for his employer, Melani D'ian.
- The Alpha Jem'Hadar establish a base of operations on Devos II. The ketracel-white manufacturing base there gives them the needed resources to sever all ties with the Dominion, and they declare their independence.
- The Cardassians dissolve the military, reforming a much smaller force as the Cardassian Self-Defense Force. It is limited to operations in Cardassian space.
- Rom pushes a bill calling for the Ferengi Alliance to formally ally with the Federation, but opponents successfully bribe enough members of the Economic Congress of Ferengi Advisers to have the bill killed.

2388

- The Romulan colony worlds reel with the loss of their homeworld and leadership.
- Rator III names itself the new capital of the Romulan Star Empire, as do Achernar Prime and Abraxas V.

- The Detapa Council votes to send a token force of six ships to assist with the Romulan relief efforts. Popular opinion is against the decision, in that Cardassia needs to conserve its remaining resources.
- Realizing that their homeworld in the Rigel system is almost depleted of natural resources and that Federation patrols are becoming a serious problem for Syndicate operations, the Orions open negotiations with the Breen and the Klingon Empire for assistance.
- Chancellor Martok refuses the Federation's request to send aid and assistance to the Romulans after the destruction of Romulus. "The Klingons will offer them no treaty, no aid, and no hand that is not holding a blade."
- The High Council, led by Councillor J'mpok, demands that the Federation be made to pay for the destruction of the fleet led by Worf to Vulcan, saying that Picard tricked the fleet into a hopeless battle. Martok refuses to attack the Federation, but the Empire's relationship with the Federation is more strained than it has been since the Cardassian War.
- K'Dhan, son of Worf, is born on Qo'noS.
- Martok orders ships to the border with the Romulan Empire, and orders them to destroy ten ships for every warrior killed by Nero. The Klingons win multiple victories.
- The Federation Council orders an investigation into the Vulcans' refusal to help the Romulans.
- Seventeen Federation planets recall their ambas-

sadors to Vulcan in protest over the Vulcan Science Academy's decision on Romulus.

- Federation President Nan Bacco appeals to the Federation Council to take a message of unity back to their homeworlds and not to ostracize Vulcan or any world. "In this time of strife we need to remain united. Assigning blame does not heal the injured, soothe the stricken, or comfort the grieving."
- Starfleet and the Federation direct immense relief efforts to the Romulans. While some colony worlds accept the help, after Taris asserts power she rejects Federation attempts at friendship.

2389

- Leaders of the colony worlds plan a conference to establish a new government, but cannot even agree on where to hold the meeting.
- General Tebok recalls Romulan ships on missions outside the galaxy.
- The Klingons take control of the Tranome Sar and Nequencia systems.
- The Federation offers to mediate talks between the Gorn and the Klingons.
- The Federation supervises elections on Cardassia Prime. A civilian coalition led by Garak narrowly defeats a hardliner faction (led by Gul Madred) calling for withdrawal from the Federation-Cardassian Treaty of 2386 and the reestablishment of the military.

- Warriors from the House of B'vat slay Aakan of the House of Mo'kai, ending a century-long blood feud between the two noble families. The House of Mo'kai is dissolved.
- The Nausicaans agree to contribute ships and weapons to the defense of the Gorn.
- The Detapa Council is reestablished.
- Ambassador T'Los of Vulcan resigns her post, citing hostilities toward her planet as the cause.
- After the destruction of Romulus, the Federation cuts funding for Cardassian relief efforts by 30 percent.
- Holoprojectors are now standard equipment in all areas of most Starfleet ships, expanding the range and usefulness of photonic tools such as the Emergency Command Holograms.
- Gul Madred acquires the rights to mine several mineral-rich planetoids in Cardassian space. He begins building a large mining operation on Septimus.

2390

- The government of Talvath requests Federation protection.
- Taris orders the Romulan fleet to concentrate on two things: rescue and relief for the colony worlds and defense of the Empire's borders.
- The Federation offers to mediate talks between the Gorn and the Klingons. Neither the Gorn nor the Klingons are overeager to accept the Federation inserting itself into what is considered to be a personal

matter, and Chancellor Martok says that one of the Klingon Empire's conditions for allowing such a summit to proceed will be the withdrawal of Federation ships from its border with the Romulans.

- Projections by Klingon military analysts show that the Empire's resources will be stretched thin by a two-front war against the Romulans and the Gorn, and that the disorganized, displaced Romulans are the lesser threat in the short term. The High Council decides to end its Romulan campaign, but holds on to the space it claimed.

- Pacifica pulls out of the Federation, citing the immense drains on resources that the Romulan and Cardassian relief efforts pose. The president of Pacifica states that his planet has no wish to subsidize its enemies.

2391

- Sela lands on Makar, an M-class planet in the Beta Quadrant with abundant supplies of dilithium and decalithium.

- Taris confronts a Klingon fleet at Zeta Pictoris and forces it to retreat.

- Colony worlds, led by Rator III and Achernar Prime, recognize Taris as the leader of the Romulan Empire. She orders leaders of each world to meet on Rator III to organize a government.

- Talks between the Klingons and the Gorn break down when Ambassador Zogozin of the Gorn is injured when a bombing disrupts the negotiations on Deep Space K-7. The terrorist group Khalb is blamed for the attack, and it is believed that their intended target was Ambassador Alexander Rozhenko of the Federation. Rozhenko is uninjured.

- The Gorn hire Lethean mercenaries to protect their outlying colonies.
- Garak enters negotiations with the Ferengi, signing contracts with Rom for both the return of several sacred jevonite artifacts as well as financial support to restart Cardassia Prime's industrial complexes. In exchange, the Ferengi get favorable trade agreements for Cardassian goods once the factories reopen.
- The Soong Foundation lobbies for the rights of sentient artificial life-forms to be added to the Federation Constitution.
- Citing the success of the extremely diverse crew of the *U.S.S. Titan*, Starfleet considers expanding the admission standards at Starfleet Academy to include races that are formally allied with the Federation but not full members.
- Starfleet Command creates a task force to investigate appearances of the race known as Species 8472 in the Alpha Quadrant.

2392

- Construction of a new Romulan capital, Roma Nova, begins on Rator III. The first building constructed is used to house meetings of the Romulan Colonial Organizational Committee.

- Formation of a new government is beset by infighting and factionalization. A group of moderates suggests that the Romulan people need someone to focus their energies, and suggests the revival of the monarchy. Taris indicates that she supports the monarchy, but that it must be the people's decision.
- Alexander Rozhenko takes a lead role in negotiations between the Federation, Klingons, and Gorn.
- Ja'rod, son of Torg (and of Lursa of the House of Duras), completes warrior training and is assigned to the *I.K.S. Kang*.
- Gorn and Nausicaan forces attack Ogat but are driven back by the Klingons. The peace talks break down, with open skirmishing on the border between the empire and the Gorn Hegemony.
- A second round of talks between the Gorn and the Klingons opens on Cestus III. Little progress is made.
- The Detapa Council enacts a series of reforms designed to promote population growth and economic stability. Thousands of displaced military officers are folded into civilian industries, with a significant minority joining the mining operations on Septimus.
- The Cardassian mining industry begins exporting large amounts of kelindide and uridium through their Ferengi brokers. The Romulans, desperate to rebuild ships and expand colonies, are one of the first major clients.
- Naomi Wildman enters Starfleet Academy.

- Aennik Okeg of Sauria is elected president of the Federation.

2393

- Taris and Tebok argue about the diversion of ships to protect what Tebok considers unimportant regions of the Empire.
- Tebok sways a portion of the RCOC with the argument that far-flung sections of the Empire can and should be sacrificed in the short term to strengthen the position of what are now the Empire's core worlds.
- J'mpok defeats Martok in an honor duel, replacing him as chancellor of the Klingon High Council.
- Natima Lang negotiates with the Remans to get additional dilithium for ships and warp drives. Cardassians begin selling their technology across the Alpha and Beta quadrants.
- Claiming that the Cardassian Self Defense Force cannot adequately protect his mining operation, Gul Madred contracts with Alpha Jem'Hadar for security.
- The Soong Foundation files suit on behalf of the hologram known as "Moriarty." Starfleet refuses to release the program.
- The Bajorians and the Tamarians are formally admitted to the Federation. Federation linguists and scientists, with the assistance of the Tamarians, set up a new facility on El-Adrel IV dedicated to linguistic research.
- The *U.S.S. Stargazer*-A makes the first contact with

the Metron Consortium since 2267. The Metrons say that the younger races are still unready for regular contact, but have made progress.

2394

- The RCOC completes its work. In a narrow vote, it rejects the idea of a monarch in favor of reestablishing the Romulan Senate in Roma Nova. It offers Taris the position of praetor, but consolidates the majority of the power in the hands of the senators.
- At a conference on Ter'jas Mor, the Orions sign a nonaggression and mutual defense pact with the Klingons, further agreeing to exchange technology and information for the rights to a planet in Klingon space. The Klingons give the Orions Ter'jas Mor to rule as a vassal state to the Klingon Empire, and the Orions begin transferring their remaining home world population from the Rigel system.
- As a gift to celebrate their new alliance, the Orions send fifteen hundred women to be servants to the great Houses on Qo'noS.
- The Supreme Court of the Federation rules that the Doctor is a sentient being, and therefore has the right to the mobile emitter. The court sets standards that artificial life-forms must pass to be considered fully sentient.
- Alexander Rozhenko resigns his position with the Federation as an ambassador and leaves to begin what he calls "a personal exploration." Reports put

him on Boreth, and indicate he may be undergoing the "Challenge of Spirit."

2395

- Ja'rod, son of Torg, is ambushed by strange tripedal aliens while on shore leave on Rha'darus. He kills two of the creatures and returns the third to the *Kang*.
- Under questioning, the alien from Rha'darus reveals itself to be a member of the Undine, a species otherwise known by its Borg designation of Species 8472. The Undine reveals that its party was sent specifically to capture Ja'rod and replace him.
- The Doctor takes a post as chief medical officer on Galor IV, allowing Starfleet to study the mobile emitter.
- After the accidental destruction of the *U.S.S Kelso*, Starfleet admits to renewed experiments with cloaking technology. The Romulans and Klingons strenuously object, and the admission leads to strained relations between the three factions.
- The Vulcans honor the 225th anniversary of completion of work on the rebuilt monastery at P'Jem. The ancient religious site was rebuilt by a coalition of Andoria, Earth, and Vulcan.

2396

- Taris orders a three-month quarantine of Kevratas to stop the spread of Bloodfire, a disease that is lethal to Romulans but curable if treated promptly. The quarantine stops all food and medical shipments to the planet in the middle of winter.

- Sela negotiates with the Dopterians to trade decalithium for ships and weapons.
- Captain Klor of the *Kang* refuses Ja'rod's request to fully investigate the extent of the Undine infiltration. Ja'rod leads an uprising of the crew and replaces Klor as captain.
- Nausicaan ships destroy three Klingon outposts in a surprise attack. The Klingons retaliate by destroying the Nausicaan starbase in the Orelious IX asteroid belt.
- An audit of post–Dominion War assets authorized by the Detapa Council finds that at least 75 warships and an undetermined amount of weapons known to have survived the war are now missing.
- Captain T'Vix of the *U.S.S Cochrane*, one of the ships assigned to monitor the border of the Neutral Zone, is removed from duty, as are two other members of her command staff. Starfleet Intelligence seals all records relating to the action.

2397

- The government of Kevratas declares independence from the Romulan Star Empire. Taris orders Tebok to put down the insurrection with force.
- Tebok refuses to order his troops to fire on civilians and instead negotiates a settlement. He agrees to

bring the leaders of the rebellion to Roma Nova to present their grievances to the Romulan Senate.

- Taris orders Tebok to step down from his position as head of the Romulan military. The Senate overrules her decision.
- Hassan the Undying moves his base of operations to the former Orion homeworld.
- After a personal appeal from the Federation, J'mpok reluctantly agrees to a third round of peace talks. His decision is in opposition to a large bloc of the High Council, which favors a declaration of war.
- The *Kang* infiltrates Gorn space in the course of its investigation of the Undine.
- Geordi LaForge is named captain of the *U.S.S. Challenger*. Nog replaces him as chief engineer of the *Enterprise*-E.
- Ja'rod and J'mpok agree to an alliance between the Houses of Duras and J'mpok. The agreement gives J'mpok the backing of many of the oldest and most influential Great Houses, and returns the House of Duras to legitimacy.

2398

- Tebok promotes Velal, who has been openly critical of the praetor, to commander of the Second Fleet.
- Miral Paris enters Starfleet Academy.
- An attack on the Klingon-Gorn negotiations kills Ambassador K'mtok of Qo'noS. A joint investigation by the crews of the *U.S.S. Enterprise* and the

I.K.S. Gorkon reveals that the instigator of the attack was Toral, son of Duras, in support of a group of hardliners that wants to destabilize the Klingon government. Toral escapes.

- Laas arrives on Devos II with two other changelings.
- The Federation Council approves rules for dual citizenship in the Federation, which allows voting and other rights without surrendering all ties to a being's home planet. The Soong Foundation and other artificial life rights groups lobby for citizenship to be extended to sentient artificial life-forms.
- Rhea, a Ferengi geologist living on Earth, is the first being to be granted dual Federation citizenship under the new program.
- Naomi Wildman becomes the helmsman of the *U.S.S. Hathaway*.
- Aennik Okeg is elected to a second term as president of the United Federation of Planets.

2399

- Tebok's ship, the *I.R.W. Alth'lndor*, notifies Romulus that it is experiencing unexplained malfunctions in multiple subsystems, but that they should not impede her progress. Engineers suspect the problems are being caused by a computer virus.
- Two hours later, the *Alth'lndor* drops out of warp and transmits a final distress signal. The *I.R.W. Kaidor* races to the *Alth'lndor*'s location. The *Kai-*

dor reports detecting an antimatter containment failure, but before her crew can act the *Alth'lndor* explodes. All hands are declared lost.

- The *Kang* returns to Qo'noS and presents evidence to J'mpok that proves the Undine infiltration goes deeper than previously believed.

- J'mpok declares war on the Gorn Hegemony with the full support of the High Council. A combined Klingon and Orion force storms across the border into Gorn space.

- The Federation Council condemns the Klingon invasion of the Gorn Hegemony and demands that the empire withdraw to its own space. In response, the Klingons pull out of the Khitomer accords.

- Starfleet formally expands its admission guidelines to accept applicants from races allied with, but not formally admitted to, the Federation. Such applicants would be allowed to apply for dual citizenship in the Federation. Hundreds of Ferengi, inspired by social reforms on Ferenginar and the example of Nog, rush to apply.

- Starfleet Command opens the first links of its transwarp network.

2400

- Sela's spies in Roma Nova alert her to irregularities in the account of the *Alth'lndor*'s destruction, and she orders her agents to investigate.

- Taris clashes with the Romulan Senate over its plans

to further restrict the powers of the Praetor. She argues that in the absence of a monarch, the Praetor needs expanded powers in order to maintain stability. She is overruled and the Senate proceeds with its plan.

- The Founders disavow any connection with shape-shifters in the Alpha and Beta Quadrants, and say that any changelings operating outside their authority are renegade.
- The combined force of the Gorn and the Nausicaans repel the Klingons and Orions initially, earning them a measure of respect for their ferocity in battle.
- The Detapa Council normalizes relations with Bajor, and opens an embassy on Deep Space 9.
- Commander Harry Kim is named head of security for Starbase 11.

2401

- Sela meets with Velal in the Zeta Volantis system.
- Velal gathers a trusted group of commanders and informs them that for the good of the Empire, Taris must be removed from power. He has allied with Sela, and her ships and weapons will give them an edge over ships loyal to the praetor.
- Natima Lang steps into the leadership of the Detapa Council.
- The Cardassian Science Ministry announces it has developed a cure for Pottrik Syndrome.
- Miles O'Brien is named head of the Starfleet Corps of Engineers.

- Captain Zachary MacAllister attempts to take the *U.S.S. Lindberg* into Gorn space against direct orders. After his crew mutinies, MacAllister steals a shuttlecraft and disappears. He is still a fugitive.
- A contingent of retired and current Starfleet officers appeal to the Federation Council to reconsider its condemnation of the Klingon invasion of Gorn space. The council denies their request.
- Naomi Wildman is promoted to second officer of the *U.S.S. Hathaway*.
- Councilor Konjah is revealed to be an Undine after he is attacked by Lethean mercenaries. J'mpok strips the House of Konjah of its titles and status and its members are either killed or forced into hiding.

2402

- Velal demands that Taris step down immediately and surrender herself to the Senate for judgment.
- Taris calls for the fleet to defend the legitimate government, and there are several skirmishes between ships loyal to Velal and Sela and those backing Taris.
- A Klingon religious group claiming that Miral Paris is the *kuvah'magh* attacks the *U.S.S. Pike* during Miral's senior cadet cruise. The kidnapping attempt fails.
- After two years of fighting, the Klingons blockade the Gorn homeworld.
- A report by Cardassian Intelligence to Natima Lang confirms that the forces led by Gul Madred may be

in possession of some of the warships missing from Cardassia Prime.

- The *U.S.S. Voyager* makes first contact with the Lorians. Federation scientists theorize that the avian race may be somehow related to the Xindi, but have insufficient data on ancient Xindi to confirm this.
- The Starfleet Corps of Engineers suggests that Starfleet begin building its ships using a modular system. The new system allows captains to customize their ships and permits quick repairs.
- Jean-Luc Picard retires from his ambassador position and settles in France.

2403

- Kevatras and Abraxas Prime throw their support behind the Romulan rebellion.
- The Second Fleet approaches Rator III. Taris' servants find her rooms empty, and an extensive search of Roma Nova finds no trace of the praetor.
- Sela and Velal land at Roma Nova and appear before the Romulan Senate. They pledge friendship with the Senate . . . not mentioning the dozens of warships they have in orbit around the planet. The Senate agrees to make Velal head of the military and Sela praetor.
- Klingon troops land on the Gorn homeworld and storm its capital. In a public broadcast, several high-ranking members of the Gorn government and military are revealed to be Undine shape-changers.

- The remnants of the Gorn government surrender to the Klingons. Councilor Marab leads the call for the execution of the Gorn royal family.
- The Klingons allow the Gorn self-rule, as long as they swear fealty to the empire. King Slathis agrees, and is allowed a nonvoting seat on the High Council.
- Emperor Kahless handpicks a crew from the Order of the Bat'leth and departs on the *I.K.S. Batlh*. He leaves a message saying that the Klingons no longer need him, so he is departing to look for new battles to fight. He promises to return when he is most needed.
- For his part in revealing the Undine threat, Ja'rod is offered a seat on the High Council and leadership of the House of Duras. Ja'rod declines to join the council, saying that until he has fully proven his worth to the Empire, he cannot rightfully take a position on the High Council.

2404

- Over a period of time, Sela uses charm, guile, and a healthy amount of blackmail to shape the Senate to her liking.
- Starfleet opens the Federation transwarp network.
- J'mpok informs the High Council that he is invoking ancient claims to the Hromi Cluster and the sectors surrounding it, a region of space that the Klingons had previously surrendered to the Federation. He tells the Federation ambassador that

they have three months to remove all Federation citizens and assets from the sector.

- The Soong Foundation gets an injunction to force Starfleet to reveal the whereabouts and conditions of all of its holographic programs, with the intention of reviewing the cases of photonic beings that have achieved sentience. Starfleet appeals, saying that the request is too broad and invades officers' privacy.

2405

- At Drax's request, General Worf agrees to be *gin'tak* to the House of Martok and advise Drax in his conflict with the House of Duras.
- The Klingons invade Korvat and start forcibly removing Federation citizens. Starfleet sends ships to stop them. The war is on.
- The Federation repulses a Gorn invasion of Sherman's Planet.
- Rom uses the profits from his trade agreements with the Cardassians to finance the passage of expanded technology and information sharing agreements with the Federation. While the Ferengi Alliance will remain formally neutral for now, Rom argues that the future of business contacts lies with good relations with the Federation.
- In a deal brokered by Slathis, the Nausicaans sign a nonaggression pact with the Klingons.
- Aennik Okeg is elected to a third term as president of the United Federation of Planets.

2406

- The Klingons invade the Archanis sector.
- A virulent plague infects the entire population of Carnegie. Federation President Aennik Okeg refuses to comment on rumors that the plague is not biological in origin, saying that Starfleet must have the time and resources it needs to treat the population and enforce a quarantine to keep the contagion from spreading.
- Admiral Chakotay is named the new head of Starfleet Intelligence. He briefs Starfleet Command on the Undine situation in the Federation. Starfleet Intelligence suspects at least thirty individuals among Starfleet and the Federation government to be Undine, and is investigating ways to better detect Undine infiltrators.
- The Starfleet Corps of Engineers says that advances in power cell technology make personal shield generators for officers on away teams feasible. They begin issuing the units to ships on a trial basis.

2407

- Forces loyal to the House of Martok battle supporters of the House of Duras in the Ghomha system.
- The Federation Council requests peace talks with the Klingon Empire. J'mpok refuses to hear their request.
- Sela revives the idea of a Romulan monarchy.

- Research on improvements to transwarp technology begin at the Vulcan Science Academy.
- A plague of unknown origin strikes the Phylosians. Starfleet is dispatching medical teams, but experts at Starfleet Medical say that the unusual nature of Phylosian anatomy will make finding a cure difficult.
- The Letheans open negotiations with the Klingons for entry into the Empire, but progress is slow and the Klingons do not consider the negotiations to be a high priority.

2408

- Sela is crowned Empress of the Romulan Star Empire.
- The Klingons and Gorn invade Cestus III. Starfleet sends ships to defend the planet and its population.
- A Starfleet committee concludes a study showing that because of retirements, deaths, and conflicts, Starfleet is facing a severe shortage of captains. It recommends revising rules on away teams to encourage more officers to seek command positions, increasing enrollment at Starfleet Academy and revising the command structure to allow for the best use of experienced personnel.
- Starfleet loses contact with Starbase 236. It dispatches the *Enterprise-E* to investigate.

ACKNOWLEDGMENTS

The author would again like to recognize the contributions of the legions who enriched the contents of these pages: editor Ed Schlesinger (who has a cameo appearance herein in the persona of Jake Sisko's twenty-fifth-century editor, E'Shles); Marco Palmieri and Margaret Clark, for their steadfast support over the years; Christine Thompson at Cryptic Studios, whose boundless patience, creativity, and enthusiasm helped to keep me on track throughout the evolution of this book's many picaresque episodes (as well as her "Path to 2409" timeline); the kind and indulgent folks at the New Deal Café (née the Daily Market and Café), where much of this volume was written; Studs Terkel and Max Brooks, whose respective oral histories of two very different previous "Good Wars" inspired this volume's format; Roberto Orci, Alex Kurtzman, Mike Johnson, and Tim Jones, whose *Star Trek: Countdown* comic-book miniseries (IDW Publishing, 2009) set up the story of Data's return and the ethical conflict that arose from it; John Van Citters at CBS Consumer Products, for allowing me to chronicle the aforementioned event, as well as the rest of the incidents recounted in these pages; David

Mack, for his astonishing work on *Destiny,* a trilogy whose world-shaking events have reverberated far and wide, affecting even Cryptic Studios' alternative *Star Trek* continuity; David Mack (again), for creating Tim Pennington (in *Vanguard: Harbinger*), the namesake of the Pennington School at which Jake Sisko matriculated; David Mack (yet again), whose *A Time to Kill* and *A Time to Heal* introduced President Min Zife; Keith R. A. DeCandido for the backstory on Nanietta Bacco and her supporting cast, including Esperanza and Nereida Piñiero (in *A Time for War, A Time for Peace,* and *Articles of the Federation*), copious details about the Cestus Baseball League, its players, and its cofounder Kornelius Yates, the invention of Sinnravian *drad* music (introduced in his *Starfleet Corps of Engineers* e-book *Cold Fusion*), and the *Meet the Press*-style public affairs program, *Illuminating the City of Light;* S. D. Perry, whose initial post-television-series DS9 novel *Avatar* Book One established Jake Sisko's middle name; Christopher L. Bennett, whose *U.S.S. Titan* novel *Orion's Hounds* introduced the term "cosmozoa(n)" to *Star Trek* literature, and whose story "Places of Exile" in *Star Trek: Myriad Universes—Infinity's Prism* established the first alternate name for Species 8472 (the "Groundskeepers"); the entire *Star Trek* Internet community, those tireless wiki-compilers whose multitudinous and serried ranks defy enumeration here; Geoffrey Mandel, for his *Star Trek Star Charts* (2002), which kept me from getting lost in the galactic hinterlands many times; Michael and Denise Okuda and Debbie Mirek, whose *Star Trek Encyclopedia: A Reference Guide to the Future* (1999 edition) remains indispensable even in this modern age of ubiquitous wikis; Shane Johnson's *Star Trek: The Worlds of the Federation,* for information about Tau Lacertae IX, the Gorn homeworld; Greg Cox and John Gregory Betancourt, who created the Xoxa colony for their DS9 novel *Devil in the Sky;* Interplay Games, whose *Starfleet Command* video game (1999) was the source of my references to the Gorn Egg Bringer S'Yahazah; Peter David (*Cold Wars*), Kevin Dilmore ("The Road to Edos" from the *No Limits* anthology), and Michael Jan Friedman (*Star Trek: New Worlds, New Civilizations*), for their stories featuring Department of Temporal Investigations agents Lucsly and Dulmer; Kevin Dilmore (again), for formulating the distinction between the three-legged Edosians and the three-legged Triexians ("The Road to Edos"); William Leisner for Denevan Federation Council member Lynda Foley, who debuted in his TNG novel *Losing the Peace;* my own work on two *Titan* novels (*Taking Wing* and *The Red King,* both cowritten with Andy Mangels) for the "continuity glitch" (oops!) that yielded Noah Powell, and John Vornholt's earlier *The Genesis Wave* series, which introduced Noah's alter ego, Suzi Powell; my Marvel Comics *Star Trek* editor, Tim Tuohy, and my longtime colleague Andy Mangels, for the references to the *U.S.S. Thunderchild* and members of her crew, as conceived for the abortive *Star Trek: Phase III* comic-book series we *almost* got to do at Marvel Comics way back in the late twentieth century; Phantom Productions' Tape

Recorder Online Collection and Museum (http://reel 2reeltexas.com/index.html), for information about Vic Fontaine's 1962-vintage audio equipment; Jonathan Coulton, whose music gave me inspiration, a nifty-sounding place name (Chiron Beta Prime), the name of the Sinnravian *drad* musician (J'Nat Cton) who sang the UFP anthem at the big game on Cestus III, and some much-needed laughs ("All we want to do is eat your brains!") when I needed them most; Scott and David Tipton, for attaching a Klingon name (Gralmek) to Arne Darvin/Barry Waddle ("Beneath the Skin," issue no. 2 of IDW's comic-book miniseries *Klingons: Blood Will Tell*); all the show runners who brought *Star Trek* to screens large and small over the past four-plus decades, with special kudos to J. J. Abrams, Roberto Orci, and Alex Kurtzman, who together crafted the new continuity tangent that spawned the *Star Trek Online* role-playing game, IDW's *Countdown* and *Nero* comic-book mini-series, and this book; all the actors whose characters participated in this volume's "interviews," but especially Cirroc Lofton and Tony Todd, each of whom made indelible imprints on the Jake Sisko character; Gene Roddenberry (1921–1991), for creating the entire universe in which I get to spend so much time playing; and lastly, though never leastly, my wife, Jenny, and our sons, James and William, for long-suffering patience and unending inspiration.

ABOUT THE AUTHOR

Michael A. Martin's short fiction has appeared in *The Magazine of Fantasy & Science Fiction,* and he is the author of *Star Trek: Enterprise: The Romulan War—Beneath the Raptor's Wing.* He has also coauthored (with Andy Mangels) several *Star Trek* comics for Marvel and Wildstorm as well as numerous *Star Trek* novels and e-books, including *Star Trek: Excelsior—Forged in Fire; Enterprise: Kobayashi Maru; Enterprise: The Good That Men Do;* the *USA Today* bestseller *Titan: Taking Wing; Titan: The Red King;* the Sy Fy Genre Award–winning *Worlds of Deep Space 9 Volume Two: Trill—Unjoined; Enterprise: Last Full Measure; The Lost Era 2298: The Sundered; Deep Space Nine Mission: Gamma Book Three—Cathedral; The Next Generation: Section 31—Rogue; Starfleet Corps of Engineers* nos. 30 and 31 ("Ishtar Rising" Books 1 and 2, reprinted in *Aftermath,* the eighth volume of the *S.C.E.* paperback series); stories in the *Prophecy and Change, Tales of the Dominion War,* and *Tales from the Captain's Table* anthologies; and three novels based on the *Roswell* television series. Other publishers of Martin's work include Atlas Editions (producers of the *Star Trek Universe* subscription card series), Gareth Stevens, Inc., Grolier Books, Moonstone Books, *The Oregonian,* Sharpe Reference, *Star Trek Magazine,* and Visible Ink Press. He lives with his wife, Jenny, and their sons, James and William, in Portland, Oregon.